AGE OF SHADOWS

R.E. PALMER

FrontRunner Publications

ISBN: 978-1-8383995-2-8
www.FrontRunnerBooks.com

Cover art by Kentaro Kanamoto
www.kentarokanamoto.com

DEDICATION

For Bern, Tim and Neve.

ACKNOWLEDGMENTS

A huge thanks to Erin Kahn, Amanda Brand and Janet Allmey for being my valuable beta-readers for this project. It's very easy to get caught up in your own work, so it's vital to get feedback from others. So, thanks to you all! I very much appreciate your time and effort.

A large version of this map is available to download and print at www.frontrunnerbooks.com/map.html

ELESSYN SEA
KARAJAN SEA
N
KERNOW
PERRAN
PYMOOR
RHYDOR
RANMOOR
PERRAN HILLS
KERNRIM
MERYN
KERN RIVER
STOWE
GWELAYN
KIRIK
CASTER
VINLAYN
HAMM
NEVERDOR
SEARITH
PORTLEA
RIVER LOE
TAMARAND
LOROMAR
HURST
TRAITOR'S ISLAND
WEST HAVEN
MENON RIVER
KOLOSSOS MOUNTAINS
VORTIMO
VYMARL
VYNMAR
TALLABAR
SAPHRIR
KRANT
EMRYST
EPHRIM
SALAHA
TELAMIR
KALMIR
CAFRA
CASTELDOR
FORANFAE FOREST
FARRAND
MUND
HOLM
SYRIS
CAERMUND
GARAMUND
ABERNOST
ARCHONHOLM
CAERWAL GATE
CAERWAL MOUNTAINS
MUNDRAKE'S ISLE
THE LOST REALMS

1. Abandon Hope

Hope writhed, tugging with surprising strength, desperate to free her hand from Toryn's grip. 'I won't take another step closer.' He let go, unwilling to risk causing harm. She sagged to her knees, sobbing into her hands. 'I won't. I can't. Please don't make me.' Her shoulders shook. 'I can't go.'

Toryn slumped beside her on the grass verge. 'It's the quickest route to Archonholm.' He looked to the dark trees of the Foranfae Forest just a hundred paces from them. 'We don't have to go any nearer. The road skirts the border. Besides, no one can enter. We're safe if we stay on this road. I promise.'

But Hope refused to listen. She turned and crawled up the bank, muttering under her breath. Toryn sighed. What other options lay open to him? He could hardly drag Hope the remaining leagues alongside a forest she so obviously feared. He stood on the edge of the Great Northwest Road and looked south. If they took the route, they would be in Archonholm in three days at most; the only other way was through the Menon Hills, which would easily add two, possibly three more days. Only the previous day he had felt confident about addressing the Archon with Hope by his side. She had made a full recovery from the incident on the ridge, hearing nothing more of the voice that had caused her so much pain. And Toryn hoped, being in the presence of the powerful Archon would bring the wise and coherent Hope back to the fore. But his raised spirits took a knock as she had quickly reverted to the muddled, old woman as they had trekked farther into the ward of Holm. And, as the road drew closer to the forest, her initial anxiety had transformed to the numbing fear now wracking her body.

Toryn surveyed the gnarled trunks and twisted branches of the Foranfae. The forest had dominated the region for as long as any could remember, yet, as Hamar was fond of saying, while few scrolls in the annals spoke of its history, it did not stop people speculating on what strange beings possibly lurked beneath her dark canopy. Not that anyone needed to read of its power from a dusty parchment — all who spent the briefest of moments close to its green border could sense this was no ordinary forest. The Archon may have forbidden entry by law, but it did not require the pain of death to deter trespassers: only the foolish, or those caring not for their sanity would dare to venture under her boughs. Of those known to have entered, the few returning to tell the tale, had no tale to tell, as none had any memory of their time inside, or for that matter, their own name or life before their intrusion. Whatever lay within would remain a mystery until Foranfae decided to give up her secrets, or an unforeseen catastrophe leveled the forest.

While Toryn was no fool, his curiosity led his feet back to the road and over the other side. He took a few paces onto the grass to take a closer look, trusting his gut would soon warn him of imminent danger. He stared into the gloom between the tree trunks, hoping the low, evening sun would allow him to see a little farther inside. His scalp tingled. He blinked, unsure if his eyes deceived him. At the edge of his vision, a tall, shadowy figure stared back. But when Toryn looked again, it had gone. He turned his head to look from the corner of his eye. There it was again. It moved among the trees, darting from one to the next with unnatural speed, making its way towards the edge, always watching but evading Toryn's effort to fix it in his sight. Wherever the figure moved, the branches swayed despite the still evening. Toryn instinctively crouched. The trees appeared to grow taller, their branches twisting towards him, their thin twigs reaching out, groping the air, sensing someone drew near. Hope screamed. She stood at his side staring, wide-eyed at the trees. He spun back. But the figure had gone, and the trees stood motionless, appearing oblivious to their presence as a typical forest should.

He took Hope's hand. 'Come on. Perhaps it's best we take the longer route after all.'

Toryn bolted upright. Sweat poured from his brow despite the cool dawn. He turned to Hope — her blanket lay empty at his side. Believing she must have gone to the stream to fill the flask, he stood and surveyed the valley to the south. If they made good progress, they could expect to cross the Menon Bridge and be in Archonholm by nightfall. Their five-day trek through the hills had thankfully been uneventful, and Hope had grown happier as the route brought them to the Menon Hills, placing the slopes between them and the forest.

He climbed a little way up the slope, hoping to catch a glimpse of the Archon's banner. But the hills at the southern edge of the range were taller, thus obscuring the tower bearing his banner.

Archonholm. All his life, he had heard stories of its grandeur. Hamar had always spoken in a rare respectful way of the city. And of the Archon, he would have no bad word uttered against him. But while Hamar had sworn the Archonian Oath to sacrifice his life, if necessary for the honor and defense of the realms, he had never gotten within a bow shot of their leader. If all went to plan, Toryn would soon find himself face-to-face with the great man. He had rehearsed his speech a hundred times ready for the first guards they encountered. But as much as he had tried, he still struggled to find the right words to say to the

Archon. But Toryn hoped the man would appreciate the importance of his message concerning the fate of the Singing Stone in the Wend Gap. His palms stung at the memory, but it seemed a long time since he and Hamar had made the grim discovery in the ruined cave.

Toryn strolled a little farther up the side of the valley to the nearby trees. He listened to the birds singing as he gathered twigs for their breakfast fire. In a way, he was pleased they had taken this route. He had also felt uneasy so close to the forest, but it had a different feel to Wyke Wood, and he could not fathom his reaction. His stomach had not recoiled as it had in the presence of Uldrak and Uleva, but he knew for sure he would not walk willingly into Foranfae. Despite Hamar's tendency to embellish his stories with weird and wonderful details with each telling, Toryn believed every word his old friend had spoken of the forest.

The flint sparked and lit the dry grass. Toryn placed the sticks over the flames and listened to the satisfying crackle. He pulled a rabbit from his rucksack and glanced towards the bend in the valley, expecting to see Hope return any moment. But this morning, he would have breakfast well underway, so at least she would have no reason to complain until midday when her empty stomach would start to grumble. After many weeks on the road together, he now appreciated how she kept going — she ate more than he would have expected for a small woman.

Toryn spiked the skinned rabbit on a sharpened stick and propped it over the fire. He wiped his hands on the damp grass and stood waiting for Hope. But still, she failed to show. He turned the rabbit over to cook the other side, then walked down the valley to the rocky outcrop where the stream flowed. He rounded the bend but found no sign. Something was wrong. Toryn ran back to their campsite to find the flask sitting beside her blanket. Where had she gone? No footprints marked her departure, but she could easily have walked from their site and leave no footprints on the thick, damp grass.

The smell of burning flesh drew his attention. Toryn decided to sit and finish preparing breakfast. Perhaps Hope had wandered into the nearby woods for privacy, and the aroma of a cooked rabbit would soon entice her back. But a nagging doubt gnawed at his stomach. In all their time together, she had never left him. Even in her most obstinate and bewildered state, she had stayed close by, appearing keen to keep her eyes on him.

Toryn tore off a strip of meat and chewed, constantly checking up and down the valley. What now? It had never crossed his mind Hope would vanish. Was she in peril? Hope had saved him from an unspeakable fate at the hands of Uleva; he should now, at the very least, look for her. But what of events in the wider world? Was there war in the north? Here in Holm, there were no signs of conflict. He had seen little activity on the main road. Had the Golesh breached the Caerwal Gate, thousands of reserves would be rushing south to defend the realm. Or if things had gone terribly wrong, he would be evading a rampant enemy surging north.

Toryn finished his meal and chose to wait a while longer. There would be no point in searching for Hope just yet, only for her to stroll back to the very place he had abandoned. If she had not returned by midday, he would walk up to the brow of the hill and look. But which way could she have gone? Perhaps another Singing Stone stood nearby? Hope had spoken of others. She claimed there were once seven, six following the destruction of the stone he and Hamar witnessed. If the remaining six were evenly spread throughout the land, possibly one could be situated in Holm. But if she had answered a call from a stone, why had she not roused him? If she had gone to a Singing

Stone protected by the old spells, would he be able to follow?

A plume of smoke rising down the valley caught his eye. Toryn kicked soil over the hot ashes of his fire, gathered their belongings, and scrambled up to the thick bushes a little way up the hill. Who could be travelling this route when the road lay close by? He retreated farther into the scrub. Did the Archonian Guard patrol the valley as well as the road? He winced as a thorn scratched his neck. It would make sense to watch the valley as fugitives would hardly be rambling along the main routes through Holm. But who were they looking for? His shoulders sagged. What if Hope had gone that way? Had a patrol apprehended her? He had to know. Toryn creeped through the thorny bushes and tramped up the hill. Sweat poured into his eyes and down his back as the sun rose over the valley. He fretted. Only a few weeks back, his clothes from the cell had offered little protection against the cold; now it trapped the heat against his body. But he was reluctant to remove his shirt as the stronger sun in the south had already burned his exposed arms and face.

Toryn left the cover of the bushes and crossed the top of the ridge. He made his way along the opposite slope until he drew level with the smoke. He crawled up to the brow and peered down into the valley. Six men sat around a campfire eating a late breakfast, and judging by their equipment, he guessed they had to be Archonian Guards. But there was no sign of a prisoner — Hope could not have come this way. Toryn turned and sat. To the west, the Menon Hills stretched another league. Between the foothills, fields of wheat and barley shone gold under the morning sun. He could think of no reason why Hope would have chosen to head towards the sea. Surely east was out of the reckoning as it would have been impossible to avoid the Foranfae. Archonholm and the Caerwal

Mountains loomed to the south, but why would she continue that way without him. He turned north. Had she fled back from where they had come?

Toryn lay on his back and stared at the sky. His spirits rose as he recognized larks fluttering high above him, enjoying the warm air, singing their lilting song. He listened, remembering Hamar's assertion they sang without pause, so they did not have to bear the silence while waiting for the Maidens to reply. For a moment, he felt as he had back in the carefree summers of his childhood. Toryn watched the larks, wishing he could join them to bask in the sunshine, blissfully unaware of the troubles besetting the realms. He sat up and found his eyes wandering to the horizon in the west. In four days, he could reach the coast. As a young boy, Hamar's tales of the Elessyn Sea had filled him with a longing to see the vast, restless waters with waves as high as houses crash against the cliffs.

He was alone. Toryn glanced south. Did he really need to take his message to the Archon? Would it make any difference? If the Golesh broke through the gate, and the Ruuk conquered the north, he may never get the chance to gaze upon the sea again. Toryn stood, took one step down the hill, then stopped. What would Hamar think of him? The old guard devoted most of his life to the service of the Archon and the realms. Toryn imagined Hamar at his side, arms folded, shaking his head in disgust. He heard his gruff voice, *Duty, lad, duty.*

Toryn turned and walked back up the hill. He had to do *his* duty and deliver his message, which meant going to Archonholm. He stood at the top of the ridge and surveyed the valley and hills opposite. Where was Hope? Had she said anything over the last few days to reveal her state of mind? But he could recall nothing. The forest had caused her distress, but as soon as they had reached the hills, she had seemed more at ease.

Below, the sound of the guards preparing to leave demanded his attention. Toryn watched as they tied on their sword belts and shouldered their packs. He held his breath, curious to see which direction they would take. He exhaled as they headed north up the valley. Toryn waited until they had rounded the bend and then made his way down the hill. He made his decision — he would go south to Archonholm. If Hope had come this way, then it made sense to follow on after her. If she had gone any other direction, he only had a one in three chance of guessing right and perhaps little chance of finding her even if he chose correctly. Besides, his objective ultimately was to speak to the Archon. As much as it pained him, he accepted his priority was to deliver his message; finding Hope would have to come later. But despite his reasoning, Toryn's heart and stomach disagreed with his head.

2. Divided Loyalties

'That's absurd!' Elodi rose from her chair. 'Bardon sailed barely a week ago, and Broon are announcing his successor?' She walked to the Great Hall's large window and looked out onto the bustling city below.

Wendel's thick eyebrows bunched in the middle as he squinted at the scroll. 'I'm afraid that is their custom, ma'am, and it's not for us to question them. Broon's charter dictates, rightly in my opinion, the realm cannot be leaderless under any circumstances. I can only assume they also have received no word from Lord Broon, and therefore he is in no position to rule. The trials would have started as a precaution as soon as Bardon took command of the Archon's fleet. But should he return within the year, their laws state he will assume his position without a challenge.'

Elodi groaned. 'A year? I dearly hope we hear from him long before then.' She followed the progress of a cart clattering along the road to deliver food and drink to the workers on the plain. She turned back to Wendel. 'And what do we know of the new lord, this Nordryn fellow?'

Wendel yawned and stretched out his arms. 'Well apart from the fact his ancestors came from the north, hence his name, we know very little. But we do know he passed the trials as decreed by the Council of Keld, so has proved worthy of taking the title.' He finished reading the note and let it drop to the table. He drew a breath. 'Ah. Oh dear.'

Elodi looked up to the ceiling. 'Oh dear, what?'

His eyes stayed on the paper. 'And… as is his right as the new Lord Broon, he's demanding Broon's spearmen return to Keld immediately.'

'He's demanding what!' Elodi shot up from the window ledge. 'But surely… he must know we…' She strode to the table, jabbing her finger at Nordryn's message. 'Demand? Or request?'

Wendel pointed to the last line. 'I'm afraid *demand* is the actual word he uses, ma'am. And to decline would be taken as an insult and, ultimately, a challenge to his authority.' He grunted as he stood and held out the paper to Elodi. 'Despite our current predicament, I believe we have no choice but to comply. I'm sure you don't want to stoke the embers of the old hostilities. The last thing we need is another unfriendly neighbor in such times.'

Elodi read Nordryn's words and brought a hand to her mouth. 'What could have befallen Bardon's fleet? Why no word? Has he failed, Wendel?'

He gestured to the nearby chair. 'May I?'

Elodi waved her hand. 'Of course, and please don't feel you have to ask my permission every time you want to sit.'

His joints creaked as he lowered himself into the chair. 'Thank you, ma'am. I find I can think more clearly these days when off my feet.' He leaned back. 'As for Lord Broon, or Bardon, as we should officially refer to him as he no longer holds that title now Nordryn—'

'He's still Lord Broon to me, but regardless of correct etiquette, what could have happened to the fleet?'

'Communicating would be a challenge, ma'am. The air is thin above the Caerwals, I'm not sure a bird could negotiate the range easily. And should it try to take the pass, they would make an easy target for the Golesh at the gate. A message sent by sea would take time, and of course, we have no idea if enemy hawks have intervened.'

Elodi snatched up the paper, screwed it into a ball, and hurled it to the floor. 'And nothing from the Archon! How does he expect me to prepare if he sends no dispatches?'

She glanced to the window as the room darkened. 'Has he opened the gate, Wendel? Are we victorious, or do we sit here in ignorance of the mortal danger we face if he's lost the pass?' Wendel opened his hands with no words to offer. Elodi returned to the window and looked up to the gathering clouds. 'If the Archon thinks I'm going to risk what small force I have at my disposal to retake the Drunsberg mines, he'd better think again. What's the point in sacrificing more soldiers? If he's gained his victory, he can send some of his *precious* resources to aid us for a change. If he's suffered a defeat, then what good is there in recapturing the mines? All will eventually be lost if Archonholm has fallen.' She turned as hail stones hammered against the window. She watched them bounce back from the glass and noted their size; even the weather appeared to have stepped up its campaign to demoralize her people. In no time, the hailstones piled up on the outside ledge, stacking on top of each other as if attempting to shatter the windows and storm the Great Hall.

Wendel cleared his throat. 'Ma'am? What of Nordryn's demand?'

'Send for Captain Ruan. I trust he's recovered fully to perform whatever duties his *new* leader has planned for him.' Elodi sighed. 'I will miss him and his spearmen. But not just for his expertise and able soldiers. Despite his abruptness, I have come to regard him as a trusted friend.'

'My sentiments entirely, ma'am.' Wendel rang the bell sitting on the table. Elodi could barely hear his words to the Officer of the Council above the barrage outside. She jumped as he joined her at the window to watch the storm. 'At least we can be thankful the enemy have stayed put at Draegnor.'

Elodi peered up to the gray sky hanging over Calerdorn. 'Yet the longer they wait, the more I fret. What are they plotting to throw against us in the days to come?'

Wendel gestured outside. 'But it's bought us time to improve our defenses. And the repairs of the fort at Dornan Pass are complete. We are fortunate the mountains offer us protection, and with relatively few soldiers, we can hold them up for a while at least.'

'But I want to do more than just *hold them up*. The enemy must have five or possibly six Ruuk for every soldier I possess, not to mention the dark arts those wykes appear to command.'

Wendel sat on the ledge. 'But let's not belittle our modifications to the city. The workforce has done remarkably well to dig the trenches, lay the spikes, and install the captured ballistae at the East Wall and docks. The enemy will struggle to bring their heavy engines within range next time. And the new ramp leading up to the gate will reduce the speed and impact of any battering ram that makes it thus far. And the bigger the ram, the more it will struggle to gain the top, to make even a dent or scratch on the gate.' He smiled and ran his hand along the solid stone wall. 'We can thank our ancestors for the foresight to build here. Unlike Archonholm, we have only two narrow fronts to defend, and both are now better prepared and equipped.'

Elodi patted his hand. 'Thank you, Wendel. You always seem to know what to say, but I fear no words can soften the blow of Nordryn's demand.' They turned as the door opened. The officer ushered in a wet Captain Ruan.

Elodi instructed her officer. 'Please bring Captain Ruan a warm drink.' She looked to Wendel, then back to the man. 'Make that three.' She gestured to the chair. 'Please, Captain, do sit.' Ruan grunted his thanks and removed his damp cloak. He sat, but Elodi noticed his movements remained a little stiff. Elodi and Wendel pulled up their chairs opposite Ruan.

Elodi addressed the captain. 'We have received word from Keld.'

Ruan nodded at the ball of paper on the floor. 'Am I to assume, ma'am, it's not a message to your liking?'

'Ah, yes.' Elodi rose and picked up Nordryn's communication. She flattened it out on the table. 'You are right to assume that, Captain.' She took a breath. 'I will get straight to the point. I don't know if you're aware of events back home, but we have been informed a new lord has been appointed following the appropriate trials.' Ruan's eyebrows raised a little, but otherwise revealed none of his thoughts. Elodi continued. 'The new lord goes by the name, Nordryn.' His brow creased. 'What do you know of this man?'

Ruan leaned forward and clasped his hands. 'A little, ma'am.'

Elodi glanced to Wendel. 'And would you care to elaborate… tell us more?'

He cleared his throat. 'His father contested the same trial in which Bardon triumphed to become the forty-fourth Lord of Broon. Nordryn's forefathers lived north of the border during—'

'Ruuk?' Elodi stared at Ruan. 'Is Nordryn descended from a Ruuk clan?'

'No, ma'am. While his ancestors were from outside the realms, they were men. It is believed they're descended from those who fought with Ormoroth in the old days. And following Draegelan's victory, they were banished from the realms.'

Elodi held Ruan's gaze. 'Can they be trusted?'

He nodded. 'Nordryn's line swore allegiance to the fortieth Lord Broon after a heavy defeat by their rivals.' Ruan sat back. 'They were given land within Lunn's border and offered the protection of Broon. They readily accepted and have been loyal since that day.'

Wendel tapped the paper. 'Will he make a good lord, Captain? Will he prove to be a reliable ally to Harlyn?'

Ruan shrugged. 'Nordryn met the standards to take the trial. And if he were not suitable, he would have failed. But he was victorious.'

'Well let us hope whoever devised the test knew what they were doing.'

The captain stroked his chin. 'The trial has served us well for all these years, ma'am. By the traditions and laws of Broon, Nordryn's success suggests he will make a good lord and serve the realm with honor.'

Elodi slid the crumpled note across the table. 'Well, he's certainly wasted no time in serving the realm. Your new lord *demands* you and your men return to Keld… immediately.'

His eyes widened. 'Ma'am?'

'As I'm sure you're aware, this puts me in a difficult position. I don't want to defy your new lord, but then I'm reluctant to lose the support of you and your valiant spearmen at this time.'

Ruan picked up the paper. His finger traced along each line as he read the words. After a minute, he looked to Elodi. 'Ma'am.' His lips formed several words before he spoke aloud. 'I was given permission to retire from the Archonian Guard following a request from Lord Broon.' His reading finger tapped the table. 'I ended my service to the Archon to take orders from Lord Broon… and as I see it, Bardon is still my commander.' Elodi held her breath. He cleared his throat. 'He gave the order to bring my men here, to help protect you, your people, and your fair city.' He sat back and folded his arms. 'And I intend to continue to honor that order.'

Elodi exhaled. 'For which I… we, the people of Calerdorn, are most thankful.' She looked to Wendel. 'But how am I to respond to Nordryn? As I said, I cannot risk animosity with the new lord at such a crucial time.'

Ruan managed a half-smile. 'Am I to assume my new lord knows little detail of the events here?' Wendel nodded. 'Then Nordryn won't know how many of my men survived.' He rested his chin on his hands. 'I will return thirty of my men, men with families in and around Keld.'

Elodi worked out the numbers. 'That will leave a little over two hundred.'

Wendel leaned on his elbows. 'And what of you? I'm certain you won't want to get off on the wrong foot with Nordryn. How will you justify staying in Calerdorn?'

'My men will tell half of the story. I was gravely injured in the siege and am unable to travel.' His lip curled up along with an eyebrow. 'They won't mention I've made almost a full recovery.'

Elodi glanced to Wendel, then back to Ruan. 'And your men are totally trustworthy? And by that, I mean, none will reveal you're in good health, and much of your force remains here.'

'Yes, ma'am. I trust them without question. I know my men each by name, and over the years we have been together, they have earned my trust and respect, and I theirs. Those returning will remain loyal to me… without question.'

Elodi retrieved Nordryn's message. 'Is it worth the risk? As much as I would dearly welcome your continuing support, Ruan, what if the new lord discovers our deception?'

Ruan leaned forward. 'May I offer my thoughts, ma'am?'

She nodded. 'Please do, Captain, as you know I value your opinion highly.'

He rubbed his hands. 'Forgive me, ma'am. Earlier, I was not entirely honest with you. But when you mentioned

Nordryn's demand to recall my men, it made me think again. It's unusual for an incoming lord to overturn an order by his predecessor, especially so soon, and in the circumstances that Bardon could yet return. Nordryn will be aware of the danger you face on your borders, and of the fall of Drunsberg, and now, Draegnor. I think, by his actions, he has set out his stall and plans to isolate Broon and tighten control of its borders yet further in the light of recent events. So, I wouldn't be too concerned about the new lord discovering our deception.' He glanced to the door. 'And… I was surprised to hear Nordryn had passed the trials.'

'What makes you say that?'

Ruan glanced to the window. 'While I have no reason to believe Nordryn and his folk are disloyal, there's always been a… wariness in Broon of those who swap allegiances from those of their ancestors.'

Wendel drummed the table. 'Are you concerned, Captain? Your fellow men of Broon may become wary of you, following your decision to stay here?'

Ruan bristled. 'My allegiance is to Bardon, who in turn offered it to you. I am not changing my allegiance.'

Elodi held up her hand. 'And for that we are most grateful. Wendel is not questioning your loyalty, Captain. Your loyalty is not, for one moment, in question. We are simply concerned you may lose face in Broon.'

Ruan sat back. 'Then I appreciate your concern. But you need not worry on my behalf. Those in Broon whose opinion I care for, will understand my decision should they discover I chose to remain in Calerdorn.'

Elodi stood. 'Good. Now, I believe we should arrange for those who will return to Keld, to prepare without delay. Wendel will pen an answer to Nordryn, and also congratulate him on his new position, although…' she looked to the water streaming down the window, 'let us look forward to a swift and safe return for Bardon.'

Elodi patted Sea Mist's neck and took hold of the reins. 'I know you disapprove, Wendel.' She looked back to the line of Ruan's spearmen chosen to return to Keld. 'But the least I can do for these men who put their lives at risk for us, is to escort them on the first part of their journey. Besides, it will also give me the opportunity to speak to the people of Dorn Plain.'

Wendel rolled his eyes. 'Then please take more soldiers to escort you for the return journey. It would help me sleep easier.'

'I have twenty of Gundrul's finest, led ably by Captain Cubric, there's been no sightings of enemy activity anywhere near the plain, and I will be gone four, maybe five days at most.' Elodi tapped her chest guard. 'And I'm wearing my armor as you insisted.' She kicked off and called back. 'And I'm sure at your advanced age you'll have no difficulty sleeping.'

Elodi took a deep breath as Sea Mist trotted out of the main gate. The cheers rang out from the hundreds turning out to give thanks to Ruan's departing spearmen. She glanced up to the dark skies, half-expecting the rain to greet their arrival on the plain. But thankfully the heavy clouds' advance had been thwarted by the snowy peaks of the Dornan Mountains, who bore the brunt of a hailstorm. As they approached the line of the new defenses, the workers stopped and waved their picks and shovels. Ruan's men thrust their spears into the air and gave a throaty roar that sounded loud enough for twice their number.

Elodi sat tall in her saddle as she observed the fine work of her city's tradesfolk. Calerdorn's engineers had narrowed the road by digging deep ditches on either side. To protect the approach, more ditches had been constructed, running out in a wide arc to shield the route to the outer wall. She winced as she eyed the sharp wooden spikes angled towards any fool daring to attack Calerdorn. A little farther on, Elodi reached the first of the two wide trenches to stop the enemy bringing its heavy weapons into range. Hundreds had worked night and day to hurriedly construct what she hoped would prevent death and destruction raining down on her people ever again. If an invading army brought wood to span the gap for their trebuchets, one accurate strike from Calerdorn's artillery would ignite the fuel sitting in the trenches, engulfing their monstrous machines before they could cross.

Elodi rose in her saddle to look back to the outer wall. Work on the second phase would soon begin. A new rampart outside the wall was to be constructed using the earth excavated from the trenches. The elevated position would house bigger trebuchets, giving them a greater range and offer more protection for the walls. If Uldrak brought his engines of death to Calerdorn, this time they would be stranded and quickly under attack before he could deploy them. But while reassured by the defenses, she was saddened by the now warlike nature of the plain. The people of the city would no longer hear the reassuring sound of grazing sheep and cattle, but it was a price all were prepared to pay. Now that much of the work outside the city had been completed, more resources could be assigned to repairing the damage sustained by the walls and buildings. But despite a number of breaches, the addition of the trenches and spikes made a daunting sight to any who sought to take the city. Elodi clenched her fists on the reins. While she did not want to see an invading army, part of her relished the challenge. Let them come. Let them suffer and die if they ever try to take Calerdorn from me again.

Captain Cubric rode at her side. The small man from Kernlow looked comfortable in a saddle, unlike his commander, Gundrul. He smiled as he nodded over his shoulder. 'You must be thinking the same as me, ma'am. If that scoundrel, Uldrak, ever tries to come back he'll get an even bloodier nose this time.'

Elodi returned his smile. 'I would hope if he were foolish enough to return, we'd give him more than just a *bloody nose*, Captain.'

Cubric laughed. 'If he wants to get into the city, he'd have to pack his Ruuk hordes in a nice, long line between the ditches and spikes. Then we could give all of them a bloody nose with one, well-aimed shot. Be almost too easy, cruel even.'

She shuddered at the memory of the last attack. 'I have no issue with that. Should he return, he can expect no mercy. I shall not tolerate the boots of his army on our plain again.' Elodi's hands unclenched. 'But yes, I am heartened by our new defenses. It's only a pity I didn't anticipate the scale of the threat earlier and prepared thus.'

'I wouldn't feel guilty, ma'am. I don't think anyone could have guessed just how strong the Ruuk had become, and we had no idea these wykes could wield so much power and influence back then.'

'Thank you.' Elodi looked back to the Archonian escort. 'How is morale among your guards?'

'Their spirit is high. They've survived their first major battle, not counting that awful storm at sea. It's all very well going through training and putting your skills to the test against your fellow guards, but it's not until you face a foe that wants to separate your head from your shoulders, that you really know if you have the nerve.' He grinned. 'But if I may say so, no one came through that battle with a quarter of the glory as you. You should hear the men talk of your skirmish in the gatehouse.'

Elodi's stomach turned over. 'I did what I had to do, that is all.'

Cubric chuckled. 'But didn't you do it well, ma'am. It makes a huge difference to your average guard to have a commander of your standing at the front. It gives them confidence to follow orders knowing you'll also be in the thick of the battle, and not standing a safe distance behind dishing out their orders.'

Elodi shuffled in her saddle. 'And what was your first battle like?'

'Nothing like the siege. And you could hardly call them battles, skirmishes more like. I've had plenty of scraps with the odd Ruuk raider, but I have to say, those young lads straight out of training did remarkably well in their first taste of a real fight.'

'It's only a pity many did not live to see it through.'

Cubric sighed. 'I'm afraid that's all part of the life of a guard. But you won't meet one who would shun the challenge. *Not a step back*, we say. And all would rather die with honor with a blade in their hands, than from the many ailments that take hold in our old age. And, of course, being a guard, we have the Archon's promise…' He slapped his thigh and covered his mouth. 'Ah, said too much. I could never stop my mouth running away with my thoughts, ma'am.'

Elodi grinned at his childlike gesture. 'Archon's promise?'

He blushed. 'Nothing that would interest you, ma'am. Just that we know we'll be looked after following our service, or... an honorable, but untimely end. That way we're happy to give our best years to the Archon.'

'Then I hope that stands you all in good stead for what will inevitably follow.'

Cubric chuckled. 'We have a saying in the Archonian Guard: There's a blade with your name on it somewhere in this world. The trick is evading the rascal who wields it for as long as you can.'

Now Elodi laughed. 'Then I live in hope they can't spell my name.'

Elodi was pleased to find morale was high in the villages along the route. At first, they had feared the Ruuk entering their territory was the vanguard of a full-scale invasion, but the news of victory at Calerdorn had spread quickly, allowing them to come out of hiding and celebrate as the routed enemy fled east. Elodi wished she could take them all under the protection of the city, but these people were needed to tend the flocks and herds that fed the realm, and much of the Archon's forces. As they had waved them off after each brief stop, Elodi vowed to keep them safe, and the plains free of marauders, but as much as she tried to convince herself, she knew it would be a difficult promise to keep.

The Dornan Mountains could not hold back the dark clouds for long. As they broke camp on the second day since leaving Calerdorn, the north unleashed a double-pronged attack of wind and hail. Sea Mist dipped his head in the face of the onslaught, while Elodi was once more thankful for her armor as the hailstones rattled their gleeful tune on her breastplate. A large, grizzled-looking spearman had tried to raise her spirits with his tales of what he called *real* weather back in Broon. He spoke of the bitter easterlies that tirelessly blew in from the seas to taunt the northern ward of Lunn. She tried to conceal her amusement as he earnestly proclaimed, she would never know true hardship until she experienced a harsh winter in Flint; a settlement clinging onto the tip of a bony witch's finger that pointed defiantly out to the icy Karajan Sea. But watching how the men of Broon marched undeterred by the driving hail, she began to believe he may well be right.

She yelled over the wind to Cubric. 'The road turns south in another league. Then we'll have the wind at our backs.'

Cubric shrugged. 'Perfect. Then we can be wet, front, back and sides, ma'am.'

'Well at least you're not miserable with it.' She shielded her eyes against the sleet as she looked up. 'This constant bad weather is enough to drain the morale of the hardest of souls.'

'Then it will have to try a lot harder with us.' He stood in his stirrups and peered ahead. 'How far are you intending to accompany Broon's spearmen, ma'am?'

'We'll make camp tonight, then see them on their way come the morning. I intend to take a small diversion off the road to visit Dorlgoth before returning to the city.' Elodi noted Cubric glance to his men on foot. She continued. 'It's a small settlement of caves inside Dorlwood. Your men can dry off and get a hot meal inside them there.'

'That would be welcome, ma'am.'

'And maybe your men would be interested to know it's the birthplace of our most famous warrior, Dorlan.' As she spoke his name, she wondered what fate had befallen Dohl. She hoped Wendel had been right in believing the old man's misery would not be prolonged as Uleva's evil would surely consume him. But she had to be sure. If Dohl believed he was indeed Dorlan, he may have returned to the place everyone in Harlyn knew to be the great warrior's ancestral home.

Cubric nodded. 'I'm sure they'll be most interested. We spend many an evening around the campfire discussing places of historical interest and their local traditions. And not forgetting of course, all those myths and legends.'

Elodi regarded his face. A flicker of a smile crossed his lips. She grinned. 'You almost had me convinced for a moment there, Captain.'

Cubric winked. 'Trust me, ma'am, you really don't want to hear what passes for conversation when my men have had an ale or two. Mind you, for most of these young men, their boasts would indeed pass for myth.'

Elodi pulled up Sea Mist and gestured for Cubric to join her at the side of the road. She watched the faces of his men pass by and hoped they would see these dark days through and have the chance to meet a good woman and live long and fulfilling lives. She turned to Cubric. 'But please inform your men the people of Dorlgoth are... how shall I say this? Not like most you'll come across in this realm. They are immensely proud of what they call their gift to the world, and still very much dwell in the old days of Dorlan. Their caves are well off the beaten track in more ways than one. Dorlan is said to have left while still young, probably for the best I imagine. I believe two of your party are from Dorn, perhaps if you speak to them, they'll give you a less diplomatic account of the inhabitants of Dorlgoth.'

Cubric nodded. 'I get the picture. We have the odd place in my neck of the woods that appear to have been left behind. But at least they produce some very fine wine. So, you need not worry, ma'am. I shall instruct my men to be *careful*, and by that, I mean not to laugh or make fun of the locals.'

The last of Broon's spearmen passed. Elodi nudged her horse to follow. 'Thank you, Captain. I can't guarantee what sort of a reception we'll receive, but I trust they still adhere to the old tradition of providing food and shelter to weary travelers, even though strangers rarely pass through the wood. They're fond of keeping themselves to themselves and are wary of outsiders.'

'But you're the Lady of Harlyn. Surely, they'll welcome the leader of their realm to their home.'

'That's not a given in Dorlgoth, Captain. Few actually recognize Harlyn as their realm.' Her jaw tightened. 'They've never accepted Dorlan died, and await his return, regarding him as their rightful lord.'

Cubric held her eye. 'In that they may be right. Do you believe that old man we took from the woods really could be Dorlan? If it was a trick by the enemy, it was a damn fine one.' Elodi remained silent as she stared ahead. Cubric continued. 'It was quite a feat to change that bent, old beggar into a young, formidable warrior. And one that could break out of Calerdorn like he did.'

'No, Captain. I cannot accept it was Dorlan. We are indeed in peril if a power exists in this land capable of bringing back a dead man from a thousand years past. But I must know if Dohl yet lives. Regardless of who he is, I cannot have him roaming the realm under Uleva's control.' Her stomach clenched. Did Uleva know of Dorlgoth's long-held belief? Sending Dohl to the settlement in the guise of their legendary hero could rekindle ancient disputes and spread division through the realm.

3. A Guest of The Archon

Toryn dropped to his knees and stared wide-eyed in disbelief. Hamar had never spoken a truer word. He had traveled the western side of the known world, and nothing could possibly match the sight less than half a league ahead. He had rounded the last of the Menon Hills to be greeted by the immense fortress city of Archonholm at close hand. His head tilted back, but still he struggled to see the Archon's banner flying from the tallest tower. A dozen or so lesser towers reached impossibly high into the sky, each tall enough to serve as a ladder to the gods. But to climb to the heavens, you would first have to scale the forbidding walls thrusting up from the bedrock protecting the immense structures. As the sun set over Toryn's right shoulder, the city glowed a deep coral in the fading light, throwing long shadows that appeared to stretch to the far east coast of the realm.

Toryn stayed on his knees, overawed by the presence of the great city. He knew well the tale of Archonholm, but his imagination had never pictured it so. Strengthened in a time of great need, it stood defiant before the vast barrier of the Caerwal Mountains. Together, the fortress and the mighty peaks served to defend the fertile lands of the Five Realms from the marauding hordes dominant in the south. Toryn had seen drawings of Calerdorn with its curved walls and tall, majestic spires. But Calerdorn, while a strategic stronghold, was conceived and constructed by hands and minds of great skill and vision in the glory days of the Seven Realms. Whereas Archonholm was built with the sole purpose of defense to keep the Golesh at bay. It may be graceless and bereft of beauty, but it had served its people well.

Toryn's eyes stayed fixed on the imposing battlements. The voice that had driven Hope to despair back on the ridge, stated the Archon was in peril. But how could the leader of the realms, sitting in his high tower amidst the solid walls of this great citadel, possibly be in danger? His eyes lowered to the Menon Bridge. Built from the same stone as Archonholm, its three piers held firm against the strong current of the Menon River as she reluctantly changed course to follow the line of the Caerwals on her final journey to the Elessyn Sea. Rivalling the Great Elda, the Menon sprang from the southerly valleys of the Kolossos to flow through the heart of the Foranfae Forest before emerging close to Archonholm. As a child, Toryn had often dreamed of drifting in a boat from source to sea, imagining the sights he would see on his journey. But even the bridge exceeded anything he could have envisaged — half of Midwyche could sit easily on its broad roadway. And how would he even make it across? The gates were shut, and he had not the words to permit his crossing. The river was too wide and strong to swim. If he attempted the water, he would find himself at the mercy of the Menon that would gladly wash him away from Archonholm and ditch him in the sea.

Toryn sank onto his haunches. What made him think the Archon needed to hear his vital message? What could he possibly say or do to aid the mighty fortress and all its armies within? Surely the eyes and ears of the city knew all that happened in the Five Realms. His account was merely a side story of little interest to the powers of the land. Toryn looked to the gigantic mountain wall. He was not needed here. He should return home and help Andryn and Jerrum tend the farm now Hamar was gone. Hope had survived many years in the wilds and would continue without him; far greater powers than he would take care of the wykes in the north. Back in Midwyche, he would be more use to the realms by maintaining the fences to keep the hungry creatures from feasting on their valuable livestock. But, above all else, he now realized, he longed to see his mother. He wondered if she stood in her herb garden watching the same sun as it drew an end to the day. Was she thinking of him? How much did the people of Midwyche know of events in the wider world beyond their borders?

Toryn turned to look back down the valley. If he went home, would he ever be able to leave again? The marshal would arrest him for his supposed desertion and throw him in the only cell the village possessed. But the urge to see his folks and at least let them know he still lived was strong. Perhaps if he arrived in the dead of night, he could see them and be gone before daylight. But then what? He clicked his fingers — it was obvious. He should search for his real father. Then perhaps he would have the answers that had nagged him since Miram first told him he was found in the barn. But Hamar's revelation of what really happened that night had served only to expand the emptiness he felt within.

He grasped a smooth stone by his side and rubbed it between his fingers. His father had disappeared over twenty years ago — did he yet live? And where would he start his search?

'Hey! You!' Toryn's head snapped up. Two Guards strode towards him from the gatehouse on the bridge. They halted a few paces away and drew their swords. One gestured at him. 'Close your mouth, get up from your knees, and haul your carcass over here.' Toryn groaned but did as told. The first guard approached. 'You better have a good story to tell, otherwise you're in deep trouble, mate.'

Toryn tried to stand taller against the overbearing towers of Archonholm. He pushed out his chest. 'I am an

Archonian Guard.' The men exchanged a glance and grinned. Toryn tried again. 'I took the Oath from Captain Roold of Drunsberg.' But they only laughed harder, the more he tried to convince them.

'Ha!' The larger guard tugged at Toryn's arm. 'So, did you choose to swap your uniform for the clothes of a beggar? Or did a nasty, little rascal rob you of your guard's armor and sword?' Toryn knew how ludicrous his claim must sound. His head dropped. The first guard scoffed. 'We hear some odd stories, but yours certainly ranks up there with the best of 'em, lad.'

The guards grabbed his arms and marched him towards the bridge, still chuckling at his preposterous-sounding story. The gate opened as they drew near. A third guard eyed Toryn. 'What you got there, Harruld? Looks like he could do with a dip in the river. Don't want him bringing no diseases in.'

Harruld hoisted Toryn by his elbow. 'Believe it or not, this shabby fellow claims he's one of us. No doubt come to swell our ranks and save the city.'

The gatekeeper stepped forward. 'Don't look like much of a guard to me.' Toryn decided to stay silent. He wouldn't believe his own story either, given his sorry appearance.

Harruld looked him in the eye. 'But then he can hardly be an enemy spy seeing as he was so easy to catch, sitting right outside our gatehouse in the open.' He nudged Toryn. 'In you go, lad.' He stood aside and smirked. 'On behalf of the Archon, I welcome you to Archonholm, principal city of the Five Realms and home to the finest hostelries in the land.' Toryn ignored the guard's mirth and trudged into the gatehouse. Once inside, they led him to a small door. Harruld leaned over and pushed it open. 'Here you go, not the finest room in the city by any means, but I'm sure it will be better than where you've been sleeping for the last week.' He wrinkled his nose. 'Or month judging by the stench on you.' Harruld sighed. 'I'll have warm water brought in, then you can freshen up for the sake of the rest of us.'

Toryn stepped into the cell, but thankfully a clean cell with a bed, table, and a bucket in the corner. He tried again. 'But I've taken the Oath. I fought with the Archonian Guard at—' Harruld appeared to lose his patience and shoved him inside. Toryn spun around. 'I know about the plain, the Plain of Ever—' The door slammed in his face.

Harruld called through. 'I'd take the opportunity to rest if I were you. You'll have some questions to answer come the morn. Then you'll have a chance to prove who you are. But if you want my advice, I'd think about whether you want to continue with your tall story or tell us the truth. It would make things easier for you in the long run.'

Toryn slumped against the door. What now? Was it such a good idea to claim he was a fellow brother-in-arms? He would have to reveal much of his whereabouts over the last three months to back up his story. But who could prove it? He had no idea what had happened to Roold and his men, and the guard would hardly go to the trouble of sending someone far to the north to investigate whether his tale was true. No doubt, there were far more pressing issues at hand to occupy the Archon and the city. Would they even care? He had broken the law and traveled without permission regardless of his status as an honorary guard. He tipped back his head and covered his face. Was he to spend the rest of his days rotting in the dungeons of Archonholm? And if Hamar was right to believe there were people in the citadel who would discover the connection to his wyke-father, he could possibly suffer a worse fate. He groaned. One thing was for certain — he would not be returning home any time soon. He was a trespasser, a deserter, and most likely a wyke; all viewed unfavorably by the Archon.

Toryn looked around his new home. At least it was an improvement on the dark hole in Wyke Wood. The bed consisted of a frayed sack of hay and sat next to the wall beneath a tiny window. Toryn had no other choice but to take the guard's advice. He kicked off his worn shoes and lay on the bed, letting his tired bones sink into the hay as he put his hands behind his head. The sack may have been thin, but it was dry and the most comfortable thing he had laid upon in a very long time. Maybe there was a slim chance the Archonian Guard would still be willing to consider him for training. Surely, in these challenging times, they would be happy to take any who could hold a sword or use a bow. He watched the pink square on the opposite wall slowly change shape and redden as it crept up the wall, then stretch out as it made its way across the ceiling and escape out the window. Toryn closed his eyes as the sun bade farewell for the day.

'Wakey, wakey!' Toryn shot up. He thought he had barely closed his eyes, but the light streaming through the open door confirmed it was morning. Harruld stood with his hands on his hips. He looked down at Toryn. 'Did you sleep well?' Toryn wiped the sleep from his eyes and nodded. The guard beamed. 'Good to hear it. And now you're refreshed from your long journey, you'll be pleased to hear you're free to go.'

Toryn slipped off the bed. 'I am? So you must have spoken to—?'

The man's belly wobbled as he laughed hard. Harruld turned and called out. 'Told you so, he believed me. That's two you owe me now.' He patted Toryn's shoulder. 'Sorry, mate, no you're not. But we have to have some fun on this posting. It's not the most rewarding duty, and when you've been on the road for as long as me and—'

'Did you know Hamar?'

'Hamar of Darrow?' Harruld frowned. 'Well, I never met the man, but of course. Every guard knows about the adventures of Hamar.'

Toryn glanced to the sky visible through the small window. 'He was my friend. We were up in—'

'Hang on a minute there.' Another guard entered the cell carrying a chair. 'You said, he *was* your friend.' He eyed Toryn. 'Has something happened to our Hamar?'

Toryn noted their concern for a guard they had never met. He took a breath. 'I'm afraid he was killed… at Drunsberg.'

The second guard sank into the chair he had brought in. 'Killed? At the mines? What was he doing up there?' He glanced to Harruld. 'Thought he'd retired years ago to work on the land.'

'He had, and he did. He worked on my family's farm. But… we had to leave and ended up in Drunsberg. It's a long story.'

Harruld sat on the bed beside Toryn. 'How did he fall?'

Toryn saw his friend's last moments. 'With his sword in his hand. He took three, no, it was four Ruuk down, before they overwhelmed him.'

The guard slapped his leg. 'Ha! Even at his great age he still had it in him, eh. That's sad news, but all the same, given the choice, that's the way us guards would want to depart this world.'

Toryn bowed his head. 'And he helped another old guard, Elwold, to the plains before the raiders could take him.'

'Good old Hamar. Wish I could have seen that. I bet…' Harruld turned to Toryn. 'Here, hang on there. How do you know about the plain?'

Toryn stood tall and pushed out his chest. 'I told you, I

took the Oath.'

The old guard frowned. 'Yet you've not done the training?'

'It was a quick initiation. We were being taken to Wyke Wood as prisoners. The captain didn't think I should fight until I'd taken the Oath.'

Harruld scratched his head. 'Wyke Wood? By the Three, you've had a tough time of late, my friend.'

'Roold… Captain Roold swore me in, along with Jedrul, a miner, before we attempted an escape.' Toryn's head dropped. 'But we failed and ended up in the wood for our troubles.'

Harruld extended a scarred arm. Toryn gripped his forearm. He nodded. 'The name's Harruld, but you already know that. And this big, ugly brute is Odrun.' He threw a mock punch as this colleague. 'Or as we like to call him, Odd'un, for obvious reasons. But don't you be afraid of him. Looks far worse than he is.'

Odrun stepped up and took Toryn's arm, almost lifting him from his feet. He grinned, pointing to his face. 'When you're this handsome, you don't have to be a bully to get your way.' His large forehead crinkled. 'Anyway, what brings you all the way down here… sorry, what did you say your name was?'

'You never ask… I didn't get the chance. It's Toryn, from Midwyche, also in Darrow.'

'Good to meet you, young Toryn.' Odrun rubbed the back of his neck. 'And yeah, sorry about the prank we played on you earlier.'

Toryn smiled, feeling comfortable with his fellow guards. 'No need. I get it. You have to pass the time somehow.'

Odrun shrugged. 'Not easy being on duty where little happens, well not after what we've seen over the years.' He turned to Harruld. 'Let's get our brother a decent breakfast, eh. I'm sure we can spare something from our… personal stash.'

Harruld licked his lips. 'I'm sure I can rustle up a feast fit for a friend of Hamar's.' He turned and left, whistling a tune Hamar used to hum while steering the plow.

Odrun turned back to Toryn. 'But anyways, what are you doing in these parts? Must be important, it's hardly a few days stroll in the sunshine to get here from the north.'

Toryn sat back on the bed. 'I'd come to bring news to the… this is going to sound absurd, but I thought the Archon needed to know there's two wykes leading the Ruuk. And one seems very dangerous. I saw her pull witches out of thin air.'

'Her, you say? I didn't know a woman could be a wyke?'

'Doesn't matter what she is, she's powerful and most definitely not on our side. And from what I heard from one of the Ruuk, there's another who poses more of a threat somewhere in the realms.' Toryn looked to Odrun. 'But what of the gate? We heard of an attack when in Drunsberg.'

Odrun shook his head. 'That's old news. Had nothing since, but things have moved on at a pace since that night. The Archon opened the seas and sent a large fleet sailing south.' He beamed. 'Twelve thousand of our finest fighters are, as we speak, giving those Golesh blighters a right good kicking. I wish I could have seen their faces when Lord Broon and General Kragan set foot back in *our* land.' He thrust out his arm, twisting his wrist as if gutting a foe. 'They're on their way to take back Elmarand. Any day now, they'll be back in the old city.'

Toryn straightened. 'Taking back Elmarand?'

'And that's not all.' Odrun glanced to the door. He whispered. 'Don't tell anyone, but we've heard rumors the best of the rest of our forces are preparing for something big.' He checked the door once more. 'Harruld and me reckon we're going to storm through the Caerwal Pass, perhaps even as soon as autumn.' Odrun puffed out his chest. 'The Archon's going to open the gate.'

Toryn's eyes widened. 'Open the gate?'

Odrun waved his hand. 'Keep it down, lad. It's just our guess. But only when Lord Broon's force have secured the capital and creating merry hell in the old realm.' He folded his arms. 'Anyway, that's what me and Harruld would do if we were in charge.' He laughed. 'Not that they'd ever trust us with a command. But if we know our Archon, then that has to be the right thing to do. Why send the elites south and then leave them stranded when we can attack on more than one front?'

Toryn found his head shaking in disbelief. He kept his voice low. 'But to open the gate? Are you certain?' He checked the doorway. 'Is that… wise?'

Odrun stood. 'Careful there, mate. Guard or not, you can't go questioning the Archon's wisdom like that. Even if it's just us thinking out loud.'

Toryn stammered. 'I never meant to… suggest he's wrong. It came as a shock.'

Odrun patted Toryn's shoulder. 'Well don't you worry about it. If we're right' — he grinned — 'and we usually are, well, most of the time, okay maybe half. But if we're right on this occasion, and the Archon sees fit to attack the south, then I trust it's for the best. Then maybe he can turn his attention to these wyke fellows… and lassies of yours in the north.'

Toryn gripped the edge of the bed. 'And take back the mines.'

'Oh, you don't need to worry about them. The good Lady Harlyn is heading up a hundred guards to oust those rascals. Probably already back in our hands as we speak.'

Toryn looked up to the small window. 'I hope that's so.

But she would've needed many more than a hundred. I saw reserves heading north, but even with their numbers, it won't be easy.'

'What won't be easy?' Harruld returned carrying a basket of bread, cheese and cold meats. For a moment, Toryn forgot their conversation as his empty stomach craved breakfast.

Odrun also appeared hungry. 'Good work, Harruld. Hope the others didn't see you.' He reached over for a slab of cheese. 'I was telling young Toryn here about Lady Harlyn's mission.' He took a bite and spoke with his mouth full. 'You've done time at Drunsberg, Harruld. What do you reckon?'

Harruld handed the basket to Toryn. 'Best dig in, lad, before we polish this lot off.' He sat. 'To tell you the absolute truth, I was shocked to hear they'd fallen. Never thought it could happen, but then I heard rumors about fire-spitting weapons and some devilry at play.'

Odrun jabbed a piece of bread at Toryn. 'He says there's wykes abroad. And get this. One of 'em is a lass.'

Harruld's mouth dropped open. 'Wykes? And a woman? Is this true?'

Toryn nodded as he swallowed. 'I've seen two. One took the mines, the other was in Wyke Wood.'

Harruld tore off a piece of bread. 'Strange times, strange times indeed. We always suspected there was one in the wood, hence the name, but they'd always seemed happy to stay put. But you said *was*?'

'She left before an attack came. Took all the Ruuk with her and went east.'

Odrun reached for the bread. 'An attack on the wood? That's news to us. Who by?'

Toryn shivered as he remembered the dank cell. 'Can't be sure. I was taken away before they arrived. But I heard word of spearmen, hundreds of them.'

Odrun thought for a moment. 'Must have been men from Broon. Harlyn don't have that many spearmen to speak of, it's not their preferred weapon of choice.'

Toryn found he relished the opportunity to share his story. 'Whoever it was, the wyke and her men didn't want to hang around to fight them.'

Harruld chuckled. 'Me neither. Tough folk with tougher spears. Can be quite a handful.'

Odrun nudged Harruld. 'And I've also told young Toryn here about what we reckon the Archon is up to.'

A lump of cheese fell from the guard's mouth. 'Careful, Oddy, we can't be telling everyone we meet, there'll be no one left in the realm who don't know of it. That's supposed to be our secret plan. Mustn't let it reach the wrong ears, eh.'

Odrun wrapped a thick arm around Toryn's neck and ruffled his hair. 'But he's a guard now. We can trust the young fellow.' He released him. 'That's right, ain't it, lad. We can trust you?'

Toryn nodded. 'Your plan is safe with me. And let's hope we'll get a chance to march alongside—'

Another guard entered the cell. A younger man, but both Odrun and Harruld jumped to attention and saluted. Toryn followed suit. The man glanced to their breakfast on the table. He lowered his gaze to Harruld. 'That'll be stealing in the Castellan's book. And you know what happens to a guard who steals from the Castellan's stores?' Toryn stopped chewing. 'You know the law.' The captain smiled and held out his hand. 'Your commanding officer gets a share of the plunder. I can hardly report a man if my mouth is full of the offending bread and cheese.' He looked to Toryn. 'And when you've finished your leisurely breakfast, kindly take our guest to the Castellan's men at the keep.'

Odrun spoke up. 'But, Captain, he's one of us, he's

taken the Oath and fought at the mines.' He put his arm around Toryn. 'And would you believe, he was with Hamar when he died taking down five' — he winked at Toryn — 'or was it six Ruuk?'

The captain's eyebrows raised. 'Hamar? Didn't know he still lived. That's quite a story. You've obviously recruited these old soaks to your side. I trust these two, so if it were up to me, I'd get you a uniform and put you on patrol. But sadly, it's not.' He took a slice of ham from the tray and tucked it in his pocket. 'My orders are to take all strangers we apprehend to the Castellan.' He turned to leave. 'And we'd be drummed out of service quicker than Odrun can down a mug of ale if I neglected to do so.' He sighed. 'But beware, young man. The Castellan has the responsibility for keeping Archonholm safe and free of spies. And he executes that duty with relish I can tell you.' He nodded to the tray. 'Take your fill, lad. You won't get such a fine breakfast once in his hands.'

The Castellan's guard made no effort to hide his disdain for Toryn. He stood before him in a wide, defiant stance with his thick, brown arms folded. If Toryn even dared to shuffle in his seat, the guard grunted his disapproval. Toryn had no option but to await the return of the Castellan's officer who had gone to report the outcome of Toryn's short interrogation. Unfortunately, the officer had not been as interested as Harruld and Odrun by his account of the last few months. And to Toryn's dismay, the main thrust of his questioning focused on why he and Hamar had been on the road in the first place. Toryn had tried unsuccessfully to convince his interrogator he was assisting an old Archonian on an important mission to Greendell, but the officer did not see fit to follow up that line of investigation. Toryn suspected the officer would have heard every excuse he could invent a hundred times already. But at least one thing worked in his favor. Due to Archonholm being in a state of emergency, few could be spared from their duties, so there had been no verification of Toryn's flimsy story. Once it became obvious he was not about to be released, Toryn tried to convince the Castellan's man that he must see the Archon as he had vital information. But the officer had leveled his eyes at Toryn and poured scorn on his claim.

The door behind burst open. Another guard, even larger than Odrun strode in and peered down at him. 'Well, ain't you a lucky fellow. I've just had word that you're to be a special guest of the Archon.'

Toryn straightened. 'A guest of the—?' The first guard grunted.

The big man grinned at Toryn. 'When I say special, I actually mean prisoner.' He smirked at the other guard. 'We only say that so as not to alarm our *guests*.'

4. Home of a Legend

Elodi was reluctant to see even thirty of Broon's doughty spearmen depart her realm. She had sat on Sea Mist as she bade them a fond farewell and wished them a safe journey back to their homelands, while desperately wishing she could find a reason for them to stay. But the new Lord Broon's command had to be respected in the absence of news of Bardon and his fleet, no matter how much it gnawed at the pit of her stomach.

Elodi ducked under the low bough, leading Cubric and his twenty young guards through the ancient trees of Dorlwood. It had been many years since Elodi had last visited, but she remembered it well, if not fondly. Her father had taken her as a special treat on her tenth birthday to see the birthplace of the legendary Dorlan. Elodi had been captivated by the homes carved in the rock and had begged her father to let her stay, or at the very least, have a room fashioned for her in the sea cliffs outside Calerdorn. But to her dismay, neither wish was granted. However, even the naïve child in her sensed the reluctance of the villagers to engage with outsiders, and she quickly decided living in a cave would not be fun after all. But while distant, the Dorlgoth folk had been polite to the young, wide-eyed girl who obviously worshipped their fabled son.

Elodi glanced back to her entourage, noting the change in their faces. While still young in years, they had already experienced a battle the likes of which their fathers had only heard about in tales. But harder times obviously lay ahead; she knew the siege of Calerdorn was just the foretaste of events to come. She ducked under the long strands of damp moss hanging from tree branches as if a mockery of festive decorations. The spikey fronds of bracken linking their fingers across the track, suggested few traveled in either direction. The roots and branches of the gnarled trees threatened to shut off their passage completely in places, but mercifully this was no Durran Wood, and despite the gloom, Elodi felt at ease.

She looked up to the gray sky barely visible between the intertwined branches. It may have passed midday, but little light penetrated the trees to shed light on their passage. But while the men behind walked in silence, she was certain it was more through awe and reverence than trepidation. Elodi suspected the trees had grown before Harlyn was founded, and judging by their apparent hardiness, would surely stand long after the fall of her realm. The odd bird, not scared away by their presence, sang, but if they greeted them or warned others, she could not tell. Otherwise, the wood was quiet, but a peaceful silence, not the foreboding and unnerving silence of Durran.

The ground either side of the track began to rise as they descended into a shallow gorge. Elodi turned to Cubric. 'It's not far now.'

Cubric grimaced. 'Can't think who'd want to live here, ma'am. It seems a bit dank and grim, even for the north.' He shrugged. 'Sorry, my lady. I know it's the home of your legend, but I speak as I see and don't mean no offence like.'

'No need to apologize.' Elodi picked off a strand of moss sticking to her shoulder. 'It wouldn't be my choice either, but the caverns are warm all year round, and according to the last census, close to two hundred people choose to spend their life here.'

Culbric peered through the gorge. 'And Dorlan grew up in this place?'

Elodi steered Sea Mist through the narrowing gap,

avoiding the moss-covered rocks jutting out from the sides. 'According to the tales. But' — she laughed — 'the same stories reckon he was conceived when a young lass coupled with a mysterious deity from deep in the woods.'

Cubric grinned. 'I'm guessing there's not much else to do around these parts, ma'am.'

Elodi chose to ignore her captain's attempt at humor. 'Apparently, when still only a child, Dorlan fought off a pack of hungry wolves armed with nothing but a flaming stick.'

'That don't say much for the menfolk of the time though, do it.'

But Elodi did not hear his words. Her head was full of the pictures formed when her father had recounted the story. She spoke as if describing the scene before her. 'It was in the dead of a bitter winter. The wolves had come down from the Caler Mountains seeking food. Dorlan begged his mother to let him fight as many had died defending the settlement. It was said the wolves retreated as he confronted them. But the leader of the pack, not wanting to be humiliated by a human child, reluctantly attacked. But Dorlan quickly slew him, then dozens more before the wolves finally fled, fearing they'd be cornered by the fierce, young warrior.'

Cubric eyed the jagged rocks. 'That's quite a tale.'

'But that's not all. There are many such stories of his bravery before he departed his home.'

'So why did this young hero leave?' He cursed as he brushed against a damp rock. 'Ignoring the pretty obvious reasons, of course.'

'Stories of his bravery and skill with a blade reached the lady of Harlyn at the time. He was thus ordered to come to Calerdorn. Whether he went gladly, or with a heavy heart, the tale doesn't tell.'

Cubric laughed. 'I would say it would spoil the legend

somewhat if he had to be dragged kicking and screaming from his mother's side.'

This time Elodi smiled. 'I'm sure it would. But the storytellers see fit to tell us the people of Dorlgoth were not best pleased, especially his mother. Indeed, according to the legend, she still lives, sustained by the hope he will one day return.' Her stomach churned, dreading she might yet live and greet Dohl in her son's likeness as her own.

Cubric nodded. 'That's a nice touch. Makes the tale more dramatic don't you think.'

'But quite sad.' She glanced at the shadows between the trees. 'Imagine, living for a thousand years waiting for your long-dead son to come home.'

'Especially in a place like this.' He smirked. 'It would seem even longer as I doubt this deity lover of hers would still have eyes for a woman of such a great age.'

Elodi chuckled, thankful for the distraction. 'I think you've spent too many evenings around a campfire, Captain.'

He sighed. 'That's very true, ma'am. Very true.'

Elodi checked ahead. 'Ah, almost there. I vividly remember this part.' Sea Mist slowed as the ground dipped sharply. A little way ahead, a thick tree trunk lay across the gap supporting a curtain of dark, green moss. She recognized the make-shift entrance. 'Ah yes. There are bells concealed in that growth to announce the arrival of rare visitors.'

Cubric grunted. 'Dare I hope it's so they can stoke the cooking fires and have a hot meal ready.'

'Sadly not, but be thankful it's not to drop that hefty log on our heads.' As predicted, the bells jingled as Elodi and her party passed beneath. Beyond the entrance, the gorge slanted downwards for thirty paces and then widened. Elodi looked up as they entered what appeared to be a long, narrow hall with a gap at the opposite end.

Above, trees jutting out from the edges of the ravine formed a high ceiling, casting a green light on the settlement. On both sides, pathways and ladders crisscrossed rock walls with three levels of odd-shaped wooden doors. At the center of the clearing, a statue of their hero stood defiant, thrusting his sword aloft as if challenging those who dared to enter. But aside from the stone Dorlan, no one greeted them — the place appeared deserted.

Cubric caught Elodi's eye. She nodded. He climbed down from his horse and called out. 'People of Dorlgoth, the Lady Harlyn requests your attendance.' She looked to the doors and checked for movement, but they remained shut fast. He clicked his fingers, directing two guardsmen to inspect the nearest cave. Elodi dismounted and took two strides towards the stone stairway. Cubric cleared his throat. 'Ma'am. May I suggest we wait down here. Just to be safe, eh. We can't have the Lady of Harlyn injured by a crude trap.' He turned to the other guards and sent them to the adjacent homes.

'Very well, Captain.' Elodi took the reins of Sea Mist and Cubric's horse and tied them to the well. She removed her cloak. 'It's been many years since my last visit, but I can remember it being busier than this.' Cubric drew his sword. She raised her hand. 'Let's not be too hasty. We don't want to get off on the wrong foot. I can't imagine they would react well to a drawn sword.'

He lowered his blade. 'If it's alright with you, ma'am, I'd rather be ready.' He surveyed the empty ground between the walls of the gorge. 'Standard procedure. And I'd be happier if you stay by your horse. Just in case.'

'Captain!' The first of the guards returned. 'Everything looks in place but there's no one at home on the north side.' Three more returned to report the same on the opposite wall.

Elodi kept her eyes on the entrance. 'Captain. Please set a watch at both ends of the settlement. But instruct your men to be polite. The people of Dorlgoth must understand this is a cordial visit.'

Cubric directed two guards to take up the watch. He eyed the doorways and muttered. 'A strange place indeed.'

Elodi ignored her captain's remark and walked to the statue of Dorlan. She noted the top of her head reached the shoulders of Dorlan's stone likeness; the same height of Dohl following his transformation. The statue had seemed so much taller and grander on her previous visit, but the sculptor had done a fine job of replicating the face as seen in the paintings in Calerdorn… and Dohl. Elodi paced around the statue, listening to her footsteps echo back from the rock walls as her sense of unease heightened. She returned to the well as Culbric sent the last of his guards to check the remainder of the homes. 'Please Cubric, put away your sword. If, for some unknown reason, they were planning an ambush, it would have happened in the narrowest part of the route on our way in.'

Cubric sheathed his sword. 'Good point, ma'am. And I see no sign of a struggle here.'

Elodi sat beside him on the rim of the well. She glanced to the trees visible through the gap at the far end of the settlement. 'Perhaps they've gone into the heart of the woods to participate in one of their customs.'

'Looking for Dorlan's dad perhaps? Might be taking another young lass with them.' He grinned. 'Perhaps looking to sire another hero?'

Elodi rolled her eyes. 'Don't be flippant, Captain. Remember what I said about these people.'

Cubric frowned. 'Apologies, ma'am.' He appeared to guess her meaning. 'Only trying to lighten the mood.' He looked to the doors left open by his men. 'But to leave all your belongings unguarded? Is that normal?'

'As I said, Captain. They're unaccustomed to visitors, and follow their own customs known only to them. I imagine the most obvious reason for their absence would be something to do with a tradition. Perhaps they're preparing for one of their many celebrations of summer. Living in such conditions among these woods means they're very much attuned to nature and her ways.'

'Would they even notice it's summer here?' Cubric shivered. 'And it's still weeks until midsummer. But perhaps it's as you say, and they've wandered off to the woods and are dancing around an old tree trunk as we speak.'

'Then we shall wait.' Elodi stood and patted Sea Mist's neck. 'Have your men stand down and rest. But maintain the watch.' She smiled. 'I assume that's standard procedure in a situation such as this.' Elodi took hold of the bucket. 'I'm sure they won't mind if we draw water.'

'Must be plenty to go around with all the rain we've had lately, ma'am.' Cubric licked his lips. 'And do they use some of it to brew ale?'

Elodi lowered the bucket on the pulley. 'I would not know. I was but a small girl the last time I was here.' She watched it disappear into the shadows. 'Maybe I shall offer the service of a builder to install a pump. That would—' The bucket hit something hard. She leaned over the edge; her voiced echoed as she exclaimed, 'That's odd.' She turned to Cubric. 'Please have one of your guards bring a torch.' She turned the handle to raise the bucket and then let it drop. Again, it clattered against a solid surface.

Cubric bent over the low wall. 'It can't be dry. The streams in the woods flowed to the brim.' He looked back. 'Might explain where they've gone though, ma'am.'

'But the whole village?'

A young guard approached with a torch. Cubric took it

and held the flames over the well. Elodi peered over as he let it drop. The walls of the well flickered as it plunged and landed besides the bucket. Cubric gasped. 'Well, I'll be.'

Elodi squinted. 'Is that… ice? It can't be frozen, not at this time of year.'

'It is ice, ma'am. See, the torch is melting it.' The flame fizzled and went out. Cubric scratched his head. 'Surely, the well is fed by the fast-flowing underground rivers. They shouldn't freeze, maybe it happens in the far reaches of Nordruuk, but not down here.'

Elodi suddenly felt a chill in her bones. 'I wonder if this has anything to do with that creature, Uleva? This could—' She ducked. The shriek froze her blood. 'By the Three. What is that?'

Cubric looked up. He shouted over the din. 'It's the wind! Picked up all of a sudden, eh. It must funnel down this gorge.' He helped Elodi back to her feet. 'Had me going there for a moment as well, ma'am. Sounded like that awful thing you defeated in the gatehouse.'

Elodi brushed the dust from her armor. 'It was purely an apparition, Captain.' The wind continued to howl overhead. 'Another summer storm, just what we need. I suggest we'll stay here for the night if this sets in.'

The storm did not abate. If anything, it grew stronger. The howling wind blowing in from the north ripped the clouds asunder, forcing them to ditch their rain on the unfortunate people below. Before long, water began to trickle through the settlement, rapidly turning into a stream, and then an angry river swelling around Dorlan's knees. Elodi and her entourage had no choice but to retreat to Dorlgoth's main hall, safely above the violent waters. As the light began to fade, Elodi reluctantly accepted they would have to wait until morning to see if the water had receded. She made good on her promise of a warm meal, allowing the men to use the fuel available to cook what scant supplies were stored in the caves. But to the guards' regret, and Elodi's relief, they discovered the people of Dorlgoth appeared not to drink ale or wine.

Elodi spent an entertaining evening beside a roaring fire, listening to what she guessed was a restrained discussion for her benefit. At midnight, she retired to a small room at the back of the cavern, welcoming the chance for a night undercover after days of sleeping in the open. Elodi closed her eyes, satisfied Cubric's guards and the storm outside would keep potential threats at bay. Despite her concern about the absence of the inhabitants of Dorlgoth, sleep soon took her.

Elodi woke with a start. Something was wrong. She could not name what troubled her, but her discomfort grew. The storm had abated. Outside was silent, and the air had changed. She rose, put on her breastplate, secured her sword belt around her middle, and called for Captain Cubric. No answer. She shivered as she stepped out of her room. Back in the hall, Cubric and his men slept, the flickering embers of the dying fire daubed the walls a deep red. But Elodi took no warmth from it. Her breath steamed in the cool air as she stepped over the nearest sleeping guard to rouse Cubric. He lay curled under a blanket close to the fire. She shook his shoulder, but he refused to wake. Elodi tried again, more vigorously, failing to rouse his cold body. She bent, placing her ear close to his mouth. He breathed, but slow and shallow. Elodi stood and was about to rattle a pot hanging over the fire with her sword, but something stayed her hand. The watch? Had the men placed at either end of the settlement anything to report?

Elodi made her way, treading carefully over the slumbering men. The air chilled farther as she neared the entrance. Her chest burned as the cold seeped deep into her lungs. She stepped outside, wary not to let her labored breathing alert the unseen threat she suspected lay close. Above, a few stars twinkled through large gaps in the storm-damaged ceiling of branches. As her eyes adjusted, the full moon broke through, shedding a pale light on the settlement. Elodi stared in disbelief. The storm river had frozen solid, leaving a path of gray ice through the village. At the center, Dorlan's statue glistened in the moonlight, wearing a hoar frost coat of armor of a thousand tiny, white spears right up to the tip of his sword.

A crunch, then a snap. Elodi spun in the direction of the sound, holding her breath, fearing the vapors would give away her position. The sound replayed in her head. It could have been a branch breaking, torn free from its trunk. Close to the entrance where they had arrived that morning, a ghostly light glimmered, but not of the moon, a cold light, tinged the rocks a faint blue. It moved. Elodi crept a few paces along the ledge, slowly drawing her sword before it froze in its scabbard.

Elodi stopped. A tall, rangy creature stooped over the prone body of a watchman left to guard the entrance. The beast held a short branch under its arm as its long, spindly fingers grasped the man. Another snap. Elodi covered her mouth. The creature twisted and wrenched the guard's leg free of the frozen body. It placed it under its arm with what Elodi knew to her horror was not a branch, but the guard's other leg. The creature crouched by its victim, raising a dismembered limb to its wide slit of a mouth in its large head. Sharp, pointed teeth closed around the leg. Elodi spun away from the sound of shattering bone. But despite her horror, she looked back. Gray sinews like cables jutted out from the creature's head as its jaws clenched, then feasted on the fallen guard's frozen flesh and bone.

Elodi's heart hammered into her ribs. A shroul! She knew the tragic tale only too well. The hardy people of the north who dared stand against Ormoroth, were captured, tortured, and defiled. His vengeance knew no bounds as he unleashed the full corruption of his dark arts upon them, twisting their flesh and bones into a cruel parody of their former selves. But if they desired a swift death, they were denied. Ormoroth set them free, forcing them to live and adapt in the hostile frozen lands. They became misshapen, hollow creatures, both despising and craving the bitter winters that sustained them. Elodi knew of no soul who had seen one, believing they remained north of the trench. But the creature devouring the guard was obviously no apparition. Elodi tried to remember the stories. Could they be killed by a sword, or should she—?'

A thud; another crunch. Elodi turned and stared wide-eyed as a second shroul stepped onto the frozen river — it too carried a dismembered limb. She groaned; the other watchmen had shared the same fate as his unfortunate brother. The shroul's large, cloven hooves splintered but did not crack the thick ice as it approached Dorlan's statue. It stopped opposite and peered into its stone face glistening in the moonlight. It dropped his plunder, extending long, spindly claws to grasp the statue's sword arm. It yanked and twisted. The cold stone snapped. Elodi stifled a moan. It may only have been a statue, but it had stood for nigh on a thousand years, cherished by the people of Dorlgoth. The shroul's jaws gaped and clamped shut around the stone arm. It took a bite but spat out the rubble. It slung the arm away and watched it skid across the ice. The creature threw back its head and shrieked. Its pitiful, high-pitched wail echoed through the gorge, dislodging ice from the broken statue while freezing Elodi's soul.

She gasped. The shroul cut short its cry. Its eyes locked

on Elodi. The creature's head tilted as if surprised to see a warm body in its icy domain. She shuffled back as the creature raised its scrawny arm and pointed a long, clawed finger at her. Elodi's chest tightened as the air grew yet colder. She forced out a breath and inhaled, her lungs desperate for warm, moist air. But none was to be had. Elodi flinched as she breathed in tiny shards of ice floating in the cold air. Her pain alerted the other shroul. It dropped its feast and stood, also raising its skeletal finger towards her. Her legs stiffened. Claws of ice grasped her ankles and held her fast to the rock. Her throat and chest burned as the shrouls' tainted air forced its way deep inside her like a blade. Unseen claws entwined her legs, groping at her torso to clutch at her arms. Paralyzed, only her eyes moved in her frozen face. But she could hear. Rock crunched and ice splintered as the two shrouls approached. Their labored rasps sliced through the air as they anticipated tearing their prey to pieces. Elodi stood helpless — the sound of splintering bones filled her head. She could do nothing to stop them from snapping off her limbs like icicles and gorging themselves on her, Cubric and all his men.

The first shroul crossed the path, strutting tall on spindly legs like the hind legs of a large hound. It moved with ease up the slope and rose up before Elodi. It tilted its head. Glassy, gray eyes glowered, turning the last warm place in her body, her heart, into a block of ice. The second drew near to her left; its glee panting coldly in her ear. The first drew its face close. The edges of its thin mouth spread across its grim face, stretching the skin, shattering its mask of frost to form a cruel grin. Its jaw quivered, gnashing its spiky teeth that chinked like hail on armor. Its cold breath smothered her numb face. The ice on Elodi's brow crackled as she frowned, curious as to why the creature reeked of sour milk.

A claw clasped her arm. A silent scream shot forth from Elodi's raw throat. *This cannot happen!* She glared back at the face of the shroul. *I will not let this happen!* The shroul's eyes widened as if recognizing something deep within her. Heat stabbed at her stomach, surging to her arms and legs. The shroul released its grip as her body warmed, snatching its claws away as if scolded. Elodi could move. She raised her sword. The blade glowed orange as if reflecting the rising sun as it had at the gatehouse. But here, only the light of the moon shone. Elodi broke free from their grip of ice. She lunged forward, wielding her blade over her head in a circle, forming a shield of light. She dropped, then swung at the first shroul's leg. Her blade sliced through the scrawny limb — its screech split the ice free from her breastplate. The leg fell and splintered. The creature collapsed, clutching the gaping wound, but before it could scramble away, Elodi brought down her flaming sword and cut off its head.

Elodi spun around. The second shroul crouched and clambered through the doorway leading to the hall where Cubric and his men lay. She strode through the entrance bellowing at the beast. 'Don't you dare touch them!' The shroul twisted to face her, stooping under the low ceiling. It raised a finger, but this time its arm trembled. The shroul's eyes bulged as they fixed on Elodi's glimmering sword. It backed away, glancing behind to find a way out. But it could not move quick enough. Elodi sprung, plunging her blade deep into the creature's hollow chest. Her ears almost split as the scream filled the cave. Elodi pulled back, then cut its cries short as she swung and removed its over-sized head. It toppled forward, crashing to the floor, quickly followed by the rest of its body as it shattered like glass, scattering a thousand pieces across the hall.

Elodi stared at the shards, satisfied she had released the

tortured creature from Ormoroth's curse. The fire within died. She staggered forward, sinking to her knees as she gasped for air. Her vision blurred as her head spun. She rolled onto her back and let her dull sword fall from her hand.

'Ma'am?' Cubric stood over her. Elodi opened her eyes to find she lay wrapped in blankets beside the hearth. She wriggled her fingers and took a deep breath. She moved to sit but Cubric placed his hand on her shoulder. 'I suggest you give yourself a little more time.' He nodded over his shoulder. 'Would that be the remains of a shroul we found in the corridor? I've never seen one, but what's left matches the descriptions I've heard.' Elodi nodded. Cubric's eyebrows raised. 'And I assume you took it down?'

Her voice croaked. 'Yes.'

He let out a long sigh. 'A shreek, now a shroul?'

'Two.'

Cubric's laugh turned quickly to a cough. 'Two! I'd say let's get you down to the Caerwal Gate and let you loose on the enemy right away.'

Elodi waved his hand away as she sat upright. 'I'm afraid I wasn't in time to save those poor watchmen.'

'Foul creatures.' His head bowed. 'We found the watchmen. Their swords were drawn, so I hope they died a guard's death and are now…' he blinked. 'May I ask you to attend their burial, ma'am?'

'Of course, Captain. We must honor them in a manner fitting to their sacrifice.'

'Then we will do so now if that is fine with you, ma'am. We rest where we fall… where possible. The locals will have to put up with that. I've placed a new watch, but there's still no sign of the villagers.'

Elodi looked to the fire. 'We shall honor those young

men then make haste. No time to search for the villagers now. We must return to Calerdorn. There are more dangerous creatures than Ruuk roaming this realm these dark days.'

5. A View from the Tower

The immense weight of Archonholm crushed Toryn against the stone floor of his cell. He had heard many tales of the citadel's dungeons, but never thought he would find himself as a *guest* of the Archon. The flickering torches in the corridor shed light on his new home through a small, barred window in the door. Thankfully, he was not chained to the wall — the many gates he had passed through, and finally the solid cell door, at least allowed him freedom to roam his small space. And small it was, with no comforts such as a bed, just a bale of old straw and a cracked, wooden bucket that obviously leaked judging by the stained floor beneath.

Toryn sat on the straw away from the bucket. The Castellan's Officer informed him he would be held in the cell until his trial, due to take place in a matter of weeks. The prison warden assured him it was purely a formality as he was unlikely to be considered a spy, and the captain at the Menon Bridge had vouched to speak on his behalf. But all trespassers were put on trial to demonstrate the Archon's resolve to uphold the laws of the land. If found guilty, which was a foregone conclusion, Toryn would likely be sentenced to another month in the dungeons, then drafted into service in one of Archonholm's many kitchens, or the stables of the First Horse. But for how long, the warden could not predict.

Toryn slumped back against the wall. Could it be months? Years even? The Five Realms could fall while he was scrubbing pots and pans, or mucking out stables. His eyes wandered up to the low ceiling. The Archon sat somewhere in his grand rooms only a few hundred feet above his head — but Toryn may as well be on the other side of the Draegelan Trench. He wondered what had become of Hope. A wry smile crossed his face; it would be quite a trick if she could rescue him from the depths of the citadel from under the Archon's nose.

The door creaked open at the end of the passageway. The prison guard's voice echoed off the thick walls. 'And this is where we keep the less troublesome folk.' Toryn was relieved to hear himself described in such a manner. The guard continued. 'But make sure you still follow the correct procedure. Even if they're no danger, we don't want them wandering out of their cells, or you'll have the warden to answer to. And trust me, young fellow, the warden is none too keen on young Archonians. He failed the trial in his day and has held it against them ever since.' They stopped outside Toryn's cell. 'This one's in for trespassing. He was apprehended at the Menon Bridge.' He chuckled. 'Seemed to think he could stroll into Archonholm and demand an audience with the Archon himself, no less.' The guard's wrinkly face appeared at the gap in his door. 'On your feet, lad. Need to check you're not dying of the plague or starvation. Can't have you dropping dead before your trial, can we, eh.' Toryn did as instructed. The guard motioned. 'Now if you could come towards the light so I can see your face, that would do nicely.' The guard turned to his colleague. 'Need to see if there's any black spots or the like. Been years since I've seen a case, but you can never be too safe. Here, you take a peek. Your eyes are probably better than mine.'

Another face appeared. 'Toryn! By the Three. How did you end up here?'

Toryn gripped the bars. 'Elrik! Good to see you.' His shoulders dropped, suddenly ashamed by his predicament.

'And look at you. You must have grown a foot since—'

'Do you know this one?' The old guard peered back through the gap, then back to Elrik. 'Best you don't admit it, lad. It won't do you any good if they know you're a friend of a trespasser.' He looked down the passageway. 'But don't you worry. They won't hear it from me. I'll finish the round and let you catch up. He don't look like a spy to me.' He turned and ambled to the next cell, repeating his instructions for the inspection.

Elrik reappeared. He whispered. 'What happened? There was a right proper commotion when you didn't show up that morning in the square. And Hamar? Did he go with you? Drakelow sent out a search party, but—'

'Hamar's dead.' Toryn leaned his head against the bars. 'I was with him.'

Elrik gasped. 'Hamar? Dead?'

'He was killed at Drunsberg.'

'You were at the mines? How did you—?'

Toryn sighed. 'If I was to say it's a long story, do you have time?'

'Try me. I'm assigned for the week. All recruits have to do time here.'

Toryn held his gaze. 'It's to do with my father… not Andryn, he's not my real—'

'What!' Elrik checked the corridor and lower his voice. 'Then who is?'

'A wyke.'

Elrik backed away. 'No. No… that can't be right.'

'Apparently so. That's why Hamar reckoned I shouldn't come to Archonholm. But here I am, and I don't know how I'm—'

'Time's up.' The guard returned. 'There's only three in these cells. Now for the dangerous ones. Come along, young fellow, plenty to learn so keep up.'

Elrik stuck his head back through the gap. 'We'll speak tomorrow. Perhaps they might let me do the rounds on my own. It's not exactly a difficult job, eh.' Then he was gone.

Toryn turned and slid down the cell door. Elrik already had the look of an Archonian Guard, yet here he sat covered in grime, smelling like a stable, awaiting trial. While Elrik would be defending the realms, he would, in all likelihood, be peeling potatoes or shoveling dung. He stood and shuffled to his bed of hay in the corner. He collapsed and lay looking up to the ceiling, and not for the first time, regretted leaving Midwyche.

Something scratched at the wall to his left. Toryn shifted away. Rodents? The last thing he needed was a hungry rat for company, but as hard as he squinted, he could see nothing. But the scratching continued, turning into a tap, tap, tap. Toryn crawled to the source of the sound in the corner of his cell. He ran his fingers along the floor and found powder. A small section of the wall, no bigger than his fist, moved. The tapping grew louder. Toryn dug his fingers around the stone and pulled it free. A voice on the other side of the wall greeted him. 'Can you hear me?'

Toryn crouched and replied. 'Yes.' He peered through the small hole. 'Who are you?'

The voice croaked. 'Oh no, you go first. How do I know you're not one of the Castellan's men?'

'But why would the Castellan—?'

'He has his ways.' The man coughed hard, blowing dust into Toryn's face. 'I could find myself dragged out of here and thrown off the bridge in no time if I say the wrong thing.'

Toryn squinted through the gap but could see nothing of his fellow prisoner. 'But what can I say to convince you? And' — Toryn thought for a moment — 'wait. How do I know you're not one of his men?' Silence. 'Well?'

'You make a good point there, young man. Never been asked that before.' He clicked his tongue. 'Fine. We'll have to trust each other. But perhaps let's keep our names to ourselves, eh. That will be safer.'

Toryn lay back on the floor. 'But we know each other's cells. You don't need to know my name to report me to the Castellan… if *you're* one of his men.'

'Ah! A clever one, I see. Ha! I'm convinced now. You're too clever to be working for that little turd of a man. I'll trust you, if you'll trust me.'

Toryn smiled in the dark. 'But I still need to know if I can. So, answer me this… are you too clever to be one of the Castellan's men?'

The man thought for a moment. 'Err… well yes.'

Toryn laughed, wondering how often the sound of a prisoner's mirth echoed down the long corridors. 'That's good enough for me. And I suppose if you were a spy, you wouldn't call your boss a *little turd.*' Toryn sensed his new friend's grin through the small gap. He peered through. 'Good. That's settled. So how long have you been here?'

The voice mumbled; Toryn heard him counting. 'Six months? Or is it a year? I can't remember which of these markings are mine.'

'Markings?'

His voice rose. 'Days you fool!' He returned to his croaking whisper. 'Sorry, it's been a long time since I've had company.'

Toryn muttered to himself. 'It's been a while since I've had company that talks sense.'

'What you say?'

'Doesn't matter. What about the markings?'

'Every time they bring breakfast, or what they call breakfast in here, I scratch a mark on the stone. Then I know… but I've forgotten where I started.' Toryn glanced to the wall above the hole to see such marks on his side.

His heart sank. Would he be adding many more of his own?

He turned back to the gap, convinced the man did not work for the Castellan. 'I'm Toryn, Toryn of Midwyche in Darrow, ward of Harlyn.'

'Never heard of it. Midwyche, not Darrow or Harlyn, of course. I'm clever remember, not stupid.'

Toryn smirked. 'Yes, you are. And you?'

'Dravic of somewhere you've never heard of either. Anyway, it's a small village in Amman, ward of Galabrant.'

'I've never met anyone from Galabrant. Well, not as far as I know.'

A grubby finger poked through the gap and wiggled. 'Then pleased to meet you… sorry, I've forgotten already.'

'Toryn.' He wrapped his finger around Dravic's and shook it as best he could.

'Then pleased to meet you also, Toryn of…?'

'Midwyche.' Toryn let go. 'What did you do to warrant becoming a *guest* of the Archon?'

'Oh no, you're supposed to go first.'

'But I thought…?' Toryn sighed. 'Trespassing. I was a long way from home without a reason.'

'Ha! It'll be the shit shovel for you then, lad.'

Toryn shrugged. 'Just like home.' Had he journeyed the length of the Five Realms only to end up with a shovel in his hand? The only difference in Archonholm being his family did not own the horses depositing the dung.

'Nah, never you mind, there's worse places to be, and you'll soon get used to the smell... so they say. And those horses… fine animals. Much better company than most here in Archonholm.'

Toryn laughed. 'Do you ride?'

'No, never had chance.'

Toryn warmed to Dravic. 'I used to ride on our farm. There's nothing like being on the back of a horse galloping across a field.' He closed his eyes, wondering if he would ever ride again.' He turned back to the gap. 'So, what about you? Why are you here?'

'Now that I don't rightly know for sure.'

'What? You've been here for maybe a year, and you don't know why?'

Dravic exhaled. 'That's the very truth. One day I was working on the Archon's new tower at the gate, the next, me and my fellow builders found ourselves down here in this hole.'

Toryn pushed up onto his elbow. 'The Caerwal Tower? You worked on the tower?'

'Up until we'd reached the top of the gate. Then one day, the Castellan and four armed guards turned up, dragged us from our beds and now here we are.'

Toryn's heart pounded in his ears. 'Did you look over the top?'

'Couldn't. Only allowed to work at night once we got that high. And when you have all those torches in your face, you can't see a thing beyond them.'

'But could you hear anything?'

'Nothing. Just our trowels scraping and our hammers tapping. We were told not to speak under pain of death. But they didn't have to tell us. Never felt more exposed I can tell you. Must have made quite a target with our torches flickering at the top of the gate. We had these thick blankets up on poles, but still, we must have been visible from the other end of the pass.'

'I was told the Archon has spied the enemy gathering for an attack. You finished it then.'

'It was, and he did. But then the enemy slung something over the top and hit the tower.'

'I heard. Has it been destroyed?'

'Of course not! We built it to last, lad. As far as the warden knows, only the roof and top floor have collapsed.

I was hoping we'd be released to repair it, but as you can tell, me and the other lads are still here. Or so I believe. We're all in different cells.'

'It's not been rebuilt?'

'Not as far as I know. I suppose it's done its job and let the Archon look over the gate. And if repaired, then it serves only as another target, don't it.' He sighed. 'Shame. It took us nigh on three years to build the darn thing. Sad to think she might be standing there all proud but with her top missing. Mind you, from the conversations we hear between the wardens, I reckon the Archon is preparing a little surprise for the swine should they break through our gate.'

Toryn's heart quickened. 'Surprise? More defenses?'

'And not one to be sniffed at. When I was still working, we'd see dozens of carts bringing in large barrels, day after day. And I tell you this, I've never seen folk handle them with so much care.'

'Barrels of what?'

'Couldn't say. But they were taken up to the new parapets, so must be some sort of ammunition for them heavy weapons. I overheard a prison warden tell of his son being recruited to work on something going on in that pass.' Dravic laughed. 'Hey, wouldn't it be funny if like me, his lad ends up in here after he's finished the work. I'd like to see his face when he opens a cell and sees his own flesh and blood. Now that would—' The gate clinked at the end of their corridor. Dravic drew a sharp breath. 'Quick, put your stone back. They'll be trouble if they find out we've been talking. Not supposed to talk—' Dravic sealed the gap on his side.

Toryn fumbled for the brick as the footsteps approached. He placed it back, brushed away the dust, and leaned against the wall to conceal the damage. A warden approached. A face appeared in Toryn's window. He checked the cell and grinned. 'Time for bed, lad. Sleep tight, don't let the bugs bite.' The warden chuckled to himself and moved to Dravic's cell, repeating the same phrase at each door along the corridor. Toryn looked to the so-called bed, then his bucket, and wondered how many others had done time in his cell.

6. Of Swords of Power

Elodi waited for the last of her captains to leave the room. Wendel stooped and peered at the map. 'If Dohl did return to Dorlgoth, where could he have led—?'

'Tell me about my mother's sword. What do you know of the weapon, Wendel?'

He turned. 'I'm not sure what you mean, ma'am?'

Elodi held his eye. 'Oh, I think you do. You know it's no ordinary blade. You must be aware of its power?'

'It's not exactly…' He gestured to the chair. 'May I?'

She waved her hand. 'Of course! Why do you insist on asking for my permission every time you want to sit down? By the Three, Wendel, I have enough to occupy my mind without having to issue a decree for the correct use of seats around this place. Just sit when you…' her shoulders sagged. Elodi took his hand. 'I'm so sorry. Please, be my guest. And never feel you have to ask ever again.' She slumped beside him. 'It's been a difficult few days… weeks… months. And the death of those poor, young guards at Dorlgoth was just tragic.' Her eyes closed. 'Such a horrible way to die. To be torn apart by those vile creatures, after all they'd endured for me.' She took a deep breath and looked to Wendel. 'May I start again?'

He smiled. 'I understand, ma'am. That's partly why I'm here. I don't just advise. I'm here for the things you cannot say to others.' He leaned forward and clasped his hands. 'About your sword, your mother's sword. It's not…' he rubbed his chin, 'it's not the sword, ma'am, not entirely.'

'Not the… what do you mean? Please get to the point.'

Wendel ran a finger across the table. 'Let me back up a little. Have you opened the trunk yet?'

Elodi frowned. 'Trunk? I'm not sure I know what you're talking about.'

'The trunk returned from Archonholm. The one with your father's belongings.'

Her hand went to her face. 'Oh my! I had completely forgotten. I've had so little time to think these last weeks. It must be sitting in the corner of my room.'

'That's perfectly understandable, ma'am. But if I know your father, if he was… thrown from that bridge by those wishing him ill, I'm certain he will have known he was in danger beforehand. And therefore, I suspect he will have made plans to send you word of… let us say, among other things, something I'm sure he had planned to tell you before he died.'

'What in the name of the Three are you talking about, Wendel?'

'It's not for me to say anything yet. But as your advisor, I would advise you to examine the contents of that trunk before I say anything more on the matter.'

Elodi eyed him. 'Does this have something to do with what you were going to tell me on the night of the siege? Do you remember? Just before I rode out, you said you had something important to tell me.'

Wendel fidgeted. 'Ah, yes, ma'am, it does.'

'I thought your explanation the following day sounded a little, shall we say, unlike anything that would pass your lips.'

He rubbed his hands together. 'I didn't think you were convinced. But you really should open that trunk.' Her advisor grimaced. 'And…'

'Yes, Wendel?'

'There's the matter of your age, ma'am. I don't need to remind you that you'll be twenty-five this coming winter. And that means we—'

'Forget it, Wendel. I have not the time... or the

inclination.'

'But, ma'am, it's the tradition. Harlyn will be needing an heir before long. We cannot risk—'

'We…? I cannot risk outgrowing my armor, or breaking Sea Mist's back at the very time I'm needed most.' Elodi prodded the table. 'You can forget the heir for the time being.' She looked to the window. 'And the last thing I want to do is leave any future child of mine without a mother. There's more to fear than the Winter Fever this time around.'

Wendel rose from his chair and stretched. 'You're right, ma'am. It was wrong of me to bring up the subject. We are in unprecedented times, well, at least in living memory. Securing the future of the city and the realm is paramount.' He rested his hands on the back of his chair. 'There's no benefit to having an heir if there's no realm to govern.'

Elodi's eyes dropped to her hands folded on her lap. 'Does it sound odd that I'm more daunted at the thought of finding a husband and producing an heir, than I am of facing the foe?'

Wendel chuckled. 'No, ma'am, not from your lips. And it has to be said, it would have to be quite a man to win your heart, if such a man even lives in the Five Realms.' He yawned. 'Apologies, ma'am. I must be off to my bed. And as for you, may I remind you your father's trunk awaits.'

Elodi's hand rested on the trunk. If Wendel was correct, what great secret of her father's lay inside? Why was Wendel, usually not afraid to speak his mind, reluctant to speak on this occasion? She placed the candle on the table at her side and opened the lid. Elodi kneeled. Whoever had packed her father's belongings had taken care to neatly fold his clothes, and for that she was grateful. Elodi carefully took out a shirt she recalled seeing him wear many times. She lifted it to her nose and breathed in her father. She buried her face in the soft cloth and let the tears flow. Elodi needed him now, and not only because of the danger facing the realm. She wanted him to stand before her, take her in his arms and tell her everything would be okay as he had done when she was a child. Elodi sobbed, soaking the shirt with her grief. The anger at the injustice of his untimely death rose. He did not deserve such a tragic end; to be pushed off a bridge by a coward not willing to look him in the eye.

Elodi straightened. She looked down to the tear-stained shirt, recalling he had worn it on the day of his departure to Archonholm. They had not long returned from their visit to Drunsberg when the request came from the Archon to attend a meeting of the Council of the Five Realms. She ran her hand along the cloth. If only she had known it would be the last time she would see him. Elodi had been reluctant to interrupt her session with Calerdorn's Sword Master to bid him farewell. It all seemed so routine at the time. Her father would be home within two months after calling upon the southern wards on his return journey. And, following every tour of the realm, he would be full of new ideas and set up meetings to improve the lot of his people. But all that had changed following his visit to the Hall of Scrolls.

Elodi looked up. Her red, swollen eyes stared back from the dark glass of the window. She spoke to her reflection. 'Enough.' She clenched her jaw. 'That's enough, Elodi.' She placed the shirt on the table, flattened out the creases, and returned to the contents of the trunk. Much of her father's official belongings had been returned shortly after his death, what lay before her now were his personal items. Apart from his clothes, she found a small carving of a horse he must have bought as a gift for her; her mother's locket he always kept with him; and finally, right at the bottom, a wooden piece from the boardgame, *Squares*. Elodi picked up the small disk and frowned. But then she remembered. She flipped it over and saw her initial carved in the wood. The tears came again, but this time she laughed. She had presented her father with the piece the first time she had beaten him at his favorite game — and he had kept it. She rolled it through her fingers, the same way he had done to her captured pieces. Elodi recalled how it used to irritate her to watch him play with her fallen comrades in such a dismissive manner. But now she understood those valuable lessons had to be learned, no matter how maddening she found his ways.

But this surely could not be the reason Wendel wanted her to open the trunk. She looked back to the pile of clothes stacked neatly on the table. If her father intended to pass a note onto her, while avoiding the prying eyes of the Castellan's men, where would…? The jacket! The old, faded brown jacket he favored for the walks around Calerdorn's walls lay to one side. She lifted it and looked to the lining. He had called it his *secret pocket*, and always hid a treat for her to eat when she accompanied him. Her hand trembled as she undid the button and reached inside.

7. Damned by his own Hands

The voice boomed. Toryn clutched his head, fearing it was about to split. A desperate cry: an anguished appeal for someone to listen and take note. The voice hailed him by name. But not the name given by his folk. Deep down, Toryn knew this was bestowed upon him in the distant past, long before he was born. But he would never be able to repeat it out loud; the name was known only to the few that could hear the Song and not meant for mortal ears. The voice urged, pleaded, beseeched him to act before all was lost. But Toryn could not fathom what had to be done.

He woke, drenched in sweat, struggling to breathe. The voice faded, echoing in his throbbing skull. He sat, staring wide-eyed into the dark. Was this the voice Hope had heard on the ridge overlooking the Foranfae? Hope had not determined whether it carried a warning to act, or an open threat — but now Toryn understood. It was a warning, directed to him alone to take action in the face of a growing threat. From where did the voice come? Hope believed it originated from beyond the Caerwal Mountains, but surely only the Golesh inhabited the lands to the south. Did the voice set out to deceive? He had to find Hope. But first he had to—

Toryn cried out. His hands burned as if plunged into Elrik's forge. The pain surged up his arms, to his chest and through his whole body. His skin blazed. He was on fire. Toryn leaped from his bedding, fearing the straw would ignite. He tore at his shirt. He yanked it over his head and flung it to the floor. But no relief was to be found. Toryn pitched forward as a thousand hot pokers thrust into his flesh — from the inside. The voice returned, hurling its words at the inside of his head as if trying to force its way out. He bounded about his cell, slamming into the walls, trying to knock the voice free, desperate for peace. He yelled, hoping his screams would drive out the intruder entrenched inside his head. But to Toryn's dismay, it refused to relinquish its hold. He threw himself against the door, desperate to break free, longing for the return of the whispers from Wyke Wood; anything had to be better than the ceaseless pounding against his skull.

The voice stopped. Toryn stood gasping, exhausted, held up only by the fire within. But that too, faded and died. He collapsed, gulping in air to dowse the pain. Now he shivered. He groped around in the dim light for his shirt and found it. He pulled the wet cloth over his head and struggled to put his arms through the knotted sleeves. Shattered by his efforts, Toryn rolled back onto the damp straw and curled into a ball. He trembled until his teeth rattled in his skull, seeming ready to split. What was wrong with him? Surely, it could not be the Winter Fever, not in the middle of summer. He wrapped his arms around his middle but found no comfort. But while his body shook with cold, his hands still burned.

'That was quite a show you put on last night.' Dravic coughed, blowing dust through the hole into Toryn's eyes. 'I thought you'd broken down your door.'

Toryn blinked and massaged his aching temples. 'Can't say I remember much of it.'

Dravic chuckled. 'Best you don't. You were ranting and raving like a madman.'

He struggled to recall anything from the night other than his pain. 'Could you hear what I was yelling?'

'Not a clue. Wasn't any language I know, and I've heard a few in my time. But I would say it was not a happy tale. You had the little hair left on my head standing on end, even though I could make no rhyme or reason from your words.'

Toryn wiped his palms on his sleeves. 'I thought I was coming down with a fever.'

'You might be right there, lad. You've been here… must be a week now. We call it the Dungeon Dread, well I do, some have other names for it, but I like my name. It can get to some like that. Could be something to do with the rats, or you're getting a little disturbed in the head by the four walls closing in.' He whistled. 'I've seen a few come down with it, but not as bad as you had it last night. Never heard any go off like that in my time here.'

'A week? Only one week? And you've been here a whole year?' Toryn looked to the bars on his door. 'How do you survive?'

'You get used to it. Not like I have to work for a living now is it. I get fed… well, sort of, it's not the food of my choosing but my stomach is never empty. And I'm dry, and it's not too cold in here, and at least it never gets sticky hot like it can outside in summer.' He let out a long sigh. 'Although I have to admit I do get a little lonely at times.' The gate at the end of the corridor opened. 'Ah, here we go. Breakfast.' He laughed. 'And I do get a breakfast that fills my belly these days, well it would be better to say it makes my gut swell up, so I don't feel hungry. And that wasn't always the case when I lived in Galabrant.'

Toryn replaced the stone in the gap. A face appeared at his door. A key clicked in the lock. The Head Warden entered, accompanied by an armed guard, but not Elrik. The warden gestured with his fingers. 'Stand, face the wall and put your hands out behind you.' He stopped. 'Don't look so confused, lad. It's the day of your trial. You'll need scrubbing clean first. Can't have you stinking up the courtroom, eh. There may be the odd lady present, and we don't want them wrinkling their noses when you enter. We wouldn't want them to think we don't look after you all proper down here. That won't do.'

Toryn clambered to his feet. 'And then what?'

'Trespassing?' Toryn nodded. The warden shrugged. 'The stables or the kitchens usually. Kitchen means you'll get leftover scraps most days, but stables are better. If you can impress the Stable Master, you might even get a proper job at the end of your sentence.' The warden stood opposite. 'Now turn around please. I know you're no danger, but we have our procedures to follow. Can't have the Castellan complaining. I don't need that bother.'

Toryn did as told and turned to face the wall. 'Is it good work… at the stables?'

'Can be, especially if you're sent to the First Horse. Even better now there's only half of them here. Should be easy going for a strong, young man such as yourself.' Toryn held his hands behind his back ready for the cuffs. The warden continued. 'If you get a job after your service, the pay is pretty good. But let's not get ahead of ourselves. Bring your hands up. Can't let you out of here until you're all secured.' The warden clicked his tongue. 'Looks like these wrists are no stranger to shackles eh, so it won't—' The warden stepped back. 'What the—?' He called to the guard. 'Bring that torch.' The cell brightened as another entered. The warden's voice wavered. 'Don't you move. Don't you move a muscle, you hear! Leave those hands where I can see them.' Toryn felt the heat of the flames as the torch was brought close to his back. The warden grabbed his wrists and tugged. Both men gasped. 'By the Three!' Toryn's arms were released. The warden yelled. 'Guards! Quick now. In here.' A strong hand grasped his shoulder and shoved him to the wall. Toryn's cheek flattened against the rough stone. He felt the tip of the guard's sword between his shoulder blades.

Toryn blustered. 'What's wrong? Why—?'

'Not a word! You keep that foul mouth of yours shut fast. Got that? Not a peep from you.' The warden had retreated to the door. 'Don't you let him say another word.' His voice broke. 'If his lips as much as move, run him through. He's not to speak. Do you hear? Don't let him open his mouth even to breathe.' More guards burst into the cell.

One spoke. 'What's the trouble? I thought this was an easy one.'

'Look. Look at his hands.'

More swords were drawn. The captain of the guard hissed. 'How was this missed? Did you not do your checks?'

'I swear there were no such markings when he entered.' Toryn sagged against the wall. He did not have to look. He knew what they had seen.

The warden fastened the cuffs. 'Bring more chains. And get a gag… and a hood. We can't take the risk. There's reports these creatures are getting more troublesome.' He stuttered. 'How did he pass the checks? The Castellan will have our guts for bowstrings when he hears about this. Oh no, this is bad news. Bad news indeed. The Archon will have to be told. Oh dear, we're all for the cells if we get the blame.'

The jangle of chains accompanied footsteps tramping through the cell door. Toryn's hair was pulled, and his head yanked back. A gag was strung across his mouth and pulled taut. A cold clasp was clamped around his neck and chains wrapped around his midriff and ankles. Another was threaded through the chains around his body and through the neck clasp. The warden panted. 'Pull that tight.' Toryn yelped into the gag as his head and shoulders arched back. The warden called out behind. 'The hood!

Where's that ruddy hood? I'm not moving until his head is covered. Can't risk looking in its eyes. Be wary, lads, don't take any chances with this one.'

Another guard entered. A rough sack was thrust over his head and pulled down. Toryn struggled to breathe. The muffled voice of the warden proclaimed his fate. 'No trial for him today. It will be the bridge for this despicable' — he spat out his disgust — 'wyke.'

8. The Family Secret

'Have you always known?' Elodi waved her father's note in Wendel's face. He blinked in the candlelight as he pushed aside his bedclothes.

'Please, ma'am. Give me a moment.' He grunted and groaned as he arranged his pillows so he could sit upright. He rubbed his bleary eyes. 'Am I to assume you have examined the contents of the trunk?' He pointed to his robe on the chair. 'May I?'

'No, you may not!' She thumped her candle down on his nightstand, spilling melted wax onto the wood. 'I don't care if you're in your nightshirt, I want to know what you've known all these years.'

He raised his eyebrows. 'If I die of exposure, ma'am, you'll be none the wiser.'

'Fine!' She snatched up the robe and thrust it at Wendel. Elodi watched him pull the robe around his frail body and felt the tension ease from her shoulders. She smirked. 'But don't think I won't throw you to the wolves if your answer displeases me, robed or not.'

Wendel managed a smile. 'At my age, I doubt they'll find much to pick at on my bones.' He gestured to the chair. Elodi relented and sat. 'Now, ma'am. May I look at the note. It will be easier if I know your father's exact words.'

'Here.' She pointed. 'This part. The rest relates to the Archon and some of what he discovered in the scrolls, but that can wait.'

Wendel reached for the candle and read. Elodi's foot tapped out her heartbeat as she waited for him to finish. Finally, he looked up. 'Where would you like me to start?'

Elodi took a deep breath. 'Were you present at my birth?' She pursed her lips but failed to prevent the quiver.

He nodded and whispered. 'Yes, ma'am. As you know, the birth of an heir has to be witnessed to verify the claim.'

'Did….' she closed her eyes. She had never wanted to know about the details of that night until now. 'Did she hold me? Did my mother live long enough to cradle me in her arms, Wendel?'

He took her hand. 'Indeed, she did. Lady Harlyn, Eleni, sat and hugged you as if you were the most precious thing in the world.' A tear ran down his cheek. 'I'd never seen her look so longingly at anyone as I saw her gaze into your eyes as they opened, not even at your father.'

Elodi's eyes stung. 'And how long before…?'

His voice broke. 'Long enough for her to name you. She held you up despite her injuries.' Wendel looked to the dark window. 'Elodi, daughter of Eleni.' He cleared his throat, turning back to her. 'And she made your father promise to tell you when he thought you were ready.'

Elodi let the brimming tears flow. 'But why did she…? What possessed her to ride north while she yet carried me in her belly? What could have been so important to risk her life just weeks before I was due?'

Wendel pulled back the covers and swung his legs over the side. 'You know the stories, ma'am. Unlike most tales, I trust the stories of their exploits are not vastly exaggerated. And I can say that after seeing your mother return. It was a miracle she made it back to Calerdorn with the injuries she'd sustained.'

Elodi grasped his hands. 'By the Three, Wendel! How did my father come to marry an Amayan warrior?'

Wendel returned her grip. 'You know your father, ma'am. He could talk a bird down from her nest in a storm. He was still a young man and not yet lord when he stumbled upon her one night on the Dorn Plain, literally. She held a blade to his throat while he explained himself. It was only his carefully chosen words that saved his skin.' He smiled. 'And then, of course, he eventually stole her heart.'

Elodi released his hands and slumped back in her chair. 'So that part is at least true.'

'Yes, ma'am. That is how they met. And most of what you know is true. Only her heritage was kept a secret to protect you. Many still fear and distrust the Amayans as a leaderless force under no direct rule. But your mother suffered for her love of your father. Her fellow warriors shunned her for many years, and she grew restless living the life of a lady of the realm.'

'I know how she must have felt. But I thought they'd all perished long ago.'

'No, ma'am. Your mother spoke little of them, but I did discover there are possibly a few dozen who still roam these lands.'

'But what in the name of the Three tempted her to ride north?'

Wendel yawned. 'Apologies, ma'am. Give me a moment.'

Elodi looked upon her elderly advisor struggling to stay awake. 'No, Wendel. It is I who must apologize. This could have waited until morning.'

Wendel returned her smile. 'I would imagine that would have been a very long wait. Let me see.' His eyes wandered up to the ceiling. 'It must have been early winter. One night a traveler came seeking an audience with your mother. I suspected later it was an Amayan, but I never actually saw her, and others told me the visitor was cloaked head to foot. But I did hear an argument between your mother and father in the early hours.' He let out a long sigh. 'The following morning she'd gone. I'd never seen your father so distraught. It was only later he spoke to me, but even he didn't know the reason for her departure, as she refused to share the words spoken by the traveler.'

'But couldn't he have stopped her?'

A faint smile passed across his lips. 'Eleni was not one to be told what she could do, ma'am. And if I was to say how much you remind me of her, then I think you have your answer. Your father loved and cherished her more than anything in his realm, and he must have feared for hers and your safety. But no, not even your father could talk her out of going, and he would have known it would have been pointless to try.'

Elodi watched the candle's tall flame flicker. 'How long was my mother gone?'

'Close to four weeks. She returned in the dead of night barely able to cling to her horse. Your father's healer treated her wounds. It was only after her death I discovered they were inflicted by poisoned blades.'

Elodi looked up. 'Like many of our casualties from the siege?'

He nodded. 'I believe so, ma'am. But Eleni was immensely strong, holding on for five more days to deliver you into this world. The people were told she had the Winter Fever to explain her absence for all those weeks, and of course, that became the official explanation for her death.'

Elodi watched the candle's reflection in the window. It was so much to take in. Not only was the secret life of her mother a shock, but her father had kept the fact from her all these years. But he had not lied, just neglected to tell her the full story. She looked back to Wendel who seemed ready to drop back to sleep. 'On the night of the siege, you almost told me this?'

He jerked awake, appearing to replay her question. 'Yes, ma'am. At first I thought it may give you strength to know you had Amayan blood running through your veins.' He shrugged. 'But then I figured it could unsettle you, and as we now know, you didn't need to appreciate your bloodline to fight like an Amayan that night.'

'And my sword, my mother's sword.' The memory of storming the gatehouse flashed back. 'I thought it had glowed in the sunrise, but it did the same at Dorlgoth in the dead of night.'

Wendel rubbed his neck. 'An ancient blade of unknown origin. In your hands it must retain some of the power of that time. I would vouch it knows your touch, ma'am. So, as I said, it is not the sword alone that wields power.'

Elodi stood. 'And what if any witnessed the sword's magic? Do we inform the people, Wendel?'

'No, ma'am. I don't think this is the right time. There are still many who remain wary of the Amayans, and the last thing we need now is to stir doubt. Your people believe in you, you as the Lady of the Realm, not as an Amayan. Let them think this is the source of your strength.'

'And the sword? What is the story the people should know?'

'It's a relic of the days of Calerdorn's and Dorlan's glory. Its power has been awakened by the threat of war. Perhaps a fitting story for such times, ma'am?'

Elodi nodded and lifted the candle from the nightstand. 'As always you speak sense. I will retire to my room and contemplate this revelation.' She glanced to her father's note. 'Keep it for now. Please read the whole message.' She turned. 'We'll discuss this at an appropriate time come the morning. And' — she tried to smile — 'apologies for disturbing your sleep.'

Elodi dearly wished she could ride away from

Calerdorn and spend a day on Sea Mist galloping across the plains. But duty dictated she should accompany the Clerk of Works to inspect the ongoing repairs to the city walls. Elodi felt a pang of guilt as her thoughts lay elsewhere as the clerk informed her of the progress to date. She needed time to clear her head and contemplate the news of her mother. But that was not all. She and Wendel had spent hours discussing the remainder of her father's letter. Her father too had doubts about the Archon, having also witnessed a similar episode as seen by Elodi and Bardon. But it was his visits to the Hall of Scrolls that revealed much. He had also suspected the leader of the Golesh behind the gate was the same who had split the Seven Realms in the dark days. He had found reference to Uluriel, the woman dismissed out of hand by the Archon. But the records her father read, must have been removed from the archive before Bardon gained access. Her father had learned Uluriel once went by the name of Sylvena and had served as the head of the influential Order of Echoes. But he had found scant information about the Order. The few archives acknowledging its existence were penned by one named Idraman. He recorded the disappearance of Sylvena shortly after she had gone in search of an ancient relic, believed to be connected to the early verses of the Song of Creation. But nothing farther could be found on Idraman, despite his obvious position of importance as author of such a significant scroll. The last lines of her father's note hinted he supposed more answers could be found in the archives, but sadly, whatever he had read on that fateful night remained unknown. But it must have been a great secret someone wished to be withheld from scrutiny, as what he discovered clearly led to his death.

Both Elodi and Wendel had difficulty comprehending such detail of the dark days, and references to the oldest tale of all: The Three Maidens. The Archon had dismissed the Order of Echoes as an ancient religion based on superstition and fairy tales. Was he right? The removal of the scrolls in question was either an act to purge the archives of worthless myths, or an attempt to hide a greater truth. And, if the latter, for what purpose? Of those dark times, only the Archon and a handful of wykes had survived. Of those, the Archon alone had authority over the Hall of Scrolls. But what could those records possibly reveal that could be damaging to the realms or the Archon? It appeared to Elodi the Lost Years held secrets that would satisfy more than just historical curiosity. Perhaps Bardon's *Age of Shadows* was a better description after all. Creatures wishing to hide from the light of day reside in the shadows. Elodi had come to believe the important facts her father sought were not lost, but concealed.

She reached the gatehouse sooner than expected. Elodi had been so deep in thought, she barely registered a word from the clerk managing the enormous task of repairing Calerdorn. To her relief, the clerk seemed not to notice her lack of attention and continued her report with obvious pride for the projects completed ahead of schedule. And Elodi agreed. Much had been achieved in so little time, but whether the work matched that of their ancestors, only a farther attack would confirm.

Elodi followed the clerk across the cobblestones, still slippery from the melting morning frost. She looked down, stepping with care on the newly laid stones over the spot where Uldrak's dark whirlwind had ripped up the old cobbles. Elodi bowed her head in respect for the many who lost their lives from Uldrak's last desperate act, just moments before Calerdorn's hollow victory was secured.

'As you can see, ma'am, the repairs to the main gate are almost complete.' The clerk patted the new beam bolstering the gate.

Elodi nodded. 'I am impressed.' But her mind went out to the plain. She imagined her mother's horse bringing his severely injured rider back to Calerdorn. Had her father kept vigil on the spot where she now stood? How had he felt when he saw the love of his life, carrying his first and only child, return from a hasty mission for a reason she had refused to divulge.

'And I can report…' Elodi tore her eyes from the plain and back to her clerk. She beamed. 'The defensive trenches, barricades and traps are all but finished. I'd like to see anyone, even Ormoroth himself, try to haul their heavy weapons within range of the city ever again, ma'am.'

Elodi smiled at her clerk. 'Good work. You have done the city proud…' she was horrified to find she could not remember the name of the woman. She continued. 'You and your workers will be honored for many years to come.' Her eyes wandered back to the plain, spoiled by the deep gouges and countless sharp, wooden spikes. It would indeed be a nigh on impossible task to bring monstrous machines against Calerdorn again. But… would the enemy need the use of such worldly weapons if they could conjure demons of old from thin air? Elodi shuddered. A single, mere apparition almost brought down her city. What if these wykes were gaining confidence and power? What horrors would they bring to the next, inevitable attack?

'Ma'am? May I have a moment of your time?' Elodi turned to see Gundrul and two men approach.

She shook the hand of the clerk. 'Thank you for your time. I trust you have more meetings and work to schedule.' The clerk opened her mouth to speak, then nodded her appreciation and walked away. Elodi groaned inside, remembering she was supposed to accompany the clerk on a tour of the inner wall. But that would have to wait. The tone of Gundrul's greeting suggested this was important. She turned to face him. 'Yes, Captain. What demands a *moment of my time*?'

Gundrul stepped aside and gestured to the two men standing wide-eyed behind him. Elodi recognized the captain from Durran Wood who had reported on the attack at Drunsberg. 'Ma'am. This is Captain Roold, and this is Jedrul of Lunn, a miner. Both fought at Drunsberg, and also the siege.'

Elodi greeted them. 'If I haven't already said so, I want you to know how grateful I am for your service to Calerdorn, especially following your terrible ordeal at the hands of that wyke in Durran Wood.'

Roold saluted. 'My…' he glanced to Jedrul, 'our pleasure, ma'am. We were only doing our duty.'

Jedrul stuttered. 'And may I thank you, my lady, your highness… ma'am, for getting us out of that cursed wood.' He looked down to his hands as he rubbed them together. 'I… I don't know how long we were there, but I do know another day longer would have…' Jedrul looked away. Roold placed his hand on the miner's shoulder.

Elodi looked them both in the eye. 'I'm only sorry we could not arrive sooner. I cannot begin to imagine what you must have suffered at the hands of that wyke.'

Roold straightened. 'We're soldiers, and of course' — he nodded to Jedrul — 'him being a miner means we can put up with more than most.' But he too looked unsettled by the mention of Uleva.

'Ma'am.' Gundrul cleared his throat. 'I overheard these two talking about an incident at Wyke… Durran Wood. I believe it may be important.'

Elodi shivered. 'Then let us take this inside. I'm sure you gentlemen would welcome a warm drink at this time.'

Jedrul nodded. 'Warm or cold, ma'am. Either is fine with me.'

Elodi laughed. 'Whatever you prefer. I have a pretty good idea what beverage is favored by the miners of Drunsberg.' She led them inside to the main dining hall and chose a quiet corner away from the workers enjoying a mid-morning break. When each had a cup of their preferred drink, she looked to Captain Roold. 'Now, please share your story.'

Roold folded his arms. 'I don't know how useful you'd find it, ma'am, but Captain Gundrul here says it might be of interest to you.'

'How about you start at the beginning and let me decide.' She held Roold's gaze.

'Certainly, ma'am. And may I begin with an apology. I realize now, the report I gave on the loss of Drunsberg and the following events was… lacking some details.'

Elodi leaned forward. 'And what details do you now feel your report lacked?'

Roold wrung his hands. 'As the weeks pass, more memories of that time come to light.' He looked to Jedrul. 'I believe much was buried deep and as such, I could not remember certain things when I told of the events.'

Elodi took his shaking hands. 'You have no need to apologize, Captain. I have seen the work of that wyke from the wood, and it is testament to your fortitude that you and your colleagues survived, let alone remember anything of the days in question.'

'Thank you, ma'am. I only hope what we've recalled has not hindered matters as such.'

She glanced to Gundrul. 'What is important is you now have something to tell. Now please, share what has since come to light and we shall determine how that may help our cause.'

Roold relaxed and took a breath. 'It's about a young man who came to the mines the same day as the attack.' Jedrul nodded at his side. The captain continued. 'He came with an old guard by the name of Hamar, a guard who's well known to us. A man who'd became the stuff of legend, who' — his head bowed — 'sadly lost his life defending the honor of his fellow guards, ma'am.'

Elodi looked to Gundrul. 'I see. And one who deserves our gratitude. But what of this young man you speak?'

Jedrul piped up. 'He was very skilled with a bow, ma'am. He took down a ballista with one shot, one that—'

Roold nudged Jedrul. 'As good as a shot that was, ma'am. That's not the story I believe Captain Gundrul wants you to hear.'

Elodi looked to the door. 'Then please, if you could get to the point, gentlemen.'

Roold nodded. 'Gladly, ma'am. This young man was captured along with the rest of us and taken to' — his face paled — 'to that dreaded wood. But he wasn't taken to the cages with the rest of us. No, ma'am. The moment that rake, Uldrak, set his shifty eyes on the young fellow, he knew something was different about him.'

Elodi checked. 'Different? How?'

'I can't say. But that gray creature pointed his bony finger and ordered an underling to take him to the *lady*. And there was only one lady there, ma'am. But not a real lady such as yourself. No, he meant the witch who lived in that forsaken tower.'

Elodi chilled at the memory of the gnarled branches forming the structure. She turned to Gundrul. 'Do we know anything about this young man?'

'No, ma'am. He's not come to my attention.'

Jedrul straightened. 'His name is Toryn, ma'am. We spoke on the journey to the wood. He's a farmworker from Darrow, a village called Midwyche, I recall. He said he was the grandson of Hamar.'

Elodi caught her breath. 'I dearly hope he wasn't in

those huts we burned, or the tower.'

Gundrul managed to smile. 'Mercifully not, ma'am. These gentlemen say he was dragged away in chains and slung on a wagon that left with the sorceress on the horse.'

She looked to Roold. 'Can you be certain he was taken as a prisoner and not as an ally.'

He nodded. 'Even in my sorry state at the time, yes, ma'am. You don't manhandle a friend like that. They seemed very keen to keep him bound up to stop him escaping.'

Jedrul put down his mug. 'And begging your pardon, ma'am. I can't say I spent much time with him, but I would bet my life he's not one of them, and by them, I mean those shady fellows in the wood.'

'Then I wonder what Uleva and Uldrak could possibly want with this young man?' Elodi regarded their faces. 'And you know nothing else about him?'

Jedrul shrugged. 'Only that he was useful with a bow, but not so much with a sword.'

The more she heard, the more Elodi became intrigued. 'Do you know how he came to be in Drunsberg?'

Roold shook his head. 'Sorry, ma'am, can't help you there either. It was unusual to see anyone other than guards on the road to the mines. They must have had good reason I guess, but seeing as Hamar was with the young man, any Archonian I know would have allowed them entry.'

'Then I wonder what has become of him. And why were his captors so keen to prevent him falling into our hands?' Elodi stood. 'Thank you, that is a most interesting tale, and I believe could turn out to be a crucial one.' She smiled. 'And one that deserves another drink and a hot meal.' She turned to Gundrul. 'Please ensure that happens, and…' she thought for a moment, 'I shall send a rider to

Midwyche and see if there's anything more we could learn about this Toryn fellow.'

Gundrul pushed back his chair. 'It's a long way, ma'am.'

Elodi's eyes flashed. 'I'm well aware of the geography of my realm, Captain.' She softened. 'But I do think it's worth the effort. If this man, Toryn, causes our powerful foes concern, I want to know the reason. And let us be honest with ourselves here, we don't have much else going in our favor right now. If the smallest crumb of hope can be garnered from learning more of this man, then I think it is worth pursuing.'

Gundrul shrugged. 'For all we know he could be dead by now.'

'I disagree. If they wanted him dead, why go to the trouble of putting him in chains and take him from the wood? We must make every effort to find this young man and bring him here. Who knows…' she thought of Dorlan, 'he might turn out to be the hero we so desperately need for our times.'

9. At the Rising of the Sun

Toryn blinked in the pre-dawn chill as his head was yanked back and the hood pulled free. He gagged anew on the iron strip clamping his tongue to the floor of his mouth. The cloth gag had been replaced by the cruel device before the commencement of his trial. But trial was a misleading word for the mere five minutes he had spent in the company of the Castellan, the Vice-Archon, and a handful of council members. One look at his hands had been enough to find Toryn guilty of the crime of being a wyke. He was not allowed to speak, and his hands had remained chained behind his back, least he wave them in the air and bring down a curse on those who would determine his fate — not that he had the slightest clue of how to wield his alleged power. But even with the restraints, Toryn noticed how people stood a safe distance from him. Eyes widened and faces paled as he was led to the small room to face judgement and his sentence. His head had dropped as the old punishment for wykes was pronounced: he was to be suspended from the Caerwal Bridge until dead.

And here he now stood on the bridge as two guards prepared him for his punishment for something of which he had no control. Toryn choked on the metal muzzle as rough hands pulled tight a leather strap around his middle. A second strap bound his ankles. A long rope was fastened to a buckle on the belt, and he watched in horror as the other end was secured to the railing.

The guard joked with his colleague. 'Make sure that's pulled nice and tight. Can't have the fellow falling to his death now can we.' He checked Toryn's belt, looked him in the eye and sneered. 'That would be far too good an end for his kind. Thankfully, there can't be many left now.' They turned him to face the Vice-Archon, the Castellan and the representatives of the Council standing a short distance from the center of the bridge. Toryn found himself oddly disappointed the Archon did not see fit to attend. Hamar had been right again. The likes of him rarely got to meet the leader of their realms.

Toryn stared at the few stars brave enough to risk the imminent rising of the fiery sun. Again, Hamar's words played over and over in his mind, *he can't go... he can't go.* He should have listened, yet he had walked willingly into the very place in the Five Realms where his secret would be discovered. He should have gone looking for Hope. She would have known how to deal with the situation.

Toryn turned to look for the Archon's banner, but his hair was grabbed, forcing him to face those pronouncing his sentence. The Vice-Archon struggled to hold Toryn's gaze as she spoke. 'In the name of the Archon, you are to be judged by the elements, as is the way of the Five—'

The guard chuckled. He hissed in his ear. 'When she says *judged*, she means slowly left to rot.'

The Vice-Archon continued. 'Your fate is in the hands of the Three, they alone will—'

Once more, the guard saw fit to educate Toryn, whispering, 'You'll dangle in the sun, wind and rain, but it makes no odds, you'll die in pain as the hunger slowly gnaws away at your guts.'

The Vice-Archon's voice rose. 'At the rising of the sun, you will be suspended...' Toryn cared not for her proclamation; as the guard said, it made no difference to his fate. He forced his eyes to look up to the tallest tower of the land, not daring to move his head. The light of the sun already painted the pinnacle a pale orange, giving the tower the look of a candle – the flame burning down the wax, hastened his end.

Toryn straightened. The solitary figure of the Archon stood upon the circular balcony at the top of his tower. He could just make out the Archon's hands grasping the rail as he looked down to the bridge. Toryn grunted to himself. So, on the last day of his life, he finally managed to see their great leader… and signatory of his death sentence. He held his gaze to the tower, and for a moment, Toryn thought the Archon made eye contact as his face tingled. But the Archon whipped his long cloak around, turned his back and returned to his quarters.

The Vice-Archon droned on, but Toryn cared not to listen. He knew all he needed to know. The cruel, prolonged nature of his execution would serve as a reminder to all who witnessed: the Archon remained committed to ridding the realms of the sorcerers of old. Without the ability to speak at his so-called trial, Toryn had moaned and groaned his innocence until his eyes felt ready to burst. But the markings on his hands were all the evidence required to condemn him.

The Vice-Archon finished. She nodded to the guards as Toryn's guests turned their backs and retreated from the bridge, no doubt keen to get a better view from the edge of the ravine. Did Elrik stand among the crowd? He wished he could have talked to him once more to try and explain his actions. Did his friend believe him? Or did Elrik now regard him as both a traitor and devious sorcerer?

Toryn was spun around to face the east. He stared to the horizon as the fabric of the sky stretched and lightened as it sought to haul the heavy sun back up to their side of the world. For the first time, Toryn pondered where the sun disappeared to at night. For a wonderful, brief moment he forgot his fate: why had he never given the matter a second thought until now? Did people dwell in another world beneath them? Did a deep rift divide their land where the Kolossos Mountains reared up in his? But regardless of where the sun had traveled, and the kind of people on which it had shone its light, its return today marked the end of his existence. He watched the light grow as if the sun rose purely for him.

The guard's breath moistened his ear. 'Ain't you lucky. It's going to be a fine day. You'll twist in the breeze and get to see the sunrise *and* the sunset. Can't grumble at that, lad. Quite a sight this time of year as the sun nears the line of the Caerwals.' He yanked on the belt. 'But that's more than you deserve.' He appeared to read Toryn's mind. 'The last *wyke* I saw hanging from this bridge suffered six days before *it* died. And that was a young lass, and in the middle of winter. You're a tough lot, eh. I'll give you that. A mortal would be stone-cold dead within two days at most.' He tugged on Toryn's restraints. 'So, who knows? If the rope holds, or the eagles don't gouge your eyeballs out first, you might manage eight days. That suits me. I've put a week's wages on it being eight.' He laughed. 'But if you make ten, that fool over there will make enough to buy a month's worth of ale.'

The pink rim of the sun appeared. The guard rubbed his hands. 'Here she comes, showing her pretty little face just for you, eh.' He nodded to his colleague. 'Right. Over he goes.' Toryn was lifted by the chains on his wrists and shoved towards the rail. He cried out and bit into the tongue guard, filling his mouth with the taste of warm, sweet blood. Toryn moaned as he stared at the rising sun, silently pleading for the forgiveness of his folks back home. He heard the murmurs of the gathering crowd anticipating the spectacle; an old man coughing in the cool air; a horse's hooves clattering on the same cobbles Toryn had taken his last steps. He felt the breath of the air on his face as it rose from the ravine; the scrape of his dungeon rags against his bruised skin; the deep ache in the muscles between his shoulders. But none of that mattered now.

Toryn's mind raced, searching for a way out of this doom. But he found nothing. He groaned. He thought of Hamar on the Plains of Evermore, hoping his old friend was content, spending his evenings drinking ale and swapping tales with Elwold and his fellow guards. Wherever Hamar was, he dearly wished he could not witness his fate. Would the old guard return on Hallows Night and wonder at the absence of his young colleague? Toryn would not get to roam the plains now. He had taken the Oath, but he had no sword in his hand, and no enemy of the realm to fight — he was now considered the enemy. He would die a stinking wyke in the eyes of his peers. His head dropped.

'Right, let's get this done, I'm ready for my breakfast.' The guards hoisted him to the level of the rail. 'A little higher.' The man grunted. 'We want a nice clean throw. Can't have him banging his head and ending it before he's over the edge.' Toryn screwed his eyes shut, trying to see Caranach's snowy peak peering over the treetops of Midwyche Wood, or hear his mother calling him in for supper, but all he heard was shouts now rising in anger from the people reveling in his suffering.

Toryn was heaved over. His stomach lurched as he dropped. His jaw clamped shut on the metal bit. His body bend double against the belt when the rope ended his fall. He tasted fresh blood and blacked out.

10. The Waiting Ends

Elodi's hair blew across her face as she looked out upon the plains from Sea Mist's back. But her thoughts were far from the scene before her eyes. The watch placed on the cave dwellings of Dorlgoth reported no sign of the inhabitants returning. But where had they gone? Two hundred people could not simply disappear without trace. The people of Dorlgoth were not wealthy, and to leave all their belongings so carefully gathered over their lifetimes, made no sense. This left only one explanation. Elodi dreaded the worst: Dohl had survived and fled to his believed home in the guise of Dorlan. The people, who had waited centuries for his return, would have readily fallen for the deception. It would have taken little persuasion for them to drop everything and willingly follow their honored son. But how long could Uleva maintain Dorlan's likeness? Unless it was not a guise…

Elodi turned north and let the breeze take the hair from her eyes. The wind had changed direction overnight, bringing cooler air from the north in defiance of the efforts of summer to bring some much-needed and long-awaited warmth to Calerdorn. She had ridden hard all morning to stretch Sea Mist's legs to get far away from the confines of the city and, if she was honest, the responsibility. Elodi needed time alone to think. Her mother was an Amayan, and the blood of these notorious warriors ran through her veins. Now she knew why she excelled with the sword and felt more at ease on horseback than in the confines of the halls of Calerdorn. But with the knowledge of her lineage came new dilemmas. Should she reveal her heritage to her people? Wendel had advised against such action, but Elodi was uncomfortable keeping her secret. If her sword revealed its power once more, surely she could not conceal her true identity much longer. Would it be better to tell them herself, than for people to find out she had been dishonest with them?

Elodi nudged Sea Mist to face the south and let the wind wrap her hair about her face once more, happy to have the world's grim reality hidden for the moment. The village of Midwyche lay six days yonder for her fastest rider. The woman she had dispatched to Toryn's village would not yet be halfway, but already Elodi grew impatient for news of the mysterious man who attracted the interest of a powerful wyke. The only other fact she knew of this man was he was a farmworker and possibly related to an old, trusted Archonian Guard. And apart from the location of his small village, she had no knowledge of Midwyche. It had never featured in any of the tales she knew, as nothing of consequence had ever been known to happen there. But the same would have once been said of Dorlgoth; and every dweller in Harlyn had come to hear of its name.

Elodi turned her horse to face home. It would be careless to place so much hope from the single account from Durran Wood, regardless how intriguing. She kicked on. Sea Mist readily responded, refreshed from his brief rest. Horse and rider sped across the road unfazed by the wind seeking to stall their progress. Elodi had been tempted to ride to Midwyche herself. She knew Sea Mist could cover the distance a full day quicker than any other horse in the realm. The prospect of days in the saddle, free of the burden of leadership, alone with Sea Mist, was almost too much to resist. But, of course, it would have been unthinkable to abandon her people at such a time.

The towers of Calerdorn rose from the horizon as Sea Mist approached the top of the escarpment. Elodi slowed him to admire the view. It made no difference how many times she returned to her city, the first sight of the slender towers standing defiant against the elements, always touched her and brought her hope. Despite the proximity of the lofty mountains hemming in the city, the towers would not be overshadowed, holding their own, undaunted by the presence of the timeless rock of the land.

Something moved ahead on the road: a scout. Sea Mist trotted on to greet the rider. The scout spotted her and slowed. 'Ma'am!' He drew level and gasped. 'We have news.' The rider drew out a note and waved it. 'There's movement… out of Fort Draegnor.' Elodi's heart sank. He gained his breath. 'A sizeable force departed yesterday. At least eight hundred Ruuk, ma'am, possibly more, heavily armed, are heading for Dornan Pass. At their current pace they'll gain our defenses at Tunduska by late afternoon tomorrow, ma'am.'

11. The Best View in the Land

He can't go. He can't go. Hamar's words repeated over and over in Toryn's head. *He can't go. They'll find out.* But he had done just that. He had walked into the very place in the land he should have avoided. He jerked awake, kicked out his legs, but his feet failed to find solid ground. Toryn opened his eyes. The sun had risen to the highest part of the sky and would soon begin its descent to the western edge of the land. He half-smiled. The guard had been right — it had turned out to be a beautiful day, and the view was indeed worth the trip. His chin itched as the blood oozing from his mouth had dried and cracked. He slowly rotated to face the south wall of Archonholm. He noted the crowds at the ravine had thinned, already weary of watching his forlorn figure dangling from the bridge.

Toryn flinched. A pebble bounced off his head. 'Oi! Get away you rascals.' He endured the pain to look up. Three young lads ran from the bridge. A guard shouted after them. 'Let him rot. And if you come back, I'll tie a rope to your ankles and throw you over so he can turn you into toads.' Toryn closed his eyes as the rope twisted. Above, the guard's captain arrived. 'Keep your eyes open, fools. Put your pipes away and do your duty. What if one had a knife and cut the rope? The Archon would have the two of you swinging from the bridge in no time.'

Toryn inhaled against the tight ropes cutting into his midriff. He grimaced. The last wyke had hung from the bridge for six days before she died — and that had been in winter. How long would he have to suffer? He thought of the young woman who preceded him. Where had she come from? Had she too felt like a stranger in her village?

He looked up to the clear, blue sky. Despite the sheer slopes of the mountains and the imposing walls of Archonholm looming either side, the sky brought relief. He could not recall the last time he had seen such a beautiful sight. He thought back to the last warm summer he could remember. He had laid on the warm grass as a young lad with Elrik watching small, fluffy clouds float by, imagining they were the ghosts of the mythical beasts from Hamar's tales. But now he was one such beast. He groaned. Word of his fate would soon get back to Midwyche. In years to come, would the children play games mimicking *Toryn the Wyke* as they chased each other between the haystacks? And what of Andryn and Miram? The secret they had kept for all this time would be discovered. Would they be driven out of the village?

Toryn wiggled his bound legs to turn towards the people on the ridge. A few more had joined the throng, possibly those finishing their morning duties who had missed the early show. He looked to see if Elrik stood among them, but his vision had blurred, and he could not make out their faces. He hoped Elrik had not come. He hoped his friend could forgive him and remember the happy times they had spent together in their short lives. But news of a wyke's trial and punishment would have tempted some to make the journey from many leagues away — it was too much to hope Midwyche would not receive the news. If the Archon was to be believed, there would be few wykes left in the land, making it worth the trip to have something to tell their grandchildren in the years to come.

Why did the people of the realms fear his kind? What had the wykes of the past done to justify such terrible treatment? Uleva and Uldrak had proved too much for the guards in the north, but surely their like could not have caused his ancestors much trouble. Dorlan and the captains of the once powerful armies had managed to overcome even the great evil of Ormoroth. Had the Five Realms fallen so far, wykes were now viewed as such a terrible threat?

Toryn glanced down. Odd. Now he faced certain death, he no longer feared the great height. He hung precariously on the end of a rope with nothing between his feet and the rocky floor hundreds of feet below. If anything, the drop would bring relief. Should the rope snap, his suffering would be over in seconds. Perhaps if he tried to swing and kick his legs, he might snag the rope against the sharp edge of the bridge and break it.

But he was not done yet. Deep inside, Toryn had yet to surrender. It was wrong of the Archon to condemn him to this dreadful end when he had done no wrong — he was only trying to help. He knew nothing of his father, but he had obviously cared for his son to go to the trouble of taking him to a safe village. If he was a bad man, he would more likely have abandoned him in the woods to die, or taken him to Uleva. Toryn glanced up to the Archon's banner hanging limp in the still air. But what of his mother? Was she also a wyke? What had happened to her? He bit against his gag. This was wrong. He would not let them win. He was not ready to give up all hope.

Hope.

Toryn thought of her, sending out his thoughts. He could not be evil. She would have sensed it in him. And he was certain Hope was on the right side. But… why had she left him? Perhaps she had sensed his growing power, culminating in the transformation in the dungeon. But where had she gone? Did she wander the fields and lanes of Farrand in her bewildered state? Toryn remembered how she had changed that night in the wood outside of time. He tried to recall her words regarding the Song as they had sat beside the Singing Stone. *Listen carefully and it's still possible to hear.* And… *I believe you too can hear these voices.* If Hope took power from the echo of the Song, and he was of the same kind, could he call upon it now? Hope had used verses to bring the past into the present to avoid their pursuers on the ridge. But how could he find the right verse? How could he use it? Even if he could access the power in the words, what would bringing the day before he hung from the bridge into the present, achieve? He guessed why the Archon chose this punishment. Should a wyke be successful in changing time, the likely outcome would be the rope ceasing to exist. He would be free — free to plunge to his death. But this was all pointless. He had not a clue how to use the powers he was accused of possessing.

Toryn let his head drop forward and closed his eyes. He imagined Hamar standing on the bridge telling him tales of his time in the Archonian Guard. Now Toryn had seen some of the world, he could visualize the scenes of Hamar's adventures in the north. He saw Hamar as a young man fighting against the Ruuk and wrestling with the strange creatures of which he spoke. He sighed. Hamar had led a long and worthwhile life. He had served the realms and, in his later years, had worked hard on the farm. And even in his old age, he fought with the strength of a young man to defend the mines. But Toryn had barely lived a third of Hamar's years, and in that time achieved little. Yes, he had at least traveled and had taken part in a battle, but for most of that time he had been a hindrance, a liability, to both Hamar and Hope.

Toryn opened his eyes. He must have passed out. The cliffs of the Caerwals had turned pink and the air had cooled. He wriggled and angled himself to face the west. The sun glowed a deep red as it skimmed the slopes of the mountain wall and touched the horizon. It was indeed a sight to behold. Despite it bringing about his demise,

Toryn could not hold such a majestic sun responsible for his death. He twisted a little to keep his body facing the sunset. She slowly slipped below the horizon to make her appearance to whatever lay on the other side of Toryn's world. He blinked as she glimmered and flattened, appearing to melt and ooze onto the rim of the land, then dip below.

One day. He had made it to the end of the first day — he could almost hear the chalk scraping on a wall somewhere in Archonholm noting his achievement. He wondered how many guards would have already lost their stake in their game. But if any had thought he would not survive a single day, he did not pity their loss. He clenched his jaw. He would show them. He would last for twelve days, thirteen even, until they ran out of space on the wall to keep count of his tally.

Toryn cried out and scratched his swollen tongue on the rough metal in his mouth. He gasped as the belt cut him in two, making it hard to breathe. Above, a silver cloud made its way slowly across the crescent of the moon. The black disk of the rest of the moon was visible and if Toryn looked at it long enough, it resembled the end of a sorcerer's staff pointing at him from high in the night sky. If he was lucky, perhaps it would cast a spell and end his misery. Away from the moon's faint glow, thousands of stars shone bright, but none could match the brilliance of those above the Singing Stone in the dreamlike wood Hope had taken him. He nudged against the rope to turn to face the north. Among the few clouds traversing the sky, he spied the bear and wolf still locked in mortal combat. Where would he go when his time came? Hamar and Elwold had their farm on the Plains of Evermore, but what of wykes? If the Archon was to be believed, would he find himself in the vaults beneath Caranach? He froze.

Was he to spend an eternity with the very demons he feared as a boy? No. He would refuse to let that happen. A new voice in his head insisted he should not accept that fate.

A guard coughed on the bridge. Another stamped his feet, perhaps trying to stay awake and avoid punishment. They spoke in low voices, but Toryn had no urge to listen in on their conversation. He had company. And the voice demanded his attention.

12. Tunduska's Rage

'I must lead the re-enforcements, Wendel!' Elodi leaped from Sea Mist as her advisor limped as fast as he could towards the gate to meet her.

His hand covered his face. 'Must you, ma'am?'

She grasped the reins and led her horse across the cobbles. 'Yes, Wendel, I must.'

He sighed. 'I agree this sounds like more than the Ruuk probing our defenses, but is it worth the risk of putting yourself in the front line?'

Elodi slowed her pace on seeing her advisor struggle. 'It's my duty. If I don't lead the fight against the sizeable force marching against us, when do I deem it fit to lead?'

'But what if—?'

Elodi patted Sea Mist's muzzle. 'The enemy have stayed put at the mines. And elsewhere? Do we have other sightings?'

'No, ma'am. No other reports have been forthcoming. We know only of their movement towards the Dornan Pass.'

'Then that settles it. I will confront them there. This doesn't look like a ruse. If they're committing the bulk of their forces at the pass, then so must we. This is an attempt to break our hold on the mountains. And then what? If they succeed and take the bridge, they'll be bursting through like water from a breached dam. Their heavy weapons prohibit an attempt to cross Mawlgrim Mire. We've spied no building of ships, so I would say the pass is our only hope of holding them... for the time being.' Elodi stopped and looked to the people in the street. 'I can't make the same mistake again. I should have focused our strength on the pass the first time. It would be a dereliction of duty to put my people through another concerted attack on Calerdorn. I have to keep these rogues as far away from here as possible.'

'Very well, ma'am. But please…' he touched her arm, 'I suppose it's futile to request you stay out of harm's way.'

Elodi rolled her eyes and headed towards the stables. 'I would hardly be performing my duty if I was *not* in harm's way.' She stopped and looked back. 'I can't make any promises, but I will do what is necessary to hold them at Tunduska's Gorge.' She handed the reins to the approaching stable boy. 'Please give him food and water, then a good rub down. He needs to be ready to go within the hour.' Then to Wendel. 'Please have Gundrul and Ruan report to me in my quarters immediately. Captain Cubric has proved himself very capable of leading, so I shall leave him in charge of defenses here. We'll march through the night. We can't allow even one Ruuk to set foot on the bridge before re-enforcements arrive. If we lose the pass, we lose control of the plain, and who knows what forces they will bring against us this time.'

The fortifications at Tunduska's Gorge had been built to last. The fort's thick, curved wall spanned the narrow valley. At its edges, the wall merged with large turrets fashioned from the mountain sides. Beneath the ramparts an archway had once housed a gate. But this was no Caerwal Gate, and Uldrak had demolished the weakest part of the defense in his first attack that led to the siege. The Ruuk had evidently attempted to destroy the fort, but the only damage inflicted were blast marks staining the walls from Uldrak's devilry. But without sufficient time to replace the gates with anything but a temporary alternative, their chances of holding the Dornan Pass relied on defending the bridge. Two hundred paces ahead, the bridge crossed the deep chasm named after the old God of the North, Tunduska. The myth came from the folk that lived in the land before the days of Harlyn. It was said Tunduska desired to create his own realm following a bitter dispute over gemstones found under the mountains. In his wrath, Tunduska had raised his great axe and had striven to cleave the land in two, splitting the north from the south. From her position, Elodi wondered if there may be some truth to the myth. The rent did indeed look deep enough to separate the mountain range, but fortunately, not too wide to prevent the building of a bridge.

Elodi was not surprised to see the bridge had been untouched. Despite their hasty retreat following the siege, Uldrak obviously intended to return this way in the coming months. She gave thanks the structure was built with defense in mind. The shoulder-high walls began only at the midway point, leaving the opposite side open to her archers, and the unprotected span making a fall more likely for assailants in hand-to-hand combat. But Elodi had wished her ancestors had included a drawbridge in their plans; evidently, they had greater confidence in their soldiers to fend off an enemy advance. But the bridge was at least narrow, and beyond the defensive wall it tapered further, leaving it barely wide enough for four attackers to march abreast. A determined shield wall could hold up a larger force long enough for the archers from the fort to pick off the easier targets at the edges.

Elodi searched the thick clouds for the sun. But the prevailing wind brought only more cover to keep her adopted talisman out of the imminent confrontation. If her blade glowed in the battle to come, it could not be explained as a reflection of the sun. She sat upon Sea Mist with Aldorman and four knights on horseback at her side. But Tunduska's Gorge was not a field of combat for horses; Tunduska was for battles of attrition, courage, and sheer brute force. Aldorman and his knights would not take part in the fighting; they were present to protect the Lady of the Realm.

Ahead of Elodi, her forces packed the bridge. At the front, a new wooden barricade blocked the path at the head of the walls. Behind, Gundrul's strongest guards, shouldered shields. At their backs, Ruan's men stood ready with their thick spears should the raiders smash through the barricade. But Elodi was under no illusion; Uldrak would not be held up by their improvised barrier for long — ultimately, it would come down to the strength of the soldiers in their tightly-packed formation. The shield and spear arrangement repeated a dozen times along the bridge with fresh soldiers ready to step forward to replace the fallen or exhausted men at the front. Elodi felt she could do no more. The best soldiers available for such a skirmish formed an intimidating barrier. She hoped the Ruuk would become frustrated if held up for long, resort to their unruly nature, and thus make it difficult for Uldrak to maintain command. It was a slim hope, but a hope all the same.

Elodi twisted in her saddle to view the walls of the fort. The hastily-constructed platform at its center, housed two of the captured ballistae from the siege. In the little time afforded them, the teams had practiced firing bolts across the gap should Uldrak bring his heavy weapons forward to clear the bridge. Elodi winced at the black, metal tips of the bolts pointing her way, trusting their aim would be true. The remainder of the wall bristled with archers. In front of the fort, two hundred men and women of the reserves stood ready, but Elodi was under no illusion they were a match for the battle-hardened regulars of Gundrul and Ruan. But any pride Elodi may have held for their show of force, was tempered by the defeat at Drunsberg. Had not the mines boasted a similar defense against a narrow field of attack? Uldrak had commanded the previously unruly Ruuk, leading them to a successful assault against what should have been a more challenging position to take. But Gundrul and Ruan had not fought at the mines, and Elodi held onto the hope that they would make the difference at Tunduska.

Ruan approached on foot. 'All set, ma'am. Captain Gundrul is overseeing the unloading of supplies at the stores, but we're ready on the bridge.' He nodded to it. 'A remarkable feat of engineering if I may say so. And one built with much thought for its defenders.'

Elodi sighed. 'Had we not feared an attack from those occupying the mines, it would have been wise to concentrate all of our forces here, and thus saved Calerdorn the pain of the siege.'

Ruan rubbed his large chin. 'Hindsight, ma'am. Every commander comes to yearn for a glimpse into the future. There's nothing to be gained from regretting a decision made with the best intention at the time.'

'Thank you, Captain. I appreciate your wisdom.' She watched him as he eyed the formations on the bridge, surprised to see his usual flat expression fleetingly slip. In that moment, Elodi thought she saw fear. 'Ruan?' He turned; the impenetrable mask returned. She held his gaze. 'Have you experienced a situation such as this before? At the siege we had our walls, but here we don't have that luxury.'

Ruan's eyes flickered, but his jaw remained set. 'Ma'am?'

'We await an unknown force, greater than our numbers, heading this way. In all your years of service, did you face a stronger enemy in an exposed situation?'

He glanced back to his spearmen. 'Just the once, ma'am.'

Elodi waited for an answer. She prompted him, suspecting he was reluctant to talk. 'And where would that—?'

'Aralak Gorge.' Ruan took a breath, then released what Elodi suspected had been suppressed since the event. 'In my second year of service. There was a breach in the fence one night. Those spiders can bend an iron spike in two when they set their mind to escape. Took three men to kill the beast that got out.' Elodi listened in silence, noting he was keen to avoid eye contact. He looked down to his hands. 'We formed a shield wall while the damage was repaired. But our torches attracted more to the breach.' He stiffened as if bracing for the attack. 'You can hear them foul creatures coming for you.' Ruan's lip curled. 'Branches cracking under the weight of their numbers, then the drumbeat of their claws as they drop from the trees and scuttle along the ground.' He swallowed. His face paled. 'We held out long enough for the men to repair the damage, but we lost a lot of good spears that night, many at the end as we retreated through the fence as the gap was closed.'

Elodi touched his arm. 'That must have been horrifying. And when you were still so young.'

Ruan looked up to the slopes on the opposite side of the gorge. 'My brother was among the fallen.'

She felt his pain. 'I'm so sorry.'

His jaw knotted. 'I could do nothing for him. He had fought at my side, protecting his younger brother, but at the last moment, two spinners pounced on him.' He grimaced. 'They pumped him full of their filthy poison… and snatched him away before I could…' Ruan's head bowed. 'Sometimes at night, I can hear his cries as they dragged him back to their lair. There isn't a moment when I wish I could have—'

A horse galloping at speed drew their attention back to the bridge. Ruan snapped back into the captain of Broon she knew. Elodi turned to see a scout appear around the rocky outcrop concealing the road to the north. The rider slowed her horse as it neared the bridge. All eyes fixed on the pair as the horse paused. Steam rose from its tired muscles as its head bobbed. It snorted at the narrow crossing, obviously wary of the dangers of negotiating the obstacle in its state of exhaustion. The rider's voice carried across the gorge as she soothed her mount. She climbed down and took its reins. Elodi held her breath as the rider took the first, tentative step, re-assuring her horse it was safe. She noted with admiration, the scout's voice portrayed none of the anxiety she must be feeling. Elodi watched in awe, knowing should the horse sense the scout's trepidation, they could plunge to their deaths. The defenders on the bridge silently urged them on as horse and rider made slow progress to the midway point. Had her scout not already proved her bravery by tracking the enemy movements? And now she had to do this, leading a nervous and shattered animal across the treacherous bridge.

They made it. Elodi breathed out. The soldiers cheered as they parted to grant the relieved horse and scout passage. Elodi nudged Sea Mist forward to greet and congratulate the rider. She dismounted and strode to meet her. Elodi shook the scout's hand. 'Your bravery is much admired and appreciated. Please, tell me your name.'

She bowed her head. 'Shelan, ma'am. And it's an honor to serve you and the realm.'

'We are very much honored and grateful to have your service, Shelan.' Elodi nodded to the bridge. 'And I'm sure your crossing with your weary mount may well become a verse in a song before long.'

The scout patted her horse's neck. 'Then let all know this fellow's name is Lightning. Fast on the straight, but not quite so speedy on the edge of a blade spanning a deep gorge, ma'am.' She straightened. 'But I'm forgetting myself. The Ruuk are not far behind me. Many, many hundreds, with some wearing armor I did not recognize.'

Elodi glanced to Aldorman. 'Their smithies have obviously made use of the plunder from our mines.' She looked back to Shelan. 'And their weapons? Do they bring siege engines?'

'Yes, ma'am. Dozens of covered wagons which I suspect carry their machines. But even from my elevated position, I could not survey the whole army. I believe I saw only the vanguard before I had to leave.'

'Thank you.' Elodi steadied her voice. 'Please report what you know of our foe's armor to the archers, then get food and water for yourself and Lightning. And when refreshed and rested, please make your way back to Calerdorn. I will write a message for you to deliver to my advisor.' The scout saluted and turned her horse. Elodi climbed back on to her saddle and nudged Sea Mist on. She approached Ruan. 'Captain. You're sure Uldrak left no surprises under the bridge?'

'Yes, ma'am. We've checked twice as commanded. But this bridge is as important to him as it is to us. I cannot think Uldrak would wish it destroyed.'

Elodi nodded. 'All the same. I do not feel we can judge Uldrak by our own standards.' She took a breath. 'Join your men, Captain. Hold your line as long as you can, allowing our archers to reduce their ranks from back here. You and Gundrul command the bridge. I will leave it to your judgment should you have to order a retreat.'

Ruan grinned. 'Retreat, ma'am? We will shovel them from the bridge in numbers that would fill a lesser gorge. It will be they who turn back.'

'Good. Let them regret coming this far south for a second time. But Captain… don't sacrifice your brave men. Pull back, if necessary. I will not view it as a retreat, more of a tactical re-alignment. The reserves will form our rear-guard to enable an orderly withdrawal to the fort if it comes to that.' Ruan nodded, spun about, and strode off to join Gundrul at the front. Elodi turned to Aldorman. 'Should a retreat be required, we shall ride to the aid of the last souls off the bridge and disrupt the raiders advance. Then we shall dash for the fort with hopefully enough time to close the gate.'

Aldorman frowned. 'But, ma'am, my orders were to—'

'Your orders were for the benefit of Wendel's ears. We can hardly sit by and witness our soldiers cut down after giving it their all at the front.'

A smile crossed Aldorman's lips. 'That we cannot, ma'am. It would be an honor to fight at your side once again.'

'Sadly, Captain, even if we succeed today, I fear you and I will have that pleasure on many more occasions. And should we have to withdraw from the fort' — she glanced to the new gate — 'which may well become a necessity, we will have a difficult journey together back to Calerdorn if the enemy choose to pursue us.'

Aldorman stiffened. 'Ma'am, if it comes to that, I will have to insist you ride ahead with my escort. I cannot allow the leader of the realm to get involved in a rear-guard action. That, I'm sure is where Wendel would draw the line, and a line I would have to enforce, ma'am.'

Elodi looked to the men on foot. 'Very well, Aldorman. Sadly, I will have no choice but to obey your order. But I trust our fire wall at the fort will afford a reasonable amount of time for my soldiers to get a good head start.' She shivered. 'Has it turned colder? The vapor from those packed guards on the bridge rises like steam from a boiling pot.'

Aldorman nodded. 'I believe it has.'

She looked anxiously on. 'This does not seem natural. Does that fiend now command the weather?'

Her captain stood on his stirrups and peered down the gap. 'It could be a feature of this unique formation of the mountains. The air is a little thin here, and the slightest gust down the ravine, aided by the cold air lurking in the gorge, would be more than enough to chase away the little warmth braving the mountains.'

Elodi wished she had hung on to her cloak a while longer. 'I hope for all our sakes you're right. The last thing we need is for the weather to side with our adversaries.' She froze. A low rumble echoed through the pass.

Aldorman's hand went to his sword. 'I'm certain that was not natural. I believe they approach, ma'am.'

Elodi tightened the straps on her breastplate. She leaned forward and patted Sea Mist's neck. 'Be brave again for me, Misty.' He flicked his head back and his gray mane brushed her face. The vapor rising from the men on the bridge thickened as deep breaths were taken as they set themselves to meet the inevitable onslaught. In the silence, the dull blows of mallets wedging the barricade supports into place, signaled the final preparations. The Tunduska Bridge was closed… but for how long?

Elodi peered to the bend in the road on the opposite side of the gorge. What horrors did Uldrak command this time? Had he learned from his mistakes made at the siege and brought more deadly terrors of old? Once more, she counted the rows on the bridge, trying to take courage from the locked shields and bristling spears. But Uldrak knew the defenses well. He must know how Elodi would hope to defend the bridge. She fidgeted again with her straps and checked her sword. Her enemy would not commit such a force to an attack he did not expect to win. What did Uldrak have in his armory to break through and take the pass?

A drumbeat rolled down the valley; slow at first but steadily gaining pace. Her heart matched Uldrak's drums.

She stiffened. Is this deliberate? Is the wyke trying to sow panic among her ranks? It stopped. The last beat bounced off the mountain walls, rumbling over their heads and down the pass as if stating Uldrak's intention. A man on the bridge coughed, but otherwise, all remained silent and ready. Elodi glanced to Aldorman, then back to the road. Why had they stopped? What was he planning?

A throaty roar emanated from around the bend. The men on the bridge braced. Thousands of cruel voices bellowed, declaring their anticipated victory. She rose in her saddle and called out. 'Stay strong! Let them come to fear the strength of the Five Realms.' Heads nodded on the bridge; shields ground together, closing the smallest of gaps between; spears lowered, the tips awaiting their prey. Another roar. Louder this time — the enemy drew ever closer to the gap. Ruan called out. As one, his men burst into song. It was one Harlyn's forces recognized, and they raised their voices in unison. Elodi's hold on her reins tightened. The song on the bridge roused their spirits, drowning out the vile howls of their foe.

But as her forces sang, the first enemy ranks poured around the bend like sludge through a culvert, dislodged by storm water. Their dull, gray shields easily looked a match for Elodi's ranks — and, no doubt, far exceeded the numbers on the south side of the gorge. Elodi placed on her helmet, flicked her visor down, and felt her face moisten as she fought to slow her breathing. Sea Mist nudged forward as those of her knights edged back. She patted his neck. 'Hold still, boy. Hold steady, this is not our battle… yet.'

The Ruuk advance halted. Elodi counted at least forty rows of shields back along the road and knew hundreds more lay concealed beyond the bend. And to her dismay, they appeared well-drilled and disciplined. In times past, the Ruuk would have charged headlong into an assault with little concern for their losses. Elodi was aware the Ruuk believed the more savage the manner of their death, the greater their reward in the afterlife. But Uldrak had curtailed their reckless nature, marshaling their aggression and strength to form a cohesive and far more dangerous opponent. She feared Uldrak had obviously learned from his errors during his attack on Calerdorn. If Elodi was to be triumphant and hold the pass, she could not rely on Uldrak's poor judgment and rash decisions to aid her on this occasion.

Elodi searched the lines for the wyke but found no sign. She could not imagine he would form part of the shield wall, and therefore commanded from the rear. Her thoughts went back to her father's notes in the trunk. What relic had led Sylvena to abandon the mysterious Order of Echoes and search the unchartered regions? Was she waylaid by some dark force wielding this relic? It must have been an immensely powerful foe to corrupt the once high and mighty leader and transform her into the traitor, Uluriel. Elodi scanned the snow-covered peaks to the north. Did this relic exist to this day?

A horn blasted. The opposing ranks split down the middle. A wagon bearing a blunt, metal head trundled through the column. The defenders' song faltered at the sight of the crude battering ram. Dozens of Ruuk pushed the heavy machine into position. Elodi's archers let loose a volley but failed to trouble the soft targets protected by the armored flanks of the wagon. With a raucous howl, the Ruuk heaved. The wagon hurtled down the slope towards the crossing. The bridge groaned as the large wheels thundered across the ancient stone. The ram gathered pace despite the incline, but to Elodi's relief, they had failed to achieve the correct line. A front wheel slipped off the ledge. Sparks flew from the squealing axel grinding the stone, but it was not sufficient to bring its heavy load to a halt, and the ram's momentum sent it toppling down into the gorge. The Ruuk who did not fall were quickly picked off by the archers as they rushed to clear the bridge.

The defenders cheered — but not for long. A second ram appeared, taking its position at the top of the slope. A whoosh. Elodi ducked. A ballista from the fort unleashed its bolt. It streaked across the gap landing short, but then skimmed the ground and slammed into the ram's belly shattering the wagon beneath. Again, the men cheered as the damaged weapon was heaved over the edge, clearing the way for a third ram taking its place. Elodi rose. How many did Uldrak have at his disposal? He only needed one to cross and drive a hole in the barricade to signal the beginning of the next phase.

The third ram was brought forward. Heavily armored Ruuk closed ranks behind. Another bolt shot over the bridge but missed, piercing a hole in the columns behind, only for the gap to be filled as if the small victory had never happened. The front ranks ran onto the bridge to clear the casualties from the first strike; Elodi noted with disgust both the dead and injured were shoveled into the gorge. Despite the efforts of the archers, the way was made ready for the third ram.

The Ruuk put their shoulders to the wagon. It gained speed. With dread, Elodi noted this one stayed true as it raced up the incline. She cried out as the blunt head crashed against the barricade. The crack sent a shiver down the bridge. The barrier held, but one more blow would surely expose the shields behind. More arrows flew at the Ruuk rolling the ram back to the foot of the bridge, ready for a second attempt. Dozens fell but were quickly dispatched into the ravine as more rushed forward to take their place at the rear of the wagon.

Elodi's eyes widened. The blunt head of the ram was removed. A long, barbed spike was brought forward and hammered into place. The first had weakened the barricade. The second would pierce the wood, embedding itself so it could not easily be removed. She groaned. A ramp was brought forward from the rear. She guessed their tactic. The ramp would be attached to the back of the wagon once lodged in the barricade, providing a platform for the attackers to leap onto the defenders. She called down to the bridge. Gundrul waved his hand. He saw the threat and withdrew the lines a dozen paces.

Two bolts from the fort flew over their heads but only succeeded in thinning the ranks of the soldiers behind — a futile gesture given the numbers keen to take their place. Elodi knew they would have no time to reload before the barbed spike breached the barricade.

The ram came. The rumbling of the wheels on the stone grew louder as it gathered pace up the slope. Elodi winced at the ear-splitting screech as the wood shattered. Gundrul! Ruan! The spike penetrated the wood and gored two men despite the gap. Ruuk rushed forward and set the ramp in place with horrifying speed. More clambered up the platform and hurled themselves, arms spread like eagles' wings, over the broken barricade with little care for their lives. But Elodi's forces rushed to greet them and fill the void. Dozens leaped over, only to be impaled on the many angled spear tips.

Another bolt from the fort cleaved its way down the length of the bridge, dispatching many Ruuk to their doom. Those that had made it over the barricade were outnumbered and quickly hacked down. But the ram stayed in place, embedded in the wooden barrier. Yet Harlyn's engineers had designed their makeshift defense well. Two engineers rushed to the front and hammered at the brackets at its sides. Satisfied the restraints were free, they marshalled the front ranks to push and dislodge the barrier with the splintered wood still empaled on the ram's spike. With a roar, the men heaved the wagon back down the bridge. Its large wheels crushed many wounded struggling to get out of the way and helped the ram to twist and tumble into the gorge.

Elodi searched for signs of casualties. Relieved, she heard Ruan bellow a command, urging his men to reform their broken ranks and raise their voices to sing their battle song. She counted half a dozen men carried back from the bridge, sadly dead or mortally wounded. More limped towards the fort, Gundrul among them. His sword arm hung lifeless with blood pouring from a nasty gash running the length of his forearm. He straightened. 'Just need to get patched up, ma'am. Then I'll return to my post.'

Elodi grimaced as she eyed his arm. 'That looks to require more than just a *patch up*, Captain. Go and get that wound attended to properly. Then return here. If you're incapacitated, I'd rather have you at my side for your tactical mind, than at the front line unable to swing a sword.'

Gundrul attempted a salute with his injured arm but gave up. 'I'm not finished yet, ma'am, but neither are those scoundrels. They've achieved their first objective. The battle for real is about to begin.' As if on cue, the horns blasted.

Elodi shouted above the din. 'Then get yourself to the fort and back here as soon as you're able.' But Gundrul could not take his eyes from the bridge. Elodi leaned over. 'Now, Captain! That is an order. You're no use to anyone until you've had that wound treated. Ruan will command in your absence.' Gundrul pulled up his right arm with his left and held it in a salute, then turned and limped to the fort.

Elodi reluctantly turned back to the bridge, not wishing to see what new terror came her way. A dull, gray shell of shields edged silently towards them — the same formation

Uldrak had used at the gatehouse. Had the approaching Ruuk chanted, she could have roused her forces to sing a riposte, but the enemy's silence troubled her. It pervaded the gorge, robbing her of a vital sense, re-enforcing the dread that these invaders were well-trained and determined to grind Harlyn into the dirt. Elodi cleared her throat. 'Ruan.' Her voice sounded weak. She tried again, calling out. 'Ruan. Have your spearmen sing.' Her captain appeared also to be entranced by the eerie calm, but he found his voice, bellowing out the first line of a new battle song. His faithful spearmen joined, but even with their numbers, the song failed to reach the spirit-raising tempo of their first rendition.

Elodi tapped her helmet, convinced her hearing had gone. But her ears did not deceive; the gorge was strangely quiet. She stood in her stirrups to check the bridge. Slowly at first as the Ruuk cleared the way, shoving the dead and dying off the sides, they reached halfway to her line of shields. Elodi twisted back to the wall. The ballistae would have to time their strikes carefully, and choose which targets warranted their attention. It would take several minutes to reload the heavy projectiles, and Uldrak knew this. He had plenty of targets to bring into range to draw Harlyn's limited supply of bolts, and then send in his attacks while her crews rearmed. The archers nocked their arrows and leveled their bows. But how much damage they could inflict against the shields was another matter.

The fort unleashed two bolts. With a whoosh they shot over the defenders' heads. One fell wide, disappearing down the gorge to join the growing stack of debris at the bottom. But the second shot across the stone, slewing beneath the shields, splintering the formation with sickening efficiency. But Elodi's initial joy was to no avail. The next row of shields rushed silently forward, forming another giant beetle to skuttle onto the bridge. Elodi guessed Uldrak's tactics. He would attack in waves with each looking to deplete her weapons and wear down her defenses. And, of course, Uldrak had little concern for his own losses.

The way to the barricade was cleared; the next attack began. The shell of the gray beast split open as the Ruuk roared and surged forward. Defenders' hands clenched shields, spears and swords anticipating the inevitable clash. The raiders gained the midway point. Elodi baulked as the two walls crashed and ground against each other. But the bridge favored its protectors. The assailants approached too fast, now dozens tumbled over the unprotected sides as the shockwave rebounded back through their ranks. With the shields open at their flanks, the Ruuk made easy targets for the archers on the turrets. Dozens more fell, pierced by arrows. Spear tips were driven at shields, some turned, opening gaps in the line briefly, but the shields soon clamped shut again and the jostling continued.

The enemy withdrew as their numbers thinned at the rear thus losing the force to push Elodi's defenses back. Men moved forward to fill the gaps resulting from the attack. But there was to be no respite. The horns blared — the next gray wave rolled in. But their attackers had learned from the mistakes of the previous strike and this time, advanced slowly maintaining their shape. Again, shield slammed against shield, cries of anger and anguish rose as the second skirmish commenced. Again, Elodi's guards held firm using the walls on the bridge to concentrate their force forward. The Ruuk fell as feet slipped on the blood of their fallen comrades. Elodi tensed, resisting every blow as if she stood with her shields. She held her breath as she willed them to hold the crucial point at the front of the containing walls. Should they lose ground and the Ruuk achieve a foothold within them, it would become harder to push back against superior numbers. Her bunched shoulders released as her defenders repelled the second wave.

Aldorman steadied his horse. 'Don't fret, girl. We're holding them.' He looked to Elodi. 'The skinny fellow is going to have to think again if he believes he can take this bridge from us.'

Elodi nodded to four more wounded being carried to the rear. 'But he has the numbers. He can inflict fewer casualties yet hurt us more.'

Aldorman glanced back to the reserves. 'We have plenty ready to take their places. We could do this all week, ma'am.'

Elodi watched as the next enemy formation took their position on the bridge. 'We can be sure he's learned his lesson from the failed siege. I don't think he'll be in any hurry. And if he gets a foothold beyond this bridge, could we ever take it back?' She kept her eyes on the bend in the road, dreading the appearance of ballistae. The narrow formation may be a good defense against advancing foot soldiers but made for an easy target for a well-aimed Ruuk bolt. With a shudder, she wondered how many rows a barbed projectile could penetrate before losing momentum. She had felt helpless standing on Calerdorn's inner wall during the start of the siege, when all she could do was watch, but this time she had no open plain to lead her knights in a daring raid.

The defenders repelled six more advances, but with each wave, Elodi lost men, but mercifully fewer with each attack as they became wise to Uldrak's tactics. Perhaps they could hold the pass for weeks. Uldrak could not take action that risked destroying the bridge — after all, it was just as important to him as it was to Elodi. But would the Ruuk stay loyal to his command should they not break through? It they failed to lay their hands on any plunder they believed stored in the fort, would they refuse to attack. Perhaps the war of attrition could work in her favor.

Elodi took the opportunity in the first pause in the battle to stretch her aching back. She turned as Gundrul returned, relieved to see he no longer limped. He lifted his bandaged arm and saluted. 'Be swinging my sword in no time at all, ma'am.'

Elodi smiled. 'You're a tough one, no doubt. I'm glad you're on my side.' She shivered. 'I only wish the weather would see fit to join us, this armor offers no defense against this chill wind.'

He grinned. 'Not made for comfort, eh. You should retire to the fort. You're the only one here who hasn't yet taken a break.' He looked up. 'It's getting dark. And I doubt you'd see your hand in front of your face down in this valley at night, even with all our torches.'

The thought of a fire and warm drink was tempting. 'Rotate the men again, Captain. I think those at the front deserve more nourishment and rest more than I. But I will retire shortly, once I'm satisfied we're prepared for the night to come.'

Gundrul saluted once more. 'And with any luck, the day to follow, ma'am.'

13. Echoes from the Past

A faint voice. So quiet, Toryn doubted at first he had heard it. His eyelids scraped across his dry eyes as he forced them to open. It was dark. Was it his fifth or sixth night? He had lost count. He could not recall when the guards had last lowered a flask of water, but his parched mouth suggested it had been many hours. And Toryn was under no illusion they cared for his well-being. This was about prolonging his punishment so the good people of Archonholm could revel in his misery. He tried to swallow but cried out in pain as if a thorny bramble had lodged in his swollen throat.

The voice? Toryn turned his head. It did not come from the bridge. He tried to recall the sound. He believed it had come from his right, originating from the towering mountain wall that disappeared up into the night sky. But it could not have been the voice that had caused Hope pain on their journey south. This was soft, a female voice, and certainly not a warning or a threat, more of an attempt to sooth and heal his torment. But in the ensuing silence, Toryn struggled to recall the voice, and it eluded all attempts. Above, on the bridge the slow breathing of the two guards gave them away — they slept on duty. Toryn tipped his head back as far as his restraints and tight muscles would allow.

The stars moved!

They wheeled above as if the great dome of the sky slowly rotated from a point far to the north. The sky brightened in the east. The sun rose quickly. He watched it climb, reach the top of the ceiling, then slide down to the horizon before it could warm his face. The sky darkened, stars appeared and swirled as before, then turning to the east, he watched the darkness retreat as the sun returned to perform the same trick. Had the days shortened to hasten his demise? But Toryn did not want to die. He fixed his eyes on the sun, determined to halt its rapid climb and ensuing descent. He failed. The great dome span faster, until night and day changed in the blink of an eye.

Toryn had but one way left to avoid death — the Song. He closed his eyes, refusing to witness the passing of time, denying its hold over him. Toryn shut out the spinning sky and attempted to clear his mind. He had to find the means to connect to the Song. Yet, even if he could hear the voices, what could he do? Hope had used her hands and voice to muster her powers, but hanging from the bridge, he had the use of neither. But he had no other option. He closed his eyes and tried what Hope suggested — listen. He strained his ears and discovered signs of activity unheard only moments earlier. A lone bird called for his mate somewhere to the west of the city; a child cried in the night; and mole dug a new tunnel beneath the manicured lawns of the Archon's Garden. But the soft voice from his dazed state remained silent.

Toryn recalled standing with Hope beside the Singing Stone in the wood. She had said all children could once hear the pure voices of the Song, but soon lost the ability once the curiosity of youth was crushed by the trials of survival. Had he heard them as a child? Hamar insisted Miram could not hold a tune to save her life, yet Toryn had vivid memories of the soothing song that helped see off the aches and pains of the Winter Fever.

Don't try! He had not *tried* to listen when young — he had no knowledge of the Song; it had come to him. Had he not been drowsing earlier when the soothing voice had sung? Toryn let his mind wander back to his childhood. The summer days had seemed long and sunnier back then, back before he had grown up and felt like a stranger among what should have been his own people. After completing his chores around the farm, he would lie on his back in the field and watch the clouds float passed. He would try to look at those strange, squiggly things you get in your eye, but as soon as he could catch a glimpse of one, it would dart away. He learned not to try, not to look directly at them and found he could watch them a while longer. Had he heard the Song on those summer afternoons? Had it seemed so natural that he took it for granted? Perhaps the carefree children also heard the voices as they had played their innocent games in the fields; maybe they had sung along with the Maidens.

Not to try. *Not to try.* Simply listen. He could manage that. After all, that's all he could do, swinging on a rope with hands and feet bound tight, and his tongue stuck to the floor of his mouth. He did nothing; just listened. Toryn made no attempt to guess what made the noises reaching his ears. He ignored the urge to make sense of the myriad of sounds; he just listened.

Toryn drifted off to another place, back through time, back across the many leagues to Midwyche. The sweet smell of the freshly, mown grass filled his nostrils, while the squeals of laughter and glad songs of the other children, brought a smile to his cracked lips. It was a different life, almost not his to remember.

The lilting song of a lark drifted in on the warm air. Toryn saw it in his mind. It hovered over a cornfield several leagues to the west. Others joined. The flute-like trill of blackbirds perched in trees to the east; the call of a lone thrush; the joyful whistle of a robin far to the north. Toryn let out a long sigh as the songs brought him relief and warmth. The bird calls merged until they sang as one.

A voice.

So faint it could have been a memory of his mother.

But there it was, unmistakably, female voices, so close in harmony it sounded like a solitary singer at first hearing. It came from a distant time, of that Toryn was sure. It had always been there, since the sun rose on the first dawn, an echo of the Maidens for all who chose to open their ears and minds. Toryn kept his eyes closed, determined not to lose the Song, convinced if he tried to capture the voices, they would be lost. He succeeded. Many verses combined. The verse summoning the bedrock to rise and form the lofty peaks of the Caerwals; the verse calming the restless waters, tempting them to withdraw from the land to form the deep oceans. As the land dried, they sang to entice saplings to spring from the fertile earth, to flourish, to open their blossoms and soak up the warm rays of the young sun. And finally, the Maidens' most gentle verse, ushering forth the songbirds to grace the skies and join with them in the splendor of their Song.

Images of those first days flooded Toryn's mind. Tears flowed, soothing his dry eyes as he witnessed the Maidens' creation of beauty from the chaos. Toryn no longer cared for his fate — he had witnessed the birth of his world and heard the Maidens' Song of Creation. He joined, humming along as best he could. The Song responded, combining their voices with his humble refrain. Despite his gag, Toryn laughed. He continued, letting the Song ease his pain. He hummed as the voices rose, bringing more themes to the tune. His whole body tingled; nourished and healed by the verses. The tightness around his torso lessened as his body appeared to float, allowing his chest to expand as he took his first deep breath for many days. His body pulsed with the rhythm; he grew hot. His flesh suddenly seemed too thin, too weak to hold the fire that burned within.

A new voice! But this was no Maiden. This had to be a singer of the Dark Verses — had they sensed his entry into their world? Toryn's jaw clenched tight as the fell voice sought to drown out those of the Maidens. Its words strove to break him and drag the pieces to its dark cause. Toryn kicked out his legs, desperate to break free from the harsh voice cracking his skull from within. He twisted and swung on the rope; eyes wide-open, forcing himself to wake from his trance.

He awoke to find night had fallen. A starless sky bore down on the land, but if he thought he had escaped the attention of the fell voice, he was mistaken. Toryn cried out as the dark presence crossed over into his waking world, seeking to drive him to madness.

A yellow slither of light appeared at the top of the Archon's Tower. A slender, black figure stepped out onto the balcony. The Archon raised his arms. The voice stopped. Toryn hung like a dead leaf about to fall. He slowly revolved on the rope to face back towards Archonholm. The great edifice of the city glowed a faint silver as the crescent moon rose to the east. A few lights shone out from the walls and Toryn knew a vigil kept watch on the Lower Gate, but otherwise the city slept. He looked up to the tower. The door had closed and now only a speck of light shone from a single window in the Archon's quarters.

The pain reduced to a ringing in his ears; his breathing slowed; the straps cut deep into his aching body. The stars returned. They no longer wheeled as before, but their light hurt like a thousand tiny needles pricking his eyeballs. Horses approached. Toryn guessed three at most, but he winced as their hooves hammered on the bridge as if a whole army rode in anger to the Caerwal Gate. They clattered to a halt. A few words were exchanged. Toryn grunted as the rope was tugged. He cried out as the men hauled him over the railing and slung him onto the back of a horse like a sack of grain. But he no longer cared.

Exhausted, he let sleep take him. He had heard the Song. He had joined the Song, but there was something concealed within he never wanted to hear again.

14. A Hammer Blow

'Ma'am?' Elodi blinked in the torchlight at the dark figure looming over her. She jerked upright in her chair. The figure stepped back. He stuttered. 'Apologies, ma'am. I didn't mean to startle you.'

Elodi rubbed the sleep from her eyes and recognized one of Gundrul's young guards. 'No, please, it is I that should apologize. I had not intended to sleep so deeply.' She glanced around the others napping where they had collapsed from the exhaustion of battle. Elodi stood. 'What is it? Is an attack imminent?'

'Not as yet, but Captain Gundrul believes they may be about to try a different tactic.'

Elodi reached for her breastplate. 'And what makes him think that?'

The young guard frowned. 'Something's changed, something that don't seem quite natural.' He glanced back to the door. 'It might be nothing, and maybe we've woken you for no reason, ma'am.'

'Nonsense. I'd rather be woken for no reason, than sleep through something important.' Elodi fastened her sword belt. 'What is your name?'

His eyes widened. 'Lorek, ma'am. But I'm no captain, or even hold rank. There's nothing special about me.'

'But you're an Archonian Guard, Lorek. Surely, that makes you special.'

He blushed. 'Oh, I know, ma'am. Don't get me wrong, I wasn't saying… or meaning… I, I meant I'm not in any position to command.' He straightened. 'But I'm as loyal to the Archon and the realms as the next guard, ma'am.'

Elodi smiled. 'I'm sure that goes without saying. I wouldn't dream of questioning the loyalty of an Archonian.' She completed the last buckle on her armor and reached for her helmet. 'You're right to bring the situation to my attention. I shall come and see for myself.'

'What about your knights? Should we wake them, ma'am?'

She stepped over Aldorman and his men, noting with amusement they had arranged themselves in a circle around her chair. 'No. Let them sleep for now. As you say, it may be nothing.' She picked up her gauntlets. 'Right. I'm ready. Please, lead the way.'

Elodi followed the young guard, treading carefully through the slumbering men. At the entrance, the two guards on watch saluted. Elodi braced as she stepped out of the warmth into the cold night. Lorek stopped. 'Please watch your step, ma'am. The cobbles are covered with a frost. I slipped twice on my way here.'

She glanced down. 'At this time of year? This isn't natural, even up here.' They walked along the path to the main gate. 'Where are you from, Lorek?'

'Tamforth in Darrow. Where the river meets the sea.'

'Ah yes. I've yet to visit, but I hear it's a fine place.'

'That it is, ma'am, especially in summer down by the shore.' He laughed. 'But the gulls can be a pest. One snatched a morsel of fish clean out of my brother's…' He looked to the ground. 'But listen to me. I'm sure you're not interested in such lowly talk.'

Elodi followed Lorek through the arch. 'At this moment, such talk, while a very welcome distraction, also reminds me of why we stand against this enemy. You mentioned a brother. Is he too an Archonian?'

His voice lowered. 'Yes, ma'am. I have… had two brothers.'

Elodi's stomach clenched. 'Had?'

'Porek and Dorek.' He sniffed. 'And yes, we had our fair share of leg-pulling when we were young. But my mother had a thing for names that rhymed. Said it made them easier to remember.'

She smiled. 'That much is obvious. But what of your brothers?'

'They were serving at the mines when they fell. The survivors rescued from the wood told me what happened.' Lorek's pace slowed. 'Both lost, and in the most terrible of ways.'

Elodi took his cold hand and stopped. 'I'm deeply sorry to hear that. Although there's nothing I can say to heal your hurt, I do regard their service, and ultimate sacrifice they made to the realms, most highly. I shall send word to your mother to—'

'Please don't, ma'am.' He withdrew his hand. 'Oh… I'm so sorry. I didn't mean to interrupt, it's just that I, I…'

'Please, Lorek. Speak your mind.'

'I have yet to send word of their loss. It would break her heart to hear of their fate, and I'd rather tell her to her face. She lost our father not long after my birth. We were all she had left in the world, ma'am.'

Elodi saw the pain in his eyes. 'Then I shall relieve you of your duty. You must return home. Should the worse happen and you are lost, it would break your poor mother's heart beyond repair.'

Lorek glanced to the bridge. 'But I can't go, ma'am. I've made my oath to the Archon and I'm not afraid to die for him, or for you.' A wry smile crossed his lips. 'And my mother would be the first to berate me for not carrying out my duty, despite losing her other two sons. I'd be in more danger from her if I abandoned my post.'

Elodi sighed. 'Then I shall not put you through that trial.' But her insides trembled. How many families in her realm had made such a terrible sacrifice? And how many more would follow?

They reached the bridge. Vapor rose like fog from the men standing guard. Elodi admired their straight lines and defiant stances, despite the cold and palpable dread hanging over the gorge. But they also knew their duty, they knew the fight had to be fought here, on this narrow bridge, in the dead of night if they were to defend their flesh and blood back home.

Lorek straightened, taking on the guise of a proud Archonian again. 'I'll take you to Captain Gundrul, ma'am.'

Elodi touched his arm. 'Thank you, Lorek. I am heartened to see such fine, young men as yourself in service to the realm. Now, please, do lead the way.' She met the eyes of every guard as they stepped aside to make a pathway along the crowded bridge.

Gundrul turned and saluted her approach. 'Sorry to disturb you at this hour, ma'am.'

'Not at all, Captain. Lorek tells me you believe our *friends from the north* are up to no good.'

'That I do.' Gundrul pointed to the slither of sky down the valley. 'Can you see that? It might take a moment for your eyes to adjust, but over there, beyond the flickering light of their fires. Something don't look right to me.'

'Is that…?' She looked passed the orange glow reflecting on the snow of the upper slopes. 'Is the sky turning green?'

Gundrul grunted. 'I have seen a night sky that color before. But much farther north and higher in the sky. And that moved like a curtain billowing in a breeze. This looks more like it's the mountains that glow, contaminating the sky by some foul means. It has to be something in the pass causing it.'

Lorek stepped up. 'May I speak, Captain?' Gundrul

nodded. Lorek cleared his throat. 'Remember what the guards at the mines said? They spoke of a green sludge seeping into the rock. The wyke had a cursed stone that poisoned the ground.' He looked to Elodi. 'That's what did for Dorek, and none could endure its touch for long, ma'am.'

Elodi peered at the tinged sides of the mountains. She ran her tongue across her teeth, convinced she could taste the corruption. 'This is grim. If we abandon the bridge and leave it open to the Ruuk, the same devilry could be used on the fort. But if we stand? Will it infect the bridge and us with it?'

Gundrul looked down the rows of shields and spears. 'The green stuff was said to crack the rock, ma'am. I don't think Uldrak can risk destroying the bridge.' He rubbed his chin. 'I'd say he's got something else planned. He can't go on losing his soldiers at the rate he did yesterday. We know he doesn't care for the Ruuk as such, but Uldrak is aware he needs the numbers to take Calerdorn, if that's his intention.'

'Oh, I believe that truly is his intention. I'm certain he's still seething from his previous failure.' Elodi stood on her toes. 'Is it my eyes, or are more of the slopes turning green?'

Gundrul's voice rose. 'Their fires are going out. Something approaches.'

Elodi's hand went to her blade. 'Rouse the men in the fort please, Lorek. Whatever is coming our way, we need to be alert and ready.'

The men on the bridge shouldered shields, stamped their feet, and checked their blades were free of ice. Elodi stood beside Gundrul behind the first line. He kept his eyes on the slopes ahead. 'I was going to suggest you retreat, ma'am, but I know it would only be a waste of my breath.' He grinned. 'And it would strengthen our line to have the slayer of shreeks and shrouls at our side.'

'Those were very different fights, Captain. Who knows what we face this time?'

'Nothing I'm sure you can't handle, ma'am.'

Elodi shivered. 'I wish I had your confidence. Uldrak obviously thinks he has the means to take this...' she froze. 'Captain! Look.' The unnatural green light grew, staining the road where it rounded the bend, shedding a dull light on a thin, black figure.

'Uldrak.' Gundrul glared at the silhouette. 'I see he's finally chosen to make his grand entrance.' He turned and waved at the fort. The archers read his intention. Three stepped forward, and three arrows streaked towards their target. But Elodi predicted the outcome — all three froze in the air, turned white, and then clattered harmlessly onto the ground.

Elodi stared. 'The arrows are covered in ice.' Her teeth chattered. 'Does he command shrouls?' Footsteps crunched on the frosty ground behind. Dozens of torches were brought forward, flooding the bridge with their yellow light. But Elodi felt no warmth from the flames, and they failed to rid the gap of its nauseating, green hue. More boots pounded across the cobbles as the reserves took their positions at the rear. Behind, the glistening spears of Broon's men returning from their rest, made their way through the tight formations on the bridge.

Ruan's large frame squeezed through the shield walls to join them at the front. He nodded to Elodi. 'A little chilly, ma'am. Reminds me of home.' He looked over the barricade and scoffed. 'Ah. I see the skinny rake has finally decided to show his ugly face.'

Elodi clenched her cold hands inside her gauntlets. 'He does like to make a dramatic entrance. And I dare say he's not about to disappoint with his next act.' She felt the crush as more defenders packed the narrow pathway.

'Ma'am?' Elodi turned to find Aldorman had followed Ruan. 'I must insist you take your position at the rear.'

'Insist all you like, Aldorman. My place is here. This is to be no ordinary attack.'

'Then please allow me and my knights to do battle at your side, ma'am.'

Elodi nodded. 'It would be a pleasure. Permission granted, unhorsed of course.'

'He's moving, ma'am.' Gundrul pointed his blade. Uldrak's robed form appeared to glide above the road to take his position opposite the bridge. More arrows flew to be met with the same fate as those before. Uldrak sneered at the archers' futile attack as he set his stance. He bowed his head and folded his arms across his chest. Above, a lone cloud masked the sliver of the moon. The gap fell silent. Elodi's teeth ached as Uldrak muttered a foul incantation. His rasping voice rose, echoing through Tunduska's Gorge, promising to bring a new horror down upon their heads. She looked to the dark, mountain slopes and wondered whose side the old God of the North would have chosen.

Elodi shuffled. All they could do was wait for Uldrak to reveal his hand. They could not risk rushing forward, forsaking their position on the bridge to run into some unknown threat the wyke had planned. They did not have to wait long. The sleeves of his robe flapped as Uldrak wove his hands about his head. He clasped them together. His voice rose higher as he slowly drew his palms apart. A sphere of rippling, green air formed between his splayed fingers as if a restless animal was trapped within a cage. He spread and lifted his arms. The sphere grew, rising above the foot of the bridge. Bile rose in Elodi's throat; the defenders stiffened. Uldrak raised one finger, guiding his abomination of the air slowly along the line of the bridge towards the shield wall.

The click of his fingers ricocheted over Elodi's head. The sphere split, oozing its contents like pus from an infected wound into the still air. Gundrul growled to his guards. 'Steady, hold the line. Not a step back. Remember your oath, brothers. Not a step back!' But every fiber in Elodi's body wanted to retreat from the swelling, putrid air creeping towards them. The line recoiled as Uldrak's mist rolled over them and the stench hit the back of their throats. Elodi gagged. She tasted festering wounds, rotting corpses and a violation of all living beings. The air froze. In turn, the torches across the bridge spluttered, hissed, and died.

Elodi stared as the spear tips of Broon, poised above her head, turned from dull silver to emerald. She flinched, glancing up to see the solitary cloud in the sky drift south to reveal a defiled, thin sliver of a green moon. Her fingers and toes tingled as its sickly, pale light merged with Uldrak's foul fog. The guards braced, tightening their grip on the shields, pulling them closer in a futile attempt to shut out the corruption tainting the air.

Ruan muttered under his breath. 'This is going to get ugly.'

Gundrul whispered back. 'Always the prophet, eh, Ruan.' But Elodi shared not their nervous humor. Tonight, she had no walls for protection. She stood exposed with only a thin line of shields between her and Uldrak's devilry. She fixed her eyes on the slim, dark figure of the wyke. He stood motionless, but she could sense his satisfaction from the dread taking hold in the hearts of Elodi's ranks. Uldrak mocked them. His disdain was obvious. His right arm shot into the air. A clash of drums, dozens of them, sent their message of doom rumbling down the pass. A horn blared, a second followed, then many more joined the cacophony to decree the violent death of all who dared to stand in their way.

A solid, black line thundered around the bend, stomping in perfect rhythm. Hundreds of raw throats bellowed their challenge.

Ruan yelled. 'Norgog!'

Gundrul grasped Elodi's arm, yelling in her ear. 'Hammerskulls! Ma'am, this is no place for the Lady of the Realm. You must retreat. You cannot be trapped here.' But it was too late. The bridge shuddered beneath the bare feet of the squat creatures hurtling towards them. Elodi gasped. They carried no shields, only cruel-looking hammers shaped like their heads. These were no Ruuk. Their ranks were chained together. Uldrak had learned; those on the flanks would not fall to their death over the edge. They would strike as a solid, gray mass, concentrating their strength at its center.

The Norgog charged in perfect formation, raising their weapons in unison as they slammed into Elodi's shield wall. The air was forced from her chest as the frontline reeled back under the shattering blow. The Norgog carried the momentum, gaining the first footholds within the bridge's defensive walls. Large hammers rained down, splintering shields, severing arms, splitting helmets and skulls.

Ruan's men fought bravely back. Spear tips drove hard into the Norgog. Elodi was lifted from her feet in the crush. She thrust her blade through the breached shield wall. But to her frustration, her blows carried little force as she was unable to set her stance. The dark eyes of the creature opposite glowered with a malice sending a chill deep into Elodi's soul. The Norgog growled and grunted, but Elodi noted no vapor poured from their wide nostrils and slit mouths. More about her fell. The defenders lost ground. Wedged between the lines, Elodi somehow found the strength to drive her blade down the throat of a snarling Norgog. Her sword appeared to strike rock. She grimaced as she twisted and snatched it back. The creature's eyes bulged. It dropped its hammer and slumped forward onto the crumbling line of shields. But it was a short-lived victory as another clambered over the dead Norgog's back to take its place.

Ruan and Gundrul bawled their commands, fighting like men possessed, slashing, thrusting, blocking, and parrying. The dead could find no place to rest — they moved with the line, heads lolling, propped up by those desperate not to join the macabre ranks. More Norgog forced their way into the small gap between the walls. Elodi fought to breathe, but her ribs had little space to move in the crush. Her sword arm was pushed up into the air. She fought to bring it down, but no space could be found; it hung limp in the air like the arm of a ragdoll dangling from a child's grip. Elodi cried out. She could not fight back. She flinched as hammers slammed down with little thought for their target, but all caused pain or death. Any moment she feared her head would be rent in two and her brief reign brought to a miserable end in defeat.

But Aldorman and his knights fought to save her. They grappled and tore at the bodies to form a circle around her. Spears thrust over the top of the front lines. Elodi twisted around. The men in the shield wall behind crouched, forming a platform for Ruan's spearmen to gain height and thrust their spikes down into the short necks and broad shoulders of the Norgog. Their dead and dying now held up the attack. Elodi's arm was freed. She regained her balance and rejoined the battle. The front wall reformed; the pushback began. Step-by-step, the defenders recovered the lost ground, stumbling over the fallen of both friend and foe. Gundrul's men shouldered their shields into the enemy as they reached the front of the defensive wall. The Norgogs' dead, chained in position, now hampered the enemy. But Elodi's hopes of a victory were short-lived. The Norgog thinned their ranks, hacking free, then heaving those unable to fight off the bridge. Fresh fighters filled the gaps and their solid ranks surged forward with renewed malice. The gray wave broke over the exhausted guards, throwing them back. Elodi stumbled and went down. Feet stamped down desperate to find a foothold. Her head snapped back. Elodi's battle was done.

15. Of Hamar's Tale

The soft ground beneath Toryn's back was most welcome. He wriggled his fingers and stretched out, realizing his bonds and gag had been removed. The grass cradled his broken body, easing the deep aches and perhaps healing some of the hurt. But his head still felt ready to split in two. He opened his eyes. The stars shone, but not with the same intensity as he had witnessed from below the bridge. A fire crackled nearby. He turned his head slowly, wincing as his neck crunched and clicked. Four dark figures huddled around a campfire. In the flickering light of the flames, Toryn could see these were not Knights of the Archon, or men from any of the realms' forces as described by Hamar. These were tall, broad men with dark hair and stern faces, and when they spoke, Toryn struggled to pick out their words in their thick accent. Behind them, powerful horses with plain livery stood alert with dark eyes reflecting the flames. These were not Knights of the First Horse, or even Archonian Guards. Yet they must serve the Archon.

Toryn looked back to the stars. Why had they hoisted him free from the bridge? The Archon had decreed he should die. He tried to recall the last day of his punishment. The Archon had appeared when the harsh voices in his head threatened to finish him. Had the Archon spared him? But if that was so, spare him for what purpose?

The wind picked up. Leaves rustled in the breeze, leaves of many trees. He turned to see a dark line of treetops stretching out as far as he could see. They were camped near to a forest; surely it had to be Foranfae. If that was so, he must have slept for at least a day — or he had been drugged. His escorts obviously held no fear of him, not that they had anything to fear. He let his eyes wander back to the stars. How much longer would he spend as a captive? First the Ruuk, then at Uleva's foul hands in the wood, to be followed as a stint as a guest of the Archon. Not too long ago he had been a farmhand with nothing more to worry about than feeding livestock, plowing fields, or fixing and laying fences. Now every power in the Five Realms seemed to want him in chains. But while the aches in his limbs eased, his head still throbbed. He had heard what had to be an echo from the Song, but as yet, it appeared to have caused him more harm than good.

Toryn stretched and yawned, enjoying the movement after days of restriction.

'That thing's awake.' *Thing?* Toryn groaned. The accent was strong, but it could not disguise the scorn.

'Better feed him then. Can't have him dying before we get there.' A man stood and sauntered over to Toryn. He grabbed Toryn's shirt, and pulled him up with ease. Toryn grunted as pain shot up his spine. 'Shut it! Be thankful you're not hanging from that bridge.' He placed a cup on the ground and thrust something into his hand. 'Eat, drink, and be quiet.'

'But…' Toryn's voice croaked. 'Where are you taking me?'

'What did I just say?' The man's eyes glared before his mouth broke into a sneer behind a bushy beard. 'You want to know where we're taking you?' He glanced over his shoulder. 'We've got ourselves a curious one here. Asks too many questions. Wants to know where he's going.' The laughter from around the fire did not encourage Toryn. The man snarled. 'If you must know, you're off to meet someone who's taken a great deal of interest in you.

But what she wants to do with you… I wouldn't know, and if you've got any brains in that thick head of yours, I wouldn't be asking questions. I don't think you'll like the answers. That's if you want to enjoy the journey.' He stood chuckling and walked back to the fire, muttering under his breath. Toryn watched him. These were definitely not a detachment of the Archonian Guard — they had none of the guard's humor.

Toryn looked down to the cup in his hand. *She?* Surely, he could not be referring to Uleva? He shuddered. Or could it be the other wyke Grebb had mentioned at Wyke Wood. Toryn remembered his chilling warning regarding Uleva when he said, *she's not the one you need to worry about.* But who other than the Archon would take an interest in him? He drank the warm liquid and felt it burn his throat on the way down. Toryn opened his hand and found a small piece of meat. As he chewed, he searched the surrounding area exposed by the light of the fire. The trees lay beyond the circle of the firelight, but they could not be far judging by the rustling of the leaves and creaking boughs. Perhaps he could wait until the men slept and crawl to the tree line. But if it was the Foranfae, he could be in more danger among the trees than with these mysterious men. He shuffled back. Something tugged at his ankle. A chain moved against a clump of grass — the other end was secured to a spike: the forest was not an option.

The ground tilted. His head swam. The drink. They had drugged him. Toryn fell back. It was not an unpleasant sensation as the lingering pain left his body. He drifted off into a deep sleep.

Toryn shivered in the damp clothes clinging to his skin. He sat and guessed dawn was almost upon them. At his back, the dark trees appeared to hang over him, despite sitting at least fifty paces from the edge. The men lay around the embers of the fire glimmering in the light breeze; Toryn suspected their clothes would be dry. He pulled on the chain, but the spike held firm, no doubt driven some way into the ground. Thankfully, the throbbing in his head had eased. He thought back to the bridge. Could he use his new-found powers to *disappear* the chain? But how? Hope had spoken of those who could find the origins of all things in the Song, but even if he succeeded, how would he *unmake* it? One of the men stirred, but to Toryn's relief, he grunted and pulled the blanket over his head and went back to sleep. He had to try. Toryn could not allow these men to deliver him to whoever had taken a great interest in him. He had only escaped the first time with the help of Hope, but no one would aid him now.

Toryn relaxed and listened. Under the bridge, it was the call of songbirds that had allowed him to hear the Song. But apart from the odd bird cawing from the trees, few had yet risen to greet the dawn. He stared at the chain. Nothing. Toryn heard nothing. He lay back. He should not try, he had to let it happen. The stars dimmed as the light from the new sun rose far to the east. He let his mind drift, thinking of all those who had gazed upon the same sky before him. His stomach warmed. His vision blurred. He thought of the chain, where it could have been made, who had forged the links and beaten them together, when it had been plunged into cold water to complete the process. He saw the gloved hands that swung the hammer. He heard the moment the object took its place and became a line of a verse in the ever-evolving Song.

'Hey!' Toryn cried out as a boot slammed into his gut. 'Stop with your mischief.' The stars returned as the second blow landed on his temple.

Something nudged his shoulder, but Toryn was not yet ready to rise. He rolled onto his side, groaning as his head seemed too heavy for his neck to lift. His bed was soft, and he longed to spend a little longer under the warm blankets.

'Get up.' A woman's voice. Toryn dragged himself from the depths of sleep and opened his eyes. A thick blade of grass tickled his nose — he was not in his bed. And the dirty rag gagging his mouth was not there the previous evening. He shuddered in the cool, bright morning, suddenly remembering where he lay. 'Do I have to ask again?' The same voice. But it was more a threat than a question. Toryn turned and looked up. Two, long tanned legs drew his eyes to a short, leather tunic. He rolled onto his back to see a sword belt tied around a slim waist beneath curves Hamar must have marveled at in his youth. But it was her face that took Toryn's breath away as she kneeled at his side and removed his gag. The breeze tussled the woman's blonde hair about a face that could have belonged to a Maiden. His eyes widened despite the pain in his temples.

Toryn stared at her face. 'You're an Amayan.'

She stood back. 'As I live and breathe. Now do as this Amayan says and you won't feel my Amayan foot in your ribs.'

Toryn sat slowly, pressing his palms onto the soft grass to steady his head. He blinked, trying to focus in the morning light, and taking a moment to believe what he saw behind the Amayan. Three of his escorts lay dead around the smoldering campfire. He stretched out his legs to ease the deep ache and noticed his restraint had been removed. Squinting, he met the gaze of the warrior's steely, blue eyes. 'Thank you.'

She smirked. 'You're thanking me?' Toryn noticed a cut on her lip and a swollen cheek.

He rubbed his ankle. 'For the rescue? My earlier attempt failed.'

The Amayan laughed, then winced, bringing her hand to her face. 'Rescue?' She whisked the sword from her scabbard and had the tip at his throat before he could move. 'You think this is a rescue? Then you're even more stupid than you look.'

Toryn edged back but the blade stayed poised on his skin. 'But what about the Archon's men? Didn't you kill them?'

'That I did. Three of them.' She glanced to the grasslands. 'But unfortunately, the fourth got away.'

'If this isn't a rescue, why did you kill them?'

The warrior sighed as if the answer should have been obvious. 'Because they weren't too keen to hand you over. I lost my last… traveling companion, and it's getting tiresome catching and cooking my own supper.' Her eyes stayed fixed on Toryn. 'I gave them a choice, but they refused.' She examined the bloodstains on her blade. 'And then the fools decided they wanted Moonbeam.' Toryn frowned. She thumbed over her shoulder. 'My horse. And no one touches my horse.' Behind the Amayan, a fine-looking gray grazed alongside three of his captor's black horses. Moonbeam stood proud with no tack, save a leather strap around its middle for minimal supplies — Amayans obviously traveled light.

Toryn stared back at the contorted bodies of the Archon's men. Hamar had not exaggerated. He massaged his stiff neck. 'The stories are true then.'

The warrior rubbed and rolled her right shoulder. 'Don't believe everything you hear.' She grinned and tipped her head to the fallen. 'But most is true. These brutes won't tell the half of it for fear of losing their reputation as fighters. It's a pity there were only four. But over all too quickly for my liking.' The Amayan withdrew, kneeled, wiped her blade on the grass, then sheathed the weapon. She looked over a cut on her forearm. 'Don't get me wrong. I don't kill for the thrill of it. I would have happily traded with them. But I won't lie, I do enjoy the challenge if it comes down to a fight.' She twisted and checked the back of her leg where blood trickled from another wound. 'Mind you, these fellows were rather good, better than most guards.' She held out a hand for Toryn to take. 'You may look stupid, but I don't think you're foolish enough to resist.' He gladly took her warm hand. She paused. A flicker of a thought passed over her face before pulling him to his feet. But a little too fast. Toryn's head span. He staggered forward, reaching out to grab the Amayan's arm. Her hand shot out, grasping his upper arm. She waited for him to steady his stance then let go. Toryn stood a little taller than the woman, but he was under no illusion he could better her in any form of combat.

He looked at her lip. 'Shouldn't you tend to that?'

'It will heal. I've had worse.'

He held her gaze. 'What's your name?'

She frowned. 'You want to know the name of your captor?'

Toryn groaned. A fourth power in the land saw fit to hold him against his will. Her eyes flashed him a look — perhaps being a prisoner of this Amayan would not be so bad. No. Not again. He straightened. 'I'll come willingly. You don't have to be my *captor*.'

She grinned. 'Suit yourself. But why would you choose to do that?'

'Perhaps we could help each other. I might—'

'Help?' She tipped back her head and laughed. 'You help me? How do you propose to do that?'

'I'm good with a bow. I can catch your supper and cook it.'

'Fine. That's a start. But why should I help you?'

'I'm…' He looked into her eyes. Could he trust her? But as he saw it, he had no choice. 'I'm looking for someone, someone I believe could be vital to save the realms.'

The woman rubbed her swollen lip. 'That's very noble of you.' She looked at his battered body. 'So, you and this missing person are going to *save the realms* from what exactly?' A grin spread across her lips as she tugged on the sleeve of his filthy shirt. 'Are you going to give a home to all the fleas and ticks of the land, so they don't bother the rest of us?'

Toryn ignored her gibe. 'The woman I'm looking for has power. She sent a dozen or so of my previous captors into a trance to rescue me from their camp.'

But she laughed more, wrinkling her nose. 'If she's anything like you, her stench would have been enough to knock them out.'

Toryn bristled. 'Haven't you heard? An attack is imminent. From the south.'

She shrugged her brown shoulders. 'And why should that concern me?'

'Should the Five Realms fall, would that not trouble you?'

'Amayans care not for your Archon or your fancy lords and ladies. We'll survive. We always have.'

'But aren't you—?'

'Enough!' She held up her hand. 'If it will shut you up, and if you really must know my name, it's Eryn. I'm known as Eryn to my fellow warriors.' Toryn repeated her name in his head as if it invoked a spell. He could not stop staring at her fair face, and despite the bruise welling up, he had never seen such fine features. Toryn was reminded of Uleva before the wyke's mask had melted away, revealing her true hideous and tortured face. Eryn held his gaze — Hamar had not embellished the story of their beauty. She raised an eyebrow and sighed. 'If you could stop gawping for one moment, and take that ridiculous look off your face, maybe you can tell me yours.'

It took a moment to recall. 'Toryn, Toryn of—'

'Just the name. I don't care which stinking hole of a village you've crawled from.' Eryn glanced at her conquests. 'But then again. What did these men want with you? I've come across this type but a few times. Not pleasant, or as easily manipulated like the guards, and I can't think they would waste their time escorting a common thief or scoundrel.'

Toryn shuddered; the screams that tormented him as he hung from the bridge still echoed in his skull. He sighed. 'Apparently I'm a wyke.'

Eryn scoffed. 'Is that all? I thought you must have been at the very least a spy from the south.'

'Sorry to disappoint.'

Eryn turned her back and strolled to the horses. 'Makes no difference to me.'

Toryn hobbled after her. 'So, you're not going to bind and gag me?' He wriggled his fingers. 'How do you know I won't put a spell on you?'

Eryn laughed again. 'Do your worst. I've met a few of your kind, and I've yet to meet one who could trouble me or my sisters. Your kind might scare the simple folk, but it won't work on us.' She reached the horses and took a flask from a bag on Moonbeam and drank. She poured a little on her wounds and offered the rest to Toryn.

He gratefully accepted and took his fill. 'Lucky for me you were passing by, eh.'

'Lucky? Don't be so sure. I've not decided what I'm going to do with you yet.'

Toryn nodded to the fallen. 'It couldn't be worse than what these fellows had in mind.'

Eryn took back her flask and looked him in the eye. 'Here's the arrangement. You can come with me and do the menial tasks I detest. You can leave whenever you like, or when I've grown tired of you. But while you're with me, you'll have to do as I say, which is as much for your own safety.'

'And if I help you?'

Eryn patted Moonbeam's flank. 'You can amuse me with your stories of this threat you speak of, and this mysterious *someone* you seek. It's been a while since I've heard a new tale.'

'And? Will you help me find her?'

'If you can convince me it's a worthwhile cause, I and my companions may decide to assist you.' Toryn beamed, but Eryn's eyes flashed. 'Don't get your hopes up. It will have to be a challenge worthy of our skills, and we've yet to discuss our reward.'

Toryn shoulders sank. 'But I have nothing. How could I pay you?'

She took his hands and examined the markings on his palms. 'You're the wyke. Teach us some of your tricks. Perhaps there'll be one that might be useful.'

'But I'm not sure how I—'

'To work.' She pointed to the black horses. 'Remove their tack. Take what you want from their bags then throw them onto the fire. You can help yourself to their weapons.' She patted the hilt of her sword. 'But don't get any ideas. A sword is for anyone we may come up against. You'll have to look after yourself if we get into a scrap. I can't be watching your back as well as my own.'

Toryn eyed the horses. 'What about one of them? It would be easier if I could ride.'

Eryn shook her head. 'They're a strange if loyal breed. They may seem fine now, but if their masters track us, they only have to whistle, and the beast would deliver you straight back to them. And, as I assume that's a risk you'd rather not take, you'll have to walk.' She sighed. 'Now leave me and Moonbeam in peace for a while.' She turned to her horse, patted his nose and whispered in a language unknown to Toryn.

He left them to carry out his first duty for the Amayan, unbuckling the saddles, bags, and reins from the Archon's horses. He took some food, a cloak, a striking dagger, and a sword, but not as heavy as the ones used by guards. He searched for a bow but found none. Perhaps these shady fellows preferred to kill looking into the eyes of their victims. Once removed, he dumped the rest of their belongings on the smoldering fire as directed. Free of their equipment, the horses trotted over to Eryn. In the daylight, the beasts did not look as intimidating as they had bathed in firelight. She stroked each of their muzzles in turn and spoke the same words as she had to Moonbeam. They edged closer to the Amayan and appeared to listen. She then clapped her hands and the horses turned and galloped off across the plain, whinnying as they departed.

Eryn strode over. She pointed to the dagger in his hand. 'Now put that to good use and go catch us some breakfast.'

'You heal quickly.'

Eryn spoke with her mouth full. 'You cook an edible meal for a wyke. Might be useful after all.'

'I learned from an old guard.' Toryn eyed the road. 'Aren't you concerned Archonians might be heading this way?'

She cleaned her hands on the grass. 'If they're knights, I'd hear their horses' metal-shod hooves long before they got anywhere near us.' She rose with no sign of suffering from her injuries. 'And if they're guards, I'd smell them from even farther afield. So no, I'm not concerned, but that rogue who escaped last night will return with more of his folk. If you were important enough to warrant four riders, they won't let you get away so easy. And he'll also have his wounded pride to heal. He'll want to get his revenge soon enough.'

Toryn glanced over his shoulder. 'Then shouldn't we be making tracks?'

'After breakfast. Besides, where we're going, they won't dare follow.'

He stopped chewing. 'You mean the forest.'

She raised a fair eyebrow. 'Not so dim after all, eh.'

He glanced to the shadows between the thick tree trunks. 'I assume you're aware of the tales of Foranfae?'

Eryn grinned. 'Who do you think spreads most of them?'

'So, they're not dangerous?'

'Oh, they can be dangerous. It's easy to get lost and eventually die of hunger. But it's safe if you know what you're doing.'

'But why risk—?'

'Moonbeam doesn't seem to care. And if he isn't spooked, then neither am I. Besides, we've used them for years to hide out.' She turned to the trees. 'There's no doubting there's something in that forest, something that tolerates us, but not the guards or any other fool that ventures inside. But whatever lives in there isn't evil. They just play little tricks to confuse and disorientate. More like mischievous children.'

'But what about me? Will they tolerate a wyke?'

She giggled. 'You really play up this thing about being a wyke. But don't you worry your wyke head over it. You'll be fine if you stick with me and Moonbeam.' She looked over his shoulder. 'Perhaps.'

The leaves rustled. Toryn shivered. 'Can't we go around it?'

'No. Where I want to go lies within.' Eryn tilted her head. 'Shush. Time to move. Riders approach.' She kneeled and placed a palm on the grass. 'Interesting. Don't see those black-clad fighters for a year, and now they're all over the place.' She looked to her dead adversaries. 'They won't be pleased to find what I did to their brothers.' Eryn sprang up. 'We'll go now. I'm in no mood for a fight so soon after eating.' She whistled to her horse. Moonbeam trotted over. She looked to Toryn. 'To the forest.'

16. Not a Step Back

'You shouldn't be up, ma'am.' Gundrul winced as he rubbed his neck. 'You took a nasty blow from a Norgog hammer.'

Elodi's head hurt to speak. 'I'm fine, Captain.'

'Yet you don't seem confident to take your hand from the wall.'

She could barely nod. 'I must admit it helps to stop the floor changing place with the ceiling, but apart from the room spinning, I feel fine.' She took a step then steadied herself. 'What of Aldorman?'

Gundrul edged closer. 'He's in better shape than you at this moment. And I have nothing but admiration for your knights. They fought well considering they were on foot.' He peered into Elodi's eyes. 'But as for you, ma'am. I strongly suggest you stay off your feet for the time being.'

'But I cannot bear to sit out the battle stuck in here. I feel so useless.'

'You'll be no use to us on the bridge in your current state. Besides, I've seen big men drop stone dead following a lesser blow than the one you suffered. And they too insisted they were *fine* and tried to shake it off.'

Elodi leaned backed and pushed both hands against the solid wall. 'Thank you for the re-assuring prognosis, Captain. Now, enough of my predicament. Please remind me of the situation on the bridge. Lorek updated me this morning, but I have to confess I struggled to hear with all the bells of Calerdorn ringing in my ears.'

'Very well, ma'am. But I insist you sit first.'

Her hand went to her mouth. 'Is it bad?'

He grinned. 'It's not that. You're leaning so far over, I fear you're about to fall and crack your forehead on the floor.'

Elodi stared back. 'Very well.' She held out her arm. 'Then I'd appreciate some assistance.' Gundrul helped her to the chair beside the fireplace. He groaned as he lowered his bruised body into the seat opposite. 'We've lost almost a fifth of our force, ma'am.' Elodi closed her eyes. He grunted. 'Of the injured, some may yet recover to fight within the week. But a number are too badly wounded, and I fear will never bear arms again.'

'Have they been sent back to the city?'

'The wagons left this morning, ma'am.' He cleared his throat. 'I've taken the liberty of requesting fifty replacements. I hope this meets with your approval. I would have got your permission first, but you were in no state to respond at the time.'

Elodi opened her eyes. 'Approved, Captain. We must hold this bridge. While I'm confident Calerdorn is defendable, should Uldrak break through to the plains with this army, the rest of Harlyn will be vulnerable… more so. And should they occupy the plain, we'd have the utmost difficulty removing them. Even if we could, imagine the cost.' She focused on Gundrul's lined face exaggerated by the low light of the fire. 'And no more reports from the watch at the mines?'

'None, ma'am. Whoever holds Drunsberg is intent on staying there, and I'm sure we can guess that means they're mining the seams.'

Elodi gripped the arms of the chair. 'And I dread to think what devious devices they plan to construct with our resources.' She sighed. 'But thank the Three, those ghastly Norgog have retreated. Have you much experience of them?'

'More than I'd wish, ma'am. But not in the numbers

we've seen here. We can take some comfort they can only fight in the cold, and when I say cold, I mean the *freeze-the-flesh-off-your-bones* cold. Uldrak has also retreated, possibly exhausted from his efforts to bring down that freezing fog long enough for those Hammerskulls to attack.'

Elodi watched sparks fly as a guard placed another log on the fire. 'But he will recover and no doubt we'll be facing those frightful creatures once more.' She looked at the flames but took no comfort from their heat. 'What can we do against such a force, Captain? We have not the numbers, and I cannot sacrifice lives with the indifference of Uldrak.'

Gundrul slapped his leg. 'Ah! I almost forgot.' He rubbed his head. 'Those blows to my helmet have muddled my thoughts. I have good news to report that should improve matters on the bridge. The engineers have built another barricade, but this one is angled. They tell me the slope may help to deflect the full force of a ballista bolt over our heads. And the ramp is set with spearheads of the fallen. Even dead, their weapons will frustrate an attack on foot.'

'That's at least encouraging. But what new tricks does Uldrak have up his baggy sleeves?' Elodi jumped at the braying of the horns. She leaped to her feet but instantly fell back.

Gundrul rose slowly. 'Ma'am, I strongly recommend you remain here to recover. But don't you fret. Ruan and I will hold the bridge, whatever the enemy throws at us. We need you alive and well to fight the battles to come, but please, take my word, you will regret returning to action so soon after such a blow.'

Elodi held her head in her hands, trying unsuccessfully to stop the room spinning. 'I cannot… stay here. I have—'

'To be fit to lead another day. If you walk onto that

bridge in your state, you'll be a danger to yourself and those around you.' He rested his large hand on her shoulder. 'Do I have to issue an order, ma'am? You did say the bridge is under mine and Ruan's command.'

She closed her eyes. 'That I did, Captain.'

'Then please stay in the fort for the time-being. I appreciate this is your realm, but you have to trust the Archonians and Broon's men. We *will* hold that bridge. You must rest and recover.'

Elodi opened her eyes. 'You're right.' She waved her hand as she slumped back into her chair. 'Please, go on without me, but keep me informed.' She managed a smile. 'Not a step back, eh, Captain.'

Gundrul nodded. 'Not a step back.' He frowned. 'Are you okay, ma'am? You look as if you're about to—' Elodi stared at the two Gundruls before her. He spoke but the words did not match the movement of his lips. The room dimmed despite the flaming torches. The captains waved their arms and more men arrived. She blinked hard but struggled to make sense of the room as it darkened. Elodi surrendered to the force dragging her body down to the ground. She closed her eyes and collapsed.

'She stirs.' Gundrul sounded surprised.

Ruan answered. 'The lady's made of sterner stuff than she looks.'

Gundrul laughed. 'I wouldn't let her hear you say that if I were you.' He let out a long sigh. 'But for a nasty moment, I thought we'd lost her.'

Elodi opened her eyes and waited for the faces to come into focus. She lay on a sheepskin close to the fire. Her captains sat either side, both with fresh wounds. Her tongue struggled with her words. 'The bridge?'

Gundrul nodded. 'Still in our hands, ma'am. The Norgog tried unsuccessfully to take it from us again, but it's warmer now which slows them down. They faltered on the new barricade, making it easier for us to pick them off. It's quiet now. I believe the Hammerskulls may have retreated back north.'

Elodi closed her eyes and whispered. 'That's most welcome news. Perhaps Uldrak has yet to recover fully.'

Ruan spoke. 'I think we may have finally broken the rake's resolve, ma'am. He's thrown everything he has under his command, but even the Ruuk appear to have limits to how many losses they're willing to sustain.'

Gundrul smiled. 'We've seen no activity for almost a day now, ma'am.'

'A day—!' Elodi dropped back. 'How long have I been sleeping here?'

Gundrul glanced to Ruan. 'Getting on for three days now. And to be honest, ma'am, we weren't sure you were going to pull through.'

Elodi covered her face and groaned. 'Three days?'

Gundrul winced as he flexed his arm. 'But time well spent. You've got the color back in your cheeks and you're breathing easier.'

Elodi sat up and was pleased to find the room remained stable. She turned her head and rubbed her neck. 'That does feel easier. But what of the soldiers?'

Gundrul's head bowed. 'I'm afraid two of your knights have fallen, but Aldorman has come through. He turned to Ruan. 'And this ugly brute's men have fared well. But' — he grinned — 'that's only because they have longer weapons allowing them to fight from a safe distance.'

Ruan scowled. 'You'd all be splattered across the bottom of that ravine without us, Gunny.'

Gundrul chuckled, immediately regretting it as he held his sides. 'Let's just say, the combination of shields, swords, and the pointy sticks of Broon, have repelled the hordes for now. There's a small force of Ruuk keeping watch, but the only thing they throw at our lines are empty taunts. But if they think they can tempt us to attack and give up our position on the bridge, they're very much mistaken.'

Elodi swung her legs off the bench and pressed her feet to the floor. 'And for that, I and my realm will be forever in your debt.'

She turned as Aldorman strode through the door. He gasped, stepped forward and kneeled at her side. 'Ma'am? You're awake.' He let out a long sigh. 'I'd sent word to Wendel preparing him for the worst.' He beamed. 'But I see now I was thankfully premature.'

'Please stand, Captain.' She held out her hand. Aldorman helped her to her feet. She grasped the captain's arm. 'Gundrul has told me of your losses.'

He glanced to the fireside. 'Two fine knights, ma'am. But they did not die in vain. Thanks to our—' A horn blew in the distance.

Elodi cocked her head. 'That's one of ours I believe. And, if my hearing serves me right, it's coming from the south.' Aldorman led her to the door as the sound of a galloping horse echoed through the fort. Elodi stepped out in the daylight. She covered her eyes, squinting towards the road coming from the Dorn Plain. A horse appeared around the bend. The rider swayed in the saddle as the horse came to an abrupt halt. Two guards rushed forward in time to catch the rider as she slid from the horse. They propped her up between them as Elodi approached.

Elodi recognized the rider who had crossed the bridge. 'Shelan! What brings you back here?'

Shelan gasped for air, forcing herself to stand and salute. 'Ma'am. News from the watch at Durran Wood arrived this morning.' Elodi's scalp prickled. The rider took a deep breath. 'A force of Ruuk, two, possibly three hundred strong have made it through Mawlgrim Mire.

They've beaten back our small force.' She grasped the arms of the guards. 'They've turned west and heading to the foot of this pass. They'll be—' her eyes rolled up into her skull as she sagged and passed out.

Aldorman gripped Elodi's arm as she too wavered. 'Ma'am, you must leave, return to Calerdorn immediately. 'They seek to trap us in the pass. We have insufficient numbers to fight on two fronts. We could not prevent them blocking your only exit.'

She glanced at her captains. 'But the bridge? It must be held. It's the only way for Uldrak to bring his heavy weapons to Calerdorn.'

Gundrul stepped forward. 'Leave that to us. You cannot be trapped here. Should you be captured… I cannot bear to think what they'll do to you.'

Ruan agreed. 'You have to leave now, ma'am. It will be a challenge to defend both sides of the gap, but we'll find a way. The pass is narrower to the south, and without weapons, a few dozen of my spears will hold them at bay.'

Elodi nodded. 'Then I shall go. Please ensure Shelan recovers. And send a bird to Calerdorn requesting re-enforcements immediately.' She turned to Gundrul and Ruan. 'And may you—'

'Not the time, ma'am.' Gundrul held up his hand. 'Prepare and go. You must make the open plain before the Ruuk trap you here. They'll fight like wild animals if they think they have you in their clutches. But once they find you're gone, their resolve may waver.'

17. On Pain of Death

Toryn felt the weight of the trees bear down on his shoulders as if they sought to deny him access to the forest. The odd bird called from the branches overhead, but if they sang parts of the Maidens' Song, they must have been the verses for the creatures of the night, as they were grim and foreboding. He kept his eyes on Eryn's back, remaining close as they made slow progress through broad, dense ferns.

At times, his attention was drawn to the spaces between the thick trunks, suspecting unseen eyes observed their passage. He trod carefully, convinced if he as much as snapped a twig, the watchers would no longer tolerate their intrusion. The Archon had decreed those entering the Foranfae would find themselves under the threat of a death sentence, but Toryn could not imagine why such a measure was necessary. Only a fool, or desperate soul would enter willingly: Toryn was no fool, but he had entered not entirely against his will. It may have been late afternoon outside, but little light penetrated Foranfae's thick canopy. He had dared to look up soon after entering and had to suppress a gasp. High above their heads, a vast dark, green ceiling stretched in all directions, supported by the tall, ancient tree trunks as if pillars of stone in a grand hall from one of Hamar's tales. The forest did not imbue the over-bearing sense of dread as suffered in Wyke Wood, but it lacked the enchantment of the trees housing the Singing Stone. Yet, Toryn could not deny, the place undoubtedly emanated an ancient power — but he could not determine if that power was for, or against him.

Eryn walked with caution, constantly pausing to listen. Moonbeam kept his head down, seeming content to follow at Eryn's side. She stopped and whispered. 'We'll be there come the morning. You'll see them soon.'

'Where? Who will I see?' Toryn's voice sounded too loud beneath the boughs, just as it had as a boy when he spoke with his imaginary friends on his adventures within Hamar's map under his bedclothes.

Eryn glanced back. 'I was talking to Moonbeam. He misses the other horses.' She rolled her eyes. 'But if you must know, we're nearing one of our settlements.'

'You live in the forest?'

'When down south, yes. Could you recommend somewhere else? Your village perhaps? I'm sure they'd welcome us with open arms.'

Toryn sighed. 'I see your point. I never felt at ease in my village, and I—'

She turned and strode away. 'Well, there you go. Who'd have thought it, eh. Wykes are about as welcome as we are.'

'But they didn't know I was a wyke while—'

Eryn's hand shot up. 'Not interested. You'll have to do better than that with your tales if you want my help.'

Toryn stumbled through the undergrowth. 'I have plenty. Many from an old guard I knew.' He caught up as Eryn had paused again to listen. 'So, how do you travel so easily avoiding the guards?'

'We don't have to avoid the guards. We can deal with them easily enough. That's on the rare occasions they're actually awake.' Eryn laughed. 'Besides, we have our ways.'

'And what about the borders? Surely you get stopped crossing them.'

'Borders? Oh, you mean those rickety fences.' She set off, appearing happy with her decision to change direction. 'I believe they're to stop you folk strolling too far from your warm beds and getting lost. Yet to find a border we couldn't cross, or a guard who could resist a bribe.' Eryn led Moonbeam a little farther and stopped. She pressed her foot on the ground, then looked up. 'We'll rest here. There's no point trying to walk at night.'

Toryn glanced to the trees. 'Wouldn't it be best to reach your settlement before dark? I've trekked through forests at night. You don't have to worry about me if you want to get home.'

Their eyes met, but Eryn's words seemed at odds to what he saw in her face. 'I'm not concerned about you. I won't shed a tear should you go missing.'

He held her gaze. 'That's… reassuring. But I'm quite used to finding my way in the dark.'

She looked away. 'Not in this place. No one moves here once the little light the sun can offer has forsaken the land.' She pointed to Toryn's rucksack as she sat. 'That stale bread will have to suffice. We can't risk lighting a fire here. We don't want to make ourselves known to prying eyes. But don't get any ideas about straying off in the night. I may not care if you end up wandering through the forest for the rest of your life, but I do care if it means I have to catch my breakfast.'

Toryn removed his backpack and kneeled beside her. 'The Archon does not allow anyone to enter the forest. Whose eyes are we avoiding?'

'The eyes of those taking no heed of your Archon's worthless decrees.' She peered over his shoulder as she took the bread from Toryn. 'It's especially those who don't fear your Archon that you need to be wary of.'

Toryn sat, welcoming the chance to rest his aching legs. He looked up to the canopy. 'Where are you from?'

She spoke as she chewed. 'Oh no, not me. I owe you nothing. If you want to talk, you tell me about yourself.' Eryn removed something from her mouth and looked it over. She grimaced and flicked it away. 'I still haven't fully made up my mind whether you're worth having around. Perhaps, if you can tell me something fascinating about yourself, I may choose to question you farther.' She held up a finger. 'But… before you start, remember, I don't regard you being a wyke as anything remarkable.'

Toryn bit into the hard bread. He noted Eryn's apparent disinterest but suspected it was a ploy. He shrugged. 'Then we'll sit in silence. There's nothing that I haven't already told you that you'd likely find interesting. I worked on a farm in a small village you've never heard of. If I pointed it out on a map, that's if I could find one of the few maps that deem it worthy of a mention, I'd doubt you'd want to visit.' He finished his mouthful and leaned back on the tree behind.

Eryn's eyes narrowed. 'Wait. Do you expect me to believe that? You're just a simple farmhand from the back end of nowhere?' She took her flask back from Toryn. 'You claim you and this missing mysterious companion of yours are supposed to be… how did you put it? Ah yes—' she wriggled her fingers in his face — 'saving the realms.' Eryn folded her arms. 'So, don't try to convince me you're just one of the simple folk, because those ruffians escorting you would not be interested. And if I—'

'Ah ha!' Toryn smiled and tucked his hands behind his head. 'Sounds to me you're curious and therefore happy to have me around after all.'

Eryn sighed. 'Fine.' She pointed. 'There's a stream over there. Go clean yourself up and wash those stinking rags passing for clothes if you're to spend another minute in my company.'

The morning light grew as the trees thinned, the higher they climbed the hill. Eryn spoke a little louder over her shoulder. 'The settlement is up here. Perhaps you'll enjoy the view.' Toryn tripped over a rock into a clearing. Eryn laughed. 'Best stick to your cooking duties. I hope stealth is not required when you come to *save the realms*, eh. If we need to sneak up on the enemy, I'd best do it myself.' Toryn rubbed his shin. A wisp of smoke rising from behind a ridge, caught his eye. He took a step. Eryn stopped him. 'Wait. Can't be too safe.' She put her fingers to her mouth and whistled. The reply came. She held out her hand. 'We're cleared. Didn't want you to get an arrow through your throat.' Eryn grinned. 'Nothing to be gained from losing you just yet.'

'Thanks. That makes me feel so much better, valued even.' They covered the last part of the hill and approached a stockade of ancient, moss-covered wood.

Eryn held out her hand. 'Here's home… for now.'

'You built this?'

'No, only repaired. Well, not us, it was a *volunteer*. We don't do that sort of thing. The settlement stood here long before we stumbled upon it, and perhaps long before the forest grew to its present size. You find a few scattered about in here, but this is closest to the edge.' She laughed. 'A few gaps in the stockade needed filling. We borrowed wood from wagons heading south a few years back. Probably never noticed, there were dozens loaded with enough wood to build a fortress. Can't remember the name of the fellow who did the work for us. We lost him somewhere. Pity, he was useful to have around."

'But who lived here before you came across it? I didn't think any folk lived in these parts.'

Eryn shrugged. 'Haven't a clue. Probably many years before your Archon forbade entry. But they're not here now. Just us.'

A head popped over the top of the barricade. 'Eryn! About time. Hold on.' A gate opened and a warrior ran forward to greet Eryn — Toryn could not help but stare at the dark-skinned woman with hair the color of night. She eyed Toryn. 'So, what's this one good for?'

Eryn stepped in between. 'Keep your hands off, Arijan. I found him. This one's mine.'

Arijan held up her hands. 'Come off it. It's not like you've never tried to snatch my spoils.' Toryn watched, opened-mouthed as another Amayan strolled through the gate to join them. The third warrior had bright, red hair and blue eyes he swore could drill holes in his head.

She stepped lightly around Eryn and took hold of Toryn's wrists. She picked up his hands and looked at his palms. 'Ooh, a wyke. Not seen one of these in a while.' His chest tightened as she squeezed his upper arms and patted his shoulders.' Her eyebrows raised. 'Looks like he knows how to use his hands.' She winked at Eryn. 'I can see why you wanted to bring this one back.'

Eryn glared at the red-haired Amayan. 'You too, Cali. Hands off.'

She released Toryn's shoulders and grinned. 'The name's Calestri actually, but you can call me Cali. And what's your—'

'Toryn.' Eryn snapped. 'He's not a bad cook. And if he can stitch leather, then all the better.'

Calestri kept her eyes on Toryn. 'Then you should take more care of this one, Eryn. Can't have him sharing the same fate as your last servant.'

Eryn took Toryn's hand and pulled him away. 'Ignore them.' She spun around. 'I didn't see you rushing to help the poor man.'

Calestri made a face. 'It was a spinner! I wasn't going to risk getting a belly full of rank poison for *him*.'

Toryn found his voice. 'A spinner?'

Eryn sighed. 'Aralak. You'll know them as aralaks, those hideous spiders.' She made a face. 'Fat, hairy creatures. Nasty things.'

He glanced to the trees. 'You get them here?'

Arijan smiled. 'Relax. Not in these parts. This forest wouldn't tolerate those scabby things. This was in… where was it? The east somewhere, I believe.'

Eryn pursed her lips. 'A forest in Ormsk. The damn thing must have escaped from the gorge. The guards would have been asleep… or drunk as usual.'

Arijan put a long arm around Eryn. 'Shame. He was useful to have around. And not a nice way to go, eh.' She turned to Calestri. 'And he was much easier on the eye than that thing you brought in last week. Can't think why you dragged that half-dead man along.'

Calestri flashed her eyes. 'He might be old, but he could still have his uses. It's not like there's much to choose from these days.'

Eryn stepped away. 'If you two have finished, I'd like to get food and water for Moonbeam.' She took the reins and looked to Toryn. 'You as well. This way.' He followed her through the gate, along with Calestri and Arijan. Inside, a clearing about half the size of Midwyche's village green, sat within a circle of six wooden huts and a stable. The horses inside nickered as Eryn led Moonbeam into the shelter.

Arijan stroked the nearest horse inside. She spoke over her shoulder to Toryn. 'Of course, it goes without saying, now you've seen this place we'll have to kill you.' She laughed as he felt the blood drain from his face. 'Ha! This one's too easy, Eryn. It's almost cruel.'

Eryn rolled her eyes. 'Leave him be.' She patted Toryn's arm. 'We won't kill you, but needless to say, don't think you can be inviting your grubby little friends back here for supper.' She turned. 'Come on, time to meet Amyra.'

Arijan shook her head. 'She's not back yet.'

Eryn turned. 'But she went out before me… three days before me.'

'She'll be fine. Probably found some young guards to keep her occupied.'

'I hope you're right. Shouldn't take her this long for a return journey to Cafra.'

Eryn caught Toryn's eye. 'There's more of those big brutes about. Had a run-in with four outside the forest, and more followed.' She patted Moonbeam's neck. 'Good horses, mind. Would give this fellow a decent race.'

Toryn recalled the stern face of the one who fed, then drugged him. 'Do you know much about them?'

Arijan giggled. 'Curious chap, eh. Does he ask a lot of questions?'

Eryn ignored her. 'One of our sisters first encountered them on the northern border a while back.'

Toryn gaped. 'They're Ruuk? They can't be. They serve the Archon.'

'Not quite. But more Ruuk than man I'd say, but taller, broader and shrewder. They're known as Nordleng by their own tongue. They come from outside your realm.'

Calestri scowled. 'Can't say I'd want to face more than two or three at a time. Not like Eryn here.'

Eryn grunted. 'You're getting out of practice. You mustn't let that—'

Calestri glowered. 'Not now! I said, when I'm ready.'

A hunched figure shuffled into the stables struggling to carry a bucket of water. Calestri turned. 'You took your time, Grunt.' She smiled at Toryn. 'I call him, Grunt, because that's the only noise he makes.' She turned back to her servant. 'I'm beginning to think you're more trouble than you're worth.' The man turned and mumbled something under his breath.

'Hope!' Toryn rushed forward to relieve her of the bucket. Her gray eyes stared back. He spun to Calestri. 'You can't treat her like this, she's—'

'That's a woman?' Calestri gawped. 'You've got to be kidding.' She turned to Arijan. 'This fellow says the bent, old man is a woman.'

Arijan smirked. 'If that's what passes for a woman, it's no surprise there's fewer folk around these days.'

Toryn kept his eyes on Hope. Maybe a flicker of recognition crossed her face, but he could not be sure. He turned to Eryn. 'She rescued me from Wyke Wood. You must have heard of that cursed place. There's more to her than meets the eye, she—' he looked away, unsure he should reveal more of Hope's mysterious past.

Eryn frowned. 'She… what?'

He placed the bucket down. 'Nothing. Doesn't matter. Probably not important.'

Calestri grabbed his collar. 'Let us be the judge of what is, and what isn't important.' She sneered at Hope. 'He… she, whatever it is, doesn't look capable of fighting their way out of a threadbare nosebag, yet she somehow rescued you from the foul beings in that wood? Even we avoid that place if possible.'

Eryn took Calestri's hand from Toryn's collar. 'Let's calm down.' She leveled her eyes at Toryn. 'What Cali is trying to say, is, should we be wary of' — she nodded to Hope — 'this one?'

Arijan drew her sword. 'And him. He knows her. Eryn. Arijan. Get back.' She jabbed her blade at Hope. 'You. Take those gloves off.' Hope grumbled but obliged.

Arijan's mouth dropped open as she saw the markings on Hope's hands. 'I didn't think there were many left, and yet suddenly two turn up in a matter of days? And we've brought them both to our shelter.'

Calestri peered at Toryn. 'And what of Amyra? Have you done something to her?'

Toryn tried to speak. Eryn held up her hand. 'Not a word.' She looked to her companions. 'One we can handle, but if these two join forces, they could become a handful.' She pointed at Toryn. 'Get that rope over there and tie her hands behind her back. Then turn around, put your hands out, and stand still.'

Toryn let his head rest against the post. He gazed at the stars thankful Eryn had not thought it necessary to place a sack over his head. But they had gagged them both, bound their hands and feet, and secured them to a stake in the middle of the settlement. Yet, even if he could speak, he doubted Hope would respond. She had shown no signs of recognizing him and seemed to accept her predicament without as much as a shrug.

A shadow moved across the sliver of yellow light coming from one of the huts. An Amayan approached. The torchlight picked out Calestri's red hair. She kneeled and checked their bonds. Toryn caught her eye. She scowled. 'Don't you look at me. And not a word when I take off your gag. Agreed?' He nodded. Calestri removed his gag and held a flask to his lips. She glanced back to the hut. 'We haven't decided what to do with you yet, but know this, I don't think the world will grieve much for the loss of two wykes.'

Toryn's shoulders sagged as she strolled back inside. He had left home a little over three months ago. In that time, he had walked well over a hundred leagues, yet while he had seen many strange and wonderful sights, he had achieved nothing — absolutely nothing. And what of the wide world outside the forest? Had the Archon opened the gate as Harruld and Odrun suspected? The realms could be celebrating a momentous victory… or mourning a devastating defeat. Yet, stuck in the midst of the Foranfae, it could be many months before he would know. And what if the Amayans chose to do the land a favor and rid it of two miserable wykes?

Toryn tipped back his head and looked up to the night sky. Was his mother outside after a meagre evening meal and watching the same stars? He closed his eyes and let his head drop. Had the knights not come to his village, he would still be laying fences and tending to the fields and animals. He had rarely felt content with his life, but at this moment, he would gladly swap places with the younger Toryn, oblivious to much of the world and its troubles beyond the borders of his small home.

Toryn's breath caught in his throat — a foul taste filled his mouth. Behind, Hope stiffened.

18. The Burden of Blood

Elodi sat in the chair at the head of the long table in the Great Hall. She gathered her thoughts as she awaited the arrival of the rider sent to Toryn's village. Could this young man the enemy had seen fit to capture, bring them hope? She closed her eyes. Her head still refused to settle after her speedy retreat from the pass. It had been close… awfully close. Another few moments, and Elodi and her knights would have ridden headlong into a large force of Ruuk, determined to block her escape from the mountain pass. And as she well knew, they desired to take her in chains back to the north — and she dreaded to contemplate the torment a ruler of a realm could expect at their hands.

Elodi opened her eyes and looked to the high ceiling and exhaled. She had been prepared to take her own life rather than allow herself to be seized. But thanks to the speed of their horses, they had made the open plain moments before the trap could be closed. The advancing Ruuk had obviously failed to spot her flight to safety, as they had rushed up the pass and failed to pursue. A few leagues later, Elodi had met with the hundred-strong re-enforcements hastening from Calerdorn to Tunduska. She had issued a new command: they were to attack the rear ranks of the Ruuk, exploiting the narrowest parts of the pass to nullify the enemy's advantage in numbers. Elodi took grim satisfaction that the unsuspecting Ruuk would be the ones trapped in the gap.

Elodi looked to Wendel at her side. He read her impatience. 'The rider is on her way, ma'am. She's coming straight from the stables. I believe her horse is exhausted.'

Elodi's fingers drummed the armrests on her chair. 'I'm not surprised. She has made good progress. Her horse would give Sea Mist a close race.' She straightened. 'Now, remind me, the riders name please, Wendel?'

Her advisor looked to the notes before him. 'Lena, ma'am.' He peered into her eyes. 'Are you sure you're up to this? I could have her report to me.'

'I am sure. And if there's the slightest ray of hope from what Lena has learned of this young man, then it will aid my recovery.' The door opened. Her officer nodded. Elodi took a deep breath and stood. 'Please, send her in.' Her heart raced as the rider strode across the hall. Dust and grime from the road clung to the woman's face and clothes, but she held herself tall despite her obvious fatigue. Elodi held out a hand in welcome.

The rider hesitated. 'I must inform you, ma'am, I've yet to wash the journey from my person.'

Elodi grasped and firmly shook the rider's hand. 'And for that, I apologize. It was I who insisted you delivered your report the moment you returned.' She looked down to Lena's hand still in hers. 'And no need to be concerned. I'm no stranger to the wilds.' She motioned to the rider. 'Please, sit. I have arranged accommodation where you can freshen up and eat shortly. But first, I would like a brief report. We will discuss your visit more at length after you've rested.' Elodi joined Lena at the table. 'You made the journey in quick time. How is your horse?'

Lena relaxed. 'Tempest is well, if very tired. But he's a proud one, ma'am. He'd have refused if I'd tried to make him rest.' She laughed. 'I'm certain he'll be boasting to the other horses in the stables as we speak.'

'Tempest has much to boast about. But please, I'm impatient to know of your visit to Midwyche. Do tell me what you have learned of this man, Toryn.'

Lena shuffled in her seat. 'I'm afraid I cannot be sure which of the numerous accounts of this young man I've heard, is the truth.'

Elodi gripped her seat. 'How do you mean?'

'According to the marshal, a man who goes by the name of Drakelow, he was a deserter who fled when chosen for the Archonian Guard. To others, he was a quiet, surly lad who kept to himself, and they were glad to see the back of him, whether leaving with the guard, or fleeing at the first sign of duty. But all assumed I was there to have the man arrested.'

Elodi looked to Wendel. 'He doesn't sound like what I'd anticipated.' She turned to Lena. 'And others? Did you find another view of this man?'

'That I did, ma'am, but her story somewhat muddies the water.'

Elodi sighed. 'I would expect nothing less during these strange times. Please, continue.'

'I eventually spoke to his mother, Miram. Or to be more precise, the woman who raised him as her own. But note, I was not informed by the marshal that Toryn's folks had a farm in the village. The woman came to me… at night.'

'Interesting.' Elodi caught Wendel's eye. 'You'd think a rider carrying instructions from Calerdorn would gain the marshal's full cooperation.'

'I wouldn't be too hard on him, ma'am.' Lena blushed. 'Oh, apologies, I'm not saying how you should—'

Elodi waved away her apology. 'Please, not necessary. But I would appreciate why you think the marshal acted as he did.'

'I believe he's trying to protect the village from outside interference. But I'm getting ahead of myself. The mother once satisfied I was there under your command, confided Toryn was abandoned in the nearby woods as a baby. She had brought him up, and while she admitted he could be difficult at times, she insisted he was no coward and hadn't run away, in fact, he was desperate to join the Archonians. No, ma'am. He was advised to leave by an old guard going by the name of Hamar.' Lena clenched her hands. 'You see, ma'am. It appears this young man was the son of a wyke.'

Elodi gasped. 'A wyke!'

Lena straightened. 'Miram insisted he had to be one of the good ones… if they exist. He'd never hurt a soul, his palms had no markings, and he showed no signs of doing any tricks of sorts.'

Elodi gaped at Wendel. 'But even so, to be the son of a wyke casts doubt on whether he would be of use to us. Could he be in league with the—?'

Wendel held up his hand. 'Perhaps, ma'am' — he glanced to Lena — 'this is an issue to discuss later.' He addressed the rider. 'Have you anything more to report?'

Lena's eyes dropped to the table. 'I do. It seems, ma'am, you're not the only person interested in this young man.'

Elodi recovered her composure. 'How so?'

'As I said, I stayed overnight to allow Tempest to recover before making the return journey. When I went to the stables the next morning, another horse had come in the night. I was struck by the fine saddle, the finest I've ever seen. This was no ordinary traveler, and I assumed one from outside Harlyn. So, I went to see the marshal to inquire and was met by a rider from Archonholm.'

'Archonholm?' Elodi looked to her advisor. 'Then it seems we were right to take an interest in this fellow if Archonholm is also curious.' She turned to Lena. 'Did this rider elaborate on their purpose?'

'No, ma'am, and if you don't mind me saying, he was most aloof, barely acknowledged my presence.'

Elodi sighed. 'Sadly, that does not surprise me.'

'I presented your decree granting me your authority, but he just laughed, dismissing my questions as an inconvenience. He claimed he outranked me, ma'am, as he had instructions from the Archon himself.'

Elodi sprang up. 'How dare he! How dare the Archon claim such authority in my realm.' She staggered into the table as her head span.

Wendel took her arm. 'Steady, ma'am.' He helped her back into her seat. 'And again. Perhaps…' He glanced to the rider. 'This is an issue to be discussed later.'

Elodi's vision settled. 'Thank you, Wendel.' And then to Lena. 'Your effort and that of Tempest are much appreciated.' She rose, but carefully this time. 'We shall speak again, but for now I insist you retire to freshen up, eat and rest. My man will show you to your quarters.'

'It is my pleasure to serve, ma'am.' Lena nodded to Wendel and followed Elodi's officer to the door.

Elodi slumped back into her chair and brought her hands to her face. 'What am I to do, Wendel? Is this Toryn fellow a threat or a possible ally? The guards rescued from the woods seemed convinced he's a good man, and one taken by force by this Uleva creature.'

Wendel sat beside her. 'It seems the more answers we find, the more questions we need to ask.'

She let out a long breath. 'And why the visit from Archonholm? Midwyche is but a backwater, the Archon must have the same reason as us to send one of his men. But wait. How did Archonholm find out about Toryn? Either news of events at Durran has reached their ears, or… could they be holding him?'

Wendel shrugged. 'I doubt we'll find out any time soon. If this young man is in Archonholm, and the Archon appears keen to find out more, then there must indeed be something about this fellow.'

Elodi stood. 'And isn't the attitude of the Archon just typical. War or not, the Archon cannot dismiss my representative with such impunity. Do I not have any powers in my own realm, Wendel? Is this how he sees me?' She fixed her eyes on her trusted advisor. 'I may be new to this role, but he cannot ride roughshod over my authority. He certainly would not have done this to one of my father's riders. We tolerate him recruiting for his guard, but that is for the safety of all the realms… but this? He has abused his powers this time, and I will not stand for it.'

The stiff breeze brought the chill down from the north onto the walls of Calerdorn, but not what Elodi desired most; a report from Tunduska's Gorge. Her eyes were drawn to the angry, dark skies above the Dornan Mountains. Should the plan to trap the Ruuk from the south turn out to be a success, she desired to push north, forcing the Ruuk out of the pass altogether. Once secured, they could strike onto Draegnor Bridge, possibly taking back the fort to gain a foothold at the border. But she was getting ahead of herself — holding Tunduska was her immediate concern. And how many more men would die just to clear the pass north of the gorge? But thankfully, heavy rains had flooded Mawlgrim Mire, making it nigh on impossible for more Ruuk to cross. At last, the weather appeared to favor Harlyn.

Elodi looked out to the flickering torches of the workers on the plain as they neared completion of the defenses. Returning from the pass, she had been impressed by the trenches and spikes; she would not relish attacking such a formidable position. But Uldrak appeared not to worry about such things. Her eyes wandered across the heavy weapons lining the front of the wall outside of the gate. Should she have withdrawn them to behind the high walls? But as both Gundrul and Ruan had stated, all

Uldrak's army had to do was to keep them confined in the city. And if Uldrak took the docks, cutting off the vital supplies brought in by Captain Horace onboard the *Celestra*, all within would starve within a month, possibly sooner.

Elodi rested her hands on the cold stone and chastised herself. She had to stop doubting every decision once made. Housing the weapons outside the city afforded greater range. And it had to be the right course to hold Tunduska's Gorge. If the north spilled through with their siege weapons, they could blockade Calerdorn, preventing her exit, then rampage through her realm, sowing fear and discord in their wake.

She reached the end of the parapet and looked out over the plain in the direction of Dorlgoth. And what of the old man, Dohl? If he lived, was it as Dohl or Dorlan? Elodi was certain he had returned to Dorlgoth in the guise of Dorlan where the folk would have been only too happy to follow him. But where had he led them? Two hundred people could not easily move across the wide plain of Dorn without being noticed. Elodi's stomach churned. Was he yet aided by Uleva's dubious crafts? Could she conceal a makeshift army of devoted followers? And if the prospect of a legendary hero taking the side of their foe was not enough, she had to deal with the Archon. Her father had said little of his private thoughts on their great leader, but even as a young child, she had perceived his misgivings.

Elodi turned and walked back along the wall, glancing back to the torches forming into a line as the workers finished for the day. She yearned to ride Sea Mist out of the gate, deep into her realm. While the blood of her father demanded she stay to serve the people of Harlyn, her mother's Amayan lineage insisted she roam the land before her roots took hold and bound her forever to Calerdorn.

Her shoulders had slumped. Elodi forced herself to stand tall and face the north. The Lady Harlyn would not bend to the threat. She had the tenacity and boldness of her mother in her veins, and the courage and devotion of her father in her heart — she could not let her people down. If her parents watched from some other world, she was not about to disappoint them.

19. From the Bowels of the Earth

Hope groaned, writhing against the post. Toryn spat as best he could into the gag but could not rid the foul taste from his mouth. He shot a glance across the clearing to the stockade. A shadow! Two, then another moved. He cried out, wrestling with the rope, but the gag stifled his warning, and the bonds held him tight. The gate rattled. Toryn checked the huts. The Amayans slept. Did they not keep watch? They must have considered themselves safe deep inside the forest, even with two wykes for company.

Hope tugged against the rope. Toryn kicked at the ground, desperately trying to make a sound. He would rather die at the hands of an Amayan, than by some foul means of whatever ghoulish creatures creeped up on them in the night. The gate cracked. A head of a large axe glinted in the gap. It twisted, withdrew, and swung again. The second blow splintered along the grain down the entire length of the wood. It collapsed as a large boot kicked the damaged plank aside. Toryn twisted away as the stench poured through the breached defenses.

The ground beneath Toryn warmed. The post at his back grew hot. Hope's mumbling changed. Either she had shaken her gag free, or her voice sounded in his head. A part of him knew the words. He joined in.

The doors of the huts burst open. The three Amayans leaped out. Their swords glowed like the rising sun as they rushed the invaders. Toryn recognized the squat forms of two Ruuk. They braced to meet the Amayans but were no match. Toryn stared as Arijan sprung. Her blade flashed a brilliant, yellow arc as it slashed across the first intruder's neck. It cried out, snatching at the air but missing Arijan as she flipped and rolled away. Eryn hurdled a rock, dropped, then slid across the damp grass, slicing her sword across the back of the Ruuk's leg, then thrust up. He dropped, dead before he hit the ground. Calestri lunged at the second, driving her sword deep into its gut to finish it with one strike.

Toryn relaxed. But Hope's muttered words rose to a chant. The Ruuk were defeated: what troubled her? He glanced to the gate and groaned — the pair were just the advanced party, expendable, sent in to destroy the gate and distract the defenders. Five dark figures strode in; one struggled to control a long, iron rod attached to a creature on the ground. Toryn forced his body up to see. But he knew before he saw it. He choked on the reek, that deep within, he knew and feared. The Amayans looked up from the dead Ruuk, leveling their blades to face the new threat, one that would challenge their fabled skills: five Nordleng… and a droog.

Eryn whispered in the silence. 'Spread out. We're Amayan warriors. We won't let them take us.' But Toryn could hear doubt in her words. The heat at his back grew. The Nordleng handling the droog, chuckled as the distorted, glistening worm writhed, sensing the sweet scent of its prey. Toryn choked on the bile rising in his throat. He could only watch in dread as the creature slithered towards Eryn. She crouched and edged away, holding her sword back and up with the tip poised at her temple. The droog's stomach-churning slathering rose as the handler steered it towards Eryn. Calestri and Arijan fought the Nordleng but always with an eye on the droog. Arijan dropped and swept the legs away from her foe with a kick, finishing him with a blow to his neck. She rushed to aid Calestri, struggling against two determined opponents. But Toryn could not take his eyes from Eryn as she sought to anticipate the droog's inevitable lunge. It lifted its blunt head and quivered, sending ripples down its bloated, gray body. The droog's large eyes flickered a dull yellow in its large skull as its drooling mouth gaped wider. The Nordleng handler skidded on the damp grass, grappling with the rod as he fed more freedom to the worm as it closed on Eryn.

Hope stood. The restraints fell away from Toryn, fading as if they never existed. Hope's hot hand grabbed his. She hissed. 'Join me.' She raised both her arms, taking Toryn's right hand upwards, then tipped back her head and called out a stream of ancient words. He listened, recognizing a language he could not have heard before. Toryn repeated them, merging his words with Hope. The ground vibrated, his skin prickled, his hands burned. He sensed the movements of all around him. Calestri and Arijan took down another Nordleng. The droog struck. Eryn evaded, but only just. She swung, but her blade missed the neck of her predator as she stumbled on a rock made slippery by the droog.

'The worm!' Hope jabbed out their joined hands. The air about it shimmered as it shaped to dart at the prone Eryn, scrambling to recover her ground. But both moved slowly, almost coming to a standstill. Toryn sought Calestri and Arijan. They too appeared to be frozen, poised ready to strike but holding back. 'The worm.' Hope's voice from the timeless wood, calmly delivered her instruction. 'Focus on the droog, Toryn.'

His skull ached. A door to the distant past opened. Quiet at first, harsh words from a bitter throat, gave form to something deep beneath the surface. The voice rose. Toryn stared as he witnessed the birth of the abomination thousands of years earlier. Spawned from the humble worm, the droog was a hideously overgrown corruption of the smallest of creatures beneficial to the earth that, in turn, nourished the crops. Yet the droog wriggling from the churning mud would come to contaminate the very ground that gave it life; resentful of all things brought into the world by the Song of Creation.

Hope's voice sounded in his head. 'Be wary. You hear lines of the Dark Verses.' She clenched his hand. 'We must counter. We must *unmake* this creature.' Toryn's throat burned as Hope's words came through him. At the rock, the droog reared ominously in slow motion, signaling its intent to devour Eryn, yet to recover her feet, moving at the same agonizing sluggish speed. Hope's verse appeared to weave about the rasping incantation of the droog's creator. But Toryn's throat grew raw. He faltered. Hope's grip loosened as she too wavered. She gasped. 'I'm too weak. I have not the strength to undo this outrage of nature. It's too far in the past.'

'The collar!' Toryn recalled his effort with the Nordleng's chain. 'We can unmake the collar.'

Hope's spirit rose. 'Yes, the shackles will do.' She took a breath and changed her words. Toryn felt her strength return. The image of the droog blurred. Shadows flew passed the edges of his vision as they appeared to hurtle through time, back towards the present day. A forge took shape in Toryn's clouded vision. He felt the heat of the fire burning white-hot within the forge. A gloved hand retrieved and poured molten metal into a semi-circular mold, as he had seen Elrik do many times. Hope's language changed, repeating three words. Toryn added his voice.

The blacksmith's cast cracked and broke. The molten metal fizzed and evaporated.

Hope yelled. 'Be ready!' The metal brace biting deep into the droog's gray skin, flickered. Toryn staggered back as the bubble about them burst and the sounds of the skirmish flooded back. The collar on the droog vanished. Its handler cried out as he was left holding the rod with no restraint. The unfettered droog twisted and struck back at its master. Its slavering mouth slapped shut around the head and shoulders of its victim, cutting his desperate pleas from the night air. The droog writhed and flipped in glee as it gulped down the man who had enslaved him. Toryn gawped in horror as the handler's feet kicked out as he was swallowed into the gut of the worm. Hope released his hand and dropped gasping to her knees. Toryn reeled forward as the heat left his limbs, collapsing as the last Nordleng died. He pushed himself up on his hands and knees to see the bloated droog sliver towards the open gate. But Eryn and Arijan sprang before it and blocked its escape. Eryn stayed Arijan's hand as she raised her blade. 'Not yet. Let the Nordleng suffer.'

Arijan objected. 'Shouldn't we put him out of his misery? Enemy or not, it's an appalling way to go.'

'Not a chance. Do you think he would've done the same for us?' Eryn pointed at the distended stomach. 'I've heard it can take a day to die in their foul juices.' She circled the creature. 'I'll give him an hour. This creature is in no condition to threaten us while digesting its prey.' She sheathed her sword. 'Then we'll rid the world of one more foul worm.'

Toryn recovered some of his strength and stood. His stomach churned as he eyed the glistening, enlarged body of the droog. Its dull eyes fell on him as it coiled tight, aware of its vulnerability. 'Careful.' Eryn held out her hand to stay Toryn. 'Don't get too close. Its belly might be full, but it can still lash out with its tail, or vomit on you. And trust me, while that won't kill you, you'd soon be begging me to run you through.'

Toryn turned as Hope roused. He led her to a nearby rock and helped her sit. Her face began to wrinkle, and her spine bend as she transformed back to the old woman. She grimaced at the droog. Eryn nodded to her. 'Thank you. I was sure I was about to end up in its gut. How did you know it would eat its own handler?'

Toryn straightened. 'An old friend told me tales of these worms. He reckoned they detest their so-called masters more than anything. They'll turn on them at the first chance.'

Hope grunted. 'Then there's still some justice in this world.'

The muffled cry from the droog's belly turned Toryn's stomach. He pleaded to Eryn. 'Please. Cut him free.'

But Eryn was adamant. 'He's not suffered enough yet for my liking.'

'Then not for his sake. I want to know what these Nordleng, the Archon's men, are doing with such a creature. And where were they taking me?' He grimaced at the rippling skin of the droog, unable to imagine what the poor soul inside must be suffering.

Eryn shrugged. 'Is that important?'

He swallowed hard as the droog gurgled. 'They're a weapon of evil. Are these Nordleng serving the Archon or another force? And if they serve our… my side, does the Archon know they have command of these foul worms?' He thought back to when he awoke at the edge of the Foranfae. 'Or did they overpower the actual men of the Archon escorting me?' He looked to Eryn. 'I have no memory. I have no idea how long I was out cold. But I have to know if these Nordleng serve the Archon, or if they took me from those who did.'

Eryn thought for a moment. 'Very well.' She clicked her fingers to her sisters. 'But stand well back. It may be weak, but it's still dangerous.' Her nose wrinkled. 'And you don't want the contents of that swollen belly splashing on your skin. The stink alone is enough to suffocate you. It takes weeks to rid yourself of the stench. You'll be on your own if you get splattered.' Toryn was more than happy to take her advice. He ushered Hope back as the Amayans circled the droog.

It sensed their intent, unfurling and trying as best it could to raise its engorged body to meet their challenge. Eryn instructed her fellow warriors. 'Don't feel any pity for it. This worm has done grave harm in its miserable life. The land will be a better place for one less monster.' She leveled her blade, sprang forward, sliced, and opened a section of the exposed belly. Eryn leaped back before the spout of yellow bile could splash her. Toryn retched on the reek fouling the air. The droog burbled as Arijan, then Calestri extended the cut with admirable precision, both jumping clear as more liquid spewed forth. The worm thrashed and flipped, flinging its undigested meal from its gut, spraying its poisonous juices in a last defiant act before it flopped dead, landing like a torn, wet sock. The Nordleng cried out, slipping on the wet ground. He snatched at the rags clinging to his blistering skin, desperate to tear them free. He writhed, lashing out his hands to find a grip on the rocks, but found none. Arijan returned with a bucket and a torch. She got as close as she dared and threw the water over him. But it brought little relief. He vomited, unsuccessfully trying to rid his body of the ingested fluids of the droog's insides. He raised his head seeking the Amayans for help. The flames of Arijan's torch exposed a horribly deformed face. His eyes had gone, leaving pus-filled sockets that oozed as he shook his head in agony. He tried to speak, but he choked on the worm's vile juices. But words were not necessary — his splayed arms shook, pleading for a swift end to his torment.

Eryn held back her disgust as she turned to Toryn. 'Ask away. I'm sure he'd only be too happy to help you.'

Toryn closed his eyes. 'Please. Put him out of his

misery.' He winced at the sound of Eryn's blade as it swiftly granted the poor soul's last wish.

He staggered back, wondering if he would ever rid his nostrils of the reek. He strode over to Hope, who appeared oblivious of the gruesome scene. She sat yawning at the opposite end of the settlement. Toryn sat beside her, desperate for fresh, clean air to breathe. Far to the east, above the stockade, the sky began to glow pink. At his side, Hope had fully reverted to the old woman. She lay back on the damp grass and immediately began to snore. He watched the beginning of a new day and wondered if he had the stomach to take on the enemy.

'Some foul sorcery must have protected them.' Eryn's lip curled as she took the sleeve of a dead Nordleng. 'The forest wouldn't normally tolerate a fetid droog slivering across its floor.'

'Tolerate?' Toryn took the other arm. 'Do you mean the trees?'

Eryn frowned. 'Trees? No, the mischievous folk who reside among them. And when I say folk, they're not like you or me, although I couldn't say for sure as I've never seen one. But I know they're there. I can feel them watching me at times.'

Toryn grunted as they dragged the body over the uneven ground. 'An old guard used to tell me tales of the *Little Folk*, but I thought he'd made them up. But then again, I thought the same about his stories of warrior maidens.'

Eryn smirked. 'Perhaps the maiden part is a little far-fetched.' The grin faded. 'And now you're a subject of tales.' She stepped gingerly over the dead grass poisoned by the droog. 'You'll have to teach me that trick you pulled off with the collar. And, by the way, thanks. You and the old woman could have walked away and left us to fight that beast alone. It could have ended badly had you not broken the worm's restraints.' They lifted the last of the Nordleng bodies, swinging him by his arms and legs, throwing him onto the pile of his fallen colleagues and the dead worm.

Toryn kept his eyes on Eryn, trying to avoid looking at the corpses. 'That was all down to Hope. I only followed her lead. I don't exactly know how we did it.' He gagged on the stench of the already rotting carcass of the droog.

Arijan brought the torch. 'The sooner burned the better. Lucky for us that thing killed off the grass. We don't have to worry about the fire spreading.'

'What about the smoke?' Toryn looked to the surrounding treetops. 'What if there's more Nordleng out there?'

Arijan shrugged. 'Makes no difference. If they want to find this place, they only have to follow the droog's trail.' She lobbed the torch onto the sorry mess of bodies. 'We're leaving anyway. The ground is poisoned. The grass all around here will die shortly, then the dirt will smell like a decaying corpse until next spring. And I doubt anything will grow on this patch for another year at the very least.' She stepped back as the flames crackled, spreading rapidly as it fed eagerly on the fat of the worm. 'Pity. I came to like this place. Almost felt like a home.'

Calestri strode through the smoke. 'The horses are ready, but the old woman still sleeps. We'll have to wake her if we're to leave.'

They stepped back as globules of fat spat from the flames. Eryn glanced to the huts. 'That woman has power.' She nodded to the bonfire. 'And I'm certain those rogues were interested in you both, definitely not us. Four escorted you, and then they bring along a droog to this camp. While you may think you don't have power of your own, they certainly do.' She held his gaze. 'What do you know of this woman?'

'Not much. And what I learned in the brief moments when she's not confused, only led to more questions. But she undoubtedly wields magic of a sort. Did you see her change last night?'

Eryn frowned. 'Change?'

'When in danger, she suddenly appears much younger. Her face, voice, everything about her is different.'

She nodded to the bonfire. 'I was too busy fighting off a droog to notice.'

'Can't say I noticed.' Arijan frowned. 'All I saw was you and the old woman waving your arms about.'

Calestri agreed. 'Same here. Still looked like a crooked, old man to me. But I don't care what she looks like if she can take down a worm.'

Toryn stared into the flames. 'She has knowledge, old knowledge of the Maiden's Song. Are you familiar with that?'

Eryn shrugged. 'Only that it's something from the old times.'

He rubbed his temples. 'I thought that once. But I've heard it. My head still aches from what sounds like an echo.' The fire roared as it reached the plentiful innards of the droog.

'Time to retreat.' Eryn ushered them back. 'I think we can safely say that task is complete.' She took Toryn's arm. 'Are you sure it was this so-called song? From what you say, you've suffered at the hands of some unsavory folk of late. Are you certain your head has not been fooled by some dark trick?' They entered the hut where Hope slept.

Toryn spoke as he looked down at her. 'I have troubling dreams, and I suppose it's possible some of what I heard, or saw, could have been illusions.' He nodded to Hope. 'But I'm sure I was fully awake when she changed before my eyes.' He thought back to the night spent in the wood outside of time. 'Are you aware of the Singing Stones?'

Eryn appeared taken aback by the mention of the stones. She mumbled. 'Singing…? Stones that…' Her eyes wandered to the door. 'I seem to recall something about tall, smooth stones that held some enchantment.' She shook the memory from her head. 'But that must have been a long time ago. Haven't seen one for many a year.'

Toryn kneeled at Hope's side. 'They have power, and she is connected to them. When near one she changes. She's old, very old, perhaps older than the Archon, but at the stone she looks only a few years older than you. And from what she's said, I believe she once held a high position in the realms. I don't know her real name.' Toryn smiled. 'I call her Hope. I gave her that name when I thought all was—'

'Eryn!' Calestri burst into the hut. She noticed Toryn besides Hope. 'A word, Eryn?' Calestri nodded to the door. 'Perhaps outside.'

Eryn followed, glancing back to Toryn as she left. He sidled up to the doorway. Just beyond, Calestri whispered with conviction. Toryn could not make out her words, but the urgency was obvious. Eryn hissed back. 'But they saved us. We can't just leave them. They'd never find their way out of the forest.'

Calestri's voice rose. 'But we don't know anything about these wykes, and it's obvious the Nordleng turned up here because of them. We could easily have ended up as droog food. We're safer alone. Besides, that woman will slow us down.'

Eryn held up her hand. 'I won't have it. There's something about them that I have—' she looked over her shoulder. Toryn darted back inside, unable to hear the rest of their conversation. He went back to Hope and took up her warm hand just as the Amayan's returned.

Eryn spoke first. 'More Nordleng approach from the west, and I don't know about you, but I'm in no mood to face another worm… or worse. Please wake your companion.' She glared at Calestri. 'We *all* leave now.'

20. A Game of Squares

Elodi received the news she so desperately desired to know, but not to hear. Her scouts posted at Dorlwood had spotted what had to be the folk of Dorlgoth, led by a tall man with broad shoulders and long hair. They counted almost two hundred leaving the wood, heading east across the plain adjacent to the road. But where had they been until now? They had abandoned Dorlgoth long before the sighting. What had they been up to in the wood?

Elodi consulted her map. If they maintained their route, the first settlement of any size they would encounter was Greendell. Was that his destination? Like Dorlgoth, Greendell was an isolated village. Secluded at the head of the Wend Gap, it had little contact with the outside world until late autumn when they traded livestock for supplies for the winter. Many of the inhabitants were retired Archonians from Harlyn. Should the likeness of Dorlan appear, would they also join his ranks? The people of Dorlgoth had little skill with a blade, but a few dozen experienced old guards from Greendell would greatly enhance Dohl's renegade force. The man must be planning to recruit more to Uleva's side. Elodi could think of no other reason why he would leave the safety of Dorlwood. She immediately swore her messenger to secrecy. Should the people of Calerdorn hear of this, their spirits would be crushed. Dorlan or not, the likeness of their legendary hero leading his kin to the enemy would do little for Harlyn's cause. But at least she knew of his location, and thankfully, they were not coming to Calerdorn… yet. Word of the exodus from Dorlgoth would soon reach her city walls regardless of her efforts. Therefore, she had to find a way to counteract Uleva's plan to undermine her authority in the eyes of her people. Dohl or Dorlan, she had to either bring him back to her side, or, as hard as it was to stomach, have him slain. If the old man was Dohl, it seemed heartless to kill him. But if he truly was Dorlan, could she be responsible for killing the hero of Harlyn? And if he had regained his strength of old, how many would be lost in the attempt? Dorlan, had after all, fought and defeated far greater foes than what Elodi could send against him.

She pushed the scout's report across the table and turned to Wendel. 'What am I to do?'

Her advisor stared at the paper. 'This is truly a delicate situation, ma'am.'

Elodi managed a smile. 'Thank you, Wendel. Your years of experience come to my aid once again.'

His face crinkled into a grin. 'You are most welcome. Now, if you will forgive me for stating the obvious, I will offer my advice, that you may take or leave.' He folded his arms. 'They are on foot. We have time to intercept them before they depart the plain. But as you say, what action do we take? His sizeable force of devoted followers will prove difficult to reason with. And we can't deny they will do everything to prevent an… intervention of any sort. And how would that look should word get out our finest knights had attacked the people of Dorlgoth, young and old.' Wendel stretched and rubbed his eyes.

Elodi glared at the note as if trying to burn the words from the paper. 'I agree. We must intervene before this goes any farther.' She watched his eyes half-close. 'You should rest, Wendel. I will take your council on apprehending Dohl, the rest is now a tactical matter requiring experienced military minds. Have Gundrul report to me as soon as he arrives. If he's made good time, he should be here any moment. Perhaps he has dealt with such sensitive issues before, then together we can come up with a workable plan.'

Wendel nodded. 'Thank you, ma'am. I will take your advice and retire to my room, but please, do inform me of your tactics.' He turned and shuffled from the hall.

Elodi let her shoulders relax. The situation at Tunduska had stabilized. Uldrak appeared to have either lost interest, or, if she was lucky, the loyalty of the Ruuk, and had withdrawn the bulk of his force. And better still, the Ruuk trapped between the bridge and Elodi's re-enforcements had been defeated, and to her regret, all put to death. But what option did they have? This was the nature of Harlyn's fight for survival. Captain Ruan remained at the bridge, leading a detachment of his spearmen and artillery, allowing Gundrul and his guards to return to Calerdorn. But that left a nagging doubt in Elodi's heart. Where was Uldrak and his forces? And did the Norgog still bolster his ranks? She shuddered as she recalled their dark eyes and slit mouths and nostrils in their flat faces. Had Uldrak the strength to bring the cold farther south allowing them to fight? The Norgog had been a handful in the confined space of the bridge; Elodi dared not imagine what damage their cruel hammers could inflict in an open battle on the plain, or worse still, in the streets of Calerdorn.

Elodi glanced at the second note on the table before her. It had arrived that morning from the watch stationed as close to Drunsberg as they had dared to make camp. Although short, the news required more thought. The tremors that had begun shortly after its capture, had grown stronger. Rubble in large amounts were being brought from the mine and dumped into the ravine. Judging by the color of the rocks deposited, the miners on the watch concluded the abandoned seams had been re-opened. The new owners of Drunsberg were tunneling deep beneath the Kolossus Mountains.

Elodi jumped at the knock on the door. She straightened. 'Enter.' She stood to greet the weary Gundrul. 'Please tell me, Captain. Do you play *Squares*?'

Gundrul turned out to be an excellent player, perhaps even better than her father. Elodi was not surprised given his calm, mindful judgment in battle. And with Wendel looking older and more confused these past weeks, perhaps she had to find another to confide in. They had played *Squares* late into the evening, winning two games apiece. Like Elodi, the captain appeared to relish the distraction from his responsibilities as they immersed themselves in the game, but inevitably, the troubles besetting the realm could not be ignored for long.

Elodi sat on her bed and looked down to the disk in her palm. She rolled it over to reveal her initial she had painstakingly carved into the wood as a child. She smiled. Perhaps she could present the captain with another piece if she beat him. Elodi had promised Gundrul they would play a deciding match when events had settled; but when would that happen? Tunduska's Gorge may be secure for now, but the captain agreed, the situation with Dohl now posed a greater threat in the short term. As much as Elodi disliked the idea, they both accepted Dohl and his followers had to be detained before they could encounter more of her people.

Elodi lay back and let her heavy head sink into the pillow. As the moon had cast its silvery light into the hall, she and Gundrul had finally devised a strategy. It was not one she had wished to commit her forces, but it was the only course of action they believed could work. Elodi rolled the *Squares* counter through her fingers as she ran the plan over in her head. She would ride ahead of the people of Dorlgoth and take up a position in their path. She, Gundrul and Aldorman would greet the man posing as Dorlan with a proposition. His followers would be offered the chance to return to Dorlgoth, while Dohl would be invited to join Elodi's Council. That part of the plan was acceptable to Elodi, buying her more time and the opportunity to fashion another strategy. However, should her offer be rejected, and Dohl chose to press on to the east, Elodi would move to the second stage — the threat. If Dohl persisted and refused to relent, she would reluctantly give the signal to her hidden, mounted archers. Dohl would be targeted first, but if his followers chose to fight on, Gundrul had coldly calculated, twenty-five skilled bowmen could bring an end to the revolt quickly and cleanly, without the need for hand-to-hand combat. Elodi dearly hoped it would not come to this, but accepted more lives could ultimately be saved if Harlyn remained undivided. Gundrul believed if Dohl could be killed quickly, the rest would surrender thus limiting the bloodshed. But Elodi was only too aware of Dorlgoth's unerring loyalty to their legend, and feared they would fight to their last to avenge the loss of their son. Yet, it was a risk they had to take.

Elodi saw her father sitting on the opposing side of the *Squares* board. He appreciated the need to sacrifice a valued disk for the sake of the long strategy to win a game. But this was no small piece of wood sitting out the rest of the game with the chance to rejoin in the next. These were people of Harlyn, even if the folk of Dorlgoth did not see it that way, and many in her realm viewed them with suspicion.

Elodi closed her eyes, rehearsing the lines that she would deliver to Dohl, desperate to invoke some distant memory of his days, if he did indeed serve her father in Calerdorn. Perhaps if she could find a small part of him that remembered his loyalty, she would persuade the man to change course and prevent the slaughter — because as much as she tried to justify her decision, if his followers fought back, a slaughter it would have to be.

21. A Life Forgotten

Eryn stopped. 'We'll rest here.' She looked up. 'It will be dark before long, and we'll struggle to find our way. The moon is yet too new to shed much light.' Toryn helped Hope from Moonbeam's back, led her to a tree and set her down on the soft undergrowth. Eryn patted the horse's nose and let him wander off to drink from a nearby stream. They had walked late into the afternoon, heading east, then a little north deeper into the Foranfae. The ground had flattened after a short incline and had remained level since. But it was the trees that fascinated Toryn as they ventured farther into its midst. Growing to a greater height than any he had seen on his long trek across the realms, he longed to climb one and look out from its lofty crown. But he was under no illusion it would prove quite a challenge. While the thick trunks with deep, wrinkled bark offered the odd place to grip, the first branches were high above their heads.

He stepped back and looked up. The trees grew closer together here, with their branches linking with those of their neighbors as if holding hands. The canopy appeared thick enough to support treehouses and provide the perfect place to hide from your enemies. Indeed, several times during the day, Toryn thought he had glimpsed movement among the high branches. But Eryn had advised him not to look too hard, believing their passage would be tolerated if they maintained their distance. But what of their pursuers? Did the Nordleng have protection from a greater power? Toryn had begun to doubt whether the black-clad men served the Archon. He had no memory of being taken by them. He had heard horses approach him on the bridge, but had they taken him directly north? Or had their party been waylaid by the Nordleng as commanded by another? He hoped that was the case; he could not contemplate what it meant if these men in possession of a droog served the Archon.

Toryn kneeled beside Hope. She appeared exhausted but comfortable as she lay on the bed of thick moss nestling in the crook of the tree's exposed roots. He leaned over and whispered into her ear. 'I heard them. I heard the Maidens.' She smiled, then curled into a ball. He looked up to Eryn. 'I don't think she'll wake much before dawn. Would the Nordleng come this far?'

'That I cannot say. Not so long ago they wouldn't dare place one foot in the forest. But now…' She glanced behind. 'I suspect they are still on our trail.'

Toryn peered between the trees ahead. 'What lies at the center?'

She shrugged. 'That I don't know. We've never ventured much beyond the outskirts.'

He shivered. 'Will we go much farther?'

Eryn gripped the handle on her sword. 'What I do know is the deeper you go, the more *mischievous* our little friends become. My plan is to lure our pursuers far enough to entice the lurkers in these trees to finish them off. But that relies on them regarding us the lesser threat and therefore tolerating our presence a while longer.' She glanced back to Calestri and Arijan checking for signs of the Nordleng. 'We'll keep on for two more days, turn north, then west back to the outskirts. I trust that will be sufficient to snare the Nordleng.'

He kept his eyes on the shadows behind Eryn. 'Is it safe to go much farther?'

'Safe? You and your mystery woman claim to be able to *save the realms.* You perform some magical trick to defeat a vile worm, and you want to know if it's safe?'

'It was you who struck the final blow. But as I said, I don't know how we did it.'

She untied her sword belt and sat. 'I'd still rather take my chances with what's in the trees than what surely follows. If they can track us this deep into the forest, they undoubtedly have some darker power assisting them. And I assume they'll have learned from their defeat last night and be coming in greater numbers.' She shuddered. 'And perhaps bring another droog.'

Toryn looked down to Hope. 'Then I must learn her tricks quickly if I'm to help.'

Eryn turned to face the north. She sighed. 'I wish Amyra was here.'

'You mentioned her last night. Who is she?'

'Our leader. She went to' — she eyed Toryn — 'well I suppose there's no harm in you knowing, you've proved your worth against the worm when you could have walked away.' Eryn gestured Toryn join her. 'Amyra went north to meet with another band of our sisters. We think it's time to combine our strength as we encounter more of these Nordleng swine. It's not just you they're interested in. We suspect someone is paying them to capture us for some foul purpose.' She rested her head against the trunk. 'You may think we're fearless warriors, and we're happy for people to think that. Always helps if the person you're facing has it in their mind we're invincible. It means most are defeated before we even draw our blades, and often the mere threat of a fight is enough to scare them.' Eryn plucked a large mushroom from the base of the tree. 'The truth is…' she peeled the outer layer of skin, 'the truth is we're not, and our numbers dwindle as the years pass.' She tore the stem from the cap. 'And it's been getting worse these last few years.'

Toryn watched her, intrigued by her honesty. 'How many Amayans are left?'

'Of that I can't be sure, but we must number less than twenty these days.'

'But the tales? I thought there were dozens, hundreds even.'

'Sadly, not. Maybe once, but I don't rightly know how many we once numbered.' Eryn's eyes widened. 'We lost eleven a while back on just one mission.'

'Eleven? Who is strong enough to kill eleven Amayans?'

Her voice lowered. 'Oh, they're out there. We can't stay in one place for long these days. Someone is training the Nordleng in tactics and the skills of fighting, and now we're seeing more of them with every passing month.'

'But you took down four to rescue… capture me.'

She rubbed her lip. 'And that was closer than I would have liked. You saw my wounds. Not too long ago, I would have beaten them in half the time and come out without a scratch.'

'How did eleven of you come to grief?'

She dropped the remains of the mushroom. 'We had word one of our sisters had been captured and taken north. Nordleng' — Eryn's mouth curled — 'accompanied by a shroul.' Toryn took her hand. She met his gaze and continued. 'And this wasn't the first time. A sister by the name of Tanis was taken several years earlier and corrupted by some foul, despicable sorcery. We came across poor Tanis a year later. It took three of us to… bring an end to her misery.'

Toryn's grip tightened. 'What had they done to her?'

'I dread to think, but she fought like one possessed. She was stronger, and' — her voice wavered — 'her eyes. They bulged as if she burned from within.' Eryn released her hand. 'We couldn't let it happen again. When we got word of another abduction, we mustered the bands and rode north.'

'Is that how you lost your last leader?'

Eryn looked away. 'No. She left us. Took up with some young lord in Calerdorn.' She let out a long sigh. 'But Eleni redeemed herself. She rode north with us and, sadly, suffered terribly for it. We heard she died shortly after giving birth.'

Toryn gaped. 'She was with child and still fought? And you say the tales are exaggerated.'

She sighed. 'Eleni was quite the fighter, one of our finest. A great pity she fell. We could really do with her skills right now.'

Toryn glanced to Hope as she snorted in her sleep. 'Did you find your sister?'

'Yes. But we were too late. She was beyond saving. We ended her torment but lost many in the attempt.' Eryn touched his arm, glancing over his shoulder. 'Not a word of this to Cali. She suffered the most out of all of us.' She gripped his arm. 'And we found to our horror, it wasn't a shroul. We came up against a shreek and Cali bore the brunt of its wrath.'

'A shreek!' Toryn insides froze. 'Hope spoke of shreeks. She seemed wary of them.'

Eryn released her hold. 'So she should. I'd never met one before and don't ever want to face another. Cali somehow kept it at bay while we completed our… task. It may have been twenty or so summers back, but she's still not her old self.'

'Wait. Twenty years! How old are—?'

Calestri strode up to the tree. 'Pretty certain we're safe for now. Arijan will keep watch just in case.' She sat, squeezing between Eryn and Toryn. 'What are you two talking about?' She ruffled Toryn's hair. 'Not like the other simple folk are you?'

Toryn could feel Eryn's glare through Calestri. She spoke through a tight jaw. 'They're not all bad, weak, annoying, or just plain dull.'

Calestri made herself comfortable. 'I suppose you're right. Do you remember the guard who used to tell those strange stories? He was particularly impressed with my skills with a bow.' She giggled. 'Or to be more precise, how I could handle a bow with my' — she winked at Toryn — 'physique.' Toryn could not stop the smirk spreading across his face, wondering what Calestri must have been like before her encounter with the shreek.

Eryn exhaled. 'I'm struggling to remember a guard who wasn't impressed by your *physique*.'

Calestri leaned back. 'But this one was different. Liked birds. Odd for a tough guard to be so keen on birds, I thought, especially their songs.'

Toryn sat up. 'Hamar? Surely, you can't mean Hamar. That would have been fifty years ago.'

Calestri nodded. 'Yeah, that might have been the name. Nice fellow to amuse oneself for an hour or two. Do you know him?'

Toryn stood and looked at the youthful faces of the Amayans. '*Did* know him, I'm afraid. He died at Drunsberg. But he was approaching his eightieth year, yet you don't look much older than me.'

Eryn rose. 'We heal quickly and age slowly.' She looked over his shoulder. 'You keep an eye on your friend. I'll track back just to be sure it's safe to bed down here.'

Toryn turned. 'But you haven't answered—' but he spoke to the tree; Eryn and Calestri had gone.

Toryn woke. In the silence, he thought he had heard a twig snap. He sat. A horse nickered. The sliver of the waning moon cast little light through the forest's roof, but enough for him to notice Eryn had risen. Calestri and Arijan slept nearby, while Hope still huddled between the roots. Eryn must be on watch. She had returned from her foray confident the Nordleng were a safe distance behind. Nothing could move at night so deep in Foranfae. The Amayans had previously learned to their cost, the shadowy inhabitants of the forest did not abide torches so close to the trees. And the plight of their sisters trying to navigate without light was known to all Amayans; becoming disorientated in the dark and lost for years on end in Foranfae was not to be recommended.

The sound of trickling water caught his attention. His mind went back to the night he and Hamar had spent by the brook bubbling up beside the first Singing Stone. The old man's words of hearing faint echoes of the Song of Creation in the running of water and the rustling of leaves, flooded back. He tilted his head to listen, but all he heard were the stifled sobs of Eryn. Toryn fumbled in the dark for the tree and slowly stood. He waited for his eyes to adjust, then stepped towards the sound of water and Eryn's grief. He found her sitting on a mossy mound by the edge of a stream.

Eryn turned as he drew near. She wiped her face, smearing silvery tears across her cheeks. He whispered. 'What's wrong?'

She looked away. 'Nothing. I'm fine.'

Toryn sat on the soft moss. 'You cry for nothing?' But Eryn remained silent, letting her gaze drop to the brook. He laid his hand on her shoulder and sought to find words of comfort; none came. He dangled his foot in the cool stream wondering if a Singing Stone stood nearby. Toryn tried to strike up a conversation. 'Does it seem strange that I'm beginning to like this place?'

Eryn sniffed. 'No.'

A light breeze parted the leaves above, allowing more light to dance on the water. He tried again, keeping his voice low so as not to wake the others. 'I feel safer here than outside. I sort of get the feeling the trees—'

'I don't know how old I am.' Eryn turned to him. 'That's what you wanted to know earlier, is it not? And before you ask, I don't know where I hail from either.'

'But surely you—?'

'No. I don't.' Her voice was barely audible above the water. 'I have no memory of my childhood, none of us do.' Her head shook slightly as she spoke. 'The only life we've known is pretty much what you've witnessed. Over the last few years it's gotten more dangerous, but before that, it was pretty much the same year after year.' Eryn leaned forward and dipped her fingers in the stream. 'We may call you the *simple folk*, but if I'm honest, I envy you.'

'*You* envy *me*?'

'You have childhood memories, do you not? You know the history of your people, your realm. You know your parents. I have no—'

'Actually, I know little of Midwyche and its past. And I don't know who my real—'

'We have no such recollection. All we know is what you see. We hunt, we fight, we… survive.'

Toryn nodded back to where the others slept. 'What about Moonbeam? Do your horses live longer than ours?'

'No. He must be the eighth horse I can remember.' She sighed. 'I call them all Moonbeam. It's easier that way.' She turned and touched his arm. Despite the gloom, her eyes shone like a clear, morning sky. 'When I took your hand to help you up from the grass the first time we met, I… I thought I saw…' She frowned.

'What? Saw what?'

'Something of my past.' She waved her hand. 'I know that sounds absurd, but for a moment I felt… connected. I had a sense of purpose, a real and noble purpose, for the first time I can remember in my life.'

'Has it happened since?'

She looked away. 'No. Just the first time outside the

forest. But now I know you're one of these so-called wykes, I wonder whether that's the connection.'

'How about Hope? Did you get the same feeling when you met her?'

'No. Not that I held her hand, but' — she tried unsuccessfully to laugh — 'we didn't take much notice. After all, we did think she was an old man until you came along.'

Toryn grinned. 'I suppose it's not immediately obvious. But now you know of her power, do you sense anything from her?'

'Still no. We Amayans have some sort of gift. We can read each other's minds, and to some degree, your people' — she noticed Toryn's jaw drop — 'don't worry, not to the extent I can see what you're thinking, not that I'd need to when you look at Cali, but I sensed you were, on the whole, a good man when we first met.' Eryn frowned. 'Can't you?'

'What? Read the minds of other simple folk? No. Well not in a way you can.' He looked back. 'But you get nothing from Hope?'

'She remains closed. I've tried since we discovered her power, but there's little I can fathom of her past, or even if—'

The cry shattered the silent night. 'Hope!' Toryn jumped from the rock, but Eryn was already two paces ahead before he recovered his footing. They rushed to the sound of distress. Calestri grappled with Hope, while Arijan clasped her hand over Hope's mouth. She tried to bite the hand, but Arijan's hold was too tight.

Toryn tried to pull Arijan away. Calestri hissed at him. 'Hands off! She'll alert every creature within a league.'

He stepped back. 'But she's frightened. If you want her to be quiet, you need to calm her.'

Calestri held her grip. 'Then be my guest. But don't

think for one minute we're going to let her give away our location.'

Eryn sat beside Hope as she continued to struggle. 'Cali's right. Talk to her, but we can't risk another scream like that.'

Toryn kneeled and whispered to Hope. 'Shush. You're safe.' Her wide eyes darted to Toryn, then back to Eryn, but she seemed not to recognize them or her surroundings. He took one of her flaying hands and held it tight. 'Hope. It's Toryn. Remember?' Her shoulders relaxed. 'We're in the forest. With the Amayans. You're safe.' He glanced about them. 'We're safe.' The moaning ceased. 'Will you be quiet if we let go?' Her eyes closed; she nodded. But the Amayans still held her firm.

Eryn tapped Calestri's arm. 'Let her go.' For a moment Calestri appeared reluctant, then Arijan let her hand drop. Hope gasped but remained quiet. Calestri released Hope and shuffled away.

Toryn nodded to Eryn. 'Thank you.' Then to Hope. 'What happened? Did you see something?' Now she had settled, Toryn could see a little of the younger Hope; the Amayans also noticed the change.

Hope spoke slowly. 'I saw… I saw something of my past.' She glanced about her. 'I have been here before, many, many years ago.' Her eyes widened again as she seemed to recall more of her memory. 'I did something. Something terrible.' The hairs on Toryn's neck bristled. Her voice strengthened. 'Many died… thousands.' She stared open-mouthed at him. Her voice broke. 'Thousands died… because of me.' Her hands shook as they covered her face.

Toryn embraced her. 'Can you be sure? You're not evil. You must have had a reason.' Her whole body trembled as she sobbed, muttering words no one could understand. He instinctively rocked her, but she appeared inconsolable. The Amayans stood aghast; a flicker passed across their faces. For a moment, Toryn thought he saw pain, a long-buried pain from a memory so deep, it could not be recovered for fear of driving them to despair.

22. In Her Hero's Footsteps

Elodi breathed in the cool, dawn air. She shivered on Sea Mist as they sat at the perimeter of Calerdorn's defenses. If she looked east, for a few moments at least, she could forget the troubled times by avoiding the scars the ditches and spikes had inflicted on her beautiful city. The work had been completed a week ahead of schedule leaving the plain silent once more. She patted Sea Mist's neck, aware he also enjoyed the chance to escape the bustle of the city as they struggled to cater for the large numbers arriving each day.

Elodi reluctantly turned to face the main gate. She averted her eyes to look to the reassuring spires, standing tall as if trying to snag the white clouds rushing south as if fleeing the threat from beyond the mountains. She felt suddenly envious of the clouds. While they had no say in their destination, blown at the will of the wind, they could remain remote and detached from the troubles below. But her head could not stay in the clouds for long; her gaze descended to the harsh reality. For centuries, the towers and billowing banners would be the first glimpse weary travelers caught of the ancient city, instilling a sense of security so close to the cold lands of the north. Today, they would be greeted by trenches and sharp spikes angled at their faces; anything but welcoming. But Elodi knew it was a price she had to pay to protect her people, but longed for the day when they could be removed.

The clatter of hooves behind, brought her sharply back to her present dilemma: Dohl. Elodi refused to refer to him as Dorlan, convincing herself it had to be the trickery of Uleva, and she would not fall for it. But it was still a matter requiring her attention. She, Gundrul, Aldorman, along with a dozen knights and twenty-five selected archers, were to ride east to locate and deal with the threat of the renegade and his band of devoted followers. But how they would *deal* with the problem depended on Dohl.

The column of knights drew near. Elodi nudged Sea Mist, noticing he hesitated — did he understand the nature of their mission? If Gundrul had calculated the respective speeds of the two groups correctly, they should apprehend the exodus from Dorlgoth by evening on the second day. Dohl and his misguided followers were on foot, consisting of all ages that would slow their progress. Gundrul believed they would struggle to travel even six leagues a day, therefore placing them fifty leagues east at most. But Calerdorn's best horses could easily cover thirty leagues before nightfall. Speed was vital. The longer Dohl traveled the open grasslands, the more eyes would perceive the likeness of their legend, thus making it harder for Elodi to maintain the narrative.

Aldorman arrived at her side. 'Ma'am. All are fit and ready to ride.'

Elodi glanced to Gundrul. 'Then let us hasten. This has to be nipped in the bud before it grows so strong, we can no longer contain this devilry.' She turned Sea Mist and spurred him on, rising in the saddle as he gained speed. The others matched Sea Mist's brisk pace, emerging from the last of the city's defenses in little time. They would head east, then south on the West Road until they drew level with Dorlwood, then strike out across the grasslands to follow Dohl's tracks. Elodi's spirits lifted, happy to be back in the saddle with a mission to fulfill. She glanced over her shoulder to the archers, hoping they would not be needed for their grim task should Dohl refuse to cooperate.

Elodi stared at the flames as they licked eagerly at the dry wood. The campfire cast grim shadow's across Gundrul's lined face, adding more years to his battle-hardened bearing. He nodded to the dark night over her shoulder. 'We're certain to make the turn early tomorrow, ma'am. Then we'll have him in our sights by sunset.' He smiled, reading her thoughts. 'But I'm confident your skills in diplomacy will do the trick. The elderly of Dorlgoth will be tired, uncomfortable, and perhaps beginning to doubt their motives. Five days in the open and at the mercy of the elements will be seeping into their old joints and bones.' He chuckled. 'If it were me, I'd take the first chance to return to my warm cave and away from the wet grasslands.' He shuffled. 'The damp can get to places I'd rather were dry.'

Elodi returned his smile. 'I know what you mean, Captain.' She looked up to the stars. 'These clear nights invite the chill from the north, even this close to midsummer. But the people of Dorlgoth are a determined folk. They may reside but a short distance from Calerdorn, yet they live in a distant time, led by beliefs that would seem peculiar to most.'

Gundrul rubbed his chin. 'I've met many strange and interesting folk on my travels. I'm not so sure the people of Dorlgoth differ much from those deep in the forests of Ormsk, or the island folk off Emryst. He pointed to the fire. 'I'd say your drink is ready, ma'am.'

Elodi lifted her cup from the embers. She breathed in the sweet smell, relishing the warmth it would bring. She blew and took a sip. Memories of the last camping trip with her father flooded back. She looked to Gundrul over the rim. 'I've yet to travel east of the Kolossos.'

Her captain lifted his cup from the fire. 'It's a very different world on that side, ma'am. It's as if the gods decided we were too unlike and thrust up the mountains to keep us from each other's throats. But we've grown passed that now. Thankfully Broon and Harlyn settled their differences centuries ago. Where would we be today if we could not assist an ally in need?'

She drank more, savoring the heat spreading to her limbs. 'That is so, Captain. But tell me of the people. How do the folk of Broon and Galabrant compare to us?'

Gundrul grimaced. 'There are those who have some pretty outlandish ways that I imagine are like those of Dorlgoth.' He chuckled. 'But don't worry, I won't sully your ears with the tales and spoil the obvious pleasure you're getting from your mead.'

'I wouldn't worry. It would take a dark tale indeed to ruin my drink. I'm keen to know more of the east.' She glanced to the shadows behind her captain. 'At Tunduska, Ruan told me he lost his older brother at Aralak Gorge. Did you ever serve there?'

Gundrul's hand on his mug clenched. 'Can't say it's my favorite place in the realms. But every soldier of Broon must do time at the fences. And yes, many of us lost a brother or dear friend to those hairy brutes.'

'Did you ever… meet one?'

He put down his drink. 'Several, ma'am. Killed one, injured another, but there was one time we weren't so lucky. The guard next to me took a belly full of its poison. Thankfully, we fought off the beast before it could drag him away, but the poor soul took months to get over it and had to retire. Never had the strength to lift his sword after that.'

Elodi shuddered. 'I can't imagine anything worse. And I dread the thought the defenses should fail and we see them scuttling free about the realms in greater numbers.'

He exhaled. 'Well, we're in luck there, ma'am. Fortunately, they fight among themselves most of the time, and I can tell you that's not a pretty sight, even from the other side of the fence.' Gundrul picked up his cup. 'But if they ever decide to work together, we'd have a hard time containing the darn things.'

'Then let us pray to the Three that day never comes.' She looked down at the flames. 'Tell me, Captain. Did you ever come across an Amayan during your travels?' Despite the firelight, Elodi was certain the old captain's cheeks reddened.

'Ah, yes. The Amayans.' He stretched out his arms and yawned. 'I've met the odd one in my time.'

'And…? What did you make of them?'

Gundrul's memories flashed across his face. 'As warriors? Second to none. Very skilled with a variety of weapons, ma'am. If we could find a dozen and persuade them to fight for our cause, I'm sure we'd have no more troubles with the Ruuk and those shady wykes. But as ladies?' He drained the last of his mead. 'As ladies, I'd have to say, I've not met any like them. Well not in the sense that all the ladies I've known can read *my* thoughts, while I don't have the faintest idea what they're thinking. No, all ladies are alike in that manner, ma'am.' He held up his hand. 'And by that, I mean no offence. It's actually meant as a compliment… I think.'

Elodi grinned. 'And that's how I took it, Captain.' She held his gaze, despite his unease. 'But to what else do you refer when you say they're unlike other… ladies.'

'Ah, yes, by that… I mean.' Gundrul looked away. 'Let's just say they can be' — he clicked his fingers — 'friendlier than most women I've met.' He poked at the fire with a stick. 'No… that's not it. I mean they seem keen to get to know you if it serves their purpose, willing to talk about such things you'd usually only talk over with a fellow guard. But in other ways, they're quite distant, detached even, almost as if they don't really know themselves.' He rubbed the back of his neck. 'Sorry, ma'am, I don't seem to be making much sense, do I.'

'Enough sense, Captain. I think I can guess to what you allude. But let's move on from their *friendly* nature, how do you judge them? Do you believe they could make a potential ally?'

Gundrul's relief was plain to see. He relaxed. 'That I could not say for sure, ma'am. Amayans dwell in their own world, obey their own rules, and appear to do what they please, with little thought or care for us common folk. But if they had to choose between the likes of us and the creatures outside of our realms, I'd like to think they'd ride to our aid, ma'am.' He placed another stick onto the fire. 'But they'd charge you much gold and gems for their services after they'd saved your skin. But then, if they thought the other side would pay more, they might consider their position.'

Elodi watched the flames greedily lick at the new wood. 'Perhaps that would be something we must consider. And I would hope, even in these times of austerity, we could muster greater wealth than that of our foes.' Elodi stood and yawned. 'Thank you, Captain. I appreciate your candor… honesty. Now if you would excuse me, it's been a long day and we have a longer day awaiting us tomorrow.'

'Sleep well, ma'am. I'll keep the fire going on first watch to keep the chill at bay.' He grinned. 'And I'll keep my eyes peeled for an Amayan. I hear they have been known to roam these parts at times.'

Elodi stretched. 'Again, thank you, Gundrul. I will sleep easier knowing you watch over us.' Her eyebrow raised. 'And do wake me should you see one.' She went to leave but turned. 'And perhaps we'll have time for our deciding game of *Squares* before too long.'

The weather had been kind, if a little cool for the season. But Elodi was grateful the north easterly wind had decided to take its unwanted presence elsewhere for the time being. They had made good progress as the finest horses of Calerdorn seemed keen to impress. Elodi had woken in the middle of the first night and marveled at the stars shining bright in the absence of clouds. Two archers kept watch, but she decided to leave them be. She remained wrapped in her blankets, taking rare pleasure from the dazzling display in the night sky. But as much as she tried to lose herself among them, the foreboding gnawing at her stomach returned as she anticipated encountering Dohl late the following day. She may have slept at times, but Elodi was wide awake when the sky to the east turned pink.

After a light breakfast, they had set off at a canter and soon reached the turn of the West Road and headed south. Before long, the tops of the tall trees of Dorlwood came into view. At midday, her scout found the tracks of Dohl's entourage as they had tramped across the road onto the wide grasslands of Dorn Plain. In parts, the uneven, wet ground had slowed the horses, but Gundrul was still confident they would encounter Dohl late that evening.

'There, ma'am.' Elodi pulled up Sea Mist. Gundrul stood in his stirrups, pointing to the line of the horizon against the darkening sky. Elodi, who had been lost in her thoughts, followed the direction of his finger.

'Ah, yes. I see them. There must be at least a hundred and eighty, possibly more. They appear to have stopped.'

Gundrul squinted. 'Your young eyes are far better than mine. All I can see is a smudge.'

Aldorman drew level. He looked up. 'I fear it will soon be too dark for the archers, ma'am. May I suggest we wait for the morning before we engage.'

Elodi glanced to the sky. 'Agreed, Captain. But I believe we have sufficient light to allow us to select a suitable position for our… meeting tomorrow.' She viewed the surrounding grassland. 'We'll circle them out of sight to the south and make camp on their projected path. Does that meet with your approval?' Both captains nodded. 'Excellent. Let us hope this matter can be brought to a satisfactory end soon.'

The clear skies and early appearance of the crescent moon obliged, affording them sufficient light to find exactly what was needed; an escarpment adequate to conceal their camp from Dohl — and Elodi's archers when she approached the man with her offer.

Elodi sat with her two captains staring at the embers of their small fire. 'Are the archers briefed, Captain?'

'Yes, ma'am.' He moved to reassure her. 'They will shoot in short bursts. Dohl is the first objective, then they'll target the warrior-like next.'

'And they will pause? I must allow them time to surrender. Casualties have to be kept to a minimum.'

He nodded. 'You have my word. I will keep a careful watch on who has fallen, and give the command to cease if there is any sign of surrender.'

'Thank you, Captain. It pains my heart, but if my negotiation fails, I see no other path open to us.' Elodi turned. Her archers sat huddled around their own small fires to keep the glow from alerting Dohl on the opposite side of the ridge. She watched their set faces in the faint, orange light, satisfied she could trust them.

Aldorman broke the silence. 'It's quiet this evening, ma'am. Quieter than last night.'

Gundrul agreed. 'Not even the odd bird call.'

Elodi cocked her head. 'Perhaps our presence and that of Dohl and his people scare the inhabitants of the plains from their nests.' She motioned to the glow of the campfires beyond the ridge. 'I doubt the creatures of this region will have seen more than the odd traveler for many a year.'

Aldorman stood. 'The people of Dorlgoth are not known for their merriment either. They barely make a sound.'

Gundrul grunted. 'Probably listening to their great leader. There's plenty of tall tales of Dorlan doing the rounds.'

'He's just an old man.' Elodi interrupted. 'He's Dohl, not Dorlan. We cannot begin to think of him of anything other than a deception of Uleva, but a clever one, I'll grant her that.' She looked back at the firewood shimmering orange in the light breeze. 'Dorlan died a thousand years ago, on a frozen plain far to the north. He had Ormoroth surrounded, all but defeated. But our tales say he underestimated the guile and strength of that devious commander. Dorlan thought him weak following the annihilation of his hordes. But Ormoroth had one last deadly card to play.' Elodi felt the loss to the realm as if it were yesterday. 'Too many fine fighters died that day. Draegelan suspected Ormoroth had unleased a great evil from the old world to deny Dorlan his victory.' She sighed and looked at her captains' faces in the firelight. 'No. Dorlan is dead, long dead. The man we'll confront tomorrow is Dohl. I suspect he once served my father, and for that he deserves our respect and gratitude. He has suffered greatly at the hands of Uleva, but, if we cannot reason with him, we should do him the honor of a swift death. As you know, it is not my desired course of action, but if it brings an end to his years of pain and misery, then so be it. He may be strong in the guise of Dorlan' — she recalled him brushing her guards aside as if frightened children — 'but I doubt Dohl could fight for long with a dozen arrows in him.'

Gundrul added more sticks to the fire, sending sparks billowing into the night air. 'Rest assured, ma'am, we have the resources to grant this man a swift end, whether he be Dohl or Dorlan.'

'Ma'am?' Elodi turned to Aldorman. He squinted at the sky just above the ridge. 'Is it my eyes or has the glow from their fires changed color?'

Elodi turned. Her heart sank. The orange had indeed gone, replaced by an eerie green light, the same she had witnessed at Tunduska's Gorge. She stood, taking a few paces towards the ridge. 'How can this be?' Her hand went to her sword. 'We've had no sightings of wykes and the enemy for many leagues.' She looked to her captains. 'Should we withdraw?'

Gundrul kicked out the fire. 'Where to? We should stay until we know of their location. If they come in large numbers, we'll be finished if we ride right into their path.'

Aldorman put on his helmet. 'I suggest we mount and form a circle.' He whistled to his horse. 'Once we've determined their position, we ride out.'

Elodi kept her eyes on the shimmering air. 'And Dohl?'

Gundrul surveyed their perimeter. 'If the enemy approaches, we no longer have a choice, ma'am. We cannot risk losing you for the sake of this old man, regardless of his potential threat.'

She slapped her leg. 'How is this possible? Where could they have come from?' Sea Mist trotted to her side. Elodi looked at his eyes. 'He seems unconcerned.' She turned back to the direction of Dohl's camp and mounted. 'Could it be something the people of Dorlgoth burn on their fires, and not a wyke's mischief?'

Gundrul sniffed. 'If that is so, it creates no smell. But you're right. The horses appear untroubled.' He mounted. 'But best be cautious and make ready to leave.'

Elodi held up her hand. 'Can you hear that?' A single voice, a woman's voice carried through the still air. The song reminded Elodi of a lullaby her nursemaid sang. For a moment, she forgot her predicament as she was taken back to her warm bed in a safer world, wrapped up in soft sheets as she watched the candle flicker on her bedside table. But a chill entered her bones. The words changed; the voice became harsh. The ground tremored. Elodi's head span. Sea Mist knickered and stomped his hoof. Her vision blurred. Aldorman's armor shone green as the light intensified. Gundrul slumped; Aldorman swayed; Elodi slid from her saddle.

23. Shadows in the Trees

'We're being watched.' Hope spoke for the first time that day. The Amayans went for their swords. 'You're wasting your time.' She chewed her bread as she spoke. 'Swords are useless against them.'

Toryn scanned the trees. 'Useless? They came off second best last time.' But Hope ignored his words, leaned back and drank from her flask.

Eryn sheathed her blade. 'I suspect she refers not to the Nordleng.'

'Then who? Ah, she must mean the Little Folk.' Toryn searched the gloom, but the late evening sun shed little light. 'Should we be concerned?'

The Amayans rose and stood back-to-back to face all approaches. Eryn whispered. 'We've not had reason in the past, but we are deeper into the forest than we've previously been.'

Arijan kept her sword ready. 'Wouldn't hurt to be wary of them.'

Calestri nodded to her horse. 'If my girl isn't worried, then neither am I.'

Eryn peered at Moonbeam's face. 'Agreed, but perhaps it would be wise to have two on lookout tonight. Toryn and I will take first watch.'

Toryn and Eryn sat on a flat rock, opposite the tree where the others slept. He glanced over his shoulder. 'The horses appear fine.'

Eryn shrugged. 'Or is it because they don't fear them or… they can't sense them.'

'Hamar reckoned these Little Folk lived in the land before we came. But he only spoke of people going a little bit strange after an encounter. I don't recall him mentioning them attacking.'

Eryn ran her hand along the fine blade on her lap. 'I'd be happier defending an attack I'm familiar with. Besides, would you want to spend the rest of your life wandering around the forest being a *little bit strange*?' She tried to laugh. 'No wait, you're already strange, but it doesn't appeal to me.'

Toryn nudged her with his elbow. 'Strange but interesting, eh.' He kept his eyes fixed on the darkness between the trees. 'But no, I guess I wouldn't want to spend the remainder of my years in this forest. This place is beginning to wear me down.' He held up the sword he had taken from the Nordleng. 'But would these be any use against them? Hope seemed dubious.'

Eryn placed her hand on his, lowering his weapon. 'Best not wave it in their faces though. But stay ready. I'd rather place faith in my sword than some magic trick.'

Toryn took a deep breath. 'Last night, after Hope had her nightmare, I saw something in your faces.' He turned to her. 'It looked to me that you remembered something, perhaps like when you first took my hand.' Eryn remained silent, but her eyes gave away her thoughts. Toryn pressed. 'You all seemed… shocked, dismayed even. Can you recall?'

Eryn looked away. 'Yes.' She bit her lip and closed her eyes. Her breath quickened, seeming to echo in the still air. Her voice wavered. 'Yes, I saw something… a flicker, a glimpse of a memory, but only briefly.' She looked up to the faint crescent moon. Her eyes moved as if trying to recall. 'I have spent the day struggling to locate it, but all I get is a flash of an image, or faint echo of a sound, but as I try to reach it, it disappears. The harder I seek, the deeper I bury it.'

'You all seemed distressed.'

'That I sensed. I can't place the memory, but my heart aches and my stomach churns at the very thought. Cali and Arijan feel the same.'

'Then perhaps you share some history with Hope.'

She sighed. 'I believe we must. Yet still I cannot read her. She remains closed to us. But we obviously have suffered a terrible event in common.'

'Could she be an Amayan? I know she doesn't look like you, but why else would you have this apparent link?'

'I doubt it. I've never met a sister as old as she.'

Toryn tried to reason. 'But when close to one of those Singing Stones, or in danger, she changes, and could easily pass for an Amayan.'

'Still no. Apart from a vague memory, these stones mean nothing to us.' She laughed. 'And how long would she have been roaming these lands to look as ancient as she does? We Amayans age slowly compared to you folk, but she would have to be thousands of years old to account for all those wrinkles and her bent back.' Eryn glanced to where the others slept. 'No. It has to be something else. What did she say last night?'

The words still played in Toryn's head. 'She'd been here before… in the forest. She'd committed an appalling act, and many had died.'

'I believe *thousands died* were her exact words.'

'But what could she have done that led to the death of thousands?'

Eryn exhaled. 'That explains the deep sense of dread I feel.' Toryn shivered. His skin prickled. She turned. 'Can you feel that?'

'Something's changed.' They stood and faced away from each other, but Toryn could see nothing in the dark. 'Anything your way?'

'Nothing. But stay wary.'

Toryn's eyes flicked from one tree to the next, fearing a pair of glowing eyes would appear any moment. He whispered. 'Nordleng?'

'I doubt it. They wouldn't risk making a move at night in here. Besides, the horses would have heard them coming a league away.'

'Then it has to be the other folk.'

Eryn touched his hand. 'Do nothing to cause alarm. Perhaps they'll leave us alone if they sense we mean no harm.'

Toryn lowered his sword. 'Hope spoke of thousands perishing, but who died? Did she willfully kill them, or was it a consequence she couldn't have foreseen?'

Eryn remained wary. 'And were my sisters involved? If so, why do we have no memory?'

'Hope described it as if a shadow concealed her past to protect her. You say you have no recollection of your childhood, perhaps it's the same for you. That would—'

Eryn spun around. 'Shush. Something draws near.' She pointed. Toryn stared but could not be certain of what he saw. It looked as if two willowy shapes creeped towards their sleeping companions — but the moonlight was not strong enough to cast a shadow. He went to move but Eryn held his wrist. She whispered, 'Wait. Perhaps they mean us no harm.' He stared as the shadows appeared to move over the ground, but then across the thick trunks, breaking up and rippling across the wrinkled bark. They reached Hope and the Amayans. Toryn held his breath. Two gray figures crouched over Hope. Hope sat, but Toryn could see she had not woken. Long, wispy fingers took her hands and helped her to rise.

Eryn yelled. 'No!' Calestri and Arijan leaped up; more shadows emerged from the trees. Toryn froze. He tried to take a step, but his knees, then his whole body locked. Only his eyes could move. At his side, Eryn also stood motionless, as did Calestri and Arijan. The shadows had formed a circle about them. The air crackled, a ghostly hue shed a little light, but all Toryn could do was witness the wraiths lead a dazed, but willing Hope out of the circle and into the blackness beyond.

The shadows faded like smoke in a breeze; the darkness returned. Toryn staggered forward, released from the invisible hands holding him fast. He groped, blind in the sudden gloom, trying to find his dagger. He spluttered. 'Quick. They can't have gone far.'

Eryn grabbed his arm and pulled him back. 'Don't. You won't find them. You're more likely get lost.'

Calestri called over. 'I'll check the horses.' Toryn saw a shared thought pass across their faces.

Eryn released his arm. 'They're not of the world we occupy.'

Toryn scratched his tingling scalp. 'Were they Little Folk?'

She nodded. 'Yes. But as you saw, they are not so little. I' — she looked back to her companions — 'we remember them now.' She stared into the emptiness between the trees. 'They are the Nym.'

He shivered. 'Nym?'

Eryn joined Arijan at the tree where they had slept. She turned back to Toryn. 'Fae by another tongue. Perhaps you have heard of them.'

He looked up, realizing belatedly how the forest had come by its name; Toryn also wondered how many more of Hamar's tall stories would turn out to be true. He shook his head. 'But I could only see shadows.'

Eryn examined the ground where Hope had lain. 'That's more than most would see. While we've always known something lives in this forest, I don't recall a time when they've ventured so close. Our sisters talk of encounters, but only sensing the odd lone figure at a distance.' She looked down to her hand. 'The ground is warmer here.'

Calestri joined them. 'The horses are fine. I'm not sure they even noticed.'

Toryn peered in the direction the Nym had departed. 'Why Hope? What would they want with her?'

Calestri caught Eryn's eye. 'It seems not only the Nordleng are wary of your friend. And if you hadn't been on watch, perhaps you'd also be accompanying them on their midnight stroll through the woods.'

Toryn gathered his belongings. 'We must find her.'

Calestri stared at him. 'Why? Besides, we don't stand a chance in this place.' She held out her hands. 'This is their domain.'

'Because she may be in danger. And, as I've said before, I believe she has a role to play to defend the realms.'

Arijan joined Calestri. 'You can believe whatever you like, but we have no reason to follow you.'

Eryn stood by Toryn. 'The fact remains the two of them saved our skins at the settlement, and we undeniably share something in common with Hope. You both felt it last night, you can't deny it.' She took his hand. 'I'm with Toryn. You two can decide your own fate.'

24. A Macabre Message

Elodi opened her eyes, crying out as the dazzling light thrust sharp daggers into her skull. She rolled onto her side and curled into a ball, clutching her numb hands over her face. Her voice croaked. 'Gundrul? Aldorman?' Neither answered. A wet muzzle gently nudged her neck. 'Misty?' He licked her hand. 'Good boy. Give me a moment please.' She took a breath and caught the whiff of smoke, but to her dismay, it failed to conceal the stench lurking beneath. Gritting her teeth against the ache in her head, she grabbed the reins and climbed to her feet. Gundrul lay close by; Aldorman a little farther away, both still coiled as if fending off an invisible foe. Elodi stumbled and grabbed Sea Mist's neck for support. She waited for her head to settle, then risked looking about her. Much to her relief, all the horses stood unscathed beside their fallen riders as they began to stir.

Gundrul coughed, then groaned. 'My head. What… happened? And what's that foul stink?'

Elodi patted Sea Mist and staggered over to Gundrul. She held out a hand. 'I fear the air brings bad news. The last thing I remember was a song, but that was no lullaby.' She squinted at the sun, already high in the sky. 'But we've slept many hours. Midday approaches.'

'Mid—? Ah!' Gundrul winced as he managed to stand. His head and shoulders moved stiffly towards the ridge. 'Are we to assume Dohl has long since departed?'

Elodi helped Aldorman up from the ground. 'That I have yet to establish. If you're fit, Captain, perhaps you and Aldorman will accompany me.' Both nodded gingerly.

'But I hold no hope for what lies beyond the ridge.' They set off with caution.

Aldorman found his voice. 'I feel as I did when you found me on the edge of Durran Wood, ma'am. But I saw no demons last night.'

'We didn't see them, but perhaps we heard one. A small mercy, but I suspect the same devilry was at play. But we can be thankful we awoke this morning without—' Her jaw dropped as they reached the top of the hill. Aldorman stumbled to a halt; Gundrul groaned; his gnarled hand went to his face as he twisted away. Elodi gawped, not wanting to believe her eyes. At the foot of the escarpment, a wide circle of smoldering grass surrounded dozens of charred, contorted bodies. Elodi sank to her knees and sobbed. But the brimming tears could not shut out the sight of the poor souls' splayed, blackened fingers as they clutched at the air in their dying moments.

Gundrul rested his hand on her shoulder. 'Please wait here, ma'am. Allow me to investigate.' He bowed his head and walked down the slope. Aldorman followed, his head shaking in disbelief. The old captain moved from one body to the next. But Elodi could watch no longer as he drew his sword and carefully turned over one of the victims. She stood to scan for tracks leading east but could find no evidence any had departed. But even a cursory glance confirmed the number of dead failed to account for all of Dohl's followers. She spat, both cursing the evil fiend that had done this, while desperately trying to rid her mouth of the taste of the despicable deed. Yes, she had contemplated attacking these people, but she would have offered clemency, and had they declined, she would have done everything to ensure a quick death — not the painful fate bestowed upon them by a callous mind.

Her captains returned with blackened boots. Gundrul spoke. 'It's as I suspected.' A tear cleared a path through the soot on his face. He blinked. 'Only the very young, and the old, ma'am. Whoever carried out this atrocity had plans for those capable of whatever task they have in mind.' Gundrul looked out from under his furrowed brow. 'And I dread to think what that task entails.'

Elodi looked back to the horses. 'But why leave us?' She shivered. 'We were out cold last night. Dohl and his people could easily have slain us in our stupor.'

Aldorman shrugged. 'Could it be they didn't know we camped nearby? The spell… I won't honor it by calling it a song, ma'am, but that spell could have been meant for the ears of the people of Dorlgoth only. We just happened to be caught up in it.'

Elodi wiped her mouth, still tasting burned flesh. 'That would seem a plausible explanation. What other—?'

'Captain!' One of the archers staggered up the ridge. He waved his arm. 'Come quick.'

The three made their way back to the campsite. The archers stood around something on the grass. They parted to allow Elodi and her captains through. Elodi gasped. A young archer lay on his back. His wrists and ankles had been tied and pegged to the ground. His naked torso bore scars of evil letters. Her heart pounded; her face flushed in anger. The distorted face of the victim made it clear he had suffered great pain. She spun away. 'Untie him and dress those hideous scrawls before you prepare him for the journey to his home. Please, treat him with the dignity he deserves. His family cannot see him like this.' She took a breath. 'And… please, as unpleasant as it is, bury those poor, unfortunate souls of Dorlgoth. Perhaps we shall find a way to honor them in quieter times.'

Elodi paced to the edge of the camp. Her fists clenched. She forced herself to stand when she so desperately wanted to drop to her knees and pound the soft grass into mud. 'Ma'am?' Gundrul placed his hand on her shoulder. 'What are we to make of what they did to that poor archer?'

Elodi bit her tongue. 'That cannot be the work of Dohl or his followers.' She shut her eyes as the tears flowed afresh. 'Those are the same foul letters we saw on that ghastly tower in the wood.'

'Why him?' Gundrul's flat tone surprised Elodi until she opened her eyes to see the tightness in his jaw. 'That could have been any of us. Did they choose him for a reason?'

'They?' Elodi glanced back to the archers gently preparing their unfortunate colleague for his final journey. 'I believe that was the work of just one wyke' — her lips pursed — 'Uleva. Of that I am certain. Only she has the power to bring about what happened last night.'

Gundrul rubbed the back of his neck. 'Then why not all of us? Or… at the very least, you, ma'am?'

Elodi shuddered. 'This is a message. She shows us she can act with impunity, and she has little to fear from us.'

'But the same question remains. Why spare you? She must have known you lay among us.'

Elodi's eyes wandered to the east. 'I fear she has other designs for me. She wants me alive for some other foul purpose of hers. But what, I cannot begin to fathom. She commands a large Ruuk force and dark beings from another age. She knows she can do whatever she wants out here on the plain. Uleva grows stronger by the day. And with the likeness of Dorlan under her control, she will use him to recruit more to her side.'

Gundrul thrust out his chin. 'All is not yet lost, ma'am. We still have Calerdorn. It presents a formidable obstacle for our foes.'

Elodi wiped her cheek. 'But do they need to take it? The way south lies open. Our dilapidated border fences will serve only to provide ample wood for their campfires.'

'But the Archon will not tolerate their boots tramping through Harlyn and Kernlow.'

Elodi let out a long sigh. 'The Archon? He's too occupied with his mission to open the gate and take back the Lost Realms. But we're getting ahead of ourselves, Captain. Finding Dohl is no longer possible. He'll be long gone by now, and I cannot risk losing more of our small force in pursuit of him. We must return to Calerdorn and speak with the Council.' She turned to face the rising breeze that thankfully blew the reek of death from the field. Her stance stiffened. 'I shall no longer sit tight waiting for the enemy to act. I cannot allow Uleva free rein in the realm. Up until now our enemy has dictated proceedings. This has to change. We must take the conflict to them in ways that suit our strengths, while catching them at unawares.' Elodi's shoulders dropped. 'But what that entails yet eludes me.'

Her captain clasped her forearm. 'You will find a way, ma'am, of that, I am sure.'

'Thank you. I dearly hope you're right.'

Gundrul strode at her side as they returned to their horses. 'And what of Dohl and his remaining followers? I see no sign of tracks, yet they must still number at least one hundred.' He scratched his head. 'It looks to me as if they were somehow plucked from the plain.'

Elodi cursed. 'Shrouded by Uleva's dark arts I should imagine.'

The captain checked the straps on his saddle, then looked down to the patch of flattened grass where he had woken. 'I still cannot figure why Uleva simply did not finish us all last night.'

Elodi stroked Sea Mist's neck. 'She does not think as we do. I suspect Uleva draws much gratification from our discomfort. It would have been all too easy for her to murder us all in our dazed state, perhaps denying her of the pleasure of the days to come. I believe Uleva relishes the prospect of our downfall, a task I imagine she has waited many years to execute. She plots our ruin, but on her terms, in her own time.'

'Ma'am!' An archer strode over the ridge. He carried a smoke-stained blanket. Another called. 'One yet lives.'

Elodi ran as best she could to meet them. The archer gently laid the blanket on the floor and lifted the cloth. The wide, blue eyes of a child, a girl of barely five years, stared from a blackened face. Elodi kneeled and laid her hand on the child's trembling shoulders. 'Oh, you poor thing.' The girl began to weep. 'Shush, my child, be still. You're safe now. We'll take care of you.'

The archer fought to stay in control. 'Horrible, ma'am, just horrible. How could anyone do this to those gentle folk? We found her clinging to the body of an old woman, perhaps her grandmother. If she hadn't cried out when we moved the woman, we might have... buried her alive. Don't bear thinking about, do it, ma'am.'

Elodi held up her hand. 'Well let us give thanks it didn't come to that.' She looked down to the frightened eyes fixed on her as if not wanting to let Elodi out of her sight. 'This girl was lucky you found her.' She nodded to the archer and whispered. 'I will take her with me on Sea Mist. But please, wash her face, then give her water, then food if she will eat.' Elodi stroked the girl's ash-strewn hair and spoke to the child. 'I must prepare for our departure. This kind man will look after you for the time being. Then you can ride on my fine horse back to a safe place.'

She turned to Gundrul as the girl was taken down to the camp. 'What sights has that child had the misfortune to witness?' She looked at the scorched grass. 'And I dread to think what would have become of her had that archer not found her. We must get her to the healers so at least some good comes from our mission.'

Elodi cradled the child as best she could to keep her warm and comfortable. As far as she could determine, the girl carried no physical injuries, but what deeper scars the incident had left upon her, only time would tell. But as much as Elodi would have liked to slowed Sea Mist to a gentle trot, speed was paramount. Decisions had to be taken, forces deployed, and resources allocated to where they could hinder Uleva. And what of Uldrak and the hideous Norgog? Where had he taken up position since abandoning his attack at Tunduska?

Elodi held the girl a little tighter and took some hope from her calm, sleeping face despite the rolling and lurching as Sea Mist negotiated the grassy tufts and wet ground. At their first camp, Elodi had attempted to find out more from the child. But the only words that passed her tight lips before she burst into tears, were *black eyes, lady,* and *fire.* Just four words, but they struck dread into her heart.

Elodi glanced up and saw the tops of the spires she knew so well. Never had she been so relieved to see them. A black speck high in the sky caught her attention. It moved swiftly against the wind, standing out starkly against the backdrop of gray clouds. A bird! It descended, growing bigger as it dipped, dropping with purpose towards Calerdorn. It had to be from Archonholm. She spurred Sea Mist into action, desperate for news of Bardon and his mission south of the gate.

25. The Archon Demands

The order carried the Archon's seal only the Lady of Harlyn had authority to break. If Elodi had felt the weight of command resting on her shoulders before, the whole of the mighty mountain, Caranach, now bore down on her exhausted frame. She read it again, but her eyes remained reluctant to traverse the page and relay the meaning of the Archon's words. She let the order slip from her fingers to drop on the table; if the parchment carried the actual weight of its message, it would have landed with a thud.

She turned to Wendel. 'He… he can't be serious? How can he ask this of me… now? At the very time I'm…' she pushed the note to him and twisted away.

Wendel cleared his throat. 'Ma'am? May I read it?'

Elodi waved her hand. 'Yes, do.' She looked out of the tall window at the end of the hall. She heard his breath catch in his throat, once then twice, and waited for the third, thus knowing he had reached the end.

He stuttered. 'What are we to do?'

Elodi turned back, fixing her eyes on the paper. 'What choice do I have? It is an order from the Archon. To decline would be regarded as an act of treason.'

Wendel clicked his tongue. 'The last thing we need is another front to defend.'

'But Midsummer's Day!' She banged the table. 'That's three weeks from now. He expects me to assemble and lead a force of two hundred and fifty of my finest soldiers? By the Three, Wendel, we're still on our knees from the opening moves of our supposedly weaker enemy in the north!'

Wendel sat back. 'That is indeed a challenge, but not unsurmountable. Ruan and his spearmen still hold Tunduska; our scouts will send word as soon as Uldrak makes his move on Calerdorn, giving ample time to prepare the heavy weapons' — he attempted to smile — 'and the defenses prohibit the deployment of Uldrak's machines against our walls.'

'But that's not the point. Uleva roams the plains striking at will where she pleases. Dohl and his entourage are at large, and who knows how many more will be persuaded by the great *Dorlan* to join him.' She snatched the message from Wendel's hand and waved it in his face. 'And while all that unfolds, I am expected to take Gundrul and the bulk of his guards, plus every knight who's fit to ride, and then sail south?' Her hand clenched into a fist around the paper. 'We may have new weapons and defenses, but our armory will eventually run out if those wykes play the long game. And if word gets out we've depleted our defenses farther, we may as well throw open the new gate and invite the enemy to supper.' Elodi pushed her chair back and stood. She paced half-way to the wall, spun about and stomped back. 'And why does the Archon need me? Does he not have the most experienced generals and best skilled fighters under his command?'

Wendel kept his eyes on the window. 'Many sailed with Lord Broon and the elites, ma'am.'

'Ah yes, who could forget this *audacious* plan of his.' She hurled the scrunched-up paper across the table and clutched the back of the chair. 'I hope this mission of his is working and he hasn't just sacrificed the lives of Lord Broon and our finest on some vain whim.'

Wendel pointed to the Archon's discarded message. 'At least it appears Lord Broon's forces are doing well, ma'am. He reports seeing smoke rising from the south, that has to mean he's taken Elmarand, and his forces are wreaking havoc as commanded.'

Elodi released her grip on the chair and slumped beside Wendel. 'But is it a sign of Bardon's success, or his defeat? The Archon also states, but with the benefit of his *farsight* and not with his eyes from his ruined tower, I hasten to add, that the Golesh have not fully taken the bait, with only half the massed forces at the gate heading south.' She flicked out her hand and dispatched the Archon's order to the floor. 'If he had seen it with his own eyes, I might be more hopeful, but can he really see what's happening all those leagues away with his so-called gift?'

'I assume he must, ma'am. Archons throughout history have been blessed with *farsight*. Lord Broon surely holds the old capital, otherwise he would not contemplate opening the gate. Now we must fulfill our obligation and strike the enemy on two fronts. Lord Broon will need our support if he's to hold what he's gained.'

Elodi sighed. 'I was right about one thing. I will no longer sit tight in Calerdorn. But I had intended to ride out against the immediate threat here in Harlyn.' She sat staring at the grain on the long table as if a map. After a full minute, she straightened and looked to Wendel. 'I shall gladly ride to aid Lord Broon. But it remains a challenge to be battle-ready and in Archonholm by Midsummer's Eve.' She let her gaze wonder to the window. 'What news of Meloni? Has the poor child spoken yet?' Elodi did not know the real name of the girl they had rescued from the grasslands, choosing instead to name her after the sole survivor of a legendary battle from the days of Draegelan.

Wendel stretched out his arms. 'The healers inform me the girl continues to improve physically, but as yet, she has said very little apart from… well, you're well aware of her limited vocabulary at present, ma'am.'

Elodi shivered. 'Only too aware. The poor child has said nothing else since we found her.' She recalled the girl's wide eyes. 'By the Three, I hope we can prevent the child, and all the children of Harlyn falling into the enemy's hands. We have to hold this city regardless of the cost.'

Wendel grunted as he bent and picked up the Archon's message. 'We can take some comfort from the Archon's promise all efforts will focus on the north following a swift victory at the gate.'

Elodi turned. 'A swift victory? He is confident, I'll give him that. And yes, it would be desirable to drive these nasty creatures from our realm and back over the old trench. But what if the victory is neither swift, nor… a victory? What if we are defeated at the gate? That would leave Bardon stranded, and Calerdorn compromised.' Her stomach clenched. 'To think this has come to pass in our time, Wendel. I shall stand before the great Caerwal Gate when, after all these years, it will finally swing open.'

26. The Waters of the Menon

Toryn would not allow himself to give up on finding Hope. It may have seemed an impossible task, but if he had learned one thing from the last few months, it was never to lose heart. He looked ahead. The forest floor had leveled, the trees now stood taller and farther apart, making their path easier. Calestri and Arijan had chosen to join the pursuit of Hope, following a discussion with Eryn beyond Toryn's earshot. But despite the Amayans' legendary ability to track, they struggled to stay on Hope's trail. At times, it disappeared completely, but Eryn guessed their line was straight, and after losing and re-discovering her tracks, it appeared to be a correct assumption.

After two days, Eryn suspected they neared the center of Foranfae. And, to their relief, the Nordleng seemed to have given up on the chase, or, as the Amayans' believed, the Nym may have intervened.

'What's that noise?' Toryn stopped. 'Is that water?'

Eryn cocked an ear. 'Your hearing is good. If we're where I think we are, that should be the Menon River.'

Toryn peered through the trees ahead. 'But how do we cross? And how did the Nym get Hope over the river?'

'They have their ways. But the Menon is still in its youth in these parts. Nothing much more than a stream. But be wary. It may be narrow, but it's fast-flowing and carries the strength to dash the unprepared against the rocks.' Eryn smiled. 'But nothing we can't manage.'

Calestri and Arijan led the way down a slight slope. As they neared the bottom, the sound of gushing water grew louder, and Toryn began to think it might present more of a challenge than Eryn hoped. The going became tougher as more exposed rocks jutted from the ground, causing difficulties for the horses. But to Toryn's relief, it left an open space where the trees could not grow. He paused and looked up to an expanse of clear sky, pleased to see it for the first time in many days.

Calestri called over. 'We're in luck. An old tree has fallen and bridges the river a little farther on.'

Toryn scrambled down the bank and almost slipped on the rocks made wet by the stream splashing up from its twisted path. Arijan grabbed his arm. 'Steady there, fellow. You don't want to be falling in.' She laughed. 'Unless you want to spend the next ten days being tossed and smashed against the rocks before being ditched in the sea.'

He steadied himself. 'Thanks. And yes, I think it's best I stay out of the river.' He looked to the water streaming over the rocks hindering its way. He guessed it to be twenty paces wide and impossible to wade across without the risk of being washed away.

Eryn leaped up onto a large boulder and glanced over the other side. 'Perfect. A pool. It's been a while since I last bathed in the Menon.' She looked down to Toryn. 'I don't suppose you've ever had the chance. But these waters have the power of healing, even old wounds and sickness you may not know you carry, especially this close to its source.'

Arijan wrinkled her nose at Toryn. 'She's being polite. What she's actually trying to say, it's time you bathed. It will help *heal* the stench of your travels.' She called up to Eryn. 'I don't see why you're concerned about upsetting his feelings. He may be a wyke, but still just one of the simple folk.' She turned back to Toryn and grinned. 'And a grubby one at that.'

Eryn shook her head. 'Ignore her. The water rejuvenates and takes away the aches and pains of a long journey. Arijan. You and Calestri take the horses across on that tree. We'll join you in a moment.'

Toryn looked upstream to the large tree trunk. 'Will they cross that? Looks a bit slippery.'

'They'll be fine. You won't find more sure-footed horses in the land.' She waved to him. 'Come up.' Eryn held out a hand. 'Your body will thank you for a reviving dip.' He shinned up the boulder and joined her. She pointed to a small pool of blue water trapped by a gap among the rocks. 'Almost as if someone carved out the stone to make a bath.' They eased their way down the mossy edge and found a large, flat rock to stand upon.

Toryn eyed the still water. 'Looks deep… and cold.'

Eryn sat and pulled off her sandals, inviting Toryn to do the same. 'That's the beauty of it. Should shock the aches away.' He tugged at his shoes not realizing how swollen and tired his feet had become; and Arijan was right — he desperately needed a freshen up. He went to remove his shirt, but Eryn stayed his hand. 'Let's clean our clothes at the same time, shall we. No need to get over familiar, eh.'

Toryn felt his face flush. He nodded. 'Agreed.'

She smiled then gasped as she lowered herself into the pool. 'Less than a day away from the mountain springs of the Kolossos and certainly potent with it.'

Toryn followed, losing his breath as the icy water numbed his legs. He panted. 'Potent indeed.' Thankfully, the shock soon eased. He trod water, wriggling his toes, letting the water soak away the fatigue from his muscles. He raised his legs to float on his back and watched a white cloud drift across the blue sky as if mirroring his movement. His shoulders lost the tightness he had not realized he must have carried for many weeks. And his head cleared as the ache in his temples eased.

Eryn tapped his arm. 'Look at this.' Toryn turned to see Moonbeam approach the fallen tree. He trotted across the trunk as if a wide road. She beamed. 'That's my boy. Didn't even pause.'

Toryn watched as the other horses crossed, followed by Arijan and Calestri in the same, confident manner; he hoped he could do the same. 'Hey, Eryn.' Calestri waved her arms. 'There's another pool this side. Big enough for us all, and the horses.' Toryn looked away as Calestri stripped off her tunic and jumped in.'

Toryn smirked. 'I see she's not concerned about being over-familiar.'

Eryn called over. 'We're fine here. Be over later.'

Toryn tipped back his head to see another cloud pass overhead; this one was shaped like Elrik's hammer. 'The River Tam runs through my village. It also flows from the Kolossos, but it never felt this good. When I was young, we used to swim in it, but only in the summer, always too cold in the winter. We'd race to the benddownstream at the edge of the woods. And you know, I never lost against those my age. They used to call me—'

Eryn sighed. 'Does this story have a meaning?'

He bristled. 'Of course. I was about to say I was known by some as—'

Arijan screamed. Eryn kicked, grabbed the bank and was out of the water in a second. She stared upstream. 'What is it?'

Arijan called back. 'Cali's in trouble! I'm going in.'

Eryn ran to her sandals. 'Quick.' Toryn reached the edge, but as he pushed, his feet stung as if a keen blade sliced open the skin. He pulled himself free and glanced down expecting to see blood pouring from a wound, but the skin only appeared pink as if scorched. He grabbed his shoes, crying out as he pulled them over his pained feet, then scrambled up the rock. Ahead, Eryn had already crossed the river and crouched at the edge of the large pool. The horses reared, kicking out their front legs as if fending off an invisible threat. But of Arijan and Calestri, he could see nothing. Toryn stumbled across the slippery stones feeling every step as if his soles burned. He reached the tree bridge, looked straight ahead, and ran. Despite the pain in his feet, he made it across.

Eryn yelled. 'Quickly, fetch that branch.' He snatched up the branch and rushed to Eryn. She held up a hand. 'Don't go in. There's something wrong.' In the center of the pool, Arijan struggled to keep her head above water as she clutched onto Calestri's limp body, face down in the water. Toryn kneeled and thrust the branch towards her. Eryn cried out. 'Take hold, Ari.' Her hand flayed but missed. 'You're close. Try again.' But Arijan's gasps for air slowed, and she slipped beneath the surface, taking Calestri down with her. 'Arijan!' Eryn took a step into the pool but jumped back, crying out.

'No! Let me.' Toryn strode into the water. Immediately his feet burned but he dived under and swam hard. The water snatched at his exposed skin as if trying to strip the flesh from his bones, but he pushed on. Shards of glass thrust at his eyes, but he spied the two Amayans as they slowly sank to the bottom of the pool. Arijan still had one arm wrapped around Calestri's shoulders, but the other drifted limply at her side. A finger seemed to point towards Toryn as if a warning to stay away. He kicked on against the stinging water as it tried to force its way into his nose and throat. His muffled cry vibrated in his skull; his lungs pleaded for air, but he found the strength to fight on.

With a thrust of his legs, Toryn reached them. He clasped onto Arijan's wrist and yanked her back; Calestri came with her. But his vision darkened at the edges — he had little time before he too succumbed to the wrongness in the water. He used the last of his energy to get beneath the two, then thrashed his legs to force them to the surface. Toryn glanced up. The water above shimmered but appeared to get no closer. He fought against what felt like two claws clutching at his ankles, loath to let him free. His legs felt like dead weights as the monster below grasped hold of his waist, eager to drag its prey down to the murky, unfathomable depths.

Toryn held onto the lifeless Amayans. He calmed, no longer feeling pain. Calestri's red hair billowed as if a slow breeze lifted it from her sweet face. He marveled at the beauty of the red strands entwining with the black of Arijan, binding them at the moment of their demise. Toryn drifted. It seemed impolite to thrash out his limbs and disturb the still water. Above, the light glistened on the surface. His eyes widened. A smile crossed his lips. *Faeries!* They had come. And they danced for him. But their performance had to be viewed from below; if he surfaced, he knew he would ruin its delicate splendor. His grip on Arijan loosened. He should let them go. He should let them be free to drift, to bathe in the healing waters of the Menon for eternity.

A voice called to him. Its urgency shattered his peace, marring the moment of serenity he shared with the Amayans. He willed it to leave him, but the voice insisted he listen. Arijan's eyelids opened. Wide, brown eyes stared at him, pleading with him to act. It worked. *Take my strength!* The voice echoed. He knew it to be that of Hope. *Rise, Toryn.* Heat surged through his limbs and filled his lungs. One more kick. Just one more kick. That was all he had left, but it was sufficient.

They burst through the glass surface. Eryn cried out their names. Toryn wrapped his arm around Arijan, who still clung to Calestri, and grasped hold of the branch Eryn held. He had nothing left; no air to waste on words; no energy to move an arm or a leg. But Eryn had plenty. She dug her heels into the ground and hauled. Toryn's numb hands began to slip. With the last ounce of will he had left, he coiled his arm around the branch, then passed out.

'You can't deny it, Ari.' Toryn recognized Eryn's voice. 'He saved you both. Now you have to admit it was worth bringing him along.' Warm hands caressed his shoulders and arms. Eryn continued. 'I told you there was more to this one than meets the eye.'

Arijan agreed. 'Fine, Eryn. You were right all along, and I was wrong. He has gone up in my estimation.' Toryn thought about opening his eyes but chose instead to enjoy their rare praise.

Calestri joined them. 'He's looking a little better. I found some more twigs for the fire, but best to keep it small. Don't want to displease the Nym.' Calestri's hand rested on his chest. 'He feels warmer. I thought we'd lost him. Never seen anyone so cold, well, one that wasn't already dead.' Her soft hand stroked his face. 'Now I see him in a new light, he looks quite handsome. I may even challenge you to a dual over him, Eryn.' Toryn grinned. Calestri slapped him. 'I thought so. How long have you been awake?'

He coughed. 'Long enough to appreciate the compliments.' He sat slowly, surprised to find night had fallen.

Eryn supported his head. 'Take your time. You were in a pretty bad way.'

'How long was I out?'

'Several hours. Dawn will be upon us shortly.' Eryn pulled the blanket over his shoulders. 'That was a brave thing you did.' She nodded to the horses. 'It spooked them, and they weren't anywhere near the pool.'

Calestri smiled. 'And for that we're grateful. But how did you get us out? I couldn't move.'

Toryn looked to the pool. 'I almost didn't, but I believe Hope saved me… all of us. I started to hallucinate.' He chuckled. 'I saw faeries dancing on the surface. They convinced me to give up the fight. But just when I thought I was done, Hope's voice came to me. Somehow, she gave me the strength to get to the surface. But the pain. Have you experienced anything like that before?'

Arijan spoke for them all. 'Never. As Eryn said, the Menon's waters are known for their powers of healing. But obviously that's changed. And it's not the work of the Nym. I can't think they would poison the water, that's not their way. From what we know of them, they see us as the poison.'

Toryn shivered. 'I've felt something similar, although not so bad. It was in Noor… in the River Wend. It stung my hand when' — he groaned — 'it was downstream from one of those Singing Stones. But when we found it, it had been destroyed. I trust that's not what this is. Hope believed there were only six left now. If another has fallen, their power will fade further.'

Eryn stared at the fire. 'When you first mentioned these stones, they meant nothing to us. But whether it's down to Hope, or to nearing the center of this forest, I'm getting flashes of a distant memory.' She looked to Calestri. 'We all are. I see tall black stones, smooth and warm to the touch, but I cannot recall their purpose.'

Toryn climbed to his feet and walked to the water's edge. 'Whatever their purpose, or who they serve, the loss of one was of grave concern to Hope.' He looked down at the still, dark pool. 'And if a second has gone… it would be a tragedy.' Toryn turned back to the fire. 'How deep is that pool?'

Calestri frowned. 'That's the strange thing. When I first waded in, it came up to my shoulders. But then if felt like claws snatched at my legs and dragged me below.' Her face paled. 'They seemed to pull me down and down as if bottomless.'

Arijan nodded. 'Same for me.'

Toryn glanced to the opposite side of the stream. 'And I felt the same moments after you screamed.' He looked to Eryn. 'It had to be something that flowed down the river. Not a creature, but something *wrong* in the water itself.' He kneeled and dipped his hand in the pool, held it for a moment then withdrew. 'It's not there now. It must have come from beneath the mountains.'

Eryn added more wood to the flames. 'It does not bode well if the powerful waters of the Menon can be corrupted. We must find Hope.' She looked to Toryn. 'You named her well.'

27. A Quiet Departure

The mobilization of Harlyn's finest was going at a pace and would be ready to set sail the following day. Elodi watched the final preparations of her depleted knights from the top of the wall. Aldorman had done well to raise forty, but almost half had barely finished training, and of the other half, many had yet to make a full recovery from the poison deployed by Uldrak. But despite her concerns, the knights made for a fine sight as they completed the drills upon their proud horses. Elodi had stood taller as she watched them practice their battle formations and maneuvers, but whether they would make a difference when the gate finally opened, was another matter.

Elodi's knights would complete a force of two hundred and fifty, combining Gundrul's guards and Harlyn's most experienced soldiers and reserves. But her heart was torn in two. While she was willing to assist the Archon to defeat the Golesh in the south, and in turn, come to Bardon's aid, she was loath to abandon Calerdorn. Captain Cubric would take charge of the city's defense, commanding a force consisting mainly of Harlyn's reserve. But while Elodi drew some comfort from Cubric's many years of service, this was beyond his experience and expertise. But then she had to accept recent events were outside the experience of them all. Wendel had tried to allay her guilt stating the new defenses had made the city stronger and better prepared for a future strike. However, more troubling news had reach Elodi's ears. Her scouts had returned from Greendell to tell of a burned-out village with the macabre sight of a pile of bones at its center. But it could not have been Dohl and his small force from Dorlgoth — her scouts judged the atrocity had most likely happened in the spring. How many more of Harlyn's remote settlements had suffered the same fate?

Elodi's thoughts went back to Meloni. The girl had continued to grow stronger yet remained tight-lipped when Elodi tried to question her about the appalling night on the plain. But to her relief, Meloni no longer repeated her refrain regarding black eyes, the lady, and fire, that had chilled Elodi's blood. And when she had tried to discover the girl's real name and more about her life in Dorlgoth, Meloni would smile and run away as if playing a game. Elodi decided not to press farther, fearing the process might trigger memories best kept buried for now. The last thing she wanted was to rekindle the terror Meloni's eyes had portrayed when they had found her clutching her dead grandmother. Perhaps with time, the young girl would recover and rebuild her life with a family in Calerdorn.

The dark skies above the Dorn Mountains drew Elodi's eye. The enemy forces known to be encamped at Draegnor could unleash its wrath upon Ruan and the bridge at any moment. And what had Uldrak devised in the face of his previous unsuccessful attempt to take her city? Despite the dogged determination of Ruan and his brave spearmen, surely they could not hold the bridge indefinitely. She prayed the Archon's victory would indeed be swift as promised, thus allowing the full might of Archonholm to drive the Ruuk from her realm. Elodi had vowed not to rest until they had pushed them well into the north, inflicting losses to prevent them ever thinking of returning. But even if a victory could be achieved in days in the south, it would be late autumn before the Archon's armies rode to Harlyn's aid — and how many would survive the conflict at the gate?

A flash of lighting exposed the snow-tipped peaks in

the late evening gloom. Elodi grasped the stone ledge and waited for the sound of thunder. She counted and waited. In the absence of thunder, it could be some new devilry of Uldrak's growing power. She held her breath, then heaved a sigh as a low rumble rolled high over Calerdorn's towers. Elodi turned her back and strode along the wall towards the docks. Her eyes fixed on Harlyn's burgundy banner fluttering upon *Celestra's* main mast. Despite the demanding deadlines, Elodi had insisted a new flag be made for the ship to raise the spirits of all who would sail south. She also wanted the people of the port of West Haven to know where they had come from — the Archon was not the only one who made sacrifices to ensure the survival of the Five Realms. But even with soldiers from across the land swelling the Archon's ranks, their numbers would still be vastly inferior to those of the Golesh entrenched behind the gate. The likeness of the Archon on the tapestry came to mind. Had he the strength of those days? Or had the artist embroidered an embellished tale simply to prevent the despair of an expected future invasion.

Elodi turned to the sound of approaching footsteps. Gundrul stood before her. He nodded over his shoulder. 'I've been watching your knights, ma'am. Your man has done well to muster so many riders. They make an impressive sight, and their skill is worthy of the colors they carry.'

'He has indeed.' Elodi noted Gundrul's new admiration for Aldorman now he too had witnessed firsthand the dark arts of Uleva and Uldrak. 'And I have every confidence they will give a good account of themselves alongside the Archon's knights.' Elodi stepped forward and gripped his broad shoulder. 'And I am in no doubt your men will also do you proud, Captain. They've grown much in stature since I first set eyes upon them at

West Haven.'

'And just as well. We face a far greater challenge at the gate.'

Elodi looked back to the ship. 'And we must hope our passage south is less eventful than our journey here.'

Gundrul's red face paled. 'I doubt we'll be as lucky should another storm find us again in open sea.'

'If I am to be honest, I dread the sea voyage as much as the opening of the great gate.'

The day dawned with a gray light that did little to ease Elodi's anxiety. But she was grateful the strong winds of the night had weakened to a tame breeze that barely stirred the waters of the Elessyn Sea. Elodi stood with Wendel on the docks as the people gathered. But this was not the same flag-waving crowd that greeted their arrival only weeks before. The folk of Calerdorn would bid farewell to their men and women with the knowledge, even in victory, many of their loved ones would not return. And, of course, if defeated, the next show of force to march through the city would be a marauding army bent on revenge.

Captain Horace approached with his eyes beaming from his ruddy face. He nodded to Elodi. 'All shipshape and ready to sail when you are, ma'am.'

Elodi feared to ask the question that had kept her awake for much of the night. 'And the forecast?'

Horace ran a red, cracked hand across his chin supporting a new beard. 'Well, ma'am. I'm not accustomed to the waters this close to the top of the world, but' — he glanced from Wendel back to Elodi — 'I'd say the wind will be at our backs and we'll be in West Haven before you know it.'

'And… the storms?'

He lifted his head and smelled the air. 'Far out to sea I

would say.' He cast his eye to the horizon. 'I'd go farther and say the storms are nowhere near these shores, causing mischief somewhere on the very edge of the sea. Maybe even on the night side of the world beneath.' He folded his thick arms. 'No. Nothing to fear on this voyage. Nothing at all. And if I'm wrong' — he tugged on his whiskers — 'you can make a brush from my beard to comb your fine horse's mane.'

Elodi laughed, grateful for the captain's confidence and good humor. 'Thank you, Horace. I'm encouraged by your conviction if you're willing to wager your fine beard. And may I say it's very becoming.'

He winked. 'Can't be a proper captain without one, ma'am. Need to have something to stroke while I ponder my next order, or which sail to raise.' Horace nodded over his shoulder. 'And the crew can hardly be expected to respect a cappy who goes bare-chinned to sea can they.'

'I expect not. And may your whiskers keep you warm at the helm.'

Wendel cleared his throat. 'Preparations, ma'am?'

'Ah, yes. And how are the horses, Captain?'

Horace straightened. 'All settled below with enough fodder to keep them happy for days. And don't you worry, Sea Mist is comfortable and seems excited to be back onboard.'

Elodi glanced to the *Celestra* sitting low in the water. 'I was pleased to hear he didn't resist the gangplank. You'd have thought his last experience would have turned him off ships for good.'

'Ah, now there you can be reassured again. Your clever horse knows. He can tell the weather will be in our favor.'

Elodi turned as the remainder of Harlyn's forces approached. A murmur rose from the crowd but nothing more. This was no ceremony. The situation called for an orderly boarding and prompt departure. She stood on the quayside beside the gangplank, catching the eyes of the men and women as they formed a single line to board the *Celestra*. Each knew their duty; each knew it could result in their death. At the gate, Elodi would lead from the front astride Sea Mist beside the Archon's forces; her people expected nothing less from her. But those departing were well aware, those remaining in the city also faced danger.

Aldorman arrived at the dock followed by his knights. All their equipment of war was already stored away in the ship's hold, making her knights look vulnerable without their armor and on foot. Elodi glanced back to the city, dearly wishing she could lead an army of Amayan warriors to the battle at the gate.

The last of Aldorman's knights stepped onboard. Elodi addressed her captains. 'I have no words for this occasion, gentlemen, as I'm sure none are needed.' She held out her hand to invite Gundrul onto the gangway.

He accepted the invitation. 'Thank you, ma'am.' The others followed in silence.

Elodi turned as Cubric approached. 'Look after my city please, Captain. I hope to return as soon as the situation at the gate is resolved.'

Cubric saluted. 'I will defend your fair realm right up to my dying breath, ma'am.'

She grasped his forearm. 'I trust it won't come to that. And please, no matter how busy, please remember to visit Meloni. Ensuring her recovery somehow atones for the sacrifice of the Dorlgoth folk and that tragic archer. Please tell her I will come to see her the moment I return. Perhaps she will be speaking freely by then.'

Cubric nodded. 'Certainly, ma'am. She's a brave one. And her bright smile reminds me why I fight on.'

Elodi turned to Wendel. He took her hands. 'Ma'am…' he clenched his jaw, 'may the Three be with you, and' — he held her gaze — 'trust in the blood that runs strong in your veins.'

'Wendel…' Elodi's eyes burned, 'I dearly hope this isn't the last time we speak, but on behalf of the realm and my father, I'd like to thank you for your many years of service, just in case…'

Wendel squeezed her hand. 'I know, ma'am, and thank you for the honor. Fair thee well.'

Elodi turned away and boarded the *Celestra.* She made her way to the bow as Wendel had suggested. She would have rather gone below and be with Sea Mist, but it would be unbecoming not to be seen. Elodi took her place alongside her captains behind the figurehead as the sailors clambered up and down the masts making ready the sails. The mooring ropes were untied and flung on the deck. Horace bellowed his commands, looking every part a capable captain. The *Celestra* stirred for what could be her most important voyage in many a century. A few children ran alongside the edge of the quay as the ship glided and quickly gained speed as if eager to return to open seas. Elodi looked up to the colors on the main mast, but the heavy fabric of Harlyn's flag remained yet unmoved by the light breeze filling the sails.

Trumpets on the walls above blared. Elodi looked up to the city's tallest tower, suddenly annoyed she had forgotten to give the order there should be no fanfares. But her heart caught in her throat. Thick, black smoke billowed high into the eastern sky. The trumpets blasted once more. Her blood froze.

This was no fanfare — it was a warning of an imminent attack.

28. A Challenge Declined

How could this happen? Elodi stood dumfounded at the top of the ramp before Calerdorn's main gate. She gawped at the seething, dark mass emerging from beneath the smoke of the burning plain, refusing to believe the unfolding scene. Her arms hung limp at her sides; her armor weighed heavily on her stooped shoulders. Elodi fought to stand tall when her body desired to sink to its knees and crumble. How had her scouts failed to send word of such an imposing force moving against them? Tears filled her smarting eyes from the fumes blowing towards the city.

Gundrul choked as he strode out of the gate to stand beside her. 'Let us be thankful of one thing, ma'am.'

Elodi stared back. 'Thankful? For what?'

'Had Uldrak waited a little longer, we'd be sailing south, blissfully unaware of the attack until it was too late.'

She trembled. 'Will we make any difference to the outcome?' Elodi reluctantly looked back to the threat. 'He's brought three times as many against us this time.' She scanned the front lines. 'Uldrak must have drained the Mawlgrim in parts. They cannot have come through the pass. Only this morning we received word from Ruan. The bridge remains in his hands. But if he's stranded…?'

'We can send word, ma'am. I trust our birds will make it past this army.'

Elodi checked the straps on her breastplate. 'How will this day end, Captain?'

Gundrul nodded to the defenses. 'Don't let your spirits drop. Even with his numbers, I'd rather be here defending than attacking from out there on the plain.'

'Yet still he approaches.' Elodi turned her back on the invaders, trying to clear her head and think. She glanced across to the crews rapidly readying their weapons on the new ramparts outside the city. More scurried across the top of the main wall towards the trebuchets. Had the drills prepared them for the terror emerging from the plain? She quickly ran through Gundrul's tactics. The main gate would remain open while the positions outside were active. If the enemy came close enough to unleash their weapons, her crews would retreat to the city, and the gate would be closed. Elodi drew comfort from the longer range available to them, plus, the addition of the captured ballistae could rip through the narrow attacker's formations needed to negotiate the gap between the trenches and spikes. Elodi had to remain strong and have faith in their defenses.

Gundrul pointed. 'The main force has stopped, ma'am. Just beyond our range.'

Elodi spun around. She peered under the billowing smoke. 'Can he burn our spikes?'

'No, ma'am. Not with ordinary fire, they're thick and well treated for such an attack. And I would say even that unnatural fire of his would take days to destroy them.' Gundrul widened his stance. 'And if he tries to bridge the trenches, our trebuchets will soon smash them. I've been impressed by their accuracy following the relentless drills.' He chuckled. 'They may have grumbled at the time, but I reckon they're grateful now.'

But Elodi had stopped listening. At the first line of trenches, a lone, cloaked figure strode with unnerving confidence towards them. 'Uldrak.' She muttered under her breath, almost fearing he could hear her words. 'I wonder what evil he's brought to Calerdorn this time.' She caught her breath. Another figure, astride a horse, emerged from the front ranks. A swirling dark cloud hung over her, darker than the haze above. Despite the distance, Elodi knew it had to be Uleva. She stiffened, desperate to stand tall in the face of two powerful wykes. This time, there was to be no rash attack. This time, Elodi feared Uleva would command a larger, better-prepared army than Uldrak alone. She scanned the defenses once more — she must not lose hope. Calerdorn represented a daunting position to conquer, and she must take control. Elodi found she spoke to reassure herself. 'We have more weapons, more ammunition, better defenses.' But today, she could not easily lead her knights out onto the plain should all else fail. Elodi clenched her fists. She would *not* fail. She must not fail.

'Those rakes are up to something. Look they've stopped.' Gundrul groaned. 'I believe there's our answer to why we received no warning.' Uldrak held up a long staff with eight, odd-shaped baubles dangling from short chains. Elodi gasped. Gundrul bowed his head. 'The swine bears a grim trophy. I hate to say this, but I'd wager those are the heads of your scouts.'

Elodi recoiled. One of Uldrak's grotesque trophies had to be the head of Shelan, the woman who had braved the narrow bridge at Tunduska prior to the attack. Her mouth curled. 'If part of this force has come from Drunsberg, am I to assume the same fate has befallen those who watched over the mines?'

The captain sighed. 'I fear you may be right on both counts, ma'am.'

Elodi's hand gripped her sword's hilt. 'I'll make him suffer for this. It's not enough for him to threaten my city for a second time, he has to do this?'

Gundrul placed his hand on her shoulder. 'Steady, ma'am. Don't rise to it. We must keep a cool head. He's done this for the very reason to get under your skin.'

Elodi relented. 'You don't have to worry about me, Captain. I shall remain in command of my anger as I gladly remove both their rotten heads.'

Uldrak rammed the staff into the ground leaving the heads to swing, looking oddly like a child's toy. Uleva dismounted and strode to stand in front of Uldrak. Gundrul spat. 'Apologies for my behavior, but the taste of that smoke is wrong.'

Elodi grimaced. 'I dread to think what burns. And, Gundrul.' She too, spat. 'You need not apologize. I think we'll both witness worse atrocities than either of us spitting in the coming hours.'

Gundrul manage to chuckle. 'Pre-battle humor, ma'am?'

'A poor attempt, I admit.'

Her captain squinted at the two wykes. 'There's something very evil about that woman… if that's what she is. I can feel it from here.' He fidgeted with his sword. 'Can't say I'd welcome a face-to-face confrontation with her.'

Elodi's tongue clicked as she spoke. 'I hope it doesn't come to that. Are they in range, Captain? I've had just about enough of this ghoulish show.'

'At the very edge I would say.'

She glanced to the walls. 'Then let them have a volley. If anything, it will throw hot dirt into their smug faces.'

'Very well, ma'am.' Gundrul turned and waved to a man on the outer wall, then splayed his fingers twice. A trumpet blared a command.

Elodi fixed her eyes on the wykes, offering a silent prayer to the Three. 'Would it be too much to finish this with the first shots?'

'That would be something, ma'am.' Elodi braced as two flaming spheres surged skyward from the rampart. A cheer from the walls urged their warning shots on their flaming way. She watched them reach the pinnacle of their trajectory then hurtle earthbound. The two wykes remained unmoved, nonchalant even, as they appeared to observe the attack with disdain. Uldrak waved his arms over his head. The shots exploded on impact, just short of their intended target. Fingers of fire snatched at the air above the wykes, only to be brushed aside by the same shimmering shield seen in the battle for the gatehouse.

Elodi slumped. 'I suspected that would happen. Perhaps a bolt from a ballista would be a better option once in range.'

Gundrul signaled to the crews to cease the attack. 'Best not to waste any more ammunition on them. We'll save it for the army behind. I can't think those two devils can protect them all.'

'Even if they had the will.' Elodi peered into the dwindling flames of their failed strike. 'They're moving again.' She glanced over her shoulder. 'I'd hoped Sea Mist would have been brought here by now. I'd feel happier on my horse.'

'Stand firm, ma'am. I wouldn't recommend riding out to *greet* them so soon. Let's see what they have in mind before making our next move.'

'But I cannot abide sitting back. I feel I have to act.'

'To sit back and wait is still to act, ma'am. You'll know when the time is right.'

Elodi took a step down the ramp. 'I see his main force are waiting.' She fixed her eyes on the two cloaked figures strolling through the outer defenses. 'What are they doing?' The dark cloud above Uleva grew, obscuring Elodi's view of the road behind the wykes. Shapes moved within, churning the air as if it boiled. A new stench caught in her throat. Her pulse quickened as she was reminded of the smell of a blacksmith's forge. With growing dread, she knew her time to act was drawing near.

Behind in the city, she sensed thousands of hands clenching weapons, handles on buckets of water, and the hands of their beloved. Elodi choked. 'We have to do something now, Captain. For all we know they're advancing beneath that damnable cloud.'

'Agreed, ma'am. Even if just to raise our spirits.'

'Good. One round from every heavy weapon we have at our disposal. Yes, that should do it.' Gundrul signaled to ready the attack. Elodi held her breath, staring at the angry cloud growing ever closer. Shouts at her sides, drew her eye. Artillery crews scampered over their trebuchets and ballistae, preparing to unleash what would be the most fearsome vedisplay of strength in living memory. Part of Elodi regretted her action, but she could not afford to allow their foe another step unanswered.

Calerdorn shuddered as she vented her fury at the veiled threat. For a moment, Elodi was appalled by the violence she had let loose upon the plain. The ramp shook. She stumbled as dozens of bolts and fireballs struck home. The ground beneath the cloud erupted, throwing up spouts of flame like giant hands above the broiling mass. But to Elodi's dismay, they quickly sank like drowning souls snatching in vain for help, as if swallowed by a stormy sea. The flames died, smothered by Uleva's dark mantle.

The two wykes emerged unscathed from under the cloud. Even from this range, Elodi's stomach recoiled at the cruel, pale white line of Uldrak's grin beneath his hood. But Uleva remained cloaked in a shroud of mist — yet Elodi did not need to see her face to fear her. The wykes stepped to either side of the road and raised their hands as if introducing an act at a play.

Elodi's heart sank; her mouth gaped. 'No… no. Not now, not here.' She knew instantly the reason for her enemy's boldness. The sound of hooves thundering on the cobbled road echoed throughout the city. A great white stallion galloped through, bearing the bravest knight in the history of the Seven Realms: Dorlan. The fog retreated before him like his foes of old upon the battlefield. Dorlan held aloft the burgundy banner of Harlyn bearing his own silver shield. If Elodi had any doubt this man was indeed Dorlan, they evaporated like the smoke. She stared wide-eyed at the glittering armor, the fluttering banner, and his sword catching the sunlight streaming through the clearing skies. Elodi groaned; even the sun appeared to take his side.

'No!' Elodi staggered back. Behind Dorlan, a row of horses formed in front of the last trench. The horses bore the twenty-two knights lost at Durran Wood. But these were not the same knights who had stood with Aldorman. Their dented armor could not conceal their distorted forms as they sat uneasily on their mounts. Elodi's hand went to her mouth, appalled at the corruption of her once fine men and women. 'How are we to resist, Captain?' She grasped Gundrul's arm. 'All is lost! We cannot fight a legend who leads our own knights.'

Dorlan drew Draego to a halt thirty paces from Elodi's position. He opened his visor and bellowed. 'Surrender! Surrender or die by my hand.' A cry of dismay went up from those on the walls and outer defenses; some abandoned their posts, fleeing to the main gate.

Gundrul tried in vain to rally the defenses. 'Hold your positions! Your realm needs you.'

But Elodi had nothing. She slumped, her head shaking in disbelief it had come to this. The great hero of Harlyn had returned, not riding to their aid as the legend promised, but leading a vile enemy to crush them.

Dorlan's burning eyes met Elodi's desperate gaze. He leveled his sword at her. She could feel the blade at her throat. She should hurl back words of defiance to reassure

Calerdorn she remained in command. But the words would not come. Dorlan's eyes bulged as if consumed by hate for his own people. He turned Draego and trotted a short way along the line of the pitiful knights who struggled to stay upright. Elodi could only look on with horror, dreading to imagine what appalling act had been performed on the poor souls.

Dorlan led his horse along their formation, performing a mock inspection. He completed the charade and took his position at the center. He sat tall and threw back his head. 'This is *my* city!' He thrust out his sword arm at Elodi. 'And you, *lady*, stand in my way.' He sheathed his blade. 'I give you a choice.' His body convulsed. 'Fight me alone, and should you win, your people will be granted a quick death when the city falls.' Dorlan looked up and addressed those on the walls. 'But should your leader retreat and cower behind your gate, Calerdorn will still fall, and all will suffer a terrible fate.'

Gundrul nudged her. He rasped. 'Ma'am. You must answer.'

She stammered, trying to find her voice. 'I… I have no choice. I cannot back down.'

'No!' Gundrul took her hand. 'You cannot fight this… this giant of a man. It will mean your certain death.' He released his grip. 'Apologies, ma'am, but it would be madness to throw your life away like this.'

Elodi's eyes stayed fixed on Dorlan's imposing figure. She would surely be defeated. How could she possibly beat this man? 'But I will lose face. And the people will suffer.'

Gundrul pleaded. 'You cannot trust his word. The mob are baying for blood. They want this city and all within. Do you think those wykes will deny these beasts the sacking of the city and their' — his mouth twisted — 'sport?'

Elodi's heart pounded in her ears. 'Then what can I do?'

Dorlan renewed his challenge. 'What say you, usurper? I claim *my* city. Do you fight, or tremble behind your walls like a frightened child?' Calerdorn stood silent awaiting Lady Harlyn's reply.

Gundrul spoke through gritted teeth. 'Think fast, my lady. You must answer.'

Elodi looked to the skies. What would her father have done? What would her people expect of their leader? She straightened, taking a step forward. 'Harlyn…' her voice croaked. She swallowed hard, bracing herself to deliver the most important speech of her short life. A whinny! Elodi spun around as Sea Mist galloped out of the main gate. His head nodded as he met her, unfazed by the sight before him. Elodi leaped onto his back, drew her sword, and held it high, despite her trembling arm. She felt Sea Mist's back rise, giving her courage.

She hurled her defiance in Dorlan's face. 'Harlyn does not recognize you, imposter!' She glared at the knight as the fire within her stirred. 'How dare you claim to be Dorlan. How dare you come before *our* gates in the guise of *our* hero and bring *our* knights to fight against us. I do not recognize you or your claim.' Elodi nudged Sea Mist forward, lowering her sword at Dorlan. Its blade glowed orange. Wendel's words came to mind, *trust in the blood that runs strong in your veins.* Heat surged through her body. She yelled. 'Your words are worthless. You have no power here. Now get you gone from my city!'

Draego took a step back against Dorlan's wish. Elodi urged Sea Mist closer, now only twenty paces from him. She saw a flicker of doubt in the great knight's face as, perhaps Uleva's hold on him wavered. Behind, Uleva stirred, as Elodi guessed the wyke sensed Elodi's Amayan blood.

Gundrul gasped. 'What the—?' He called out. 'Ma'am! Behind you.'

Sea Mist reared up, screaming in pain. Elodi grasped his neck to prevent her fall. She spun around. Blood spurted from a wound in his rear leg, splashing the cobbles… and the white nightgown of a young girl. Elodi gaped. 'Meloni!' The child grinned back as she held up a glistening, red dagger. Elodi screamed at her. 'What have you done?'

Meloni cried out with glee as she beheld Dorlan. The girl threw down her knife and ran open-armed to greet him. Dorlan leaned forward and pulled the bloodied child onto Draego. Dorlan grinned, tipped back his head and laughed. If Elodi's words had raised the hopes of the city, Dorlan's disdain now tore them to shreds. He turned to his slave knights, spitting out his scorn. 'See how even a small child causes so much mayhem. See how far the once great realm of Harlyn has fallen.'

Sea Mist settled but struggled to stand firm. Elodi gripped her reins. 'Steady, boy, steady. We must hold our ground.' The light in her blade faltered, but she forced herself upright to face Dorlan's mirth. She found her voice. 'By the power vested in me, I, Lady of Harlyn, demand you leave.' But her words had lost their strength, failing to convince those who heard.

Meloni giggled. Dorlan sneered. 'Then you are foolish, not worthy of your title.' His voice boomed, sounding too loud, even for his large frame. 'Prepare to lose everything you hold dear!' He thrust his sword skyward. A bolt of lightning shot forth — Meloni clapped her hands and screamed with joy as the air crackled. Elodi's skin tingled; her hair stood on end beneath her helm.

Gundrul pointed. 'They move, ma'am!' Elodi groaned. While Dorlan had her attention, the mass ranks of the enemy had advanced. Rows upon rows of heavily armored

Ruuk burst from beneath the last vestige of Uleva's shroud. Elodi's heart sank; they would gain the gates before they could be fully closed.

Elodi cried out. 'One more volley, Captain!' She could barely give her next command, but reluctantly she formed the words she never wanted to utter. 'Then sound the retreat.' She turned Sea Mist as her heavy weapons let loose what she guessed would be a futile gesture. They hurried up the ramp to the main gate. The ground trembled. She glanced behind to see the shots land. Many found their targets, throwing up flaming dirt and bodies of the advancing Ruuk. But none troubled the wykes or Dorlan. The trumpets blared the retreat. The remaining crews from the ramparts scampered from their platforms and dashed for the open gates as the trebuchets from the walls reloaded.

The clatter of hooves on the cobbles of the gatehouse gave her hope. Aldorman and his knights formed a line, ready to ride out to challenge Dorlan. Sea Mist rallied at the sight of the horses. He stamped his feet to prove he was fit to join them. Elodi yelled to Aldorman above the cries of the attackers. 'The gates, Captain! We must give them time to close. We have to disrupt the assault.'

But Gundrul planted his ample frame before her horse. 'Madness, ma'am! Sea Mist is injured. You'll all be lost, and the gatehouse will still fall.' The first of the Ruuk fell upon the slowest of the artillery crews rushing for the gate. Gundrul jabbed his finger over Elodi's shoulder. 'The inner gate is our only chance.' He pointed upwards. 'The archers can thin their ranks.'

Elodi wavered at the sight of the advancing masses of the Ruuk. Dorlan and his horsemen waited alongside Uleva and Uldrak at the foot of the ramp, while Meloni laughed as if playing a childish prank on her friends. Elodi slammed her hand against the armor on her thigh. She wheeled her sword above her head. 'Retreat! To the inner gate.' She spurred Sea Mist back to the city as the archers let loose a volley. The first Ruuk surging for the main gate fell, but too many were ready to take their place, clambering over the dead, anticipating their promised plunder.

Elodi and her knights made it through the inner gate. She commanded Aldorman to form a line behind the reserves taking their positions. Elodi spurred Sea Mist back through the gate to help the stragglers inside. The archers unloaded volley after volley onto the attackers, but no matter how many fell, it appeared only to delay the inevitable.

Gundrul staggered to her side. 'Dorlan and the wykes have entered the main gate, ma'am.'

Her stomach clenched. The archers faltered. She cried up to the parapet. 'He's not Dorlan! He cannot be. Take him down. Take the imposter down.' But she knew they could not touch him. Dorlan circled his sword. A shield of rippling air formed, shattering the arrows before they could reach those he protected. Again, he and Meloni laughed, mocking Elodi and her people. He roared above the din. 'You are not deserving of such a fine city, *Lady Harlyn*. Your ancestors would be ashamed of what you have become.' He caught Elodi's eye. 'Leave now!'

Gundrul pleaded with Elodi. 'Please! Get back, ma'am. The archers flee. The Ruuk will be upon us before we can close the inner gate.'

Fighting tears of rage, Elodi relented. She retreated with the last of the surviving soldiers from the gatehouse. She held back until all made it through. But just as they were about to close, she spied a large ram poke its bulbous, ugly nose beneath the main gate. The inner gate closed, shutting out the noise of the baying mob. But Elodi knew it was but a short reprieve. She dismounted and stumbled to the first line of the reserves. Gundrul stood with her as they faced the gate. Her sword felt suddenly heavy, and she doubted she had the strength to wield it.

Dorlan's voice carried over the inner wall, chiding her from the gatehouse. 'I bring a gift for you, *lady*. Wrought from the very ores of your mines.'

Gundrul frowned. Elodi felt the fight drain from her body. 'It's a monstrous battering ram. This gate cannot withstand more than two blows at most.'

He sighed. 'Ma'am. Then you have no other choice. You must abandon the city.'

She gawped at her captain. 'Abandon! I… I cannot.' The sound of the wheels trundling across the cobbles beyond the gate, left no doubt in anyone's mind of the size of Dorlan's gift. A cheer went up from a thousand hoarse Ruuk throats. Elodi despaired. 'But I cannot leave it to *them*.'

Gundrul shouted above the cruel taunts as the ram was made ready. 'You have no other course of action left. How will your soldiers fare against Dorlan? And that's just one man. We're outnumbered five to one by the Ruuk. The *Celestra* is ready to sail. Get everyone you can on the fishing boats and any vessel that can sail. You must escape while you still have the chance.'

Elodi's mouth moved, but her words took time. 'Abandon the city?' The road trembled as the great wheels of the ram hurtled towards the gate.

Gundrul yelled into her ear. 'You have no choice! The gate will not hold for long. It's all but lost. If you don't go now, all will perish, and you'll never win the city back.' The ram slammed into the gate. The metal hinges buckled as the wood shattered. A hideous, barbed nose protruded from the wound. Gundrul took her hand. 'They'll torture you, torment you, bind you, then hang you from the highest tower, but they won't grant you death.' He pleaded. 'Please, my dear lady. I cannot let them do that to you. Please, Elodi, you must go!'

The gate splintered as the metal barbs of the ram tore into the wood as it was wrenched back. The hinges bent; a dozen, dislodged bolts clattered to the flagstones. Dorlan laughed. 'Is my gift to your liking, lady? I shall bring more should it not please you, *Elodi*.' The use of her name hurt. The child in her would have given anything for her hero to speak it, but now, the name chosen by her mother, was defiled by Dorlan's cruel mouth.

Gundrul thrust his hand towards the dock. 'We must sail. Go to Archonholm. Defeat the enemy in the south, then return with the Archon's forces.'

Elodi's knees buckled. 'Then you come also. We'll get as many onto the boats as we can, then we'll head south.' She barely felt the stone beneath her feet as she allowed Gundrul to lead her and Sea Mist to the docks. She was vaguely aware of the stench of sulfur; people rushing by her; the screams and cries of despair, but she remained numb to the grief of the city as it yielded to the old enemy. Elodi could not contemplate losing Calerdorn. For more than a thousand years it had stood, even in the face of the greater evils of the past. But it would be lost on her watch. Elodi cared not for how history would judge her actions — even if there were survivors to speak of the disaster. She cared only for the suffering of the thousands who trusted their safety to her leadership and the walls of Calerdorn.

Gundrul halted and spun to face her. He frowned. 'Ma'am? Your orders.'

Elodi blinked, surprised to find herself at the wharf. She stared at the dozens of overcrowded fishing boats already heading for the open sea. Fresh smoke billowed over their heads as more people rushed to the quay, many slipped and fell into the water, many would drown as no one had the time to stop and rescue them. The sounds of panic burst Elodi's ears. She cried out, clenching her fists. She had to act. Captain Cubric hurried to meet them. She grasped his shoulder. 'Where is Aldorman? Where are the knights?'

Cubric pointed. 'Boarding the *Celestra.* More are on their way. The horses are all on board, let my man take Sea Mist, ma'am.' He glanced to the wound on his leg. 'He needs attention now.'

'That… girl? How could she do that? We saved her on the plain.'

Cubric frowned. 'Meloni? She wounded Sea Mist?'

More cries went up. Elodi jumped. She glanced to the opposite side of the docks used by the fisherman. Hundreds more poured onto the jetties, desperate to find space on a boat. She searched the crowds. 'Who supervises the evacuation?'

Cubric threw up his hands. 'No one. It's everyone for themselves, ma'am. There was no time to organize a proper retreat.'

'And Wendel?' She scanned the panicked faces of the crowd. 'Is he here?'

'No, ma'am. I've not seen him.'

Her heart raced. 'Where is he? I need him here. Please, Captain. Send one of your guards. He has to be located.'

Cubric stared back. 'But where? Ma'am, where would he be?'

Elodi's mind began to clear. 'The archives! He'll be in the library trying to save the scrolls.' She grabbed his shoulder. 'Send someone immediately. We only have minutes before they're all over the city.'

Cubric saluted. 'I'll go myself. Be sure if he's there, I'll get him onboard the *Celestra.*'

'Bless you, Cubric. Please, be quick. He must be saved.'

She turned to Gundrul. 'We must get word to Ruan. But the Ruuk will be watching for our birds. He cannot be left stranded, but who could possibly—?' She spied Lena, the rider who had made the journey to Midwyche. Elodi waved frantically. The rider saw her and pushed her way through the crush. She took Lena's hand. 'What I ask of you is more than I could expect you to deliver. But time is short, and the need is great, very great.'

Lena nodded. 'Whatever you command of me, ma'am.'

'It is not a command, it's a plea.' Elodi winced at the sound of wood splintering from a strike on the harbor gates. 'Word needs to reach Captain Ruan at Tunduska's Gorge. He must withdraw immediately and head south' — Elodi's mind raced — 'to Seransea if he and his men can make it. Tell him of the fall of…' her voice faltered, 'the fall of Calerdorn. He has to withdraw before he is surrounded.'

Lena eyed the gate as it buckled. 'Will you meet him at the port, ma'am?'

'No. I must sail with haste onto Archonholm. I shall set up my Council at the port and leave word of my mission. Tell the captain to seek the Town Steward. I will inform him of my plans.' She grasped Lena's shoulder. 'What I ask of you is fraught with danger, but you are the fastest rider in the realm, and I can entrust this task to no other.'

'Tempest and I will not fail you, ma'am.'

Elodi gritted her teeth, determined not to show her apprehension. 'Leave by the postern gate to the north. If we're lucky, their attention will be focused on the main entrance, and you'll find a way through the foothills.' Lena nodded, but the enormity of her mission could not be concealed from her face. Elodi held her gaze. 'Ride well, ride true. Your service will never be forgotten.' But as the words left her mouth, Elodi dreaded it would be Lena's sacrifice that would remain with her until her dying day. She watched in awe as Lena turned and strode with purpose through the panic of the docks.

'Ma'am!' Gundrul nodded to the harbor gates. 'We must depart. The *Celestra* is as ready as she can be.'

'But Wendel? He's not here?' She stood on her toes, desperate to see his face among the crowd.'

Gundrul pointed. 'There! Cubric has him.' She turned. Cubric and a guard carried Wendel between them. Her advisor gasped for breath, looking paler than she had ever seen him. In his hands, he clutched a small box. She rushed to him.

Cubric yelled over the din. 'You were right, ma'am. We found him staggering down the steps from the library. Then he passed out.'

'May the Three thank you, Captain. Get him onboard and find a healer.'

Gundrul gripped her arm. 'Now you, ma'am. You must leave while you still can. Should the enemy take the quay, they'll sink the ship before we're out of dock.'

Elodi's stomach churned. Few vessels remained in the harbor, yet hundreds of people still packed the quayside, desperately searching for a means to escape. 'Very well, Captain. But not until we have as many as we can get on board. We can take them to Seransea before sailing on to West Haven.' She tried to work out the numbers. Even if the *Celestra* was packed to the point of sinking, scores would remain stranded, and how many had already fallen at the hands of their assailants?

A cry went up as the gate shattered. The thin line of reserves staggered back at the sudden onslaught of Ruuk, heavily outnumbering the brave few who tried to hold the entrance. Elodi bit her lip as her soldiers fell to savage blows, but still they held. Archers hastily formed on nearby steps and shot over the defenders' heads. Yet, despite their efforts, the attackers advance could only be slowed, delaying their predictable victory for a few precious moments. But it brought time enough for more to clamber onboard the *Celestra*. Elodi backed towards the ship, not wanting to take her eyes from the final battle before the city fell.

'Ma'am! It has to be now.' Gundrul took her arm. 'She's ready to sail.' He bundled her onto the gangplank, apologizing as they crossed. She stumbled and fell onto those cramming the deck to bursting. Two sailors untied the plank and threw it into the water, having no time to secure it onboard. Elodi struggled against the massed bodies and the sway of the *Celestra* as the sails unfurled, but she had to know what was happening at the entrance to the quay. She cried out as the last of the defenders toppled over the wharf and crashed into the water; she doubted any would survive. Elodi longed to turn the ship around and pull them free, but had to accept more lives would be lost. Tears streamed down her face. But the horror had not ended.

Dorlan led his sullied knights galloping into the harbor. Elodi was thankful to see Meloni no longer rode with him. The enemy cheered as he charged his horse at the stragglers who had failed to find a boat. They had no other course but to leap from his path into the water. Elodi's eyes burned at the atrocity unfolding in her once peaceful city. Dorlan's gaze fell upon the ship. He slowed Draego and trotted along the pier taunting those on the *Celestra*.

But he saved his last words for Elodi.

Dorlan halted Draego at the end of the quayside. His face twisted and his eyes glared as if throwing bolts of fire at Elodi. 'The city is mine! All Harlyn will bow before me.' He leveled his sword at her. 'You may flee south, but don't think you can avoid me. You and the Archon will come to feel the pain of my swift blade.'

29. March of the Vanquished

'We've seen no tracks for over a league now.' Eryn stood and wiped her hands. 'They must have changed route once they crossed the river.' She looked back and sighed. 'Or they never came this far and doubled back.'

Toryn caught up with Eryn and scanned the trees behind her. 'Hope came this way. I know she did.'

Arijan eyed him. 'We could walk around in circles for months and still not find her. The Nym are no fools. They won't make it easy. We came close to drowning in a shallow pool yesterday. If some power in this forest wants us dead, they won't have to try much harder next time. And what makes you think this *friend* of yours yet lives?'

Toryn recalled the voice in the water. 'She lives. And just as well, otherwise we wouldn't have made it out of that pool.'

Calestri put her arm around him. 'A few days ago, I struggled to believe a word that came out of your mouth, but now…?' She squeezed. 'After your heroics yesterday, I'm happy to listen to what you have to say. And you, Eryn? Should we continue?'

'We should. Let's find Hope, she has the answers to the mystery that now pains us. We find her, solve this puzzle, then we seek Amyra. Her skills and counsel will be vital in the coming months.'

Moonbeam stamped his hoof. Eryn turned. 'What's the matter, boy?' She patted his nose. 'Hold up, he's nervous.' She followed his gaze. Eryn whispered. 'Something lies up ahead.' She pointed. 'There. See. The trees thin out. I can see open sky beyond.' Toryn peered through the trunks and, for a fleeting moment, thought he could see patches of blue. But when he looked again, they had gone.

He checked. 'Are you sure?'

Eryn straightened. 'Yes, can't you see, it's…' she frowned. She asked Calestri. 'Did you see it? I was certain I saw blue sky.'

Calestri shrugged. 'Sorry. I was looking out for tracks.'

Arijan squinted. 'All I can see is more trees.'

'You stay. I'll check.' Eryn strode on, calling back. 'I'm sure the trees are thinning.' She returned and stroked Moonbeam's muzzle. 'It looks safe. We'll press on once the horses have calmed. There's plenty more light left in this day yet.'

They walked for another hour. At times, they all thought they caught a glimpse of open sky a little way ahead. But each time they neared what they believed to be a clearing, the trees thickened and blocked their way.

'Stop!' Eryn held up her hand. 'Look. There. I can definitely see an opening ahead.' She turned as she pointed. 'Can you all see that?' Toryn nodded, but the other Amayans could not be sure. Eryn threw up her hands. 'This wretched forest.' She thrust her finger to the trees ahead. 'There. Just over there, it's— Aargh! It's gone again.'

'No wait.' Arijan took a step. 'I can see the edge. And yes, beyond that, there's open sky. We should—' she gasped — 'Eryn? Cali?'

Toryn blinked. Arijan had been at his side, but now she stood twenty paces from him. He spun around. Eryn appeared farther away still, but he could not locate Calestri. He called to Arijan. 'Can you see me?'

She nodded. 'But where are the others?'

'Over here.' Eryn's voice seemed muffled. 'Don't move. I can hear Cali, but she's very faint. I'll get her to come to me, then we'll find you.'

'Toryn is nearby. I'll get him to join me.' Arijan waved her arms at him. 'Keep your eyes on me and walk.' She beckoned. 'Whatever you do, don't take your eyes off me for one moment. Don't even blink.' Toryn forced his eyes wide-open, fixed his gaze on Arijan and walked, deliberately lifting his feet so he did not trip. His eyes began to smart, but he forced himself not to blink. To his relief, he finally stepped up to Arijan. She smiled. 'Here. Link arms.' Arijan called to Eryn. 'Toryn's with me. Have you found Cali?'

'She's here. Now keep talking and we'll find you.'

Arijan grinned. 'I'll do better than that. I'll sing.'

Eryn's voice echoed back as she laughed. 'No don't. Please don't. The last thing we need is for you to sing. You'll bring the forest down on our heads. Tell us a story. How about when you challenged those knights to a duel.'

Toryn gaped as Arijan told the tale Hamar had lately struggled to remember. He recalled his old friend's face as Arijan recounted the time she had taken on five knights in a disagreement over stalls in a stable; Hamar had told the truth! Arijan enjoyed the retelling. 'We agreed only to the point of drawing blood.' She laughed. 'So, I nicked a finger on each of them.' She winked to Toryn. 'I didn't want to hurt them. Perhaps only their pride.'

Eryn sounded closer. 'Don't be modest, Ari. If I remember, you did it in order. You nicked the thumb on the first knight, then through them all finishing with the little finger on the last.'

Arijan beamed. 'I did enjoy that part. A nice touch I thought.'

Eryn and Calestri stepped arm in arm from behind a tree. 'And one not lost on them. I bet that story is still doing the rounds. Perhaps told only by the guards to put those aloof knights back in their place when necessary.'

Toryn nodded. 'You're right. Many in my village know

of it, although the details may have become a little hazy over time.'

Eryn tucked her arm under Toryn's to form a circle. 'As good as it was to hear again, it doesn't help us get out of this trap.' Eryn eyed the ground. 'It has to be a faery ring.' She looked to Toryn. 'It's a favorite trick of the Nym. But at least we know we're on the right track. But obviously they're aware we're on their tail.'

Toryn looked to Calestri. 'I've seen faery rings. We call them mushroom circles in my village. We get them in our meadows, but you could step in and out of those without becoming confused.'

Calestri scoffed. 'Because that's what they are: just a circle of mushrooms. Don't flatter yourself. The Nym wouldn't waste their time in one of your villages. And do you seriously think they would set a trap by marking it with *mushrooms*? Hardly much of a trap then, is it!' She jabbed her finger to the ground as best she could with their arms linked. '*This* is something completely different. We know of people becoming so lost and befuddled, they die of hunger while the spell of the ring holds.' She glanced to Arijan. 'We found two such souls not so long back.'

Toryn shrugged. 'Then how did you know it was due to a faery ring?'

Calestri sighed. 'Because the ground tingles under your feet for days afterwards... and there were no mushrooms.'

Eryn looked up. 'Can we please stop. This isn't helping. We're losing the light. If we attempt to leave the ring now, we'll never make it out together. This enchantment could stretch for some distance in all directions.'

Arijan laughed. 'But if we're lucky, the Nym will have planted the border with mushrooms, so we'll have something to eat.'

'Enough!' Eryn glared. 'We need to stay calm. And we best stay linked together until morning. Then we'll figure it out.' She withdrew her sword and placed it on the ground in the center of their circle. 'Just so we don't get disorientated. Can we all remember, the tip points to the way we're heading. Best to play it safe, eh.'

Calestri looked about her. 'I wouldn't be so sure. Those creatures could easily move your sword in the night.'

Eryn stepped on the blade. 'I'd like to see them try. But no one can sleep. If you nod off for one minute, you could be whisked away and who knows where you'll find yourself come sunrise.'

Supper proved a challenge, requiring coordination and cooperation as they tried to prepare the food while keeping their arms interlocked, as was tethering the horses to the closest tree. But none complained. All were keen not to break the circle and risk becoming lost. Now they sat facing each other as if playing a childhood game. Toryn found he welcomed their predicament. He thought of Elrik and grinned to himself — his friend would never believe his story should he ever meet him again. He looked around their faces. Despite the late evening light, their eyes appeared to glisten. Whether it was part of the enchantment, or a trick of the light, Toryn could not tell, but they looked almost ethereal as if the moon shone from within them. He listened intently to their stories of past adventures, but felt like a trespasser sitting among them.

At first, their spirits had been high as Eryn was convinced the spell would be spent by dawn. But Calestri had her doubts, concerned they had ventured deeper into the forest than any she had known. She suggested the power of the Nym had its source close to the center. And should the secret the Nym wished to conceal lie ahead, perhaps the ring surrounded the whole area and be permanent. As the evening gave way to night, Toryn sensed the others began to share her unease.

'That's strange.' Arijan glanced past Toryn. 'I'm sure that's moonlight ahead.' She looked up. 'But I can't see the moon or stars above.'

Toryn shivered, mindful of the shroul Hope had faced at the farmhouse. He whispered. 'It's only between those two trunks, surely too narrow to be moonlight.'

'Turn away.' Eryn spoke with certainty. 'It's a trick. If you see anything, it's a trick. They want to lure one of us to break the circle.' But Toryn found he could not take his eyes from the ghostly light. Eryn yanked at his arm and hissed. 'Look away! I don't care if you see the Three Maidens, you're not leaving this circle.'

Arijan kicked his shin. Toryn twisted back. 'Sorry, but I thought I saw—'

'Don't!' Eryn scowled. 'Don't for a moment even think about what you thought you saw. And don't you dare tell us. They're trying to get into our heads. I've heard tales of this. They'll come in all forms, people you love, dead friends, creatures you fear. Shut your eyes, all of us, shut our eyes.'

Arijan sighed. 'Our Nym friends obviously know where to start. You're the weak link, Toryn, and by that, I mean the dumb one. And I'm including the horses.' He felt her grip tighten. 'But I'm not going to let you be the one to break this circle.'

Toryn's spine tingled as the faint voice of a woman echoed through the still night. He clenched his jaw, trying to block his ears without the use of his hands. She called again; her mournful cry tugged at his heart as if his long-lost love waited for him. He groaned as he tried to resist the silken words of the woman, promising her body and soul, if only he would reach out and take her hand. He bowed his head and groaned.

Arijan whispered. 'I don't care what you think you've heard, it's not real.'

Toryn murmured. 'But I know her, I'm sure I know her. She's calling for me. She loves me.' He spluttered. 'And I love her dearly. We've been separated for years.'

Calestri spoke through a clenched jaw. 'And I think we can guess how they're tempting this simple man.' She stamped on his foot. 'She's not real, fool. She doesn't *want* you. What part of you can possibly imagine there's a woman wondering this forest at night, that just happens to desire your company.'

Arijan chuckled. 'I think we can guess which part, Cali. You of all people should know that.'

'Enough, Ari.' Calestri pressed down harder on Toryn's foot. 'Stay focused for the sake of us all.' She tutted. 'You can be thankful you've not been to sea. You'd be on the seabed in an instant once the sirens beckoned.'

Eryn spoke. 'Has it stopped, Toryn?'

'Yes.' But he could still hear the echo of his love as she wondered heartbroken into the night. He tightened his hold on the Amayans' arms, yet his heart yearned to follow before the woman was lost forever.

Eryn softened. 'Then keep in mind it's you they'll target. Sorry to be the bearer of bad news, but you're the one the Nym view as most likely to succumb.'

Toryn straightened. 'Don't worry. I won't let you down.'

'Too right you won't.' Arijan shoved her elbow into his ribs. 'I'll slit your throat and prop your dead body up before I'll let you break this circle.'

Eryn exhaled. 'Please, let's try to stay calm. No one is going to slit anyone's throat. Arijan, can you be sure that was your idea, or are they playing with your mind now?'

Arijan snorted. 'I think we know who is next in the

order of gullibility… eh, Cali.'

'Leave it.' Calestri struck out her foot at Arijan. 'Not now! Don't you bring that up now. Of all people, Ari. And don't think I wouldn't break this circle to throttle your scrawny neck.'

'Please! All of you.' Eryn lowered her voice. 'This is exactly what the Nym want. We must stay strong, stay together. We'll see this through to the morning and find another way out.'

'I'm sorry, Cali.'

'And me, Ari.'

Toryn's face flushed. 'What about me? Do I not deserve an apology?'

'Oh, you can go hang. No one cares about your puny—'

'Cali!' Eryn groaned. 'Stay focused. They're still in your head. That's the Nym speaking.'

But Calestri chuckled. 'Not that time. Sorry, Toryn. And don't you worry. I wouldn't let Arijan slit your throat. Well, not before me.'

'The horses!' Eryn braced. 'The horses are scared. They're in pain.'

Toryn listened. 'Are you sure? I can't hear them.'

Calestri agreed. 'Me neither. Eryn, it's you now. We all know you value Moonbeam over the rest of us. They're in your head.'

Eryn slumped. 'Sorry. I should have known. But it sounded so real. They were in so much pain.'

Toryn peered through one eye at Eryn. 'Now you know what it feels like. They go for your strongest feelings.'

Arijan chuckled. 'And now we all know yours, farm boy. Even now, in this dark hour, you're first thought is rutting with the first available woman that comes your way.'

'Rutting? She's the love of my life! How dare you suggest—'

Arijan kicked out again. 'I don't want to share this circle with a hound like you. We should—'

'Silence!' Eryn tried to calm them. 'They've started on you, Ari. Can't you see? Toryn. I don't know who she is, but I'm certain the love of your life is *not* strolling around this forest. Arijan. Toryn is just a man, and the Nym can read his mind. Look, at least we've learned something of the Nym. It looks like they can only get into one of our heads at a time. So, from now on, perhaps no one talks. Keep your eyes and mouths shut. Don't share your thoughts. If you hear anything, keep it to yourself.'

Calestri grumbled. 'This is going to be a long night.'

Eryn reasoned. 'But one we can get through if we stay strong.'

Toryn kept his eyes shut. He was sure he had heard a woman calling to him, but now felt foolish. He could not name the woman he believed he had loved with all his heart — it had to be a trap and he would not let them trick him again. Toryn imagined walking through his village to the trees at the edge of Midwyche Wood. A light breeze chilled—

A horn. A faint, somber call of a horn drifted through the trees. Toryn held his breath. Another illusion? It sounded again, but this time it was louder. He clenched his jaw and tightened his hold on the Amayans at his side. It continued, rousing the blood in Toryn's veins. The horn rallied all who heard to join its noble cause. He groaned. To decline would be an act of betrayal, allowing others to answer, marching to the defense of the realms while he remained behind.

Eryn hissed. 'Can you all hear that?'

Toryn let out his breath. 'A horn?' Arijan and Calestri agreed.

He resisted the urge to open his eyes. 'But how can that be? I thought they could only reach us one at a time.'

Eryn's voice shook. 'Unless they grow stronger.' More horns joined the call.

Toryn's toes clawed, desperately trying to resist stepping out of the circle. 'Have you heard horns like that before?' The Amayans could not be sure. He reasoned. 'I certainly haven't. Could it be real? How can the Nym tempt us with something unknown to us?'

Eryn whispered. 'That is true. We must know if it's real. Is it a threat? Or help? I'm going to look.' She gasped. 'This is not the work of the Nym. See for yourselves.'

Toryn opened his eyes to see Eryn's face bathed in blue light. He turned. A faint glow poured from between the trees. It took a moment to focus, but within the light, figures moved towards them. He knew they answered the plea of the horns. Toryn gaped as the phantoms drew near. Proud knights sat tall on majestic horses, adorned in grand, shining armor. They glided passed Toryn and the Amayans without a sound save the horn. He stared in awe at their bright eyes set in stern faces, fixed to the front as they marched to confront what Toryn knew to be a dark, powerful foe. Banners, many Toryn did not recognize, fluttered above the magnificent army, determined to fulfill their duty at a moment of dire need. They stood and turned to watch as the last of the ghostly army marched passed their spot.

The horn faltered, then silence. Toryn's heart lurched as the horses at the front reared. Their distant screams tore at his chest. The riders threw their arms up, shielding their faces from unseen horrors. Swords and lances fell from their hands as they were tossed from their mounts. Their anguished cries echoed through the forest from what Toryn knew had to be a long-gone age. Suddenly, the air above the stricken knights, rippled then flashed with the light of the sun. As one, the knights perished. The light died, leaving Toryn to gawp into the darkness as the echo of the tragedy faded.

It seemed an age before Eryn whispered. 'Have you ever…?'

Calestri wept. Arijan stammered. 'Is that not the most appalling waste of—?' But she too was overcome for the loss of souls to continue.

The ghostly afterglow stayed with Toryn. He instinctively knew he had witnessed knights from the distant glory days of the Seven Realms. But what enemy had they faced that could obliterate their finest so completely and utterly?

'I need to sit.' Calestri did not wait. Her body sagged. They helped her to the ground, arranging themselves so they sat back-to-back, but still with linked arms. Despite their sorrow, Toryn felt the strength of the Amayans' backs supporting his own. But he could barely hold himself up, shattered by the crushing defeat of his kin from the old world. His chin dropped to his chest as all his strength deserted him. A voice repeated over and over in his head, so faint at first, he could not be certain if it came from memory or was real. But even if the pure voices of the Three Maidens sang the first verse of the Song of Creation, it could not have prevented Toryn drifting off into a deep sleep.

30. A Great Wrong

'The horses!' Toryn shot up. He blinked in the daylight to see Eryn, holding up the frayed ends of the reins. 'They've gone.' She stood by the tree where they had tethered the horses. 'But where?' She paced about the trunk, frantically seeking for their tracks. Eryn stopped. Her hands dropped to her side, still clutching the reins. 'I can't see any sign of them.'

Arijan went to her side and took the reins. She held them up. 'They bolted. These haven't been cut by the Nym, they're frayed. The poor creatures must have taken fright.' She put her arm around Eryn as Calestri joined them.

Calestri crouched and examined the ground. 'Eryn. Look. In your panic you missed them.' She patted the earth. 'See, the undergrowth is thick and has sprung back, but here, beneath in the dirt, I can definitely see their marks.' Calestri stood and pointed. 'Thankfully, they went the right way.' They've headed west. Don't fret, Eryn. They'll be out of this place before long. I'm sure Moonbeam and the others will be waiting for us when we finally make it out.'

Eryn wiped her cheeks. 'If we ever find a way.'

Toryn climbed to his feet, still drained from the night's events. He looked past Eryn. 'There's the clearing we thought we saw yesterday.' He took a few steps, careful not to stray far from the others. 'It's still there. Can you see?' The Amayans turned, then nodded with visible relief. Toryn straightened. 'It has to be where they've taken Hope.'

Arijan returned to where they had stood in their circle. She pointed to Eryn's sword. 'The question is, do we follow the point or the hilt? Find Hope? Or the horses?'

Eryn took a deep breath. 'It has to be Hope. If the Nym still hold her, she's in danger. I don't know what or how, but what we saw last night is obviously related.' She picked up her sword and touched the ground. 'I feel nothing. No enchantment. Those fine souls marching through may have broken the spell.'

Arijan took Toryn's hand and squeezed. 'I'm sorry for what I said last night. I hope you realize it was the Nym speaking through me' — she grinned — 'well some of the time.'

Toryn managed a smile. 'Accepted. And please, I wouldn't have broken the circle, not even for the love of my life… well maybe not.'

Arijan laughed. 'Then let's agree those Nym know how to get inside our heads.' She glanced to Toryn. 'And can read what's in there, eh.' Her grin faded. 'But who were those knights? And what dark power could annihilate such a strong force?'

Toryn's heart still bore the scars of the loss. 'I recognized only the banners of Harlyn, Kernlow and Farrand, the home of the Archon, but the others were unknown to me.'

Eryn asked. 'What of Broon and Galabrant? We care not for your flags and colors, but did you see theirs?'

His head dropped. 'I'm afraid I wouldn't know them if I saw them.' He sighed. 'I spent my time on a small farm in a backwater no one has heard of. All I know of the world came from my old friend. He may have mentioned them, but I'm ashamed to say I didn't always listen.' He recalled the sight of the ghostly soldiers. 'But I do know the armor, horses, and weapons of those knights, are way beyond the skills of our smithies today. We have nothing resembling such fine quality. Or if we do, it's from the old days.'

Calestri agreed. 'And I suspect their skills were far superior. One glance at those fellows on the horses would make me think twice before engaging.'

Arijan looked up as if trying to recall the scenes from the night. 'But did we see *ghosts* of such an army? Or could it have been an illusion conjured up by the Nym?'

Eryn shrugged. 'But what purpose did it serve if it was the work of the Nym?'

Arijan held her gaze. 'Isn't it obvious? Look what happened to all those soldiers. Is it not a threat? It looks to me as if they're warning us to go no farther. Or if we do, we'll share the same fate.'

Eryn disagreed. 'Not a way I would have chosen. I'm convinced we witnessed a real event from the past.' She turned to Toryn. 'Did this Hamar fellow ever speak of a battle fought in these parts? I can't say I know of any.'

But Arijan still appeared unsure. 'Come on, Eryn. Here? The center of a dense forest seems an odd place for a battle of such magnitude.'

Toryn thought for a moment. 'If a battle did occur here, it must have been before the closing of the Caerwal Gate. According to Hamar, the Golesh landed many ships along our coast, enough to form a large army.'

Arijan scoffed. 'You listened to some of his stories then.'

'The interesting ones. Certainly, those involving the big battles. Anyway, for a hundred years, the Archon fought on two fronts. He held them back at the Caerwal Pass after they'd overrun the southern realms, while his armies struggled to defeat those causing havoc here in the north. The banners I didn't recognize, could be those of Houses from the two Lost Realms south of the mountains. They must have fled north following the invasion to fight for the Archon. Hamar told me the Golesh commanded terrible dark forces, otherwise our knights would have finished them off with ease.' He shivered and looked at the trees. 'If Hamar's stories were accurate, a battle could've taken place here around four hundred years ago. Perhaps when the forest was still young.'

Eryn ran her hand down the nearest tree. 'The Foranfae is an ancient forest, surely it has been here longer than a few centuries. But that doesn't mean a battle wasn't fought here. Perhaps your enemies used it as a hideout. And if they possessed such dark forces, they didn't have to be concerned about the Nym.' She eyed the clearing. 'But regardless, would we abandon Hope if it was a threat?' She looked to her sisters. 'When have we ever backed away in the face of danger? I say we go on.'

Calestri slung her bag over her shoulder. 'One thing is for certain. Those ghostly knights have broken the Nym's spell.' She looked to Arijan. 'Would the Nym have removed their own enchantment? I think not. We know they have the power to trap us until we starve' — she glanced at Toryn — 'or died by our own hands.'

Eryn tightened her belt. 'That settles it for me. The knights had to be real. And even if it was a threat, who here thinks we're not up to the task?' She smiled. 'Good. We go on.'

Without another word, they shouldered their bags and headed for the bright, morning light visible in the clearing a short distance ahead. As they neared the end of the trees, Toryn's scalp prickled. He squinted as they stepped from under the thick boughs of the last tree. He pulled up.

Calestri gasped as her eyes adjusted first. 'That's the last thing I expected to see.' Toryn could see nothing at first save the ground beneath — it was bare, cracked and pained his feet to stand upon. The air did not smell right, and he got the same acrid taste as he had at the burned-out settlement of Greendell. He shielded his eyes from the sun and looked up, fearful he would see another pile of ashes of innocent souls. But all he saw was a wide, barren plain of gray earth stretching out a league towards a faint line of trees on the horizon.

Eryn pointed with her sword. 'Are those trees, rocks or… people?' Toryn thought he saw a line of thin, dark shapes at the center of the clearing. His breath caught in his throat. He could not see the opposite side, but the curve of the formation suggested the trees or rocks stood in a wide circle. But as hard as he tried, he could not see what lay inside the formation. The air rippled, appearing darker, refusing entry of the sun's bright rays.

Toryn hopped from one foot to the other. 'Can you feel that?' He spat. 'And what is that smell?'

Eryn retreated to the trees, gesturing the others to follow — they gladly accepted the invitation. Once off the tainted earth, she spoke. 'I don't think I exaggerate when I say something terrible once happened here. The ground is poisoned, but that's not the work of one droog.'

Arijan grimaced. 'Perhaps a thousand worms? Imagine facing them?' She stared back to the cracked earth. 'Now I believe a great battle must have taken place here.'

Toryn kept his eyes on the dark circle at the center of the ruined plain. 'Then those banners must have been of the Lost Realms. No one has marched under them north of the Caerwals for centuries.' He coughed, still tasting the corruption.

Eryn looked back to the clearing. 'Regardless of the timing of the battle, it doesn't help us locate Hope.' Her lips moved as if chewing a bitter fruit. 'I don't like the look of that circle, but I suspect that's where we'll find her.'

Calestri shivered despite the warmth. 'It reminds me of… well, I'm sure you know.'

Toryn straightened. 'How much do you know of the Nym?' He looked at the blank faces of the Amayans. 'You said they wouldn't tolerate the Nordleng and their like, but they don't seem too keen on us either.'

Eryn shrugged. 'We know very little. The strange thing is I'd forgotten their very name until that encounter. And now we stand in this place' — she looked to her sisters — 'it's like a mist clears to reveal more.'

'Just like Hope's shadow.' Toryn held her gaze. 'She believes she's protecting herself from some terrible event, which I guess is the one we witnessed. Could it be the same for you?'

Eryn's eyes never looked bluer as her face paled. 'The same great wrong? Did we take part in what happened here?'

Arijan held up her hands. 'But four hundred years past? Are we that old, Eryn?' She gaped at Calestri. 'We can't be... surely? We don't age as quickly, but I can't think we've spent all those years doing... well, the same every day.'

Toryn sensed their confusion. 'Perhaps not you, perhaps it was your ancestors. You appear to know each other's minds. Could you have the knowledge or memories of your sisters from that time?'

Eryn spoke. 'It's possible, but there's still plenty they can't have known judging by the gaps in our knowledge.' She lifted her bag from her shoulder and reached inside for her flask. She took a gulp, swilled, then spat. 'Ah, that taste. It must have been some mighty source of wrongness that fouled this place.' She wiped her mouth and looked back to Toryn. 'From what we can now recall, the Nym serve no one, good or evil. They're an ancient force unto themselves, here long before ours or your kind came to these lands. But why they want Hope, and more to the point, what they desire to do with her, is beyond me. If she were indeed responsible for some great wrong in the past, if it didn't impact the Nym, they would have no interest.'

Toryn's blood froze. 'But what if it did? What will they do to her?'

Eryn shrugged. 'What could she have done to cause harm to the Nym? Hope is closed to us, but what I've seen of her, and from what you say, I cannot believe she has an evil bone in her body.'

Arijan nodded to the trees. 'If the Nym wanted Hope dead, for any reason, they could have done it the other night. We were frozen, she was defenseless, they could have finished her there on the spot… and us.'

Eryn peered back to the clearing. 'Then we must assume Hope still lives. We are linked to her somehow.' She looked skyward and sighed. 'It appears our only course of action is to endure the stench of this contaminated plain, reach the center, find a way to enter that circle… and then, somehow locate and rescue her.'

Calestri groaned. 'I thought you'd say that.' She brushed the dirt from her shoes. 'Spending our days doing the same old thing is beginning to sound inviting.' She took a step towards the edge of the trees. 'But there's no point delaying this any longer. Let's find Hope, then Amyra, and perhaps life could get back to normal.'

31. A Captain's Wisdom

Elodi could not tear her eyes from the smoke hanging over the towers of Calerdorn as it dipped below the horizon in the twilight. She yearned to turn the *Celestra* around and throw everything she had in a last, futile attempt to retake the city. But she knew it would be pointless and only result in more death. Tears flowed down her face as her heart fractured in her tight chest. Only a day before she had vowed to make her departed parents proud, and not let her people down. But she had failed; so utterly failed and lost the city. And she had not even brandished her sword in its defense. She had not struck a single blow against the enemy when they surged through the cobbled streets, burning, looting, and slaughtering the very people she had sworn to keep safe. And what of those stranded in the city and docks? Had the lucky died first?

The Ruuk had always craved Calerdorn, but not for its beauty and history. The city held a strategic position, protecting the northern lands against those wishing ill of Harlyn. And now the enemy held it, Elodi's ability to retake it would be difficult, if not impossible as the occupiers benefited from the hard work of her people to fortify the city.

Elodi slumped against the taffrail as the futility of her position sank in. Everything she held dear would be ransacked and defiled; those left behind, the relics, the art, and on a personal level, her father's belongings. A thousand years of the city's fine history would be wiped out in just a matter of hours. Thanks to Wendel, only the most valuable scrolls from the archives had been saved.

But all else would be reduced to smoldering ashes by dawn. She clenched the rail and let the splintered wood dig deep into her palms. Why had she not devised a plan for an orderly evacuation? She knew Uldrak would return, but in her pride, had never contemplated a rout. If only they had planned for such an event. Boats could have been kept in a state of readiness; people assigned to designated areas of the quay; and everything of value and importance, packed and stored for rapid loading. Her head dropped. But no, nothing had been done to prevent the resulting panic and carnage.

Elodi stared through the tears she had not the will to blink away. The cliffs of Dorn rose to hide the evidence of her failure from view. Now her only hope to take back her city from the enemy's vile hands, would be a sea-based attack. But the *Celestra* would make for a large and vulnerable target if she tried to sail into the docks. One strike from a fireball slung from the quay, and all onboard would quickly be engulfed in flames. And Elodi knew only too well, the dreadful results of the evil fire Uldrak deployed.

Elodi squeezed her eyes shut, determined to stop the flow of tears but failed. How had she lost Calerdorn? How could a city, bristling with new, heavy weapons, fall with barely a blow landed on its assailants? The screams of the people fleeing the onslaught still resonated. How many had made it out alive? She would not know the true number until they made landfall at Seransea. Elodi tried to take some comfort in the numbers escaping, waiting for as long as she could, using the *Celestra* to shield the dozens of fishing boats as they fled. Gundrul reported at least one hundred and fifty civilians had boarded the *Celestra*, and estimated thrice that number had escaped on the flotilla. Many looked fit and ready to fight; but were they capable of fighting the likes of the Ruuk, the wykes, and the possessed Dorlan?

Elodi released her grip and examined the cuts on her hands. She looked back to the darkening coast. The lights of the odd house, nestled in the few inlets on the shoreline, twinkled as if nothing had happened. Perhaps they would be safe in their remote settlements, shielded by the rugged landscape from the rest of the realm. But with the fall of Calerdorn, Harlyn could do little to prevent the Ruuk from rampaging through Dorn. She slammed her hand down hard on the rail, aware Noor and Darrow had insufficient resources to defend against such a force. As soon as the *Celestra* gained the open sea, she had sent word to Archonholm. She had watched the bird shrink to a tiny speck as it flew along the coast, but with the Archon committed to the Caerwal Gate, would he spare resources for Harlyn? Kernlow would be sending its army south; could she convince the old lord to send reserves to her aid?

Elodi groaned. Now it became clear why Uleva had spared her on the grasslands. Humiliation. That cunning wyke desired to belittle Elodi in her own realm. She wanted to humble her before the city, demonstrate she had nothing to counter Uleva's strength. And to destroy Elodi's belief in her own ability to lead and defend her people. Why kill her in her stupor when Uleva could savor the moment, leaving Elodi to live in dread of worse to come while suffering the loss of Calerdorn.

She leaned over the edge. The swish of the water lured her thoughts from the tragedy and soothed the deep ache in her heart. The waters whispered to her, promising Elodi lasting relief from the pain. The cold depths offered peace and anonymity. With one movement, she could plunge into the icy waters and purge the shame. One movement. Elodi tore herself away from the convincing claim of the sea. She cried out in despair and anger, then quickly covered her mouth, desperately trying to control herself in front of Horace at the helm.

The captain looked over from the wheel. 'Let it all out, ma'am. There's just thee and me up here, and you don't have to worry about me.'

Elodi clenched her jaw, but only succeeded in squeezing the pooling tears from her stinging eyes. She took a breath. 'I have to stay in control, Captain. I cannot let my people see me like this.'

Horace tried to smile. 'I know how you feel, ma'am.' He patted the rim of the wheel. 'I'd be the same if this old lady went down.'

'But I believe the custom is you'd go down with your ship.' Her voice wavered. 'I shouldn't have left the city. When she fell, I should have fallen with her.'

'But what would that have achieved, ma'am? You must live to fight another day for the sake of your realm. If the *Celestra* sinks I have no other ship to sail, and therefore no longer serve a purpose.'

Elodi placed her hand on his shoulder. 'I appreciate your kind words, Captain, perhaps I will someday come to think the same, but at this moment' — she turned away — 'I feel my heart has been ripped from my chest and shredded into a thousand pieces.'

Horace stroked his beard. 'From the stories I've heard of you in action, I have no doubt you'll retake your fine city before autumn is done.'

Elodi returned to the rail to gaze at the coast of Harlyn. She whispered to the craggy cliffs. 'I wish I could believe that.'

'Ma'am?' Elodi jumped as Gundrul stood at her side. He leaned on the rail but pulled back as it creaked loudly. His brow creased as he appeared to consider his words.

'Don't let one defeat deflate your spirits. My first commander used to say—'

'One defeat?' She kept her eyes on the wash below. 'I lost a whole city. And not just any city. Calerdorn. I lost the seat of my ancestors, Gundrul. Hundreds remain at the mercy of my foe. And where do I begin to take her back?'

Gundrul spoke softly. 'I have no such love for my own home, ma'am. When only sixteen, I left a small settlement in Lunn, so far to the north even the people of Keld regarded us as Ruuk.' He looked her in the eye. 'What I'm trying to say is… I can't begin to guess how you're feeling, but I do know your passion and courage will ensure you win her back.'

Elodi wiped her face. 'We fashioned the city to withstand a determined attack from an enemy with greater resources than mine. I appreciate your faith, but it will take more than my passion and courage.'

Gundrul glanced back to Horace. 'Ah yes, maybe for an ordinary soul, but we both know there's more to you than meets the eye, ma'am.'

'How do you mean?'

His eyebrows raised. 'Your blade. At the gate when you raised it against Dorlan. I've seen a sword do that before, but only in the hands of a… shall we say, certain type of warrior.' Gundrul grinned. 'Come on, ma'am, even that Dorlan fellow had a moment of doubt.' He leaned closer. 'I began to suspect after your exploits in the gatehouse at the siege. And when you asked me at the campfire, I knew for certain.'

Elodi drew a breath of salty air. She nodded. 'You are correct, Captain. I only learned about my mother's *secret* a short time ago.' She touched his forearm. 'But I would ask you not to share your knowledge. There are many still wary of… well, we both know.'

'My old, cracked lips are sealed. But if I may say, you might want to reconsider. It's true many are suspicious of the warriors of which we speak, but you won't find a brother or sister at arms who wouldn't be honored to fight at the side of such a warrior.'

'Then I will consider it. Perhaps I shall seek Wendel's view. He is the only other man who knows.' She looked down to the deck. 'Is he about?'

Gundrul's brow creased. 'He's taken to his bunk. I think recent events have taken their toll on the old boy. Maybe it's best he's allowed to sleep for now.'

Elodi nodded. 'Wise council, Captain. I shall let him rest. His mind has to be sharp. I've never needed his wisdom and experience more than now.'

The ancient port of Seransea predated the building of Calerdorn. Ramshackle roofs clung precariously to the tops of the poorly maintained buildings, looking ready to spill over onto the quayside and tumble into the water. Fishing boats returning with their nightly catch, and the early risers preparing for the coming day, tore a fresh wound in Elodi's heart — could those bustling about their duty, oblivious to the loss of Calerdorn, ever forgive her? The sight of the *Celestra* sailing into the harbor had been a common sight over the last few weeks, so few took notice of her arrival. But today, the Old Lady brought terrible news to change the ways of the port for good. Elodi turned to scan the horizon out at sea. It would be midday before the remaining vessels fleeing Calerdorn reached the port, and only then would she discover how many had escaped. And of the survivors, how many would be able to bear arms against the unrelenting foe?

Sailors scrambled up and down masts preparing to dock. Elodi went below, not wanting to be seen. She felt guilty going to wake Wendel. The old man had barely been able to stand, following his valiant effort to save selected scrolls from the archives. He had appeared pale and wore every one of his eighty-odd years on his troubled face. Elodi hoped he had regained some of his dogged strength following a few hours' sleep; but she had not slept a wink.

She entered the cabin where Wendel and members of her council bunked. A healer sat beside Wendel. She looked up as Elodi entered. She stood. 'Ma'am. He sleeps after a troubled voyage, but I advise he not be moved just yet.'

Elodi looked down on a face whiter than the pillow beneath his head; his smoke-stained robes appeared too large for his frail bones. She dared to ask, 'Is… is it serious?'

The woman held her gaze. 'Yes, ma'am. I have done all I can to aid recovery, but while his spirit is strong, his body is weak.'

'Is it the fever? He appears calm.'

'Mercifully, not the fever, ma'am. I believe it's an accumulation of the last few months, and of course, yesterday's events and the shock of Calerdorn's fall.'

Elodi's head dropped. 'I fear the fault can be laid squarely on my shoulders.' The protests of those present in the cabin failed to allay her guilt.

The healer took Elodi's hand. 'Not a single soul in Harlyn would blame you, ma'am. You too are in shock. If it were possible, I would prescribe rest, but alas, I know the current predicament will not allow you such a luxury.' She patted the back of her hand. 'But please, do not hold yourself responsible as your health will deteriorate, and with that, the fate of our realm.'

Elodi held her gaze. 'Thank you, Healer. I will heed your advice as best I can in the circumstances.' The shouts of the sailors on deck announced their imminent mooring. Elodi turned to Wendel. 'Sleep well, my old friend.' She looked up to the healer. 'He's a stubborn one. I trust he'll be fighting back in his dreams.' The *Celestra* nudged the quayside. Elodi braced. 'Now I must be gone. Please keep a close eye on our friend here, and let me know of any change, no matter how small. I wish to stay informed of his condition. His counsel is vital to Harlyn.'

32. The Heart of the Foranfae

Toryn's toes recoiled from the wrongness beneath his feet. The shimmering circle in the center of the spoiled ground lay farther away than at first appeared, and for a moment, he feared they had walked into another faery ring. None spoke; each kept their heads down as if suspicious the corrupt earth had laid traps to hamper their progress to Foranfae's heart. When Toryn did look up, he struggled to find the words to describe what awaited them. The black shapes protruding from the ground, resembled teeth of a gigantic creature lurking below the surface about to burst through and devour the forest. But inside the perimeter, the air defied attempts to see what lay within. At times, a wall of swirling, dark water seemed to climb impossibly high to the very gods, jealously shielding the circle's secrets. But when he looked again, Toryn thought he saw shapes, perhaps figures, dancing around the edges. Yet this was no joyful dance, their disjointed movements seemed to mock him, promising Toryn he would die should he defy the will of the forest and enter its domain.

As they progressed across the parched earth, Toryn had the unpleasant sensation of being crushed. It seemed as if an invisible hand repelled him, yet at the same time, another shunted from behind compelling him towards the center. But which guiding hand should he trust? Was he being encouraged to turn back for his own good? Or was the force behind willing him forward to his doom, or to find Hope? Regardless of his doubts, his legs continued to trudge across the rotten ground.

Toryn's eyes played tricks. On more than one occasion, he believed he was about to tread on a discarded sword, or a plate of armor, or worse, severed limbs, and helmets still worn by their once great warriors, each with the heart-breaking look of dismay and shock. He would stumble, not willing to defile the fallen with his grubby boots, even with the knowledge they could not be real. Toryn slogged on, despite the conflicts within. He set his jaw and clenched his fists, determined to find Hope. She had done the same for him, now it was time to repay the debt.

Finally, they drew near. How long it took to reach the center of the foul plain, Toryn could not tell. It could have been an hour; it could have been two days; it could have even been a month — he had no way to keep track of the time. His stomach did not feel empty despite knowing it had been a long time since he had eaten. But the stench of decay would take the edge off the appetite of a starving soul.

'They're trees… of a sort.' Eryn's voice sounded strange, as if her words were the first Toryn had heard in many years. It took a while for the meaning to penetrate his muddled thoughts. He looked up. A tree like none he had ever seen, stood a little way ahead. It was small, barely twice his height, with a smooth, dark trunk. Twisted branches sprouted halfway up, growing sideways, then splitting to resemble gnarled fingers. Toryn stared, convinced they reached out to their neighbor as if holding hands to form the circle.

'What now? Do we enter?' Calestri stepped between him and the tree. He turned to the others and gasped. The Amayans looked pale, their once fine limbs were thinner, their hair unkempt and gray, and their faces tired and gaunt. How long had it taken to cross the gap? He held out his arms and turned them over, but he alone appeared not to have aged.

Toryn croaked. 'Do you have the strength? You look

too old.'

Eryn frowned. 'Old?' She regarded her colleagues. 'Perhaps it's your eyes that have decayed. I see nothing out of the' — she looked at him differently — 'except you are shorter and look… frail.'

Toryn straightened. 'I may feel tired, but frail?' Again, he examined himself. 'I can assure you I am as before. Look at yourselves before you start calling me *frail*.'

'What do you see?'

He shrugged. 'Three weak, old women with gray hair and wrinkles. And as for your arms, I doubt you could swing a sword or nock an arrow.'

Calestri bristled. 'Weak? Wrinkles?' She placed her hands on her hips and strutted. 'You're calling this body old?'

Toryn smirked. 'Now I come to think of it, if you did have the strength in your skinny arms, you'd have no trouble drawing a bowstring now. Your chest is well out of the way.' He pointed to her feet. 'But you'd struggle to tie your laces.'

Calestri glanced down. 'Why you—!'

'Gray?' Arijan strode towards Toryn. 'Who do you think you are?' She drew her sword, swung it over her head, thrust her blade towards his throat, then sheathed it before Toryn had time to take a breath. She grinned. 'Satisfied. I could've removed your dumb head from your scrawny shoulders, then put an arrow through your puny chest before your thick skull had landed at your feet.'

Eryn held up her hand. 'Wait! Please. I think we can guess what's happening here. It's the same spell the Nym placed on their ring.' She leveled her gaze at Arijan. 'How about we calm ourselves before we regret any actions that can't be undone.'

Arijan scowled at Toryn. 'Fine, but don't you dare call me a gray-haired, old woman again.'

Toryn brought his hands to his face. 'I'm sorry. Eryn's right.' He rubbed his eyes and was relieved to see the three Amayans appeared as he had known them. 'Now you look better.' He held up his arms. 'How about me? Still short and frail?'

Eryn smiled. 'Taller and stronger.'

Arijan jeered. 'Don't flatter him. I've seen better, far better.'

'Enough, Ari. Take control.' Eryn turned to the circle. 'Now if we can please see past the Nym's mischief-making, let us figure a way to enter.'

Toryn peered through the branches. He had not been wrong. Inside, it looked as if the surface of a slow-flowing river had risen from its bed to block their way in the manner of a wall. Eryn took a step closer. 'Do you all see what looks like water?' They agreed. 'Then this has to be an illusion. I hear no sound.' She tipped back her head and looked up. 'And I can't imagine how this wall of water could support itself.' Eryn drew her sword. 'Wait here. I'll find out.' She strode through the trees, but as soon as she met the barrier, she was flung back as if slapped by a giant's hand. She climbed to her feet and put away her sword. 'Well, I think we can presume it's not an illusion. And it appears we cannot just walk through it.'

'Can we walk around it?' Toryn paced towards the next tree. 'Perhaps there's a way through at the northern edge.'

Eryn shrugged. 'Wouldn't hurt to try.'

They set off but soon Toryn began to experience the same conflicting forces as before, except this time the hands pushed and pulled at his sides. Again, they seemed to walk for hours but the scenery did not change. With the circle of trees to his left, and the thin line of the edge of the forest on the horizon to his right, he could be walking on the spot for all he knew.

'This is hopeless.' Eryn stopped and gasped. 'It's dark! When did night fall?' She unbuckled her sword belt and collapsed. She groaned. 'I don't know about you, but I'm not prepared to press on when I can't see my hand in front of my face. And I certainly don't rate our chances of making it back to the forest across this cursed ground in the dark.'

Toryn was happy to sit. His bones ached and had not even the strength to lift his chin from his chest. He lay back. 'Then we have no choice but to wait for morning.'

Arijan slumped beside him. 'Then for your sake I hope the love of your life doesn't show up again. You'd be lost for good wandering these parts.'

'If the very Maidens called for me, I wouldn't have the will to stand, let alone walk to them.' He looked to her, barely able to keep his eyes open but managed to smile. 'If they want to take me, they'll have to carry me.'

Arijan grinned. 'Only in your dreams, farm boy.' But she too collapsed. 'Perhaps come the morning we'll be in better shape.'

Toryn wondered if the night would ever end. He knew he had slept as the dreams had seemed too strange to be reality. But he was certain he had to be awake now. He lay staring at the clouds passing slowly across the night sky for what seemed like days. Surely the turning of the dome had slowed. The Amayans stirred, and at times, woke and sat up, but they appeared as if on the other side of a window unaware of his efforts to speak to them. They would turn and look towards him but fail to acknowledge his presence. They also appeared oblivious to each other, looking about themselves, confused, perhaps wondering like Toryn whether they were awake or dreaming.

The ground before him lightened. Toryn glanced up to see the half-moon slide out from behind a cloud. He blinked. The moon moved, whereas the clouds sat motionless. He followed its meandering ways around the thick clouds as if playing a game with him. It would peer around one, then hide, only to appear from behind another. Toryn scratched his head. How could it move across a patch of open sky and not be seen? He lay back and closed his eyes. 'I'm not playing if you're going to cheat.' *Now he was talking to the moon.* He must be losing his mind.

Horses! Frightened horses. Toryn sat. The Amayans slept. Had they not heard? Surely their love of their animals would shake them from their slumber. He searched the cracked plain, now dark as the moon had ceased its childish game. More horses squealed, until hundreds cried out in fear. He stood and stumbled to where he thought Eryn lay, but in the gloom he failed to find her. He jumped. The sound of steel clashing on steel, echoed all around. Toryn's breath came in gasps as he desperately sought the Amayans. He froze. A screech ripped the air asunder, to be joined by another, then a third, tearing the sky to shreds. Not screams of fear; this was fear itself, paralyzing the ghostly battlefield with dread.

The stench of burning flesh hit the back of his throat. Toryn recoiled as the memory of Drunsberg flooded back. The air erupted with the tortured cries of a thousand souls. He dropped to his knees, covering his head. He could see nothing, yet felt everything. But among the turmoil, a single voice could be heard. Repeating what had to be an incantation, a woman spoke: Hope. Toryn sensed her trepidation at what she recited. She remained in control, fighting back against the terror, desperate to invoke powers to end the torment of those falling at her side. Her voice rose against the shrieks as the heat scorched Toryn's back. Hope yelled her last words. The ground shook. The sky exploded. Toryn's ears burst; a blinding light seared his eyes; the heat burned the flesh from his bones. Silence returned to the heart of the Foranfae, but not peace.

Toryn awoke oddly refreshed. He stood as the sun made its long-awaited appearance in the east. The mist rose from the dew-laden trees as it had for centuries at the start of each new day. He turned and almost toppled over. The wall of rippling air, concealing what lay inside the tree circle, had gone. Toryn teetered on the edge of an enormous crater, hundreds of feet deep. Its sides sloped towards a middle shrouded in thick fog. At the center, four black stones protruded from the haze as if dark claws reached out to pluck the sun from the sky.

He shuddered as a thick band of gray cloud shrouded the sun, determined to deny the forest its warmth. All about was silent and dull. He took two steps back and turned to the Amayans — they still slept. He kneeled at Eryn's side and gently shook her shoulder, but she failed to stir. Her skin was cold to the touch, and her lips tinged blue. 'Eryn?' His voice echoed back. He shook a little harder. 'Eryn!' He placed his ear close to hercalese and was relieved to find she breathed, but very shallow. Toryn tried to rouse Arijan and Calestri but knew neither would wake. An invocation entrapped the Amayans, that much was obvious. But why them and not him? Did the Song protect him? Or was it a trap to lure him alone and defenseless into the heart of Foranfae?

A moan escaped from the hollow behind. Toryn knew it had to be Hope. He covered his companions with their blankets, then reached for his sword. His hand stopped. A sword would prove no use against what awaited him inside the circle. He turned to face the crater and the four, dark stones jutting out from the dense fog. Mindful of what happened to Eryn, he edged with caution to the lip of the dell. He held his breath, lifted a foot, and stepped beneath the branches. He exhaled as his foot touched the ground within the trees. Toryn glanced back to check the Amayans, but the curtain of shimmering air had drawn behind him. He had no choice but to proceed.

Toryn's feet made no sound as he approached the center of the hollow. The pressure he had felt outside the circle had gone — no power repelled or forced him on; this was his decision. His feet pained him still. He looked down. The scorched ground resembled the crater he and Hamar discovered in Greendell, yet this was many times larger. He stopped at the edge of the fog. But this was like no fog he had seen. It had the look of a lake of cloudy water, reluctant to reflect the sky above, denying it the pleasure of gazing upon its beauty. The dense surface barely moved in the still air. The four stones stood taller than had first appeared from the edge; standing at varying heights, twisting as if forced from the rock beneath the fog. But from what depths did they spring? And who had set them? With a growing sense of dread, he knew the secrets it held would soon be revealed.

Toryn waded into the fog, gasping as the cold froze first the blood in his legs, then up to his middle and shoulders as the ground beneath dropped. He paused with his head above its surface, unable to feel his body beneath. Something moved on top of one of the stones. Toryn tried to see, but knew it was not intended for a mere mortal's eye. He bowed his head and descended into the fog.

33. Into The Circle

Toryn entered another world. Ahead, the bases of the stones now stood as pillars in a great hall shoring up the high ceiling of fog.

The whispers began.

But these were not akin to the cruel taunts of Wyke Wood — they did not speak to him; they spoke of him. Shapes he could not fix his eyes upon, whirled about him. Wisps of white smoke darted this way and that, stopping for a moment to allow the trails to catch up, then dash away. Toryn twisted and turned, but they moved too fast for him to get a proper glimpse. He took a step forward. The ghostly forms swirled about him but did not hinder his progress. With purpose, he strode towards the center accompanied by his ethereal watchers. From the lip of the crater, he had not fully appreciated its size. But his feet no longer pained at the touch of the ground, and, as he noted, his footsteps made no sound. He clapped his hands in front of his face but heard nothing. Only the whispers of his pursuers filled the air. He knew them to be the Nym; but should he fear or welcome their presence?

As he neared the center, more Nym emerged, forming as a large, billowing cloud. The whispers rose, sounding as a gale howling down the Kolossos Mountains — yet the air remained still. Then, as if a door had shut, silence. Toryn halted, suddenly finding he stood just inches from the base of one of the stones. The dark surface defied attempts to identify its color, appearing to change from a gray, to green, to blue, yet never allowing sufficient time for Toryn to be certain. Instinctively, he reached out to touch it, hoping it would feel like a Singing Stone. His hand recoiled at the faintest contact. He stared at the tips of his fingers turning white. The stone was icy cold. He tipped back his head. From its thick base, the stone tapered as it rose, wending its way to the foggy dome high above. But what purpose did they serve?

Toryn edged back to see what lay at their center. The ground amid the four stones appeared empty at first. Yet, when he looked again, he saw a tree, the same as those forming the circle outside. This stood a little taller and held something in its branches. He groaned. Hope. He tried to run but his legs struggled as if wading through a fast-flowing river.

The voices spoke, but this time he understood. *It knows. It is troubled.* Nym whirled around him as he strode on, brushing his hands about his head as if swishing away flies. He reached the tree. Hope's forlorn body hung spread-eagled among the branches. Her head bowed forward; her damp hair draped about her face. He tried to call her name but could make no sound. The Nym gathered before him, merging until they formed two solid shapes, human-like, but twice Toryn's height with long limbs and slender torsos. They bowed, bringing their faces close to look upon him. A chill passed through Toryn as he sensed they read his thoughts.

It committed great wrong. Toryn staggered back as a hundred murmurs echoed inside his head. He knew they now spoke to him; it was Hope who had committed the great wrong.

He looked up. The heads of the Nym were draped by hoods as if made by mist; their faces revealed little, save two oval, gray eyes a little darker than their pale skin. Toryn cleared his throat. His voice echoed. 'What have you done to—?'

It must atone. The answer flooded back.

'Why? For what?'

It recited a forbidden verse.

His hand raised through the thick air towards Hope. 'She must have had good reason. She has knowledge of an ancient power.'

The Nym faded at the edges, smearing the air as they came closer. *It corrupted the Song.* Then louder. *It must atone.*

Toryn groaned inside. 'And how must she *atone*?'

Their voices rose. *Remain 'til the land is healed.*

He stared to Hope. 'And how long will that take?' He asked, knowing the answer would not be to his liking.

The healing begins.

He gasped. 'Begins…? But it has been hundreds of years since—'

It annulled the Song of Creation. All was unmade. One figure dispersed, then shot straight at him, solidifying inches from his face. Toryn held firm as the being's mirror-like eyes bore into him. A spindly hand floated towards him and caressed his chin. His jaw froze at the touch. *It has union with the destroyer.* The Nym floated back to its full height. *It will also atone.*

Toryn's body jolted. His arms and legs flew out to his sides. He rose from the floor. He cried out. 'She serves the Singing Stones. She defends against those of the Dark Verses.' He hung in the air, hovering a few feet above the ground.

The Nym returned, reaching out a translucent hand to his temple. *It speaks of the Amanach.*

Toryn could not hold the Nym's searing gaze. He twisted away. 'There were seven, but one was destroyed.'

It has union with the Amanach.

'Who? Me? Hope? Her mind is lost when she's far from a stone. She spoke of a veil she placed there herself.' He turned back to the Nym. 'She protects herself.' The Nym released its hold and retreated. Toryn drifted back to the ground. They tilted their heads as if regarding him in a different light. He tried again. 'You say *it* has *union* with the stones? Do you speak of me'— he pointed to the tree — 'or Hope? Perhaps we can help. I have seen one destroyed. I know what—'

It has knowledge. Toryn groaned as he began to rise. *It poses a threat.* The Nym stretched out a thin arm towards the tree. Spindly fingers tickled the air. Toryn watched in horror as a black, fist-shaped knot broke through the ground besides Hope. It twisted as it grew to his height before splitting into a dozen branches, splintering into finger-like twigs. Toryn's body floated towards the new tree that gladly reached out, wrapping its shoots around his wrists, ankles, and lastly his throat.

The Nym swirled and rose, gathering about the trees. They bowed their heads. *It will atone.*

Toryn yelled. 'No! There is a greater wrong rising. She is needed. We are needed.' But his feeble voice failed to convey his desperate plea.

The Nym formed a circle, proclaiming his fate. *It will remain 'til the wrong is righted.*

He tried to call out, but the Nym took his voice and dispersed like smoke in a breeze.

34. A VOICE LOST

'The defenses are in desperate need of repair, ma'am.' Gundrul cast his experienced eye along the ancient walls surrounding the oldest part of Seransea. 'And it doesn't make matters any easier having so many buildings outside the boundary.'

Elodi stood with her captain in front of the small gatehouse. She looked to the narrow streets lined with wooden homes, alehouses, workshops, and market stalls. 'Should the town be attacked, and I can see no reason why the enemy would not, I doubt all the people who live outside could be sheltered and fed for long inside these walls.'

Gundrul tutted, shaking his head. 'I don't think that would be the main worry, ma'am.' He pointed to the new town outside. 'To an attacker, that's a big pile of kindling just waiting for a spark. A dozen fire arrows would soon start an inferno. And even if we had more heavy weapons and thrice the number of archers on the wall, they'd struggle to pick out their targets behind the palls of smoke.' He took a few paces along the base and kicked at the loose masonry. 'And I wouldn't want to be on top of this when the war machines unleash their fireballs.' He stepped back and looked up. 'As I see it, how long the inhabitants could be fed is irrelevant. The walls won't hold back a determined attack long enough for rations to become a concern.'

Elodi sighed. 'Then all we can do is prepare for another evacuation should they approach. We need scouts at the Noor border fences to give them sufficient time for an orderly departure by land and sea.'

'I hope you don't mind, ma'am, But I took the liberty and started talks on the matter.'

'I wouldn't expect anything less from you, Captain.' Elodi looked over his shoulder. 'How did it come to this? It seems only a few months ago I was occupied with minor raids from Nordruuk.' She clenched her fists until her nails dug into her palms. 'I could never have envisaged Calerdorn…' she turned away.

Gundrul kept his eyes on the wall. 'This has been planned for years. I guess the raids were just a cover to keep your eyes from what they didn't want you to see.'

'But even if I had been suspicious, my options were limited. And the Archon's invitation to witness the *grand opening* of his tower didn't help matters.' Her eyes wondered back to the busy market. 'How could I have allowed this to happen?'

'Allowed, ma'am? No one could have foreseen Dorlan leading an army up to the very gates of Calerdorn.' He looked her in the eye. 'I assume you've accepted this man is the real Dorlan?'

Elodi took a deep breath. 'There are three possibilities as I see it. The wykes created an entity in his likeness along with his powers; or, they have, by some foul means, brought him back from the distant past; or lastly, they have had him all this time, sustaining his life well beyond his years. And even his horse. Draego, looks the same as in the portraits. I'm not sure which of those explanations bothers me most. All require powers far superior to ours.' She watched the people of Seransea going about their business. 'The Archon must be made aware not all our foes lie south of the gate. I've sent dispatches but have yet to receive confirmation they arrived.' She turned her back on the bustle. 'And another thing concerns me. If Dorlan didn't fall at the Battle of Talaghir, did Ormoroth also survive?'

Gundrul shuddered. 'It doesn't bear thinking about. But surely, if he did, we would have seen his dark form on the battlefield.'

'Perhaps he bides his time, waiting to see how the Archon fares against those in the south.'

Her captain's hand went to his sword. 'Do you think they may be in league with the Golesh?'

'Ormoroth is of a distant age, I hope that is where his life ended. But I have to admit to knowing little of that time aside from the escapades of Dorlan. Ah! At a time when I need him most, Wendel lies on his sick bed showing little sign of recovery.'

Gundrul nudged another piece of displaced stonework with this foot. 'Is he not yet well enough to be brought ashore?'

'The healer advises he remain onboard the *Celestra*. A move now could cause him great harm.'

'I had not realized he was in such bad shape. Have you… another to take his place?'

Elodi pursed her lips. 'I have reluctantly given it some thought. Perdew is Wendel's obvious successor, but he's not much younger himself. Wendel's shoes will be difficult to fill. But I will make no decision until the situation at the Caerwal Gate is resolved. What happens there determines all else.'

They walked back through the gatehouse to be greeted by the sounds of wooden swords thudding against shields. Elodi observed the faces of young and old reserves performing drills in ill-fitting, battered armor. 'And what of these brave folk, Captain? How long could we expect them to delay an enemy advance should it be necessary to send them north?'

He spoke in a low voice. 'Those who fought at the first siege have acquired some skill and experience, but the fresh faces here have much to learn if they're to survive.'

He stroked his chin. 'If those scoundrels choose to consolidate their position at Calerdorn, your reserves may yet have time to improve. But in open ground?' He shook his head. 'I fear you'd lose more lives trying to buy time for a full evacuation, than those you'd save.'

'Alas, it's as I suspected.' She waited until out of earshot of the reserves. 'Calerdorn fell with barely a whimper. Is there an outside chance the port itself could be held? It's vital we keep at least one open.'

'As you know, ma'am, I do like the odd wager every now and then, but I wouldn't want to bet on such an outcome here. If we focused all efforts on the port itself, we'll only succeed in presenting a smaller target with tightly packed soldiers. One shot will cause more fatalities. And should Dorlan make an appearance, or if they attack by sea…'

Elodi's shoulders dropped. 'Then if they move to attack, an evacuation it will have to be. I can see no other option but to install the Council at Eldamouth, and get as many of the folk here farther south.' She sat on a low wall surrounding the training area. She watched young children carrying buckets of water for the reserves to quench their thirst after just a short session. She kept her voice low. 'Eldamouth boasts superior defenses and has the benefit of surrounding water.'

'Agreed, ma'am. The cost of lives to hold this port would be too high to justify, even if possible. Eldamouth would be my choice to maintain a foothold in your realm.'

'But how much farther can we flee? Do we end up abandoning Harlyn altogether?'

The captain grunted as he sat. 'When you played *Squares*, were there times when you thought you had the better of your father, only to find he came back to defeat you?'

Elodi managed a smile. 'Indeed, there were many

games before I could second guess his preferred strategies.'

'The stakes are obviously much higher, but war is no different. You have to know when to retreat so you can regroup and fight another battle. You can't win if you have no counters left in the game.'

'Yet I am duty-bound to take my best *counters* to the aid of the Archon.'

'Err… please excuse the intrusion, ma'am?' She looked up to see the drill master fidgeting with his wooden baton.

Elodi stood. 'Yes, Master?'

'I… err' — he glanced to Gundrul — 'I'm sorry to interrupt, ma'am, but I was sort of wondering whether you had the time to maybe address my lads and lasses? A sort of—'

Elodi smiled. 'Morale-boosting speech?'

He breathed out loudly. 'Yes, ma'am. That would be just perfect.'

'Very well. Have your reserves gather round.' The master beamed and strolled back two inches taller. Elodi sighed. 'I could hardly decline. But what can I possibly say to raise their spirits? What have we got up our sleeves that could bring them hope?'

The captain rose and held out his hand. 'May I suggest you can start by standing on this wall. Always worked for me to be taller than my audience.'

Elodi agreed and climbed onto the low wall. She looked down at Gundrul. 'Any more advice?'

He gave a wry grin. 'Perhaps start with a compliment, then give them the news on the situation, but maybe miss out some of the worse parts, then…' he scratched his head, 'the rest I'll leave up to you, ma'am.'

The first of the reserves drew near. Elodi whispered. 'Thank you, Captain, that affords me a minute to work out the remainder.' She held up her hands to greet thirty or so makeshift soldiers, many still out of breath from their exercises. 'Please, gather round.' Now they stood closer, she was shocked to see just how young and old they appeared. But it was the obvious awe in their faces as they looked up to her that caused concern. They would have heard stories of her confrontation with the shreek at the gatehouse. But that was a mere sideshow compared to their current predicament. As Lady Harlyn, they rightly expected her to lead them to victory. But as she surveyed the group, Elodi wondered how many would survive an encounter with a ruthless and experienced enemy.

She took a breath. 'May I start by saying how impressive you all look performing your drills. I am heartened by your skill in combat.' She caught Gundrul's eye at her side — his thoughts remained hidden. Elodi looked at their faces caked in dust: had she overdone the praise? She continued. 'Times are difficult.' Her three words understated their dire situation somewhat, but she felt it needed no more explanation. Her voice wavered. 'As you know, Calerdorn is lost.' A few heads bowed among the reserves, but she could tell they waited for her reassurance. 'And you will, by now, have heard the enemy have one of our… own. By some dark power, they have corrupted the once-great warrior, Dorlan. But he is not the Dorlan of the legends. He is but a shell, a vessel those rogues have filled with their hatred, a figurehead, but nothing more.' Gundrul nodded. She raised her voice. 'We have nothing to fear if we stay true to our values. We fight for what is right. We fight for our families, our traditions, our lives. Our enemy has nothing to lose, but we do. So, we fight with a fire in our bellies that they will never understand. And that fire will ultimately bring us victory.' The reserves cheered.

Elodi waited for them to finish. She took a breath and lowered her voice. 'Yes, we are in a difficult position, I will not deny, but we are the men and women of Harlyn. Our realm has stood for over a thousand years.' Elodi felt her own spirits rise. 'And we are not alone. I sail south to stand side-by-side with the Archon to defeat the Golesh at the gate.' She could see them stand a little taller. 'We will be victorious, then I shall return with a force the likes we've not seen for many centuries to drive the marauders out.' Elodi took hold of her sword. 'The few that survive our onslaught will have learned never to churn the soil of Harlyn with their boots ever again.' She drew her sword and thrust it into the air. 'To victory!' The reserves cheered louder, raising thirty battered wooden swords in reply. Elodi took Gundrul's hand and climbed down from the wall. The master barked an order, sending the soldiers back to their training with renewed vigor. She looked to her captain.

He grinned. 'Nicely put, ma'am. I think that did the trick.'

She recovered her breath. 'You don't think it was perhaps a little over done?'

Gundrul beamed. 'Not at all in the current situation. Better a soldier goes into battle with hope in his heart than despair.' He glanced to the drill master. 'And he'll feel less guilty training these folks not to die for a lost cause.'

Elodi turned from the square. 'Ah, just when I was beginning to believe my own words.'

'Ma'am!' An aide skidded to a halt before her. He quickly gathered his breath. 'Please, ma'am. You must come, err… I mean your presence is required at—'

'Please, deliver your message and don't be concerned about etiquette.'

He blushed. 'Apologies, ma'am. The healer asks you to come quickly. The Chief Advisor has taken a turn for the worse.'

Elodi descended the dozen steps to the cabin. She threw open the door to find the healer at Wendel's side, surrounded by members of her Council crammed into the small cabin. He looked frail and small even in the modest bunk. Wendel tried to raise his head as Elodi approached.

'Don't. Please, Wendel, don't try to move.' She kneeled by his bed and took his hand, suppressing a gasp as his deathly, cold fingers trembled, barely able to return her grasp.

The healer whispered in her ear. 'I have tried every herb and tincture I have at my disposal, but he is old and greatly weakened. And the shock of the loss of Calerdorn weighs heavy on his mind.'

Elodi nodded. 'As with us all, but for Wendel, it must inflict a greater blow.' She leaned closer and rested a hand on his shoulder. 'I will retake the city, Wendel. I swear in the name of my father, and for the pride of my mother's kin. I will retake the city.'

Wendel attempted a smile. He croaked. 'I know, ma'am. I have no doubt you—' he coughed, spitting flecks of blood onto his whiskered chin.

She tightened her grip on his cold hand. 'Don't give up. I need you, more than ever, I need you at my side, Wendel.'

His lips moved. 'Don't let the healer tarry here any longer, ma'am. There are others who will benefit from her care. I've not the strength. I'm old. I've had my time.'

Elodi nodded to the healer. 'He's right. You've done all you can, and for that I'm grateful.' She looked to her Councilors. 'And please, you also, give us a moment alone.' In turn, they each bade their farewells to Wendel and departed.

Perdew was the last to leave. He placed his hand on Wendel's arm. 'Hang on in there, old boy. We have yet to finish our debate on the finest wines of Gwelayn.' He glanced to Elodi, then followed the others from the room.

'Ma'am?' Wendel's voice was now barely a whisper. He struggled to lift a finger to point to a small wooden box. 'In there… I just had time to retrieve it before the fall. The scroll contains information you should—' He spluttered, losing his voice.

A tear ran down Elodi's cheek. She had always viewed Wendel as an old man, seeming ancient when she was a young child, thinking he would live forever. She stroked his hand. 'Even in the midst of a losing battle, you had the wherewithal to think ahead. My dear, Wendel, you never cease to amaze me.' He winced in pain. His grip loosened. Elodi pleaded. 'Not now, Wendel. Please.' His gray eyes held hers as all their years together came flooding back. Her voice broke. 'I won't allow it, Wendel. You can't go. You don't have my permission.'

A faint smile spread across his pale face. He whispered. 'I know, ma'am, but this is one request I cannot fulfill.' His voice faded. 'May I, ma'am?' Wendel's eyes closed, his breathing slowed, but the smile remained.

Elodi blurted out, unable to contain her grief. First Calerdorn and now her trusted friend. She buried her face in his shoulder. 'Of course, Wendel. Close your eyes, take your rest.' She sat up, concerned she may have caused him pain. 'Wendel.' His eyes flickered. 'My father said you were the wisest man he had ever known, trusting you above all others.' Another tear ran down her cheek and onto his hand. 'And I came to believe the same. I will retake Calerdorn, I will, Wendel. Go on your way now, my dear friend. I am certain we will meet again.'

Wendel let out a long sigh. Elodi watched, certain she saw his spirit leave. 'Go in peace, my sweet man. Go in peace.' Elodi let the tears flow, hugging him, dearly wishing she could entice him back. But she had to let him go. Wendel had served Harlyn all his adult life — he deserved peace. She sat back and crossed his hands on his stomach. His many loyal years of service had afforded him a quiet life for his final days. Elodi should have insisted Wendel retire to a comfortable residence out in the country long before now. But where in the realm could he have been safe? And as she straightened his clothes and bedsheets, she knew he would never have accepted retirement. Elodi looked down and stroked Wendel's face. 'Goodbye my dear, dear friend.'

35. The Shadow Retreats

The branch creaked. Toryn lifted his head and looked over to Hope. Her fingers stretched out and extended towards him. He reached out. Their fingertips touched. A pinprick of warmth reminded him of a Singing Stone. He whispered. 'Hope? Can you speak?'

Her voice croaked. 'You've heard them.'

'The Nym?'

'No. The Maidens. You heard them, did you not? At Archonholm.'

Toryn recalled their voices. 'You know? How?'

'The shadow retreats a little. Enough for me to see more of my past and learn of my purpose, but also to regain some of my powers. I sensed your presence… in the Song.'

'Long enough to hear the other voices? I thought my head was about to split. Was it you who stopped them?'

'Yes, I heard them, but no, it was not I who saved you. Another entered, but not a voice known to me.'

He sighed. 'Whoever it was, saved my life. I was close to breaking. I can't say I'd readily want to listen to your Song again.'

'You entered too early. I can show you how to deal with the lesser mischief-makers, but it will take time to develop your powers to handle the real threats.' Hope looked up to the dome of fog. 'But I cannot achieve this while we're detained.'

Toryn struggled against the twigs entwined about his wrists. 'What happened here? And why must you and I atone?'

Hope's head dropped. She muttered into her chest. 'A terrible battle. Thousands died.'

'But how was that your fault?'

She turned to face him. 'The shadow over my past yet conceals much from me, but I believe I fought with another of my kind.' Hope looked over his head as if trying to recall. 'His name was… Mordram. Yes, Mordram. He was of my Order. But we grew weary.' As she spoke, Toryn's vision blurred as if he hurtled back through time. His head spun as he slowed, then came to an abrupt halt. As his sight recovered, he found he stood at Hope's side on a wide, grassy plain at the head of a great army, the last army of the Seven Realms: the ghost army he had seen from within the faery ring. The ground trembled. He turned. A vast horde of fierce fighters advanced, outnumbering the Seven Realms many times over. But it was not the host of the enemy that troubled Hope.

The dark ranks parted. Tall, gangly creatures emerged from a whirling funnel rising from the ground and strode directly at them. Toryn shrank back as the shroul-like forms drew near. Yet these were larger, more fearsome, and had wide gaping mouths, seeming too wide for their narrow skulls. They thrust their hideous heads forward and screeched a terrible cry, turning Toryn's bowels to water. Shreeks! They had to be shreeks, the spawn of Ormoroth. The plain shuddered as they stamped their cloven hooves, crushing the first ranks rushing forward to defend Hope. The shreeks broke through. Toryn felt Hope's heart lurch as she and Mordram braced for the onslaught.

Toryn found his voice among his horror. 'When did this happen?' The vision faded. 'The last great battle fought in these parts was long before the closing of the Caerwal Gate.' He turned his head to see she had changed: the young Hope looked back. 'Are you that old?'

Hope shook her head as much as the tree would allow. 'That I cannot tell. The battle was fought here, but I have no recollection of when.'

'What happened? Why do the Nym hold you guilty?'

A tear trickled from her eye. 'I had no choice. I killed many… many thousands. Fine people.' Her voice broke. 'I had no choice.'

Toryn found himself back in the midst of the battle. The shreeks led the hordes of the dark forces, baying for the blood of the defenders of the Seven Realms. But for all their honor and bravery, the finest knights of the age were exhausted, barely able to lift their spears and swords through willpower alone. Unable to hold back the tide after hours of battle, the enemy slaughtered them. None had the strength to resist. They fell beneath hooves and rough-shod boots who gleefully stomped them into the dirt.

Toryn caught his breath as he flinched, trying to evade the attack. 'The Nym said you recited a forbidden verse.'

Hope's voice quivered. 'I had no choice. I recited one of the… Evil One's verses.'

Toryn gasped. 'Evil One? From the tales?'

'There is but one.'

'How did you come to use such… such devilry?'

Hope closed her eyes and tipped back her head. 'Had I not, all would now be lost. I had to make the choice. If I had not acted, the enemy, the Ul-dalak of the Dark Verses, would have triumphed and overrun the entire land. Mordram and I were all but defeated when' — she opened her eyes and looked passed Toryn as if hearing something from afar — 'yes, a voice from south of the mountains. He gave me the strength to counter.'

'The one you heard when we sat upon the ridge!'

Hope nodded. 'Yes. I believe it to be the same. And one of my Order.'

'But those lands south of the mountains were lost to the Golesh.'

'I believe he must be imprisoned. Held for many centuries. Yet he still lives. I sense his presence in the Song. But he is weak, nearing the end of his long life.' She drew a sharp breath. 'I know his name. The one from beyond the mountains.' Her eyes moved as if searching. 'He is Idraman, the head of the Order of Echoes.' More memories appeared to flood back. 'I stood here with… ah, yes. There may have been more than one, perhaps the last few of my kind. But, despite our combined strength, we fell. So many… so many. The Immortals of Elmarand, Spearmen of Keld, Lancers of Tallabar, Phalanxes of Rhydor, and the Knights of Calerdorn' — her head bowed — 'so many fine fighters, all overcome as the shreeks screamed their foul curses, driving horses and men to madness. I'd fought shreeks before, but these were more terrible than any I had encountered. These were' — she gasped — 'not shreeks, no… not shreeks, they were something from before our time, they were… the *Draedalak*. Ah! The *Draedalak*. We had not the strength to resist for long. One-by-one we fell. Those of my Order… lost.'

Toryn's heart sank as he saw the proud ranks of the Seven Realms crumble beneath the onslaught. 'How did you survive?'

Hope took a few moments. 'From south of the mountains, Idraman gave me his remaining strength so I could… I had no choice. With Mordram's help, I found the most potent lines of the Dark Verses, and… and I used them. I recited the Verse of Unmaking.'

Toryn shivered in the damp air. 'And it caused this?'

Hope nodded as fresh tears streamed down her face. 'Those from my Order were protected, but every other soul was' — her lip curled — '*unmade*. I annulled the Song of Creation within a league of where I stood. All was undone. They just… fragmented. Torn apart as the force that brought them into this world was ripped from inside them.'

Toryn beheld the dying moments of the battle. Hope threw back her head and thrust her arms open. Her scream cut the cries of conflict from every throat. In an instant, the air erupted, a flash of a white light so intense, the vision alone scorched Toryn's eyes.

Hope sobbed. 'All those who fought, whether for good or evil, perished, snatched from the land as if they had never existed. The foul beasts from the past were hurled back to their time, sadly escaping to fight another day. All other mortals perished. I cannot penetrate the darker shadows over my past, but I know those of my Order present, were saved. But while our lives were spared, our minds were lost. The memory buried deep to spare us the horrors we endured. What you saw outside this circle was how the land was before the Maidens' Song. The forest is, I believe, the work of the Nym to heal the great wrong, but much has yet to recover. I, unfortunately, did much harm to the land which will take many centuries yet to recover.'

Toryn felt her pain. 'But if you hadn't acted, you said the evil would have triumphed. What else could you have done?'

She turned; her gray eyes moist with tears. 'The guilt rests heavily upon my head.' She tried to stretch her back as best she could. 'But the Nym are right. I must atone, but not in this place. I have much to do to redress the wrong I committed. But I cannot do that if held here.'

He pulled against the tree. 'How do we escape?'

Hope's voice strengthened. 'We have the means. In a way, the Nym have done me a great kindness. Bringing me here has allowed me to connect with much of my lost knowledge… and a vestige of my power.' She watched him. 'But before we leave. There is something else you must know.'

'Must?'

'I cannot be sure of the others who fought at my side. Apart from Mordram, I remember just one other. His name was Finromir. He too escaped.' She held his gaze. 'The reason the Nym believe you should be held here is, because' — she took a deep breath — 'Toryn, I can see now that Finromir is your father.'

Toryn choked. 'My father!' He gaped at Hope, gasping for breath. The words failed to come. Ever since Miram told him he was adopted he had wondered about the man. He knew he was a wyke, but he had not considered for one moment his father could have played a part in such a key battle. His mind cleared. He turned back to Hope. 'My father? He was here, with you, all those years ago?'

Hope nodded. 'And as his kin, I'm afraid the Nym hold you responsible for what they perceive is an atrocity committed against the land.'

'But… how? It was hundreds of years before Hamar found him in the woods outside my village. I can't see how he could have fought here.'

Hope touched his hand. 'Of that, I am certain. He was one of the last who stood against the evil that day. When I recited that verse, he survived, and I suspect, like me, he roamed the lands for many, many years, lost, confused, not knowing of his past.'

Toryn stared at the ceiling of fog hoping he could see his father's last moments on the battlefield. 'What could have happened to him in those lost years?'

Hope finally smiled. 'You are proof he must have found a wife and lived a vestige of a normal life for a time. I should imagine he found happiness for a few years at least. But… something must have happened to restore his mind. Yet, as soon as he remembered his past, his presence in the Song strengthened, attracting the attention of the ever-watchful Ul-dalak. I can only speculate they found him before he sensed their approach. Perhaps they slayed his wife… your mother, explaining why he fled with you alone to find a safe place for you to grow.'

Toryn's voice shook. 'Hamar was right. Desperate people do desperate things in desperate times.' He closed his eyes. 'Does he live? Would you know?'

'He does.' Toryn's heart lurched. Hope sighed. 'But I'm afraid he is in dire need. I feel his anguish. I'm afraid he is now held by the Ul-dalak.'

If Toryn's hands were free, he would have covered his face. 'Hamar believed he had spent years evading his pursuers.' He bit his lip. 'But he must have finally succumbed.'

'Have faith. Your father is strong. The Ul-dalak seek to corrupt and recruit him to their cause. Our kind hold great powers, powers that would prove most useful to the other side. They strive to turn him, yet I know still he resists, enduring great pain to hold back their attempts to break him.'

His father's agony twisted a blade in Toryn's gut. 'Where is he?'

'Alas, that I cannot tell. While I know he lives, his location remains hidden, leading me to suspect he is held deep in some dark pit of the enemy's making.' She caught his eye. 'But he stays true to all that is good. I believe he will endure yet. His captors cannot afford to let him die, and in a way, this is good news. This reveals to me some of my Order still live, and we may yet hold an advantage in numbers.'

'But surely he cannot resist forever. Will we ever find him?'

Hope nodded. 'Sadly, the day will come when he finally breaks. But I believe, as I recover my strength, I will find him, then together, as your powers grow, we will have the chance to free him from their domain. Of that I am certain.'

Toryn clenched his fist. 'And what of the other who fought with you here? You said his name was Mordram. Could he aid us?'

Her eyes scanned the air above. 'Alas, I can find no evidence of him, not even within the echoes of the Song. I can only think he must have perished in the years I wandered these lands in my confused state. Ah! This is a great loss. Mordram was a knowledgeable and powerful ally. He will be missed in the months ahead.'

Toryn recalled Hamar's stories. 'Could the Archon be one of your kind?'

'That I cannot tell. If he is, his mind is closed to me, and he leaves no trace in the Song. He may yet be, but he may also shield his mind from his past. I will have to converse with him in person for confirmation. If he is from my time, he may possess knowledge that will push back the stubborn shadows that yet linger.'

'The Archon fought a great battle south of the mountains in the last days of the Seven. Surely, he couldn't have held back the Golesh and their dark creatures if he were not one of your Order?'

'When I meet him, I shall know.'

Toryn looked about them. 'So, how do we get out of this place? We can do little if we must *atone* here until the land is healed. Can you get the better of the Nym?'

She managed to smile. 'They are a formidable force, but not as challenging as they once were. Their powers have declined over time as the forests fell with the coming of new races, and the poisoning of the land by dark forces.

I suspect they may already know of my—' A rush of wind snatched Hope's words from the air.

The Nym returned. They circled the trees, slowly taking shape before them.

One formed in front of Toryn, another before Hope. *It speaks truth.* He chilled as the Nym's face met his. *It has purpose. It serves to protect the Amanach. It will atone by other means.*

Hope spoke to Toryn. 'They can read my recovered memory.' The Nym waved a hand, leaving wisps of fog where its fingers had been. The branches moved, lowering them to the ground and releasing their hold. Toryn rubbed his wrists and went to aid Hope as she stumbled forward. They stood to face the two visible Nym.

They bowed their shrouded heads, speaking directly to Toryn and Hope for the first time. 'We have delayed your quest. We must atone.'

Hope raised her hands. 'You have no need. You have assisted by revealing what lay hidden.'

They stood tall over them. 'Then we will aid where we hold dominion.'

'And it will be gratefully accepted.' She winked at Toryn. 'We have a powerful new ally. Their help may yet prove a deciding factor.'

Toryn peered ahead. 'This is taking longer than when I entered. We're still beneath the fog.'

Hope turned. 'Time and distance are irrelevant to the Nym. They have their ways.'

'Who are they? Did the Nym set the Singing Stones?'

'No, not the Nym. They may be from the earliest of days, but they have not the means to raise the Amanach. The stones were set by an ancient race many centuries ago, perhaps with the assistance of the Nym. But what fate befell them, I do not know. Little evidence remains of their existence, so I regret it may have been a catastrophic end, possibly at the hands of Ormoroth and his dark hordes.'

'Did you fight Ormoroth here?'

She looked to the sky. 'I doubt it. Even if all my kind stood together, we could not have resisted his power, unlike the great Archons of the past. No. We faced his minions and still struggled. Thankfully, Ormoroth was driven from this land by the combined might of Draegelan and Dorlan at the height of their power.'

Toryn felt his chest swell at the mention of Harlyn's greatest warrior. 'But ultimately such a sad tale.'

'I called on the very verse Ormoroth is believed to have invoked to deny Dorlan's ultimate victory at the Battle of Talaghir.'

'And what became of Ormoroth? Is he gone forever?'

Hope stopped. 'Alas, I think not. I cannot sense his presence, but I believe his spirit is preserved by the corrupt verses in the Song. It has taken me all these years to recover from reciting those abhorrent lines, or at the very least, regain some of my memory and skill. But Ormoroth was vastly more powerful than I. I suspect his influence still taints this land, but should he recover his physical form and cross back into this realm, we will be challenged to our limit, if indeed we have the strength to challenge him at all.'

Toryn felt the cold for the first time since leaving the stones. 'Where would we begin to fight the likes of him?'

Hope took his hand. 'Certainly not alone. I must seek your Archon and perhaps together we can locate the remnants of my Order. If we can yet discover the First Verse of the Maidens' Song, and unlock the secrets of the Amanach, we may yet resist. We believe if we're able to recite the first, uncorrupt verse, we may complete the Song, close the circle and rid it of the stain of the Evil

One. That alone would cast out Ormoroth and his foul servants.'

Toryn took courage from her resolve. 'Then I will do everything I can to aid you, for what that is worth.'

Hope squeezed his hand and smiled. 'Your aid is worth more than you can imagine. You are strong, your heart is true, and the blood of your father flows through your veins. And with my guidance, you will grow stronger… in time, if that is a luxury we have.'

He straightened against the weight of responsibility suddenly bearing down upon him. 'But where do I begin? I have not the first idea of how to use this power you say is in my possession. I would dearly love to help with the fight, but surely at present, I am just a burden.'

She rested her hand on his shoulder. 'We will find a way. As my powers recover, I will guide you along the path. But I will not make false promises. It is not an easy path, and the need is great, and you will have to learn fast. But Finromir was a fine man, and I know you will follow in his footsteps.'

Toryn bowed his head. 'I wish to honor my father, and perhaps someday make him proud.'

'Of that, I am confident.' Hope looked ahead. She set off. 'But first, we must evade the enemy and seek out your Archon. From what you say, I believe he must be one of my Order and is hindered by the same shadow as me.'

Toryn followed. 'But the last time I was in Archonholm, I was hung from a bridge to die. They condemn wykes to death. That is the law of the land.'

'Not this time. I'm certain I can free his mind from the shadow. Then he'll see you're the son of Finromir, and therefore accept you as a worthy ally.'

'Imagine. Me a farmhand. An ally of the Archon.'

'You are of the blood of Finromir, Toryn. You will be welcomed into the Order.' She winked. 'And remember, we now have the Nym on our side.' Hope pointed. 'And look. The mist clears. I can see the edge of the circle.'

36. A Master Stroke

Elodi could almost believe the *Celestra* was pleased to be back in the warmer waters of the south. An obliging, stiff breeze had assisted a safe passage in good time. The gods of the deep, still exhausted from their efforts to entrap her on the voyage north, had no choice but to allow her to sail across their domain as they suffered to observe from the depths.

Elodi fixed her eyes on the green hills of Tamarand basking in the noonday sun. Her eyes still smarted, but these were no longer tears for Calerdorn or Wendel, but the work of the salty water thrown up by the *Celestra's* bow as the old lady struck home for the harbor at West Haven. Her clenched jaw ached but she could not relax for one moment. The thought of her people in the hands of the enemy hurt as if a sharp blade twisted in her heart. But she could do nothing for them now. She had to focus on the immediate task ahead.

The *Celestra* had docked briefly at Eldamouth to assemble the surviving council members into a working body with Perdew at its head. Elodi decided Perdew would best serve the realm remaining at Eldamouth. And Elodi believed she now knew all she needed to handle the likes of the Castellan and Vice-Archon. As for the Archon, none in the Five Realms had the expertise to second guess him.

Elodi's gaze wandered back to the north. She had tasked Perdew to coordinate the total force of Harlyn's reserves from Eldamouth. But some difficult decisions lay ahead. It would not be easy to determine which parts of the realm to defend. Elodi hoped many of the small settlements would be of no interest to Uldrak, thus allowing their scant resources to be focused on strategic bridges and passes that could be defended with fewer numbers. But the thick walls of Eldamouth had given her some hope. Set on an island within the Great Elda's estuary, three wide bridges spanning the gap provided the only land-based means of entry. Gundrul suggested two could be destroyed as a last ditch attempt to hold the port if necessary. And while Elodi still had the *Celestra* and a fleet of small boats, they could at least supply the town.

Elodi looked to the skies. And what of Ruan and his spearmen? Had Lena succeeded in delivering her vital message? She hoped Ruan's experience would see his men make it across the Dorn plain to seek refuge in Seransea. His force would be a valuable addition to the reserves and their likely evacuation to Eldamouth. The upturned faces of the reserves as they had listened to her improvised speech, filled her thoughts. Had she given them false hope? She had vowed to bring aid from Archonholm, but it would be late summer at the earliest before she could fulfil that promise. But how much of her realm would be under the control of its new rulers by then? What would she find on her return?'

Elodi grabbed the rail as the West Haven trumpeters sounded their greeting from the harbor wall. Gundrul and Cubric stood at her side, but she could not help noticing the gap Wendel should have filled. The ropes were thrown to the men on the harbor, the sailors scurried about the masts and decks, preparing to dock. She looked to her captains, but no words were needed. Elodi checked her armor, buckles and re-arranged her sword, then followed her two captains to the gangplank.

Elodi's stomach unclenched as she stepped onto the solid West Haven pier. She had spent most of the journey with one eye on the horizon, dreading the rise of dark skies and a return of a storm, oddly thankful for taking her mind from the plight of her people, if only for a little while.

The Harbor Master headed a large crowd eager to cheer those who would march alongside the Archon to defeat their great foe in the south. But as Elodi stood by his side to watch her force come ashore, she wondered if her contribution of just two hundred would make the slightest difference, despite them being the best Harlyn had to offer. She would have preferred a day for her force and the horses to recover from the voyage, but the Archon had made it clear he would open the Caerwal Gate on Midsummer's Day. Despite Elodi's many misgivings, she knew her duty to the Five Realms, vowing Harlyn would play her part. That momentous occasion lay only seven days ahead, and Archonholm sat seventy leagues to the east. A forced march would get them there in time but leave little space for rest before facing the greatest challenge of their age.

Elodi watched the banners fluttering in the breeze as the Harbor Master spoke of his admiration for Harlyn's finest. But she was numb. Their world would change forever, whether for good or for bad. Would any of the realms' colors still be flying in the months to come? Or would all be burned and trampled underfoot before summer was done.

Despite her doubts about the Archon, the sight of his blue banner flying above the horizon gave Elodi strength. While he and the forces of Archonholm ruled, she had hope for Harlyn. As the tall spires of the great city came into view, the pain in her heart eased. And if Bardon's elite forces fared well beyond the mountains, they could muster a formidable force and drive the Ruuk out of the north for good. She glanced up as a messenger bird glided high over their heads, then slowly descend towards the city — it seemed all flocked to Archonholm on this day.

The march had been hard on Harlyn's foot soldiers. Unaccustomed to the warmth of the ever-present sun, they had struggled, but to Elodi's pride they had not grumbled. At regular intervals she had brought Sea Mist to a halt at the side of the road and watched the lines pass. She had worried her standing among her elite forces had suffered a mortal blow following the fall of Calerdorn. But Elodi need not have fretted, as all managed to raise a cheer from their parched throats as they passed by. But to what fate did she lead them? What lay behind the great Caerwal Gate? Elodi now had just two days to wait. But was the Archon capable of leading them to a great victory? She dared think ahead, imagining herself at the front of the combined armies of the Five Realms, riding to liberate Calerdorn from the grip of the Ruuk. But too many events had to go their way before she could countenance taking back her city. How many of Bardon's force still fought? Did Bardon live? And, even if she could command a large force to take back north, the new defenses and weapons they had worked so hard to install would now be deployed against her.

'Ma'am?' Gundrul cleared his throat. 'A delegation of Archonholm approaches.'

Elodi focused on the road. 'Ah yes, thank you, Captain.' She groaned. 'And I see that odious little man, the Castellan, among them.'

'Then may I suggest you wipe the dirt from your face, ma'am.'

Elodi waved her hand. 'No. It's been a hard march for all. I want them to appreciate our colossal effort and note our discomfort.' She turned in her saddle. 'They all deserve a bath and a soft bed. They've suffered greatly of late, and it's not over yet by any means.'

Gundrul chuckled as he leaned towards her. 'Good point. Then I… *concur*, ma'am.' He grinned. 'I hope you're impressed. I've learned some of your fancy words. I believe it will help when in the company of those smart commanders of Archonholm.'

Elodi laughed, enjoying the release of the tension from her shoulders. 'Then I am pleased to have been your tutor. And I have learned much from being in your presence also, Gundrul. But don't be concerned about the commanders here. I should imagine you have much to teach *them* following these last few months. I doubt many will have had your battle experience of late.'

Gundrul shuffled in his saddle. 'Yet I have still to master the art of riding a horse. But at least I now have more words at my disposal to describe my discomfort.'

The Archonholm delegation stopped a short distance ahead. Elodi turned to Gundrul. 'Have Captain Cubric sound a halt.' She nodded to the Castellan and his riders. 'Let them come to us, eh.'

Gundrul beamed as he waved to Cubric behind. 'I fear for the Golesh behind the gate, ma'am, once you're set loose upon them. I truly do.' The horn sounded and the long columns of Harlyn's soldiers came to a welcome stop.

Elodi turned her attention to the road ahead as the welcoming party relented and rode to meet them. 'But first we have to deal with the scheming Castellan. I don't trust that man, Captain.'

Gundrul lowered his voice as the Castellan drew near. 'You and me, ma'am.'

'Ah, Lady Harlyn! We meet again.' The Castellan looked taller on his horse.

Elodi forced a smile. 'Indeed, we do, Castellan. And may I say what an honor it is.'

'You flatter me, ma'am.' If the Castellan bowed his head, it was barely a nod. 'The honor is all mine.' He stood in his stirrups and looked along the column. 'And what an impressive, if small, force you have assembled for the Archon. But then, we do have to consider your circumstances. May I say it was with great sorrow I heard of the fall of Calerdorn.'

Elodi's face reddened with the shame of hearing her failure voiced by the Castellan. She swallowed. 'It is but a temporary setback. I will retake my city before the winter.'

'Of course, ma'am, of course.' He clapped his hands. 'But we have more pressing matters to deal with.' Elodi clenched her jaw. The Castellan spoke to one of his aides. 'Have the captain of the West Barracks show these fine soldiers of Harlyn to their quarters.' Then back to Elodi. 'The Vice-Archon has prepared your room as before, ma'am. I trust that is to your liking.'

Gundrul whispered. 'Accept it, ma'am. You can't bunk down in the barracks. It wouldn't be fitting.'

Elodi shook her head. 'But we'll all stand shoulder-to-shoulder at the gate.'

Her captain smiled toward the Castellan as he kept his voice low. 'Begging your pardon, ma'am, but I should imagine you'll be at the front.'

'And that's where I should be.'

Gundrul nodded towards the waiting Castellan. 'Ma'am?'

Elodi sighed and turned. 'Thank you, Castellan. That would be acceptable. But I am keen for my soldiers to have the best available resources. They have had a long, difficult journey and thus require time to prepare for the battle ahead.'

'Rest assured, Lady Harlyn, your force will benefit from the best we have to offer.'

Elodi leaned over to Gundrul. 'If you feel they are not getting what he's promised, please let me know immediately.'

Elodi washed away the dust from the road, but not her guilt. While she had bathed in a warm tub, she guessed her fighters had little more than a slosh down with cold water from a bucket. She dried herself and walked to the window. Outside, all looked well with the world. The Foranfae Forest exhaled its morning mists as it had done for hundreds of years. White, wispy clouds streaked high across the blue sky, prompting the direction of her gaze: north. But as settled as the ward of Holm looked, she knew the situation in Calerdorn could not be worse. In an odd way, she now welcomed the opening of the Caerwal Gate. If, as the Archon promised, a swift victory could be achieved, she would soon hasten back north leading a stronger force than the one she had brought south. But was she capable of commanding? After all, she had lost a well-defended city in less time it took to ride around its walls.

Elodi tore her eyes from the clouds and dressed. Her meeting with the Vice-Archon was in two hours and she was determined to walk the terraces to clear her mind and prepare. Gundrul assured her the accommodation for her soldiers was adequate and they were recovering from the long march. And to her relief, Sea Mist appeared happy to be stabled with the proud beasts of the First Horse. But still her heart raced. She felt as she had as a young child as Midsummer's Day drew near in Calerdorn. The young Elodi had found it close to impossible to sleep as she anticipated the music, dancing, and giving of gifts for the celebrations. Elodi would spend many hours making her present for her father, but if she was totally honest, it was in the belief the better she gave, the better the gift she would receive. And seeing as she had never received anything to disappoint, her theory held true. Yet there would be no exchanging of gifts this year in the usual manner for most — but a victory at the gate would easily surpass anything from previous years.

Elodi fastened the buttons on her tunic. She regarded herself in the mirror, keen to see an Amayan warrior looking back. But the tight muscles on her face laid bare her unease, and not the confident determination of a skilled fighter. She spun away and strode from the room, hoping the warmth of the southern air would alleviate her guilt and trepidation. But as she neared the end of the corridor, an aide of the Castellan approached.

He pulled up. 'Ah, Lady Harlyn. The Vice-Archon requests your attendance immediately.'

'But it is not yet midday.'

'Apologies, ma'am, but the Vice-Archon has other pressing matters to attend today and has therefore brought forward your meeting.'

Elodi wondered what could be more important than a meeting with the leader of a realm bringing her scant forces to support the Archon. She breathed out. 'Very well.'

The aide held out his hand. 'Then please, this way, ma'am.'

Elodi reluctantly abandoned her walk along the terraces. But of course, this was the way of the Vice-Archon. Even on the brink of the most decisive day in the history of the Five Realms, she still played the game of unnerving the leaders of the lesser territories. Elodi strode faster, overtaking the aide, forcing him to catch up; she was not going to let the Vice-Archon's scheming worry her today. She turned to the aide. 'On my last visit, Tombold was assigned to me. I wish to speak with him again. Could you inform him I would like to see him this afternoon, no, make that midday.'

The aide frowned. 'Ma'am? You would like a meeting with one of our aides?'

'Yes!' He jumped. She lowered her voice. This man had done nothing to warrant being on the receiving end of her frustration. 'Not a meeting as such. He was assigned to Lord Harlyn in his last days, and I simply want to reminisce.'

They turned the corner. 'I see, ma'am. But I'm afraid it is not possible. Tombold was retired by the Castellan just two months past.'

'Retired? Does he reside in Archonholm?'

'I think not, ma'am. He will have returned to his family home. I believe they owned a small vineyard in Gwelayn.' They stopped outside the Vice-Archon's room.

Elodi stayed the aide's hand as he reached for the door. 'That is a shame. I would have dearly liked to speak with him once more. And what of his sons? I believe they serve at the gate.'

The aide appeared taken aback by her interest. 'That I do not know, ma'am. I cannot say that I knew Tombold well, only that he was retired because of… a disciplinary matter.'

Elodi assumed it must be related to returning her father's trunk. 'Well, I hope he wasn't denied his allowance. He had served the Archon well.'

The aide seemed impatient to gain entry. 'Again, ma'am, I would not know.' He looked to the door. 'If I may?' Elodi nodded. The aide knocked and awaited the Vice-Archon's reply before opening. He nodded. 'Ma'am.' Then stepped back and retreated down the corridor. Elodi entered to find the Vice-Archon sitting at a small table beside a window overlooking the Caerwal Bridge. Elodi took some satisfaction that the woman appeared to have aged ten years since their last meeting.

The Vice-Archon motioned to an empty seat. 'Please sit, Lady Harlyn.' But before Elodi had pulled back the chair, she added. 'I trust that is still the correct way to address you.'

Elodi gasped. 'Of course, why would you think otherwise?'

The Vice-Archon's eyebrows raised. 'Having lost Calerdorn to a ragtag bunch of Ruuk, I wonder how much longer Harlyn will survive.'

Elodi remained standing. Her fists clenched. 'How dare you!' The Vice-Archon stiffened, but Elodi pressed. 'I stood in the Great Hall not a few months back and warned you of the forces assailing our borders in greater numbers. I sent messages to the Archon about a dark entity commanding these *ragtag* soldiers. Yet I did not receive a single reply, let alone any offer of help.' Her face burned. She yelled. 'How dare you! I will not take a lecture from you on this matter.' Elodi spun away, fearing she may strike the Vice-Archon. She paced to a smaller window and looked out on the mountains.

The Vice-Archon took a breath. 'You will apologize for your outburst. I appreciate your emotions are running high in your current predicament. Apologize and nothing more will be said.'

Elodi turned slowly and held the Vice-Archon's eye, speaking calmly. 'I will not apologize. If there are any due, it is from you and the Archon.' The Vice-Archon went to speak. Elodi raised her voice. 'You left me to defend Harlyn with depleted resources while insisting I send my produce south to pay *your* levy. Food and supplies that would feed my people in the event of a siege.' She strode to the table. The Vice-Archon shrank back as Elodi slapped her hand on the polished wood. 'And even now, I bring the best of my army to assist the Archon.' She lowered her voice as she glared at the woman. 'I offer my help, but do not expect an apology any day soon.' Elodi sat. 'I have plans for the rest of the day, so I would appreciate you move on to the subject of this meeting.'

The Vice-Archon stared back aghast. Elodi suspected only the Archon spoke to her in such a manner. She muttered. 'Plans?'

'I wish to visit my soldiers in the West Barracks, and I demand an audience with the Archon.'

The Vice-Archon stuttered. 'Demand? The Archon prepares for his greatest challenge since Gormadon Plain. He has not the time for an individual audience.' The Vice-Archon recovered some of her confidence. 'When the time is right, he will address his commanders and leaders of the realms. You will be informed when that meeting will take place.'

Elodi stood. 'Then inform the Archon, I will take my force back north if he refuses to see me… today!' She turned and marched from the room. She grasped the door, intending to slam it in the woman's face, then stayed her hand and left it open. Her heart pounded in her ears and her stomach churned as she walked away. She turned the corner and waited for two aides to pass before gasping for air. When she had entered the room, she had every intention of complying with the Archon's wishes. But the attitude of the Vice-Archon had staggered her. She slowed her pace. What had she done? If the Archon turned down an audience, would she abandon the mission at the gate? Elodi paused at the top of the stairs. Should she return and offer her apology? She half-turned, ready to undo her words of haste. No! Elodi straightened and descended the stairs. Let the Vice-Archon stew. She would have no option but to pass on Elodi's threat to the Archon. If their great leader needed Harlyn's help, he would relent. And if he did not, it proved Harlyn's presence was purely for show, a ceremonial parade for the Archon's gratification. Elodi stopped at the entrance to the South Terrace. She smiled. Her rash words had in fact turned out to be quite a master stroke. A walk in the morning sun would be possible after all.

Elodi returned from her stroll on the terrace much refreshed. She doubted the Archon would respond quickly to her request for a meeting, so took the opportunity to finally read the papers Wendel had rescued from the archives. But the box he had clutched in his hands contained but a single sheet. She carefully removed it, concerned the ancient document would crumble at the first touch. Elodi carried it to the window and laid it out on the ledge. It took her a moment to understand what the faded, sketchy map revealed. But as her eyes wondered across the faint lines and words beneath, her heart lifted. She looked to the skies above Foranfae. How many people in Calerdorn knew of this? Her father had never alluded to it. Did he know? In the wrong hands, the knowledge contained in the map could bring down the city. But in these troubled times, it could liberate her people.

Elodi looked back to the plan. Close to the cell where Dohl had been held, a slab of rock concealed a spiral staircase that descended deep beneath the city. At the foot, a narrow tunnel stretched beyond the south wall and surfaced in the Calern Mountains. It must have been constructed at the time of the city's inception. Had the founders of Calerdorn foreseen such a need? She closed her eyes and thanked them for their far-sightedness, and Wendel for his bravery. Already, her mind set about formulating a nasty surprise for Calerdorn's captors. Now she could not wait for Midsummer's Day to come and pass. But first, there was the small matter of defeating the Golesh at the Caerwal Gate.

37. Sisters of the Stones

The Amayans slept where Toryn had left them. He whispered, not wishing to disturb their slumber. 'Eryn believes they have a connection with you. Do you know of them?'

Hope beamed. 'Now I see them again, yes.' She clasped her hands. 'So much I had forgotten, but the more I remember, the more I am encouraged.'

'Who are they? And why could they not enter the circle?' The Amayans stirred.

Hope explained. 'The Nym did not allow them entry because they had done no harm and thus had no reason to *atone.*'

Eryn sat and wiped the sleep from her eyes. She stared at the young Hope; it was obvious to Toryn she instantly recognized the woman. Eryn glanced to Calestri and Arijan as they stood. As one, they drew their swords, planted them in the ground, then dropped to their knees. Eryn gasped. 'Nyomae. You have returned. Please forgive us. We failed to remember you, and thus treated you poorly.' They bowed their heads. 'We are ashamed.'

Hope winked at Toryn. 'Ah yes! That is my name. Nyomae.' She spoke it as if remembering.

Toryn smiled. 'Should I call you by that name?'

'That would be preferable. With each mention, it will help keep me on my path. I would not wish to return to my older self.' Nyomae motioned the Amayans to rise. 'And you, my sisters, have no reason to be ashamed. We have lived many years in a world of shadow, our purpose concealed from us. But you have stayed true to the land, resisting evil, even if your way has been lost of late. You have waited long, far longer than any could foresee.' She turned to Toryn. 'The Amayans stood with me in this place. They too were shielded from the horrors. The Amayans are protectors of the Amanach, the Singing Stones. A vow taken many centuries passed. A vow that sustains them through the ages.' She nodded as she recalled more of their shared past. 'Yes. That is your purpose, Guardians of the Amanach, or as I prefer, Sisters of the Stones.'

Eryn looked to Arijan and Calestri. Tears filled their eyes and streamed down their cheeks as the veils slipped away to reveal their true selves. Their faces changed, and if possible, looked finer than ever. They stepped forward and threw their arms around Nyomae. She laughed, holding out her arms to invite Toryn to join them. They stood clasping hands as her eyes shone. 'We have much to do, much to remember' — she glanced to Toryn — 'and much to learn. And sadly, while in our slumber, the dark forces have not been idle.' Her head bowed. 'One of the stones has been destroyed. We cannot let another share its fate.' Nyomae stepped back. 'You must gather the remainder of your sisters.' She closed her eyes and tilted back her head. She gasped. 'You number fewer than I'd have hoped.'

Eryn glanced at her sisters. 'How many of us remain?'

'Twelve… no, thirteen.' Nyomae sighed. 'One is in dire need. She—'

'Amyra!' Calestri cried out. 'She must have been' — her face paled — 'captured by Nordleng.'

Nyomae released their hands. 'Not yet, but she is pursued. She flees through Emryst... on foot. You must go to her aid before she's taken. Go north. The Nym will not hinder you. Your horses will come to your aid. You will find them at sunrise. Take the road to Telamir. But you must hurry. Her strength fades and will not be able to resist much longer.' Nyomae scanned the Amayans' faces.

'Amyra is resourceful, but you must hasten if you wish to save her.'

Eryn clasped Nyomae's hand as Calestri and Arijan packed their belongings. 'We shall not fail her. I sense her too, and our sisters. We shall unite, save Amyra, then renew our vow to defend the Amanach.'

Toryn's stomach churned. 'The stone in Wend Gap was undone by a circle of rocks placed about it. Hamar recognized the writing on them, the same as he had seen in Wyke Wood.'

Nyomae grimaced. 'Lines from the Dark Verses.' She looked to Eryn. 'You know how to counteract such devilry but take care. The strength of the Ul-dalak grows, and I fear, will soon match their powers of old.'

Eryn held up her sword. She bowed her head; the blade glowed a faint orange. 'But we too recover ours.' Her eyes widened. 'Let them once more cower before us as they feel the tips of our swords at their throats.'

'We're ready.' Calestri handed Eryn her pack.

They gathered about Nyomae. She looked to each in turn. 'Don't delay. I go south with Toryn to seek council with the Archon. We shall push back the darkness yet.'

Arijan clasped Toryn's shoulder. 'I owe you an apology. I may have… overreacted at times.'

'There's no need. I think I gave as good as I got.'

Arijan grinned. 'That you did. I look forward to meeting again and fighting together.'

Eryn took Toryn's hand. 'Take care. I can see in you now the blood of Finromir. You grow strong.' She held out her bow. 'And please, accept this as a gift. I suspect you'll be needing it shortly on your travels, and it will serve where your scavenged Nordleng blades are useless.' She smiled. 'And when we meet again, I suspect you will make a worthy opponent.'

Calestri laughed. 'May take a while longer to give me a decent fight. But I hope we will get the chance to put your new-found skills to the test.' With that, the Amayans turned and ran north. Toryn watched as they quickly reached the far side of the ruined plain and disappeared beneath the trees.

Nyomae placed a warm hand on his shoulder. 'Now we too must press on. I am hopeful the Archon will help to bring sunlight into the remnants of the shadows still lingering in my mind.'

Toryn remembered the words of the guard at the Menon Bridge. 'I heard the Archon is planning to open the gate and strike south. But if he's made aware of the growing dangers here, he might consider delaying.'

She held his gaze. 'Then there is also a third reason we must hasten to Archonholm. I fear my awakening has alerted the Ul-dalak of our location.'

Toryn's scalp tingled. 'Uleva and Uldrak?'

'The very same. Servants of Ormoroth.' She turned to the tree line. 'Foranfae is a good place to lead them a merry chase, but we cannot remain here forever, and I fear not even the Nym can resist them as their power grows. There are other places safer than Archonholm for you at present. But Archonholm is where we must head. You would be a most welcome convert to the enemy if they captured you now. You're not strong enough to resist, but far enough along the path to turn you quickly to their ends. And perhaps used as a pawn against your father.'

Toryn glanced south. 'It's a long road to Archonholm. Are we safe?'

Nyomae bowed her head. She whispered. 'They come.' Her head turned to the west. 'And it's not just Nordleng. I could handle them alone, but another leads them.' Her eyes widened. 'It is Uleva. She is dangerous. I would not wish to face her at this time.'

Toryn struggled at first to keep up with the renewed Nyomae. She strode fast, requiring little rest as she spoke of her remembered past.

Born at the height of the Seven Realms' prosperity, close to five hundred years ago, Nyomae soon earned a reputation in her village for taming wild animals and predicting the weather. As word of the abilities of the young girl spread, she drew the attention of the Head of the Order of Echoes, Sylvena. Nyomae was invited to Elmarand, the seat of Draegelan, the greatest Archon who ever lived. But Draegelan was in his dotage, having lived many years beyond that expected of rulers, and he died shortly after Nyomae's arrival. His successor, Malendra, was a great warrior in her youth and had served under Dorlan on the Nordruuk border, five centuries earlier. Having witnessed the horrors of Ormoroth, Malendra feared he would one day return, and therefore set up a watch on the north.

Malendra also tasked the Order of Echoes to find new ways to defend against Ormoroth and his spawn. By this time, Nyomae had become a respected member of the Order and assisted Sylvena in the study of the earliest known verses of the Song. After many years, Sylvena believed she had found what they sought: a source of immense power that would protect the realms. Believing she had discovered the location of a lost relic, Sylvena, despite Nyomae's concerns, ventured to the far north. But Sylvena had been deceived, and to Nyomae's dismay, Sylvena vanished from the Song before the year was out.

Nyomae, along with others from the Order, had raced to Sylvena's aid. But as they approached the Nordruuk border they were driven back by severe snowstorms and dark shapes that loomed within. But if they thought Sylvena had perished, they were mistaken. A fate far worse had befallen her. Sylvena had been captured by the Ul-dalak, tortured, tormented, and crushed. They remade her in their form and bestowed upon her a new name: Uluriel.

Within a decade, she rose to lead all who opposed the Archon, proving to be a formidable addition to the servants of the Dark Verses. With this new powerful force at their helm, the Ul-dalak formed a large army to challenge the might of the Seven Realms.

Nyomae stopped beside the bank of the still youthful Menon River. She sighed. 'It was this force I, your father, and the thousands who perished here, faced. But others from my Order must have survived. Once I consult this Archon of yours, I'm certain my memory will return and we will know the full story of those dark days.'

Toryn rested his hand on her trembling shoulder. 'And what of Uluriel? What happened to her following the battle?'

'That I cannot know until my memory is restored. My guess is she may have fled south and sought to rouse the Golesh you speak of.'

'Then perhaps it was Uluriel who led them through the Caerwal Pass once the Second Realm fell?'

Nyomae nodded. 'That is where the Archon must have held her at bay while the gate was completed.' She looked to the opposite bank. 'We will rest here a while.' She sat on a large slab of rock overhanging the fast-flowing river. Toryn joined her, letting his tired legs dangle over the side. Nyomae tossed a pebble into the water. 'It is a great pity I could not have stood with your Archon at such a vital time. But I imagine following our defeat here, I and your father must have wandered these lands in our dazed state while the Archon fought on in the south.'

'How many were in your order?'

'Before Sylvena was lost, we numbered seven for as long as any could remember. Following Sylvena's fall, a man named Idraman took the mantle of leader. I, along with Mordram, had served the Order for almost as long as Idraman.' Her eyes flickered as she watched the Menon flow on its way south. 'Then there was your father, Finromir, and… ah yes. Then Dormarl, then Elysia, the youngest and most recent addition to our ranks.'

Toryn took some berries from his bag and shared them with Nyomae. 'Please. Tell me more about my father.'

Nyomae gratefully accepted the fruit. She smiled. 'Gladly. He was born in a settlement not far from Saphrir on the coast of Emryst. But once his powers became known, like me, he was summoned to Elmarand.' She nodded as Toryn's eyes widened. 'Yes, your father also lived there.' Toryn's chest swelled. He had heard only a few tales of the great, mythical city far to the south, but he could see it now. Its tall towers of smooth, white stone glistened in the hot sun, reaching high into the bluest of skies. Its mighty walls stretched for many a league, protecting the thousands who resided within. And his father had lived there!

Toryn beamed. 'The Archon has sent a force of our finest soldiers to retake it. If the Archon achieves his victory at the gate, I would dearly love to visit.'

Nyomae patted his hand. 'You have that same determined look of your father when he spoke of victory. Finromir was one of the bravest, yet kindest men I've met. I know nothing of your mother, but he would have chosen well, and her blood will surely complement your father's strengths.'

'I wish I knew more about her.' Toryn looked to the trees. 'Where she was from and what did she look like.' He turned to Nyomae. 'How long had you known him before you fought the great battle?'

'Many years, too many for me to count now. We traveled far and wide together. Always seeking answers to the mysteries of the Song before the Ul-dalak uncovered them and used them against us. Finromir is clever. He often saw signs in places we thought to be insignificant. His powers grew quickly, and had events turned out differently, I have no doubt he would have become head of the Order.' Nyomae clutched his hand. 'That is how he has resisted the devious arts of Ormoroth's servants for so long.'

Toryn shivered. 'Earlier you wondered whether Ormoroth may have survived the Battle of Talaghir. Do you think it's possible he lived, while Dorlan was lost?'

'Of that I cannot be sure. If he still has physical form in this world, I am certain I would sense his presence. But if he were forever lost, I doubt the Ul-dalak would have the strength to rise as they appear to be doing so. I suspect his spirit cannot be vanquished, and he gives sustenance to our foes as we speak.'

Toryn's nostrils wrinkled. 'That explains the droog.'

'You did well in that unfortunate encounter, Toryn. Many would have succumbed to just the mere hint of its horror.'

'I still don't understand how I came to be a captive of the Nordleng. From what the Amayans say, they don't sound like the sort who would serve the Archon.'

Nyomae finished her fruit. 'I may have an explanation. Once you heard the Song you would have become known to the Ul-dalak. Your verses would have strengthened, standing out among the myriad of all others. If the Archon has powers, he too would have noticed, and perhaps even figured you were the son of Finromir.'

Toryn's hand went to his stomach. 'Thankfully, it wasn't a moment too soon. Any longer and I wouldn't be standing here.'

'That was an unfortunate misunderstanding. It appears in the long years of the shadow, those of our Order and others with such skills have become outcasts, treated as sorcerers. I do not like this word, *wyke*.' She smiled. 'But as you might say, luck intervened. When you heard the Song, it must have elicited a response from your Archon. He may have recognized your importance to our cause, but also of potential use to the enemy, thus took steps to hide you.'

'But where? I was being taken north. Surely, Archonholm is the most secure place in the land.'

'That may be so for mortals. But remember when I said I could not locate your father. There are rocks from the dawn of time undisturbed by the ages. The echoes of the Song cannot penetrate, making them ideal for certain purposes. If I wished to conceal you from the enemy, I would secure you in such a place. I imagine the Archon knows of these places and sought to hide you. But you were in a bad state after your encounter with the fell voices lurking in the Dark Verses. While on the open road, you would have attracted the Ul-dalak like a flaming mountaintop beacon. The enemy must have had its resources closer than the Archon could have known. I suggest you were waylaid by these Nordleng folk acting on behalf of the Ul-dalak.'

Toryn sighed. 'Then it was a stroke of luck that Eryn discovered me when she did.'

'There is that word again. Luck? Or destiny? There are many forces that act upon this land of which we know nothing.'

He laughed. 'You sound like my old friend, Hamar. He spoke of such unknowns.'

Nyomae stood. 'Then he was a very wise man.'

'That he was.' A splash of water soaked Toryn's feet. He jumped back.

'Does something trouble you?'

He checked his shoe. 'When I came through these parts with the Amayans, they almost drowned in a pool. It was if they were stung, poisoned by the water. I too was effected, but not as badly as them.'

Nyomae bent and scooped water from a puddle formed in a groove in the rock. She quickly released it and dried her hand. 'It is… changed.' She stood and looked up stream. 'These waters come from deep beneath the Kolossos. For as long as I can remember, the Menon has had the power of healing. It is a bad omen if these waters have lost that power.' She brushed the grit from her robe. 'It is time for us to leave. And we must move quickly. It's imperative I speak with the Archon.'

38. The Archon's Pledge

'You are very persistent, Lady Harlyn, I will grant you that.' The Archon gazed out of the doorway leading to his balcony. 'I would not, in normal times, grant such a *request* made in such a manner.' He turned. Elodi suppressed a gasp: the man looked worn. His eyes, gray and sunken; his body frail.

Elodi felt her head bow. 'I am grateful for your time, Archon. I am fully aware you need time to prepare for—'

'But these are unusual times, as you, above most, will appreciate. I trust your soldiers are being well cared for, Lady Harlyn?'

'Yes, thank you. They have had a challenging few—'

'You… you appear different.' The Archon stepped closer, appearing to grow. His head tilted. Elodi's ears ached, and her throat tightened as his eyes suddenly widened and glimmered blue, then green as they met hers. His thin lips pursed. 'Something has changed, Lady Harlyn.'

Elodi stammered. 'I have fought against dark enemies since our last meeting. I have seen things I did not believe could exist but a few months ago. That would be sufficient to change anyone, Archon.'

He stroked his smooth chin and retreated. 'That may be the case. Brushes with such powers will often *change* us.' He spun away. 'Such sad news to hear of the fall of your city. And so quickly followed by the death of your Chief Advisor.'

'Wendel. His name was Wendel, Archon.'

'Ah yes. Such a tragic loss I should imagine.' The Archon turned back to the room. His eyes had returned to gray, and his statue once again, hunched. He shuffled to his chair and lowered himself slowly. He beckoned Elodi to sit opposite. 'But rest assured. As soon as I have dealt with the Golesh ruffians beyond the gate and secured the south, I will devote all my efforts to taking your city back.' He waved a trembling hand. 'I may even lend a hand myself. I would welcome a trip north. It has been many years since I've ventured outside Farrand.' He attempted to straighten his bent neck with little success. 'I'm sure it will be but a trivial matter to drive out the Ruuk from your realm.'

'With all due respect, Archon, you underestimate the strength of the force led by these wykes, if wykes is what they truly are. The legend that is Dorlan rides with them. I have witnessed powers that I thought not possible…' The Archon's head dropped. Did he sleep?

He snorted, sitting up with a start. His eyes focused on Elodi, taking a moment as he appeared to remember the purpose of their meeting. 'Fret not, Lady Harlyn. I have a few' — his eyes flickered into life as his mouth curled — 'tricks of my own that may surprise you yet.' He waved his hand across his face. 'Don't be deceived by my appearance. I have passed through a series of preparations that, for the time being, have taken their toll and left me fatigued. But come tomorrow, I will be stronger than I have been since my trials on the Gormadon Plain.' He nodded and grinned. 'Have no doubt, Lady Harlyn. I predict a swift victory over my stunned foes at the gate.'

Elodi let out a sigh. 'Then I am encouraged, Archon. A swift victory would be most welcome.' She glanced to the window. 'May I ask what numbers we possess, Archon? How many ride from Broon, Kernlow and Galabrant?'

'We have sufficient numbers.' He closed his eyes as if bored by the conversation. 'I suspect the rogues will flee once they witness what I have in store for them.'

Elodi leaned forward. 'So, am I right to assume all realms have committed their full strength?'

The Archon dismissed Elodi's question with a wave of his hand. 'I do not trouble myself with the actual numbers. I have left the finer details to my generals.' He shuffled in his seat. His brow creased, his dull eyes fixed on Elodi, but this time she sensed no discomfort. The Archon's voice weakened. He spoke as if to himself. 'Kernlow and Galabrant are weak. They are the soft belly of this land sitting comfortably between the realms of the north defending the border with Nordruuk, and Farrand in the south guarding the gate.' He noted Elodi's attention and sat straighter. 'We've already taken their finest fighters for the First Horse, knights and my guard. They have little to offer and will provide a token force made up from their small armies.'

'And the lords? Will they partake?'

'That they will, Lady Harlyn. The old lords will accompany us at the gate, but purely for ceremonial purposes you understand.' He laughed. 'Though I cannot imagine how they could offer us any advantage on the battlefield. Their reserves would only be but a hindrance, getting in the way, tripping up our fighters when they inevitably fall. That is why I have placed them at the rear.'

Elodi recalled Lord Kernlow's large frame struggling up the steps when the gate had been attacked. 'That is true, Archon. And Broon? What of the new lord, Nordryn? I see the gold and green banners of Kernlow and Galabrant in the fields outside, but not the black of Broon. Will they be here in time?'

'I see no need for Nordryn to commit here. He is a new—'

Elodi stood aghast. 'No need?' The Archon was taken aback by her reaction. But she pushed her point. 'I have lost Calerdorn! Yet still I bring my best soldiers to your aid. How can you expect me to *commit* while Nordryn sits idly in Keld?'

The Archon regained his composure. He held up his hand. 'Please sit, Lady Harlyn. There is no need for anger. I have sufficient numbers for my purpose. Once I have slept and recovered from my trials, I will be the major force to be feared at the gate. You have no need to be concerned. All I ask is you and your force accompany me to the pass. As I have already stated, I have all the strength I require. The enemy will not be able to endure me for long. You and your soldiers will simply have the task of mowing down those who turn tail and run after I have dealt with them.'

Elodi looked to the open skies outside the doorway. 'What news of Lord Broon in the south?'

'Come!' The sudden vigor shocked Elodi. The Archon rose, strode to the door and out onto the balcony. She followed, shielding her eyes as she stepped out into the red light of the early evening sun. He held out a hand. 'See for yourself.'

Elodi peered through the Caerwal Pass but could make out little other than the dark line of the top of the gate. 'I do not possess your power of *farsigh*t, Archon. What am I meant to see?'

The Archon recovered more of his strength, standing as strong and straight as a statue. 'Smoke rises in the southern skies. Broon holds Elmarand. My elites create havoc among their hordes. The enemy at the gate had no option but to send a force to aid their stricken comrades. Thus, they are weakened further at the pass.'

'And you can be sure the smoke is a result of Lord Broon's victories?'

The Archon bristled. 'Of course! To date, my plan has delivered as I promised. And I am ready to deliver my part of that plan.'

Elodi gripped the rail. 'You have received word from Lord Broon? How many does he yet lead?'

He kept his eyes on the pass, appearing not to hear her question, nodding his head in satisfaction. 'Come Midsummer, have no doubt, Lady Harlyn, I shall deliver a crushing blow upon all those who attempt to stand against me.'

Elodi held her breath. 'That is tomorrow, Archon.'

His eyes glinted. 'Indeed, it is.'

39. Hands Beneath the Water

Nyomae stood tall on the riverbank. 'While its waters may be tainted, it may serve to hasten our way.'

Toryn stepped out from the trees. 'You're thinking of sailing?'

She nodded. 'Archonholm is an arduous six days on foot. By boat we could make it in two, possibly less.' Nyomae glanced to the opposite bank. 'We would be visible on the river, but it will give us a better chance of outpacing our pursuers. And as the river widens, we'll be at less risk of a poisoned dart.'

Toryn felt his spirit rise. 'There's plenty of fallen branches back there. And those reeds look thick and strong enough for binding. I could construct a raft. When I was young, we made them in the summer and dreamed of sailing out to sea.' He sighed. 'But, of course, we were never allowed to go farther than the old bridge.'

Nyomae looked over his shoulder. 'That may not be necessary. I have another option. Allow me an attempt first. If I fail, then you can build your raft. But I fear such a vessel would be difficult to master as the currents grow stronger. If we're not careful, we could end up watching the towers of Archonholm disappear as the river takes us to the coast.' She held out her hand. 'Come. See what I found while you were catching supper.' Nyomae led him to a cove. Toryn wondered whether it was a natural formation, or if hands from long past had fashioned the inlet as it offered some protection against the fast-flowing water.

Nyomae crouched and pointed. 'See? Down there on the water's edge.'

Toryn stooped. 'All I can see is moss clinging to the rocks, and… wait' — his eyes picked out a shape beneath the growth — 'is that a rowing boat?'

'Granted, it's almost decayed after what must be many years of neglect. But look closer. It is well-made by gifted folk.' She stepped back from the ledge. 'The trees were not always so dense. I suspect there must have been settlements in this place being close to a river, and with wood for building and fuel.'

Toryn nodded. 'Do you remember the settlement the Amayans used? They believed it had stood for many years before they came across it.'

'Thankfully, much of my time as… what name did they call me?' She laughed. 'Ah yes, Grunt, the bent, old man. My time as *Grunt* seems much like a dream, but yes, I do recall something of that place. There may be many such settlements within the forest, but perhaps most have crumbled as their foundations were disturbed by the roots of these great trees. But lucky for us people did once live here.'

'Luck or destiny?'

'Ha! A point well-made.' Nyomae turned back to the inlet. 'That boat was built to navigate this tricky stretch of the Menon. Perhaps with your rafting skills, you could do the same.'

Toryn scratched his head. 'That may be so, but surely that boat is well beyond repair.'

She beamed. 'I don't intend to repair it.'

'Then how…? Ah! You're going to bring it from the past to here?'

'The Song can be used for good as well as evil. Just as I recall concealing us from those rogues on the heath, I can bring that boat from the time it was abandoned to the present day. And, hopefully equipped with oars and two comfortable seats.'

Toryn chuckled. 'And maybe a figurehead of a swan?'

'Let's not get ahead of ourselves. A simple boat will suffice. But even a simple boat will be a challenge. I suspect it is from many hundreds of years ago. I shall need time to recover.'

'Can I help?'

'No. While you would be able to assist, your entry into the Song will alert our enemies. Given time, I can teach you how to evade as best as possible those who are also present. But now is not that time. And if Uleva enters, I doubt I could elude her attention for long.' She took a deep breath. 'You must make ready for our departure. If I succeed, I will be in no state to help for many hours.' She pointed. 'There was a pond back there. It should be safe to drink. Please fill our flasks for the journey. I would hope the Menon loses its corruption the farther south it flows and is joined by other streams, but it's a risk we need not take. And we'll need food for two days.' She took his hands. 'Please be wary on your return. If I appear… different, I may have encountered a powerful foe who could take control of my actions while I recover.'

Toryn shuddered as he recalled Uleva. 'Different? How would I know?'

'That I cannot tell. If I am indeed under the influence of the Ul-dalak, they would not make it obvious. Perhaps on your return, it would be a wise precaution to bind my hands with those reeds.' She smiled. 'Ah! And when I awake, ask me what name the Amayans gave me. I don't believe that would become known soon to any should they capture my mind.'

'But what if we capsize while you sleep… you would drown.'

She nodded grimly. 'Should I be possessed by one such as Uluriel, that would be better for us both. But I believe that boat will not capsize.' Nyomae gestured to the trees. 'Now please, find us water, food... and reeds. If I am successful, it will take only minutes in our time so don't delay. If, on your return, I lay by a fine-looking boat, please tie my wrists, put me in the craft and get us away from this place. The Nym may have offered their support, but they are creatures from a different time and may not appreciate the urgency. And if the Ul-dalak come in force, they may possibly be able to resist the Nym.' Nyomae looked up to the sky. 'Evening draws near, but with a cloudless night and light from the moon, you will be able to navigate us safely for many leagues. The waters of the Menon may yet constrain the dark powers of our enemy.' She glanced across the river. 'But we must make haste. I fear we have tarried here too long. Our enemies approach.'

Toryn lowered Eryn's bow as he eyed the white markings on the rabbit just visible in the fading light. The Amayan weapon sat comfortably in his hand as he nocked the arrow. At Nyomae's request, he had filled the flask, cut a few lengths of reed, picked two handfuls of berries, and now leveled the point of his arrow at tomorrow's dinner. Toryn slowed his breathing, not wanting to miss and delay his return a moment longer. He let fly and secured their supply. He hurried to his prey and pulled out his arrow. Eryn had given him eight in total, and he suspected he may be needing them again. They would have to leave the river at least once on their journey to rest and cook the rabbit. Toryn would have preferred to keep going, but Nyomae insisted she would need sustenance following her efforts to acquire the boat. And she assured him the strong currents of the Menon would soon tire his arms and he would struggle to keep them on course without rest.

Toryn tucked the rabbit under his arm and headed back to the river, wary of what he might find. As he approached the edge of the trees his scalp tingled. Toryn crouched behind a thick trunk. Previously, his stomach had churned in the presence of the Ul-dalak, so as it had remained calm, he assumed it was safe. He stepped out to see Nyomae as she had predicted: laying besides a rowing boat with two slender oars. The air appeared to shimmer and crackle but carried no threat he could perceive.

Toryn kneeled beside Nyomae. She slept, breathing slowly. Her face looked calm, but as she had warned, if she had been taken by dark forces, it would be unlikely he would be able to tell. He gently placed her hands on her stomach and bound her wrists with the reeds, then checked they were not too tight. He lifted her and laid her in the stern of the boat where he could keep an eye on her. Toryn checked the opposite bank as he packed the last of their belongings in the bow. He climbed aboard and took his seat. The oar felt light in his hand as he planted it on the bank and pushed. He placed the oars in the rowlocks, then looked once more to the bank across the river. The boat appeared to know its way as one pull on the oars took them out of the cove and onto the Menon. They quickly gathered pace as the water took hold and swept them south. Toryn soon mastered the oars to guide them to the center and navigate safely around the odd rock jutting up from the river.

He kept one eye over his shoulder and the other on Nyomae. She appeared to sleep peacefully, so he hoped all was well and she was not fighting a desperate battle for her mind. But Toryn needed a third eye. In the moments he had no rocks to negotiate, he glanced uneasily to the trees on the west bank.

Nyomae moaned. The hairs on the back of Toryn's neck prickled. Something was out there. She muttered and turned in her slumber. Did she sense it? Or had the Ul-dalak possessed her? He checked the river ahead, and then the trees. But in the gloom, he saw nothing in the forest.

Nyomae cried out. Toryn's stomach clenched. He searched between the thick trunks as he fought to control the boat. She writhed, arching her back and throwing up her bound hands to the sky. But she did not wake. The boat glanced off a fallen tree trunk. Toryn forced down the oar to steer away from the east bank. He had to get back to the middle of the river to avoid running aground. But Nyomae's distress grew.

Toryn's head snapped back as if claws snatched at him. He tussled with the oars as his shoulders locked. He chanced a look to the river's edge. He cried out. Dark shapes darted from one tree to the next. Some were tall, rangy creatures, the others he recognized as Nordleng. But one moved ahead with unnatural speed unhindered by the trees. A faint blue light seeped from beneath the figure's hood. Uleva!

Uleva traveled fast, but to Toryn's relief, the Menon flowed faster. He regained control, keeping the boat in the middle to ride the strong current. But Uleva was not to be denied. Her silken voice reached into his mind, shutting out all other sounds. *Deliver Nyomae to me.* Toryn's jaw bunched as he tried to yell his defiance. *She is worthless. Don't sacrifice your life for the old woman.* The boat lurched as the water surged through a narrow gap between two steep banks. *Give her to me, and I shall let you go.*

Toryn forced his answer through clenched teeth. 'Never.'

Uleva persisted. *Surrender to the Ul-dalak. You cannot win.* He twisted away, searching the river for a safe passage to his right. But the banks rose higher as far as he could see. Still Uleva spoke in the eerie silence. *I'll make you a glorious warrior, Toryn, son of Finromir.* She knew! He turned his head away but could not shut her out. *All will fear and kneel before you, Toryn.* Uleva showed him what he could become if he yielded to her will. He saw himself leading Uleva's armies, vanquishing all who stood against them. Toryn could take anything he craved, perhaps even the great city of Elmarand for his own. All its riches would be his to dispose of as he wished.

He shook his head, screaming into the night. 'Leave me alone!'

Surrender to me, and I am yours, Toryn.

'You're a wyke. I don't want you!'

The vision of Elmarand blurred. Uleva stood before him naked: the young, beguiling Uleva he had seen briefly on the plains of Dorn before the veil concealing her true form had fallen. *I know you, Toryn.* She held out her arms. *I know what you desire.* His face tingled as the image caressed his cheek. *And I am everything you have ever wanted.*

Before he could stop it, Toryn raised the left oar and pulled down hard on the right. The boat reeled towards Uleva. He cried out. 'No! Never!' With all his remaining strength, he fought back, forcing both oars under the water to take them back to the middle.

Uleva screamed. Her face distorted into the hideous wyke he had seen. The image shattered as she cursed him. *Fool. If you desire a life of thralldom, I shall grant your wish.* He would be her serf, compelled to execute despicable acts at her whim. She promised him life beyond his natural years to witness the decline of the land he held so dear.

But Toryn's resolve returned. Heat flowed from deep within his soul. She could threaten him with her worst punishment, but he would not surrender. His head cleared, leaving only the echo of her wrath. The boat steadied, appearing to lift as it regained the current, leaving Uleva and her creatures behind. But his grip on the oars loosened, exhausted by the encounter. Toryn's vision blurred. He wavered; the boat yawed as he lost control. But just as he feared they would run aground, the craft steadied, correcting itself to avoid the banks. He glanced over the side and thought he saw the wispy forms of the Nym in the dark waters, perhaps steering a safe passage as he recovered his strength. All he knew was the threat had passed, Nyomae breathed slowly, and they were clear. The river widened and the boat settled in the calmer currents.

Toryn tipped back his head to watch the stars drift by overhead. He became drowsy and tried to fight the urge to close his eyes. His head dropped forward. A voice assured him he should rest. The Nym would see them safe while the river still flowed through the center of Foranfae where they held power. Toryn accepted their offer and gladly let the voice sing him softly to sleep.

Nyomae had passed the test. She awoke from her slumber the following morning and had smiled as she recalled the ugly name the Amayans had given her. Once Toryn had recovered from his ordeal with Uleva, the Nym had faded away, leaving him in control of the boat. He had guided the small craft through the many twists in the youthful Menon waters while keeping a close watch on his sleeping companion. When she awoke with a ravenous appetite, he had moored the boat on the east bank under a large, overhanging tree, satisfied he had put many leagues between them and the Ul-dalak.

Toryn turned the rabbit on the spit as Nyomae watched eagerly on. She ate a few berries as she waited and looked through the trees. 'I'd say we'll arrive at Archonholm by early evening.'

He recalled his last attempt to enter the city. 'We should ditch the boat on the south bank before we come into view of the Menon Bridge. There'll be guards and trust me, they don't miss any comings or goings. And they'll take some convincing to allow us to see the Archon.' He turned to her. 'Unless you can pull the same trick you did on the grasslands.'

Nyomae sat by the small fire. 'Not this evening. I'll need another night's rest before I'm able to work another one of my… *tricks*.'

'Then we'll best camp upriver and sneak in tomorrow morning.' Toryn took a stick, pulled the cooked meat from the spit, and passed the breast to Nyomae. 'Looks good and tender. Should help to recover your strength.' He looked downstream. 'How do we convince whoever greets us to take us to the Archon?'

Nyomae gratefully accepted the meat. 'I have my ways.' She grinned. 'Ways that work better when we're visible.'

Toryn took a bite of his early lunch. He glanced up at the sun between the dark leaves. 'It'll be Midsummer tomorrow.' His eyes dropped to the flames. Back in Midwyche, they would be decorating the hall come evening, and the preparations for the feast would be well underway. He and Hamar had left early in the spring. A little more than three months had passed but it felt like a different age now. So much had changed, including every belief Toryn had held while living in the isolated village. In a short time, he had seen more of the land than any in Midwyche, save Hamar. He wondered how Miram and Andryn would celebrate the day, as surely by now, they would assume their adopted son had fallen with Hamar. Toryn hoped he could return before winter to let them know he still lived. But other pressing matters had to be dealt with first. He had a thought. 'Ah! Perhaps it might be easier to enter Archonholm than last time. If they celebrate half as much as the sheriff and his men do in my village, they won't even notice.' He laughed. 'If we wait until the afternoon, they'll have passed out and we'll just need to step over them.'

Nyomae looked up from her lunch. 'I don't care much for celebrations myself. And I trust the Archon abstains from such frivolity. I need him to be coherent tomorrow. He has to know of the rising threat behind him if he's planning to open the gate.'

Toryn recalled his time at the gatehouse on the Menon bridge. 'Two guards I met reckoned their forces wouldn't be ready until autumn, so perhaps they'll be time.'

Nyomae placed the stripped rabbit bone on the fire. 'Are you rested?' Toryn nodded. She stood. 'Then we must be moving. I'm reluctant to spend too long in any one place, and I doubt the Nym will be able to assist this far south. Their powers wane as the trees begin to thin.'

Toryn kicked dirt onto the fire and ensured it had gone out. 'Surely we'll be safe camping close to Archonholm.'

Nyomae sighed. 'Perhaps best to be cautious and maintain a watch. The enemy would indeed be strong if they can venture with impunity to under the very shadows of the walls of your city, but it is a risk I would rather not take.'

40. A Secret Revealed

Elodi rose before sunrise on the longest day of the year — and a long day it promised to be. As she dressed, she wondered whether she would survive the forthcoming battle and see the sunset. Determined to maintain the tradition of the Five Realms, she strode to the window and out onto the small balcony to witness daybreak on Midsummer's Day. The pink tinge spreading from the horizon across the clear sky, announced the imminent arrival of the sun. She shivered in the light breeze but was reluctant to miss even one second to fetch her robe. A lone thrush sang its flutelike song from the edge of the forest below. Elodi tilted her head to listen, waiting for others to join the chorus. The lilting whistle of a robin followed, and soon the treetops of the Foranfae was filled with birdsong. Elodi made a promise to herself; if she lived to see the day out, she would rise early tomorrow to listen to their unbridled joy at the coming of the dawn.

As the sky brightened, Elodi thought of Bardon. What would he see this morn as he looked out across the plains from the walls of Elmarand? Did he truly hold the old city? The Archon seemed confident the elite forces had been successful, but Elodi wondered how he could be so sure. The evening before, Elodi, along with the Lords Galabrant and Kernlow had sat once more in the Great Hall as the Vice-Archon briefed them on the Archon's tactics. Dozens of generals and captains of Archonholm had swelled the numbers at the meeting, and all sat eager to hear how the newly-named Battle of Midsummer would unfold. And they were not to be disappointed. Prior to midday, a combined force of close to ten thousand knights, archers, spears, and foot soldiers would assemble at the gate. Then, as the sun gained its highest point directly above the pass, the weapons on the parapets would launch a deadly barrage over the gate to, in the Vice-Archon's words, *soften up* the Golesh. Immediately afterwards, before the enemy could recover from the shock, the Archon would give the order to open the gate.

The Archon had already taken his position in the pass, accompanied by a detachment of his Palace Guard. He would spend the night at the top of the damaged Caerwal Tower preparing for his part. When Elodi had questioned if the Archon knew the numbers they could expect to face on the other side, the Vice-Archon had assured her, the size of their own force was sufficient: their task was to protect the Archon long enough for him to unleash his new-found powers directly upon the enemy. This, the Vice-Archon proudly announced, would greatly turn the advantage to the Five Realms, who would crush the dispirited, ragged armies of the Golesh for good. The Archon then planned to split their force, sending one cohort to meet with Bardon, while others rode out to the cities and settlements of the south to bring news of victory and crush any rear-guard actions of the Golesh.

A glimmer of light caught Elodi's eye. The top of the sun peered over the horizon. Elodi pushed the looming events aside to enjoy the moment. In Calerdorn, the clouds had kept the spectacle of the sunrise hidden for many months, today she would not let anything spoil her pleasure. Elodi took a deep breath as the first rays streamed across the land and touched her face. Her skin tingled as it warmed. The sky grew lighter as the glowing pink rim of the sun slowly climbed above the dark line of the hills to the east. She knew she could not stay for long as she needed to oversee the final preparations, but Elodi decided delaying another minute would not matter. She placed her hands on the balustrade's cool stone, threw back her head, and drank in the pure, morning air.

Elodi turned to the forest. For a moment, she had the strange sensation she was being watched — but not an unpleasant experience. She searched the tree line but saw no sign of her observer. The tales of the Foranfae had not been exaggerated. Perhaps something did indeed live under the protection of its canopy, but whether friend or foe, she had not the first idea.

Elodi turned her attention back to the wonder of the sunrise. She sighed. How she wished she could ride Sea Mist to the fields east of the city and watch the sun paint the craggy slopes of the Caerwals orange. But while Elodi wished to see that spectacle, Lady Harlyn had a duty to her people to fulfill. As the leader of her realm, she would have to confront the foe she had been taught to fear above all else. Then if successful, she would return to her realm and take back Calerdorn. But she dreaded what atrocities and horrors awaited her behind its walls.

A single trumpet blew the call to muster. Elodi took one last look at the sun as it cleared the horizon, wondering once more if she would be around to see it sink in the west.

'Morning, ma'am.' Gundrul strode across the courtyard in full battle armor with his helmet tucked under his arm. Despite the age of both the wearer and the armor, he looked like a warrior from the legends of old. He grasped her arm in the fashion of the guards. 'A fine day for a momentous occasion.' The wrinkles on his face deepened as he smiled. 'Let's hope the bards will be singing of a glorious victory in the years to come.'

Elodi returned his strong grasp. 'While not omitting the verse dedicated to your deeds of the day, Captain.' She grinned, certain he blushed beneath the weather-worn skin of his cheeks.

Gundrul released her arm. 'Come now, ma'am. The likes of me are not meant for such songs.' He winked, lowering his voice. 'And perhaps by then you will have made your true lineage known. I can imagine the bards clambering over each other to be the first to sing of that tale.'

She found herself laughing. 'Perhaps we should focus on the job at hand before we get too carried away with the music and glory.'

'I know, but you can't deny it would keep folk captivated during the cold, dark nights in the winters to come.' Gundrul fidgeted with the straps on his helmet. 'But if I'm to be honest with you, ma'am, when I think about the gate opening, it feels like every butterfly of the Foranfae flutters in my belly.'

Elodi checked her sword belt. 'That goes for us all, but I know I can rely on you once the battle starts.' She smirked. 'And I eagerly anticipate your pre-battle humor at the gate.'

Gundrul grimaced. 'I wouldn't hold your breath. I'm not so sure it will flow today. And I don't have Ruan's dumb face for inspiration.'

She turned to the north. 'I hope he made it to Seransea, and not only for his support in the difficult months ahead.'

'He's a resourceful man, ma'am. If anyone can make it, he can. I wouldn't want to be the one getting in his way. He's a stubborn one, I'll grant him that.'

'Then let us look forward to the day we will all meet again.' She nodded to the Caerwals. 'How would you rate our chance of a quick victory today?'

Gundrul rubbed his chin. 'I like to see what I'm about to face before I raise my hopes. I'd feel happier with Ruan's spears protecting our flanks, but we won't know nothing until the big, old gate swings open. Who's to know what stands on the other side.'

'But don't forget we have the Archon with us this time. He has spent many years preparing for this very moment.' She looked up. 'Ah. Captain Cubric approaches. She turned to greet him. 'Are our soldiers ready, Captain? Have they had sufficient rest from the march?'

Cubric nodded to Gundrul briefly, then turned to Elodi. 'Yes, ma'am. All in good order and have been well looked after. And Sea Mist, and the other horses for that matter, are champing at their bits and seem eager to ride out.'

'Thank you, Cubric.' She caught Gundrul's eye. 'Then let us hope we're all in good order to meet the challenges of the day.' Elodi glanced to the west wall of the courtyard as the sunlight liberated the top from the shadows. 'The sun waits for no one. I imagine it will take well over two hours for our forces to cross the narrow bridge. I believe it is time for us to take our position alongside our soldiers.'

The three strode out of the courtyard and through the bustling streets of Archonholm. Elodi watched merchants, smithies, cooks, stable hands, and families rush to their doors to witness the gathering of the army that would determine their destiny. Their faces revealed a mix of hope and anxiety. Elodi returned their gaze, nodding to re-assure, trusting they would not suffer the same fate as the people of Calerdorn. Her hands clenched within her mail gloves — she could not let that happen again. They reached the South Gate. Elodi recalled how she had stood with Bardon on that misty morning they had awaited the Archon to lead them to the gate on the opening of the Caerwal Tower. On that occasion, she had shivered in the cold dawn in anticipation of seeing the renowned structure that had saved them centuries earlier. But in the warmth of a fine summer's day, her blood suddenly chilled as they passed beneath the thick wall. Today, she was to witness the great Caerwal Gate open, and then face the unknown beyond.

Sea Mist whinnied as they emerged from the South Gate. Elodi strode to his side and stroked his nose. 'Good morning, Misty. I need you to be brave again for me today, boy.' She watched his eyes, convinced he understood her words. She mounted and waited for Gundrul and Culbric to saddle up. She smiled. 'You look more like a rider with each passing day, Gundrul.'

He grimaced, rising from his saddle. 'Then I wish my *rear guard* agreed with you, ma'am.'

They rounded the corner of the South Wall. Cubric beamed. 'Well don't they make a fine sight, ma'am.'

Elodi turned to see Harlyn's burgundy banner flutter in the light breeze. Beneath, Aldorman and his knights sat straight in their saddles, behind, the men and women of the realm's small, but skilled fighters, stood proud. And beside them, the remainder of the Archonian Guards who had accompanied Elodi from the day they had first sailed north on the *Celestra.* Elodi stopped and held back a tear. She whispered. 'They do indeed make a most splendid sight, Captain.' Their armor glistened in the sun as her force turned to greet her with a loud cheer. Elodi felt suddenly she owed a great debt to those who would follow her into danger. As a young girl she had attended many a parade with her father. She had watched in awe as the Knights of Calerdorn had marched through the streets to mark the numerous celebrations of the city. But it was not until she was ten years old that she understood the position of power and responsibility that came with her father's position. As the knights had turned and saluted Lord Harlyn, her eyes had seen him in a new light as he acknowledged the loyalty and commitment of his forces. And now, here she stood, not watching a ceremonial parade, but about to lead them into the biggest battle in centuries.

Elodi pulled back her shoulders, pushing out the doubts of the young child.

Now was the time.

She nudged Sea Mist up a low mound and turned to face Harlyn's force. She drew her sword and held it high to catch the sunlight. The warmth in her stomach grew and spread to her limbs. Elodi knew if she let it continue, her blade would glow and reveal her lineage. She glanced to Gundrul. He smiled and nodded.

Elodi unleashed the power inherited from her mother's kin.

The heat surged through her arm to her sword. The blade burst briefly into flame then shone bright, casting an orange hue upon all around. The cheers caught in her soldiers' throats, then erupted as they grasped the significance of her sword: Amayan blood ran strong in the leader of their realm. Comrades grasped arms, slapped each other's backs, and thrust weapons into the air, elated to follow a warrior of the legends to the gate. The forces of Harlyn stood a foot taller and broader with renewed admiration for Elodi, the Lady of Harlyn, and an Amayan warrior. No words were needed. She watched their faces, feeling a deep love and admiration for all who stood with her under the banner. Tears of pride brimmed; her love for Harlyn swelled her chest; the loyalty of her forces steeled her spine.

Elodi let the display last a moment longer, then sheathed her sword. She turned to Gundrul and beamed, yelling above the cheers. 'You were right as usual.'

Her captain nodded. 'All true fighters respect the Amayans, ma'am.' Gundrul laughed at Cubric. 'And for the first time I can recall, this one is speechless.'

Cubric's mouth gaped, his wide eyes gawping at Elodi.

But his silence did not last. He gasped. 'Well, I never… I never thought… well that explains a lot. I was proud just to march under your banner alongside you and the Knights of Calerdorn, ma'am. But now… now I serve under an Amayan.' He chuckled. 'I only hope my armor can restrain my expanding chest as we cross the bridge and enter the pass.'

Elodi grinned at them both, but as she beheld them, it faded. 'Whatever the outcome, it is I who will be proud to march beside you on this historic day. Your service has been exemplary. Your bravery, unquestionable. Your loyalty, unbendable. Your skill, unsurpassed in our time. But above all, your friendship and support, is most welcome.'

Gundrul rubbed the back of his neck. 'Thank you, ma'am. That is very good of you to say so.' He sat straighter in his saddle. 'And I believe I speak for us all when I say, it has been an honor to serve you, and indeed to watch you in action.' He looked up. 'But this will not be our last day together. I'm certain I… and Cubric, will ride with you to drive those rogues out of your city very soon, ma'am.'

Elodi blinked away a tear. 'Of that, I am sure. I only wish Ruan and his spearman could be with us to share this moment. I do hope they survive to fight with us another day.'

Gundrul smiled. 'As I said earlier, if anyone could, it would be Ruan. And if he did come across those scoundrels on the plain, it wouldn't be him coming off second best.'

A single horn blared from one of the towers. Elodi pick up her reins. 'Well, gentlemen. This is it.'

41. The Gates of Dawn

Toryn stretched the aches from his tired shoulders and walked the short distance to the edge of the Foranfae. The thinning of the trees allowed just enough moonlight through to guide his way over the large, protruding roots. He thought back to the night he and Hamar had left Midwyche and how he had stumbled numerous times in the dark. If all had gone to plan, Toryn would be asleep in a warm bed in Greendell, resting after a hard day's work of caring for livestock and repairing fences. Yet, for all those years Toryn yearned to escape the confines of his village, would he now exchange his current situation for that warm bed? He could not be sure either way.

Toryn stopped at the last trees and gazed out on the Caerwal Mountains on the opposite side of the chasm. His eyes traced the jagged, black line as they stretched out towards the east coast and the lighter skies. He emerged from under the heavy boughs, took a few paces across the dew-laden grass, stopped, and took a deep breath. He had spent a little over two weeks in the forest, yet it had seemed far longer. Toryn looked up to the welcome expanse of the open sky. The stars overhead vanished one-by-one as they made way for the coming day. In the growing light, he could just make out the line of the Great Northeast Road as it wend its way around the forest and through the rich farmlands of Holm. Toryn called to mind its route on Hamar's old map. From an early age he been curious of what lay on the opposite side of the Kolossos Mountains, fueled by Hamar's tales of the strange people and places he had encountered.

Toryn strolled a short way through the long grass

towards the road. The centuries-old route would hasten his way to the mysterious lands of the eastern realms. If he followed its route, it would take him around the edge of Foranfae out of Holm, then through the foothills of the Kolossos to Emryst, the southern ward of Galabrant. Following a three-day trek, he would discover if the strange black tower of Telamir truly cast no reflection on the lake in which it stood. Hamar had told him it was the most peculiar building he had ever looked upon, and according to the old man, he had seen many in his travels. Beyond the Telamir Tower, the east fork in the road found its way to the grand old cities of Tallabar, Saphrir and lastly, the twin towers of Karrock. If Toryn continued north, he would pass close to the fortress of Vortimo, built into the sides of the Kolossos Mountains. Crafted by skilled stonemasons of a distant age, the city now stood abandoned, but while none knew the reason, few braved the steep road to venture inside its ghostly walls. Toryn wondered if he would have the stomach to enter Vortimo, or whether he would opt to hurry on his way. In a little over two weeks, he would find himself in Ormsk, being wary not to fall into the deep chasm of Roth's Doom. Here, it was said, Ormoroth rent the earth with his great axe as he fought to free his master from the vaults beneath the mountains. But seeing as the land remained free of the Evil One, all could safely assume Ormoroth had failed in his attempt.

Farther on, Toryn would pass beneath the eyes of the watchtowers at the head of the Kolossos Pass. From there, the road took a wide berth, avoiding the dark, web-strewn fences of Aralak Gorge to reach the next junction. The fork on the right would take Toryn to Keld, the seat of Lord Broon, whereas only the hardy fools chose to undertake the last punishing leagues to the end of the road. And those who endured the beast from the east, howling in from the icy seas, could not expect respite in front of a roaring fire at Lindmar. Hamar had told the walls of the old fortress had finally capitulated to the relentless battering of the elements. Large, unrepaired gaps left the interior exposed and few relished serving within its walls for long.

Toryn turned his back on the temptation of the road. As much as he desired to explore the lands on the other side of the Kolossos Range, he had another, more pressing task at hand. He looked to the city. The first time he had set eyes upon Archonholm, its immense walls and tall towers had glowed a deep pink in the setting sun. In the pre-dawn light, it stood silent as its cold, gloomy walls awaited the sun's arrival on the longest day of the year. In the dark, the walls appeared more daunting, and its towers even taller, as if it were a mountain itself. A few torches flickered high on the eastern terraces and watchtowers, but otherwise it seemed the whole city still slept. But Toryn knew this was not true. Hundreds of eyes would be fixed on the Caerwal Pass, ever watchful for movements in the south.

Toryn spun around as Nyomae whispered. 'I see your people still follow the tradition of observing the Midsummer sunrise.'

He nodded, pleased to have company on this special morn. 'All over the land, people will be rising early to watch. I thought about waking you, but you looked deep in sleep, in need of your rest.'

Nyomae smiled. 'I am well rested now, thank you. And I thought you wouldn't want to see in this day on your own.'

Toryn took her warm hand. 'You're most welcome. Back in my village we hold hands in a long line reaching almost to the bridge. When I was young, I sat on Andryn's shoulders to watch it rise between two mountain peaks. I used to think it was like a great gate opening to let the sun through.' He laughed. 'Of course, being west of the mountains, we'd have to wait over an hour longer than those on the other side.' He grinned. 'When I was little, I thought it unfair the east would see the sun first. But Miram, my mother, assured me they would be jealous of us later as it dipped below the mountain ridge, allowing us to see it set the sky ablaze a deep red in the evening.' He traced his hand in an arc over his head. 'But here in Farrand, I guess we'll get to watch it for longer than both sides of the Kolossos.' His stomach knotted. 'Well, that's if we're not both chained to a wall in a dark cell, or hanging from the bridge come the end of the day.'

Nyomae smiled. 'You'll get to see your sunset. I promise.' Toryn looked up as voices echoed from the terraces of Archonholm. She pointed to the Archon's Tower. 'It rises.' He tipped back his head to see the top of the flagpole glisten gold as the first rays descended, turning the rippling banner blue. The last time he had seen the sun touch the tower, it signaled the guards to heave him off the Caerwal Bridge and leave him to die. On this morn, while its arrival wasn't quite so final, it still brought in a day that might not end well.

Toryn watched as the veil of night slowly withdrew as if pulled from the city to make way for dawn. The light rolled down the conical roof to the balcony on which the Archon had observed Toryn dangling over the chasm. He pushed the memory aside and turned back to face the horizon. The snow-covered peaks of the Caerwals were already tinged pink as they proudly laid claim to the first of the sun's light. The deep crevices and rocky outcrops threw sharp, dark lines down their steep slopes as the rays crept ever westward. Toryn stood on his toes as, far to the east, the shimmering lip of the sun appeared. On Midsummer's Day, it rose exactly in line with the Caerwals, almost as if that is what the Gods of Old intended; he often speculated what other wonders they could have created had the Evil One not taken their daughters.

Toryn held his breath as he had always done as a child, believing it would bring good luck if he could delay inhaling until the full disk of the sun appeared. But he had never managed it as a child, and unfortunately, could not achieve it now. He chided himself for still believing such superstitions, but part of him thought it could yet turn out to be an ill omen.

Voices drifted down to where Toryn and Nyomae stood. It was tradition for the folk of Broon and Galabrant to sing at the rising of the Midsummer sun. But those of Harlyn, Kernlow and Farrand had always stood in awed silence, preferring to listen to the dawn chorus of the birds greeting the new day. Here in Farrand, the birds sang verses unknown to Toryn, but it still cheered his soul.

The sun climbed, turning the east-facing walls of Archonholm first pink, then slowly orange as it cleared the world's edge to bring its full strength to the land. High on the terraces, Toryn could see hundreds of people watching, shielding their night eyes against the glare. The sunbeams found their way along the north side of Archonholm, chasing away the shadows on dozens of balconies jutting out from high on the smooth walls. A few inhabitants observed their vigils alone from their viewpoints.

One caught Toryn's eye.

The sun shone on a red-headed woman. He watched, captivated, as the breeze tossed her long hair about her slender shoulders. For a moment, Toryn was convinced she had to be an Amayan as she stood tall, defiant even, as not even the vast city of Archonholm could diminish her presence.

'A fine sight indeed.' Nyomae released his hand.

Toryn gasped, realizing he had been holding his

breath; perhaps that would prove to be a good omen after all. 'She is… err yes, indeed it is.' He glanced back to the balcony, saddened to find the woman had gone.

Nyomae sighed. 'It is a grand city worthy of the sun's attention at Midsummer. But it's time to prepare. I am rested and believe I can easily convince the guards into taking us to the Archon.'

'Convince? How?'

Nyomae winked. 'When I say, convince, I really mean, trick.' She clasped her hands. 'But first, breakfast. We'll need all our strength for the coming day.'

Toryn grinned. 'Then lucky for us I caught two fish while they still slept in their beds this morning.'

'Fish? Sleep?'

He laughed. 'You see! I also have a few tricks up my sleeve.'

They ate the fish cooked over a small fire that Toryn was careful to hide from prying eyes high on the wall. He was happy to wait a few hours before taking to the road that led to the main North Gate. He was certain the guards would soon be distracted by the events of the day, especially once the maidens of Archonholm began the time-honored dances with their hair adorned with summer flowers. He wondered if the red-haired woman would also partake — she would certainly help take his mind from his troubles for a few precious moments.

The time came when they had to make their move. Toryn shouldered Eryn's bow, and concealed the Nordleng sword and dagger, not wishing to rouse any suspicion among the guards more than necessary. They arrived at the road beneath the over-bearing walls of the city. Once more, he turned his attention north as the road beckoned him to the east of the Kolossos.

'Toryn? Are you ready?'

'Yes. Sorry. For a moment I was elsewhere.' His feet,

though tired, would welcome the chance to turn left, but his head urged him to the right and take the short journey to Archonholm's gate. He smiled to himself. And perhaps, the road would also take him to the woman with the flowing red hair from the balcony. But as he took the first steps beside Nyomae, a horn sounded from high upon a tower. Its urgent call echoed across the city and over the walls to be swallowed by the Foranfae Forest.

Toryn looked to Nyomae. 'I don't know what that means, but it sounds important.'

42. Crossing the Chasm

Elodi turned in her saddle and admired the long line of Harlyn's force stretching back to the city. A large crowd had gathered along the route leading to the bridge, and many more watched from the high terraces on the south wall. Harlyn's banner fluttered ahead of them, and Elodi had never felt so nervous and confident at the same time. She had detested standing on the walls of Calerdorn waiting for the enemy to strike. Today, the Five Realms would take the initiative, and she longed to strike back against an enemy that had posed a ceaseless threat for three centuries. And the sooner they could deliver their decisive blow, the sooner she could ride back north. Any doubts she had of the outcome of the battle had melted away as she laid eyes on the magnificent ranks waiting to cross the bridge. At the front, the glittering rows of armored knights with their lances held high, looked ready to impale any who dared to stand in their way. Even without Broon, the remaining four realms had assembled an imposing force to support the Archon.

Trumpets at the head of the column blared, and the knights, led by the Castellan, stepped onto the narrow bridge. Half of the First Horse had accompanied Lord Broon and the elite force on the mission to retake Elmarand. The remainder now trotted confidently ahead of the main force, eager to make their contribution to the Archon's historic plan. Elodi's pulse rose as the waiting columns began to edge forward. All now appeared keen to take their place besides the Archon, and she hoped, their place in the annals of history that, for years to come, would be celebrated throughout the land.

Elodi nodded to Gundrul and Cubric. No words were necessary. In the few months they had fought together, they had endured so much hardship and many dangers, forming a bond she knew could never be broken. Without a second thought, she would lay down her life for them, and she knew they would do the same for her. Elodi beamed at Cubric as his chest did indeed look ready to burst through his armor. Sea Mist's head nodded, seeming impatient to join the proud horses of the knights on the bridge. Above, the sun continued its climb, gaining height over a world that would drastically change before its departure.

The riders of the First Horse arrived on the far side of the chasm and began filing through the Lower Gate. The Archonian vanguard now filled the bridge, marching proud and in perfect step. Many wore new armor made in the smithies across Farrand in time for the momentous day, and thankfully before the supplies from Drunsberg had ceased. Elodi held back Sea Mist. 'Wait, boy, wait. But not long now, just you see.'

The Archon had granted Harlyn the honor of leading the rest of the realms behind his own forces. And she had been happy to accept the role. Of all the realms, Harlyn's soldiers had by far the most experience of late. She turned one more time to take in her army. Those catching her eye, nodded with grim determination, leaving Elodi assured they would serve Harlyn well. All had been brought up with tales of the injustice dealt out by the Golesh on their people south of the Caerwals. Today, they would avenge the wrongs that had for far too long, gone unpunished.

'We're off, ma'am.' Even Gundrul, the grizzled veteran, could not disguise the excitement in his voice.

'Indeed we are, Captain.' She nudged Sea Mist, who needed no encouragement to take his place. Her scalp prickled. For the second time that day, Elodi sensed eyes upon her. Thousands of people watched, but one among them was different. She rose in her saddle and searched the crowd of upturned faces. But with so many flags waving, she could not find the one she sought; the one she knew who had observed her from the Foranfae at first light. But Elodi had no time to investigate. Sea Mist's hooves clattered onto the foot of the bridge. She shook off the sensation and turned to her captains. 'May the Three be with us all.'

Cubric held his head high. 'I'm sure the fair Maidens ride with us today, ma'am.' He glanced to his commander. 'And even old Gunny here looks the part, despite being on a horse.' He laughed as Gundrul scowled, but the old captain grinned back.

Gundrul patted his horse's neck. 'Perhaps I'll challenge you, Cub, to a race when this day is done. I think I may be getting the hang of this riding lark. I might even consider taking it up once I retire.'

Elodi laughed. 'Then let's make it interesting. I'll wager you both, your mounts can't beat Sea Mist on the straight, even if you ride in relay.'

'You must think me and Cub were born yesterday. We'd be foolish to put our money against an Amayan and her horse, ma'am. We may be simple soldiers, but we've heard all the tales. We appreciate your offer but will have to decline that challenge.'

Harlyn's vanguard reached the top of the bridge and began the descent to the Lower Gate. Elodi looked up to the steep sides of the pass. 'Then I'll settle for a gentle trot with you through the fields south of these mountains and watch the sunset instead.'

Gundrul muttered as they approached the gate. 'That would be a most welcome end to this day, ma'am.'

Nyomae, true to her promise, had easily fooled the

guards at the Menon Gate and were waved through without a second glance. But Toryn remained wary of being recognized and had kept his eyes to the ground, avoiding showing his face. But he need not have worried. Every inhabitant of the city appeared to be preoccupied with events elsewhere. At first, Toryn thought the crowds thronging to the south walls were taking part in the festivities of the day, but as they followed the masses, he soon realized this was not to be an ordinary day of celebration. An excited young woman informed them that today, at noon, the Archon would open the Caerwal Gate.

Toryn stood aghast. Odrun and Harruld had been right. The guards from the Menon Bridge had spoken of their hunch, yet Toryn had not thought it would be so soon. But now he saw the assembled forces of the realms, he was left in no doubt. From their position at the top of the slope dropping away from the South Wall, he could see over the heads of the crowds eager to find the best viewpoint. Stretching out in the distance, the lines of straight-backed knights, guards and horses tugged at his heart. He should be marching to the bridge. He should be doing his duty and fighting alongside them. Toryn searched the Archonian lines, wondering if Elrik was among them. He was tempted to weave through the spectators and somehow join the waiting ranks. But Nyomae took his hand, reading his mind. 'This isn't your destiny, Toryn. Your skills are required elsewhere.' She stroked his arm. 'Trust me. You will play your part when the time comes.'

But Nyomae's words did little to ease Toryn's guilt. He watched as the Archonians formed behind the First Horse. He scanned the banners fluttering proudly above those awaiting their turn to rally to the Archon's call. Toryn found the one he sought: the burgundy and silver of Harlyn. Beneath the colors sat Lady Harlyn. He stood on his toes and gawped. She sat resplendent on a majestic, white horse, and like all in Harlyn, Toryn knew his name: Sea Mist. Lady Harlyn's helmet gleamed in the morning light, but it was the braid of red hair draped over her shoulder that caught his eye. He didn't have to see her face to know this was the woman from the balcony. Jedrul's words came to mind when he had described Lady Harlyn: *hair the color of a sunset.* Toryn's heart lurched into his ribs. But not purely from awe. Something else wrenched at his soul. With every fiber in his body, he knew for certain, he had to be at her side on this day. He turned to Nyomae, calling out above the cheers. 'I have to go. I have to go with them. I must be with her.'

Nyomae frowned. 'But what can you do? You have yet to master your…' he took her hand. She nodded. 'I understand. You're right. We both have to be at the pass today.' They weaved their way through the masses, down towards the foot of the bridge. Toryn kept his eye on Harlyn's banner as it neared the edge of the ravine. He could not put his trepidation into words, but somehow, he knew they both would play their part earlier than Nyomae had envisaged. If they were not present at the gate when it opened, he was sure a dreadful fate would befall the realms and Lady Harlyn. But what fate that entailed, and how he could prevent it, he had not a clue. By all accounts, Elodi was an accomplished sword master and rider. And she would be surrounded by the Knights of Calerdorn once the battle began. How would his presence at the Caerwal Gate make any difference? Eryn's bow would count for little in the close hand fighting, and he had not the first idea how to wield the innate power Nyomae believed he possessed. But regardless, he would allow no one to stand between him and the gate.

Toryn and Nyomae reached the front row of the crowd as Harlyn's banner approached the bridge. Lady

Harlyn had yet to shut her visor and, despite the dangers ahead, Toryn lost himself gazing upon her fair face. He had found Uleva's hidden beauty breathtaking before the illusion had shattered. But Lady Harlyn outshone Uleva and her beauty was most definitely not a deception. And undoubtedly, she had to be an Amayan. He saw the same confident and ageless look of Eryn, Calestri and Arijan. He saw a woman, a fighter, and a leader deserving of his enduring service and loyalty. In that moment, the purpose of his life suddenly made sense — Toryn vowed he would follow her to the very edge of the world. And he would gladly fight the demons lurking beneath Caranach, should she demand it of him. And, despite knowing very little about her, he knew he would love this woman unconditionally, and her name would be on his lips as he drew his last breath.

Lady Harlyn glanced in his direction, searching the faces of the exuberant folk of Archonholm waving flags, flowers, or anything they could lay their hands upon. Toryn struggled to catch her eye, knowing she sensed he watched. Did she detect his, or Nyomae's power? He called out but could not make himself heard above the din. But she turned as her horse trotted onto the bridge. Toryn's heart faltered as the dread growing in his stomach took hold. Should anything happen to her, he would never forgive himself. Nyomae shouted in his ear. 'You never told me Lady Harlyn was an Amayan.'

'You see it as well? I didn't know until now.'

Nyomae nodded. 'This is encouraging. The more they number, the better for us all.'

But they could go no farther as the crowd stopped at a line of Palace Guards blocking the way to the bridge. Toryn watched anxiously as Harlyn's forces began crossing the chasm. He glanced to Nyomae. 'Can you get us over?'

She eyed the guard. 'We'll wait until they've all gone.

Then I will find a way.'

Toryn grasped her hand. 'You must.' He followed Lady Harlyn's progress up to the apex of the bridge, groaning inside as her red braid, then plume disappeared below the path. He turned and scanned the long lines of Kernlow's and Galabrant's soldiers waiting patiently. It would take at least another hour before they could attempt entry. But they had no choice. He and Nyomae were jostled by hundreds of excited and nervous people keen to find another viewpoint of the bridge. Toryn pushed his way a little farther to his right and saw Harlyn's banner reach the other side. The colors tilted, then passed through the Lower Gate and out of sight.

Toryn tugged at Nyomae's sleeve. 'We have to get away from this crowd.'

'Agreed. I require time to prepare for our crossing. And we need somewhere away from the bustle to talk.'

The pair made their way out of the masses and found an inlet in the south-facing wall where they could not be seen or overheard. Toryn clutched his stomach. 'Can you feel it? I cannot rid myself of this dread.'

Nyomae took his hand. 'I do. I couldn't say anything among those people, but I'm getting snatches of a warning. I can't be sure, but I believe it could be the voice from the other side of the mountains.'

'Warning or threat?'

'I cannot tell, and to make it worse, I'm hearing another voice, just as powerful, but I cannot determine its origin.'

Toryn's heart sank. 'It seems every soul in the land desires to be at the opening of the gate.'

The crossing of the Archon's army took longer than Toryn anticipated. But the delay allowed Nyomae more time to prepare. The crowds dispersed as many chose to watch from the high vantage point of the terraces along the South Wall, perhaps hoping for a glimpse of the promised barrage preceding the opening. But Toryn wondered if it was to witness the attack, or to feel safer should the Golesh overwhelm the Archon and come surging through the pass.

Toryn looked to Nyomae. 'Can you conceal us long enough to cross?'

'That is one way, but it would take too much of my strength, and I'd rather conserve that for events to come.' She looked over his shoulder. 'There's only one guard remaining on duty. I suppose no unarmed person in their right minds would be looking to enter the pass now. And I can see no guards at the Lower Gate. A simple guise may do the trick.' She held his gaze. 'Ready?'

Toryn took her hand and managed a smile. 'More than I've ever been.' Nyomae closed her eyes; his face tingled as the air shimmered about them.

She nodded to the bridge. 'I've located a memory of the sentry that will suffice. He will see us as two Palace Guards. I will inform him we must deliver an urgent message to the Archon. But don't dawdle. I can only maintain the illusion until we reach the top and disappear from his line of sight. But should he choose to follow… that will prove a challenge.'

43. Into the Maw

Elodi shivered, feeling the same chill in her bones she had experienced when first entering the Caerwal Pass. The steep slopes of the mountains kept out the warmth of the sun still climbing to its Midsummer high. It would be noon before it shone directly down into the pass — the exact time the Archon intended to open the gate. Ten thousand soldiers marched in silence with only the odd clink of metal, and clip-clop of horseshoes on rock, breaking the eerie stillness. Elodi glanced behind to her captains. They nodded offering support and encouragement, but as they drew closer, she could not shake off her sense of foreboding. Her eyes were drawn to the sheer, dark slopes. Elodi shuddered; the mountains greedily sucked them down its gullet to their fate, drawing them inexorably to a confrontation with their nemesis. But the time to withdraw had passed — there was to be no turning back.

As they progressed, the Caerwals loomed ever higher, shutting out the sky as they looked ready to crash down upon their heads. Elodi suddenly felt insignificant. To what names did these mighty mountains answer? They cared not for the petty labels on the maps drawn up by the fleeting inhabitants of the land. When thunder rumbled across the range, did the peaks call out to one another in their ancient tongue known only to the gods?

Elodi looked ahead to the Archonian Guards. What would the mountains make of the coming conflict? Surely, the people marching through the pass, carved out at the cost of their lower slopes, were nothing more than tiny insects to them, a minor irritant at most. Two swarms of these creatures were about to do battle — it mattered not to the mountains which side claimed victory. It made no difference to them. Whether it was the Five Realms or the Golesh, the mighty peaks of the Caerwals would not ultimately be disturbed again. They would stand long after all had departed their world.

For the tenth time since entering the pass, Elodi looked back along the line of her soldiers. She trusted they would fight courageously and face whatever awaited them on the other side of the gate, but something nagged at the pit of her stomach. As she had approached the bridge, Elodi knew the same person who had spied her on the balcony at sunrise, also shared her misgivings on how the events of the day would unfold.

Elodi beheld the gate. Being later in the day than her one and only visit, no mist obscured her view. She still had some distance to cover before she entered its shadow, but already it stood large and seemingly impenetrable, despite being dwarfed by the mountains. Even now, she wondered if it would be wiser to leave it shut fast. But she knew Bardon urgently needed their support, and if Calerdorn was to be taken back from the hideous wykes, unruly Ruuk and corrupt Dorlan, the realms had to put a permanent end to the threat from the south. She glanced up. The thin line of blue sky gave no indication of when the sun would make its presence felt in the pass, but the hour of the Archon launching the attack was nigh. To her right, the Caerwal Tower rose to reach the top of the gate. The damage inflicted by the attack in the spring was, as yet, unrepaired, and the missing roof and fractured wall, served only to add to her growing unease.

Harlyn's finest reached the assembly point. Elodi noted the Castellan had the honor of directing each cohort to their positions. It was with some pride, Elodi and her force formed their lines besides the mounted Knights of the Archon at the front. But of course, this also meant they would be the first to ride through and crash headlong into the enraged Golesh hordes.

Elodi leaned forward and patted Sea Mist's neck. She dared not even whisper and give away the Archon's intention, but her faithful steed knew her mind. Now they would wait. She wondered how the battle would come to be written. Should the Archon carry the day, many songs and tales would entertain and enthrall folk for centuries to come. Should the Golesh be victorious, a vastly different story would be told — but who would be spared to listen?

Elodi shifted in her saddle. Uncomfortable beneath the immense presence of the gate, she turned to survey the parapets. The widened platforms stood almost one hundred feet above the floor of the pass. The Archon's new heavy weapons stood ready to unleash their fury; her stomach churned as she was reminded of the machines Uldrak had brought to Calerdorn. She watched as the black-clad artillery crews lit their torches ready to ignite the projectiles. The Archon promised the barrage would be like nothing witnessed for many centuries, and the mayhem caused in the narrow pass would pave his way to a comprehensive victory. Elodi's hands clenched her reins — the same preparations must surely be underway just a short distance on the other side of the gate. Whoever launched the attack first would undoubtedly gain the upper hand. But did that mean the Golesh were yet to detect the Archon's army? Otherwise, why would they wait?

The gate. Of course. Why waste valuable ordinance on the gate if you suspected your enemy planned to open it. The Golesh must know the Archon was preparing to send the remainder of his strength to aid the forces holding Elmarand. But if they anticipated the opening of the gate, what awaited Elodi on the other side? Defending such a narrow pass would be made easier if they drastically thinned the Archon's ranks. Wedged within the steep slopes, the massed armies of the realms lay vulnerable to the dreaded weapons of the Golesh. Elodi's stomach clenched at the thought of a deadly trap waiting to be sprung. If the defenders crushed the best of the Five Realms, they could stroll through, meeting with little resistance to take the realms one-by-one without breaking step.

Elodi turned her attention to the top of the tower, determined to rid herself of her reservations. Was the Archon ready? Had he looked upon the Lost Realms and sincerely believed they could be victorious? She took a deep breath to calm her nerves. The Archon must have seen their formation and assembled an appropriate force. She cocked her head. If the Golesh waited on the other side, they too remained silent. Elodi would have thought any sound would be amplified by the steep sides of the pass, or would the height of the gate prevent sounds reaching the other side? What would an eagle see if it chose this moment to soar overhead?

Gundrul touched her arm. He pointed to the door at the base of the tower as it opened. The Archon strode out. His bright blue robe appeared to glow, as did the markings on his skull. Even from a distance, Elodi sensed the air change as he took his position on a small platform at the center where the two great iron and stone gates met. The Archon did indeed appear vastly stronger than at her meeting with him the previous day. She took encouragement from his demeanor. Gone was the weakened man she had witnessed ready to jump from his high tower. Before them stood the Archon of the Five Realms: strong, confident, and in command of immense power. Whatever his preparations at the top of the tower had entailed, they had obviously proved effective.

The Archon's gaze moved to the parapets and the heavy weapons. Elodi noted he gave a slight nod to the artillery commander. The awe of the retaliation she had witnessed from the terraces of Archonholm had been great. How would it feel this time to stand beneath the weapons as they unleashed their deadly onslaught? She stroked Sea Mist's mane, hoping the horses would not be spooked by the barrage. And what of the enemy's weapons? Timing would be key. If the enemy did indeed anticipate the attack, would they have positioned their engines farther down the pass? The Archon's first volley could achieve nothing but signal the onset of battle, allowing time for the Golesh to bring forward their war machines to launch their reply, before those on the parapets could reload. Or were the Golesh about to unleash a pre-emptive strike? Elodi fidgeted in her saddle, willing the Archon to begin proceedings, and not be such a stickler for ceremony and wait for the appointed hour.

Nyomae's trick worked. Toryn had felt a pang of guilt as the Palace Guard waved them through with enthusiasm, even apologizing for delaying their progress. They had crossed the bridge and reached the unattended Lower Gate before Nyomae released her hold on the deceived sentry. Hamar had spoken of the Caerwal Pass, but even his old friend's tendency to exaggerate had not done it justice. Despite Toryn's anxiety, he marveled at the achievement of his predecessors. It must have taken an age to form the pass, blasting away the lower reaches of the mountains, allowing the mainly straight road to take the shortest route. But now he focused his attention ahead, desperate to reach the gate.

They walked a hundred paces behind the small force from Galabrant. Toryn was as yet unsure of the role he and Nyomae would assume. But of one thing he was certain — he had to be present. He stopped. The gate! Again, Hamar's description failed to prepare him for his first sighting. Hamar had only ever seen it from half a league, now Toryn would see it unlock and hauled open. But how could something of such huge dimensions be moved? It had remained shut for hundreds of years; how many would it take to shift the vast gates on their runners?

Another feature drew his eye. At either side of the pass, great ramps had been carved out of the rockface, climbing to ledges high above the road. Thick wooden beams from gigantic weapons jutted out, directing their ominous destructive force over the top of the gate. Toryn counted four on each side. Dark figures scurried over them. He remembered Dravic, the man in the adjacent cell in the dungeons beneath Archonholm. Dravic had told him of the ongoing modifications to the parapets, but he could never have envisaged their scale.

A robed figure moved across the foot of the gate, appearing to glow in its shadow: the Archon! Toryn instinctively pulled his hood a little farther over his head. But surely the Archon could not recognize him from this distance, especially with his mind focused on the attack. Ahead, the force of Galabrant halted. Toryn watched another who had condemned him to death: the Castellan. The man marched through the lines, guiding the soldiers to their positions at the rear with extravagant gestures, obviously enjoying his role in the proceedings. Toryn turned away as the Castellan drew near. He and Nyomae moved off to the side and made their way a short distance up the ramp leading to the weapons.

Toryn took the opportunity to look for Lady Harlyn. As he saw her plume, the same dread he had felt at the bridge, intensified. She sat ready on her horse beneath Harlyn's banner, right at the front, almost opposite the Archon. He blinked. The air around the Archon glimmered. Power radiated from his slender body, seeming to fill the pass and bounce back from the mountain walls. The Archon glanced up and nodded to someone on the parapet. Toryn followed his gaze. His stomach lurched.

44. The Archon's Crushing Blow

The snowy peaks on the west side of the pass glistened bright in the sun. Elodi watched, barely able to breathe, as the light slid slowly down the sheer slopes towards the ramparts bearing the war machines. Midday approached. The gate would soon open. Their world would change.

Elodi's bones vibrated as the Archon spoke. His voice, deep, yet soft, almost a whisper, emanated throughout the pass. Each who heard his words, felt as if he stood by their side speaking only to them. The Archon appeared to grow taller as he addressed his army. 'I stand before the largest force gathered since the day the Caerwal Gate closed.' No one moved. 'You stand before your Archon, stronger, more powerful now, than the day the Caerwal Gate closed.' The lines on his head burned like glowing embers, but not red as before, now a bright orange, bordering on yellow. The Archon's body shuddered as if struggling to contain the energy surging within. He drew his blade and held it high. The Sword of the Realms shone bright as the sun appeared over the lip of the eastern peaks. He bellowed. 'Today, all my enemies will fall!'

Elodi gasped. The Archon held the pose she and Bardon had witnessed on that eventful day in his room; the same, dramatic stance on the tapestry depicting the final moments on Gormadon Plain. The markings on his head blazed with a brilliant white light, appearing to widen, until Elodi feared his skull would crack open. His voice changed. 'Today, I take back what is rightfully mine.' Elodi struggled to understand his words as two voices now issued from his throat: the second, higher voice, dominating that of the Archon.

Elodi's mind raced against a dullness growing inside. She stood in her stirrups and stared at the Archon. Her head numbed; her eyelids grew heavy. Think! *What were his words at the last battle?* She forced herself to recall the relapse he had suffered in his room. *Rise and send these demons back to the darkness.* In his desperation, the Archon had tried to command the sun! But that meant… no, it could not be true. If he raised his sword to his right, the Archon must have faced north at the last battle. Elodi shook her head, trying desperately to stay awake. He should have faced *south* — the threat came from the south! Unless…

Elodi turned to Gundrul, fighting against her tight chest to breathe and give her voice the fuel it desperately needed. She managed barely a whisper. 'Captain. Something's wrong.' But Gundrul's glazed eyes stayed fixed on the Archon, appearing not to hear her. She tried to rouse the others, but all stared glassy-eyed at the platform, spellbound by their leader.

Toryn gripped Nyomae's arm. 'Up there. On the parapet. They're… Nordleng!'

But she failed to respond. Nyomae staggered forward, clutching her head. Her teeth ground together as she tried to speak. 'That voice… the Archon's voice. It's not—' Nyomae collapsed. Toryn checked she still breathed. He placed her at the foot of the mountain wall away from the foot of the ramp, then sprinted up to the parapet. He reached the top as the Archon's voice escalated. It was as he feared. The crews were not artillery divisions. The Nordleng stood not by the large weapons, but close to the edge.

The first black-robed figure turned, surprised by Toryn's sudden appearance. Toryn lunged at him before the man could draw his sword, shoving him over the side. Seven more lined the parapet, but all were too focused on the Archon to notice Toryn. A flaming torch lay beside a shaft where his first victim had fallen. He glanced down. His head spun. 'No. It can't be.' He thrust out his hand to steady himself against the giant, redundant trebuchet. His body froze. Toryn turned his stiff neck to find the Archon glared directly at him. His limbs locked, rooting him to the spot. But his will was strong, and the Archon's attention laid bare the leader's mind. It could not be! He had to act. Toryn delved deep inside to find the strength. Heat rose from his core, bursting through his chest and up into his throat. He yelled, shattering the air the Archon had forced against him.

Toryn threw back his cloak and unshouldered his bow — he had five arrows. The Archon would no doubt be shielded, and he would waste his precious few shots attempting to bring him down. He kneeled, nocked his first, and took down the closest Nordleng crouched beside another shaft with his flaming torch. The next along the ledge fell with an arrow in his throat before the others noticed. Lady Harlyn! Her plume stood out among the thousands of mounted knights at the foot of the gate. He searched the end of the parapet looming over the massed forces. A man stood poised with his torch awaiting his order. Without a second thought, Toryn fixed the dark figure in his sight and let fly.

The Archon's mouth curled into a grin. 'Today, I shall not open the gate.' He faltered, staring up to the rampart as if another took his attention. Elodi followed his gaze. A man kneeled, aiming an arrow. She found her voice, shouting at Gundrul. 'Forward! Take him. Forward, Harlyn, forward!' This time her captain responded.

But the Archon's frenzied scream halted their charge.

'All who dare oppose me shall be crushed!'

Elodi hurled back her defiance. 'With me, Harlyn. With me!' She spurred Sea Mist. He readily responded and sped towards the Archon. The ranks of Harlyn followed, surging forward, loyal to their leader to the last.

The ground buckled. Sea Mist stumbled, throwing Elodi from the saddle. The air exploded. Elodi's ears burst as the Archon laughed. The sides of the mountains erupted, raining rocks and rubble down onto the largest force the Five Realms had mustered in its short history.

Toryn was flung through the air as the ledge disintegrated. His arms flailed, desperate to find a hold and prevent falling to his death or being crushed by the trebuchets as they toppled over. He lost his bow as his hands grasped solid rock securing his safety. Dust filled his eyes, ears and mouth. He coughed hard, gasping for air. The ground settled. A thunderous wave hurtled down the pass, fading to a rumble as it departed, seemingly oblivious to the carnage left in its wake.

Toryn scraped the grit from his eyes and climbed to his feet. He gaped at the floor of the pass, just visible beneath a cloud of billowing dust. Where once a formidable force had proudly filled the gap, rocks and rubble lay. Much of the ramparts had gone. The large weapons lay shattered among the rocks like a child's discarded toys. But fortunately, the four Nordleng he killed, had spared some the dreadful fate of their entombed companions. Hands, spear tips and the odd banner protruded from the debris. The silence gave way to the cries and moans of the injured and trapped. Stunned survivors staggered over the rocks, desperate to free the buried. Toryn frantically searched the ruins. Those closest to the rear on his side of the pass, had survived, and mercifully, some of the ranks at the front had been spared the landslide, although many lay dead or dying, dashed by flying rocks. He checked the foot of the ramp and to his relief found Nyomae had avoided the slaughter.

Nyomae looked up and pointed to the gate, then began to find her way through the rubble. Toryn turned. Harlyn's bedraggled banner stood defiant amid the rubble at the foot of the Archon's dais, but thankfully it was not as deep as the rest of the pass. He spat out the last of the grit and ran along what remained of the ledge towards the gate. Of the Nordleng, only one remained. The cloaked figure drew his sword, but as he moved to swing, the loose stones gave way, dispatching him to the floor of the pass to share the fate of his victims.

Toryn reached the end of the parapet, clambered over the side, and half-climbed, half-slid down the slope of dislodged rocks. At the foot, the full horror struck. The screams of the wounded horses and soldiers was unbearable. But he was relieved to find many of the First Horse and Knights of the Archon had escaped the worst of the blasts. But few were spared the flying debris, and dozens had been thrown by their panicked horses. Some staggered, dazed by the shockwave, those who could, had begun the enormous task of retrieving those trapped beneath.

But Toryn had not the time to help them — he sought Lady Harlyn. He stumbled over the rocks strewn across the front of the Archon's platform. For a moment, the enormity of the Caerwal Gate overwhelmed him. He looked up to the huge slabs held in place by a lattice work of iron. It appeared to waver, as if about to fall and flattened the survivors. But it was a trick of the clouds as they floated idly by, unconcerned by the follies of the little folk below.

Toryn looked for Lady Harlyn. Here, the stones lay only a foot or so deep, but still enough to suffocate an injured soldier trapped beneath. He drew up. Her distinctive helm lay on its side a short distance ahead. But where was she? Toryn scanned the scene and found her horse. Sea Mist nudged at the rubble with his nose and had uncovered a braid of red hair.

The Archon! Toryn's heart raced as the Archon stumbled towards the prone Lady Harlyn. The markings on his head now glimmered a faint red. He looked weakened by his efforts to shield himself from the detonation, but he did not need his powers to bring an end to her life as she lay defenseless. The Archon stooped to pick up a rock; his eyes fixed on Lady Harlyn's exposed head.

Toryn yelled. 'No!' Sea Mist turned and reared up to the Archon, kicking out his hooves to defend his mistress. But the Archon had enough strength to deal with a determined animal. He shot a glance at the horse that sent a shudder through Toryn. Sea Mist whinnied, backed away but refused to bolt. The Archon turned his attention to Toryn. The air crackled, pushing him back as he tried to gain a foothold. The Archon raised the rock above his head and stepped towards his prey. But Toryn was not to be denied. He too grabbed a stone and launched it at the Archon. His eyes were fixed solely on Lady Harlyn and failed to see the rock. For the fourth time that day, Toryn's aim was true. No shimmering shield of air protected the man. The stone struck the Archon squarely on his temple. He cried out and staggered back. The remaining force holding Toryn fell away, releasing him to rush forward. He picked up another stone and threw, hitting the Archon on his shoulder as he turned and stumbled towards his tower. Toryn almost laughed. What would Hamar have made of him hurling stones at the Ruler of the Five Realms?

Toryn waited until the Archon had entered the tower, then ran as best he could to Lady Harlyn's side. Sea Mist followed and began to kick at the rubble covering his mistress. He took her hand — it was cold. 'My lady? Can you hear me?' To his relief, she gripped back. His fingers bled as he tore at the jagged stones on her back as Sea Mist licked her face. Once he had cleared the largest, Toryn sat beside her, slid his arm beneath her back and carefully rolled her onto her side. She coughed, spat out dust and tried to sit. He moved to calm her. 'Careful, my lady, you may be a little dazed. You were buried under rubble.' She grasped his hand tighter. He read her thoughts. 'No, not all are lost. And Sea Mist is here by your side.' Toryn felt her body relax. He laid her on his lap and cradled her shoulders. 'Ma'am? May I clean your face?' She managed a slight nod. He picked the small pieces from her eyes, and brushed the dust from her cheeks, being careful not to scratch her. Toryn held his breath as her face revealed itself. Despite their desperate situation, he marveled at her beauty, the smooth skin of her cheeks, miraculously unblemished by the blast. She blinked away tears and dust; Toryn's heart stopped as her green eyes opened and found his. He stared deep into them, losing himself for the moment as all else around faded.

Lady Harlyn stirred. 'Please' — she spluttered — 'please, tell me your name.' But she asked as if she already knew.

He cleared his throat and straightened. 'Toryn, ma'am. Toryn of Midwyche.'

Her eyes closed as she sighed. 'Yes, yes I thought it would be you.' She sagged against his arm.

'But how… how would you know my name, ma'am? I'm just a—'

'Please. How many? How many survived?'

Toryn surveyed the pass, unsure if the truth would hurt her. 'Difficult to tell right now. The First Horse were spared the worst. There are quite a few riderless horses that must have thrown their knights in the panic and bolted, and there's movement among the debris close to the gate. But farther back… unfortunately, I fear not many could have survived, ma'am.' Toryn felt her pain. He moved to console her. 'But your action helped. I saw you lead a charge moments before the blast. That took many out of harm's way.'

Her body shook as her hand went to her face. She wept. 'We've lost, all is lost.' She winced as it pained her to cry.

'But you're Lady Harlyn, you can save—'

She sobbed. 'No… no, I'm not. I'm just Elodi. I don't deserve the title. I have no realm to speak of, I doubt I have much of an army left to command.' Her voice grew weak as if the effort to speak drained her. 'I have no title. I have failed.'

Toryn's heart lurched. 'You're still Lady Harlyn to me, ma'am.' He looked about him. 'There's more emerging from the rubble. It's not so deep here. I can see more of your knights and soldiers climbing free. They may look a little dazed, but they're alive. And you still have Calerdorn.' More tears flowed; her pain renewed. He stuttered, reading her mind. 'Calerdorn's lost? But that can't be…'

She moved to sit but could not find the strength and gave up the struggle. 'I didn't even raise my sword. Dorlan. He's back. He's taken the city.'

'Dorlan? Lady Harlyn, you must be mistaken.'

She choked. 'No, it's him, I'm sure. Raised by the enemy.'

'Dorlan… back?' More tears flowed. Toryn tried to console her. 'But all is not lost, ma'am. The Amayans still ride… your sisters. Yes, I know. I can see it.'

Her head turned. She wiped her face. 'You've met them? How many?'

'At least a dozen, ma'am.' But Toryn chose not to

mention the current danger they faced.

Her voice croaked. 'My armor. Please remove my breastplate, I can't breathe.' Toryn loosened the straps and gently lifted the dented armor. Beneath, her body was warm and growing hotter. He noticed she had sustained injuries where the metal had been struck by larger rocks, but already the wounds had stopped bleeding.

Toryn looked up, searching for Nyomae. 'And we have a new ally, one from the old days, ma'am. She fought with the Archon before the last battle. And… my father, he's another with power. He lives but is held prisoner. They are both like the Archon and perhaps—'

'All too late, I fear. We should never have—' Lady Harlyn let out a long breath. Her head lolled to one side as beads of sweat formed on her brow.

'Ma'am?' Her eyes flickered. 'You have a fever.' Toryn lowered his ear to her lips and was relieved to feel her shallow breath on his cheek. 'I'll go for help. You need water.'

Toryn shuddered. Malicious eyes were upon him. He spun around to see the Archon had reached the top of his ruined tower. The Archon held out his arms and splayed his fingers. The air rippled between his hands as he fashioned a glimmering sphere. Toryn's scalp tingled. He placed Elodi on her side and stood. *Be ready, Toryn.* Nyomae's voice sounded in his head. He turned to see her stride effortlessly across the rubble as if strolling through a meadow. She pointed to the tower as the Archon thrust out his arms, hurling the sphere across the floor of the pass, expanding as it made its way over the debris. Toryn staggered back as if caught in a gale. But as fast as it came, it died away.

Nyomae arrived at his side. 'He seeks to divide the survivors. If we don't stop him, they'll be killing each other before long.'

'But the Lady Harlyn! She cannot defend herself in her state. She's vulnerable. And I think she has a fever.'

Nyomae kneeled and placed a hand on Elodi. 'She will live. She's an Amayan. It's not a fever. The healing has begun.' She glanced back to the pinnacle of the tower. 'But we have to confront the Archon now. If we don't, he'll grow stronger and even together, we will not defeat him.' More survivors climbed out from beneath the debris. Nyomae watched them. 'They are yet too weak to cause much harm, but the Archon will give them the strength as he recovers, strength to tear each other apart if we don't stop him.'

Toryn peered over his shoulder. 'And he could still open the gate. We're in no state to face the Golesh. They'd be in Archonholm before the day is out.'

Nyomae took his hand. 'Then we have no choice. We must strike now. But we have just moments before he regains all his powers. He is who I suspect. Your Archon is the one I knew as Mordram. The one who fought with me at Foranfae. He was once a fine and powerful man, but I fear he's been corrupted by the Ul-dalak.'

They reached the foot of the tower. Nyomae quickly removed the spell the Archon had placed on the door. They entered. Toryn gasped. 'There's no stairs. How do we get up?'

Nyomae managed a smile. 'A small victory.' She pointed to a timber frame that disappeared up into the gloom. 'I recall seeing these in the towers of Elmarand.' She walked to a wheel attached to a rope. 'Turn this, a platform will descend.'

Toryn did as instructed and noticed a large stone rise as the wheel turned. Nyomae watched it ascend. 'It appears the Archon is either expecting our company, or in his madness, he thankfully forgot to lock the mechanism.'

Toryn stared up through the dust. 'Or he feels

confident he can resist our efforts to defeat him.'

'Either way, I am relieved we don't have to climb a thousand steps to challenge him. But challenge him we must.' As she spoke, the air grew heavy as if a great hand pushed down through the tower. 'And challenge him now.'

The platform descended and came to rest at their feet accompanied by a loud click. They stepped on. Nyomae nodded to a lever. Toryn pulled and immediately the platform rose against a force that appeared to resist their ascension. He glanced up. Far above, a tiny circle of light grew. His heart raced. Nyomae took his hand. 'Stay calm and follow my lead. You may not yet know how to use the power in the Verses, but your presence will lend me strength.' She squeezed his hand. 'You have the resolve of your father, Toryn. Trust it, and we will prevail.'

The air cooled. Claws of ice groped at Toryn as if seeking to rip his heart from his chest. He slowed his breathing and stood tall. The platform approached the top. The light grew. Toryn squinted as they emerged through the shaft into the cold air high above the pass. They stepped off into a roofless room, smaller than the one at the base, no more than a dozen paces in diameter. Much of the wall had gone, demolished by the attack in the spring. Only a remnant of the stonework remained, adjacent to the gate containing steps that once led to the top floor — the floor that afforded a view into the Lost Realms. Toryn had time to take in the view. They stood just below the ledge of the rock wall that housed the great hinges of the Caerwal Gate; he could almost reach out and touch the cold iron.

But they had not come to admire the view. The air throbbed, hurling waves of heat at their faces. Its source was at the foot of the crumbled stairs. Toryn dipped his head, trying to protect his eyes. The Archon had his back to them as he kneeled facing the wall. The lines on his head glowed yellow — he appeared to have regained much of his strength. The Archon rose and turned. His body appeared diminished, but his eyes glared a dazzling white. Toryn and Nyomae stiffened, held fast in his withering gaze.

Nyomae gasped. 'Uluriel!' Then to Toryn through clenched teeth. 'Alas, a dark one possesses him. It is worse than I feared.' The Archon's thin lips grinned. Nyomae's strangled voice struggled to make itself heard. 'Mordram? Can you hear me?' The Archon gave no sign. Far below, swords clashing on shields and armor, jerked Toryn back to life — Lady Harlyn was in danger. He tried to move, but his rigid muscles held him fast. Nyomae took his hand. It warmed, drawing power from within him. She muttered unknown words. Toryn's vision blurred. The Archon's body flickered and changed before them. A woman's form took shape. Like Uleva, she appeared both beautiful and terrible, but unlike Uleva, there was no sadness behind her eyes — only glee for her thirst for blood and power.

Nyomae's voice rose as she continued her fight; Uluriel's grin widened. And to Toryn's horror, he sensed Nyomae strive to maintain control as she sought to separate Uluriel from Mordram. Without the vessel of the Archon, Uluriel could not fight, and would be forced to flee back to her body. But Uluriel was embedded deep within her host and was not ready to abandon it. Toryn read Nyomae's strategy — she delved back through the Verses, seeking aid from Mordram before the time Uluriel had seized his mind. But the leader of the Ul-dalak had taken hold many, many years past.

Nyomae cried out. Her jaw clamped shut, her head was thrown back, her shoulders bunched as her grip on Toryn's hand threatened to snap his fingers. He suffered her pain. His muscles clenched until his bones would surely shatter. But Nyomae fought on, probing deeper into the past. Together, they raced back through time. A tempest raged, resisting their passage, seeking to snatch their souls from their bodies. Nyomae screamed. Then silence. Toryn gasped for air, but the moment Uluriel entered Mordram revealed itself: at the very moment Nyomae had uttered the Verse of Unmaking. Toryn saw through her eyes. The Archon had fought at her side to face the unworldly might of Uluriel and her dark hosts. *This* was the last battle.

The legend was a lie.

The Archon had not faced the enemy at Gormadon Plain. The conflict had not taken place in the south; it had been fought where the Foranfae Forest now dominated Holm. The Archon had resisted Uluriel and the Ul-dalak alongside Nyomae and the last of the Order of Echoes. Toryn stared in horror as they fell. The first, Dormarl, later captured, tortured, and spoiled, had become Uldrak; the same fate befell the youngest of the Order, Elsaya, who would become Uleva. He saw his father, Finromir, fight to the last moment, desperately holding back the attempts of the *Draedalak* to break his soul and haul him from the battlefield.

Nyomae and Mordram now stood alone on the field of shattered souls. But Uluriel grew to twice her height, fueled by the powers summoned from the Dark Verses. She snatched up Mordram as if made of straw. Toryn dropped to his knees as Uluriel vomited a stream of a foul green fluid into Mordram's mouth. She flung him to the floor, leaving him to crawl away. Uluriel leveled her fell eyes at Nyomae. She sneered, speaking in a voice that echoed across the battlefield and within the tower back in Toryn's time. 'Fool. Do you think you can defeat me?' Uluriel stepped forward.

But Nyomae was not done. She stiffened, steeling herself for one last effort to reach farther back into the

Song, seeking the unpossessed Archon. But Uluriel held sway in this realm, ensnaring their souls in the Verse at the moment Nyomae had uttered those ill-fated words. And Uluriel drew strength from the forces she had summoned at that time. Her power surged. Toryn read her intent with dread. She strove to take form in the tower, releasing herself from the limitations of her weakened host to become invincible.

Toryn's feet slipped. Both he and Nyomae were pushed back. He forced his head to look behind. The platform had gone. Only inches separated them from their death should Uluriel send them plunging down the tower's shaft. He had to act. But do what? He wriggled his fingers. Then moved an arm. Uluriel's hold on him wavered as her attention focused solely on Nyomae. He pushed against the invisible hand forcing them back. Toryn lifted a foot. At his side, Nyomae sensed his thoughts. She called upon her last reserves of power, then loosened her grip on his hand.

Toryn dipped and charged at the Archon. He hurtled into the body of a frail man but seemed to slam into a rock wall. The Archon's skin burned as Toryn grappled with the flaming demon within. Hot blades slashed at Toryn, but he held tight. He cried out. The tower trembled; the Archon glowed white hot, but still he held firm. Uluriel fought to enter his head, her curses promising to tear his skull apart and claim his soul as her own. Toryn clamped his jaw, strengthened his grip, and wrestled, trying to distract Uluriel long enough for Nyomae to gain advantage. His flesh burned; his eyes boiled; but still he held on. Nyomae's voice rose, freed from the time of her defeat, shouting new verses discovered among the cacophony of the past. The tower shook to its foundations. But still Uluriel held the advantage.

Toryn pushed. They neared the edge. There was only

one way to defeat Uluriel. He would take them both crashing to their deaths. He dropped his shoulder and shoved hard as he would against a wagon stuck in the mud. Uluriel sensed his aim. It was enough. Her attention wavered. Nyomae struck, reciting a verse of Mordram's youth when free of his possessor. It released Mordram's mind and gave him the strength to resist. His head snapped back. A brilliant, green light burst from his gaping eyes and mouth; a scream tore the air from Toryn's chest. Then a flash of orange blinded him. He was flung back against the wall and blacked out.

45. The Dust Settles

'Thank the Three. I thought you were surely lost.'

Toryn opened his watering eyes. He blinked in the light. 'Lady Harlyn! You're—' He tried to move.

Elodi stroked his arm. 'Please, remain still. You wouldn't want to fall to your death so soon after your victory.'

'Victory?' Toryn looked about him. 'Hope!' Her body lay beside the Archon slumped against the wall. His heart lurched. 'Is she…?'

'She's in a trance but appears satisfactory. But I cannot vouch for the Archon. He is weak. I'm not sure he'll survive.'

He clutched Elodi's hand. 'What happened? I recall wrestling with the Archon, scorching heat, a blinding green light before it turned orange… then all went dark.'

Elodi glanced to her sword. 'The orange flash was me. I arrived just as a vile apparition was forcing its way out of the Archon's mouth. I did the only thing I could do — I ran it through with my blade. Then, as with you, all turned black. I awoke just a moment ago, but I sprained my ankle when I was thrown back.' She looked to the two prone forms. 'Who is that woman? You called her Hope?'

'Her real name is Nyomae, and once a follower of what she called the Order of Echoes. She believes the Archon was possessed by one who turned against them. One she named Uluriel.'

Elodi gasped. 'I know that name.' She turned to the Archon. 'Has that foul creature been inside his head all this time?'

Toryn winced as he tried to move his arm. 'That I

cannot say, but there's something else you need to know. Nyomae fought alongside the Archon at the last battle. But it was not fought at Gormadon in the south. It took place where the Foranfae now stands.'

'So… he did face north. I suspected as much.' Elodi nodded to the gate. 'Then I wonder why the need for that?'

Toryn sat upright. 'Nyomae believes Uluriel's allies fled south to rouse the Golesh to their side. But she couldn't be certain.'

Elodi sighed. 'There is so much we need to learn… and fast. We are weakened, vulnerable to an attack. Surely, the Golesh will have heard the explosion and ensuing landslide.' She grimaced as she tried to flex her ankle. 'Would they not be about to launch an assault on the gate?'

Toryn moved. 'My head is clearing.' He climbed to his feet and stepped over the Archon to Nyomae. She stirred as he placed a hand on her shoulder. Nyomae mumbled a few words, her eyes flickered beneath their lids, but she remained in her slumber.

Elodi limped to join him. 'We must get them both to a healer. And then, somehow, reform our lines and prepare for a full-scale attack.'

Toryn nodded to the steps. 'I could take a look over. We may not get another chance if these walls collapse.'

'Agreed. Better you than I with this ankle. I would not trust myself on those steps. But please be quick. If they are to launch their heavy weapons and deploy the rams, we have to retreat and endeavor to defend the Lower Gate.'

Toryn stood and placed his foot on the first step. 'It feels solid.' He slowly climbed the stairs, feeling exposed in the breeze as he rose above the level of the floor. The stairs followed the curve of the wall to finish where the upper room had stood. He pushed his feet deep into the steps close to the outer wall, daring not to look through the gaps and down into the pass far below. Toryn reached the last step. He gripped the jagged edge of the stones and pulled himself up to peer over. But he was still several feet short of a clear view over the crest of the rock wall. The air rippled like a blue curtain just above the rim. His face tingled and his hair stood on end, but he could not yet see into the south.

Toryn had no choice. He would have to climb onto the top of the tower's wall, barely wide enough for his feet. He took a deep breath, pushed down on the ledge, and clambered up to the protests from Elodi below. Toryn crouched until he felt steady. Then, slowly, with his arms held out at his sides, he rose, blinking into the wind blowing through the pass.

Toryn wiped his eyes and looked over the top of the Caerwal Gate.

Elodi called up. 'What do you see?' Toryn's mouth dropped open. She tried again. 'Toryn? What do you see?'

He mouthed the words twice before he could find his voice. 'Nothing. I can see nothing.'

The pass to the south lay empty.

No armies, no weapons, no parapets, not even a road. If the Golesh had once occupied the pass, it had long been abandoned. A lone structure stood in the empty space, a few hundred yards from the foot of the gate; a monument, perhaps a memorial to the fallen. But would the Golesh have built such a structure for those lost in battle? Toryn looked closer. Wild creepers grew around the stone, tainting it a dark green. If it was indeed a memorial, no one had tended to it for many years. He peered farther down the pass to where the mountains ended abruptly less than a league away. But no gate or wall sealed the southern exit. Beyond that, a stubborn haze concealed any towns or settlements that would provide a clue to what fate had befallen their long-lost kin.

Toryn turned to Elodi below and shrugged, still unable to accept what his eyes witnessed. 'Nothing. I see nothing.'

Elodi gasped. 'But there must be some sign of the Golesh.'

'None. Just an old statue.' The stone beneath his feet moved. 'I'm coming down.'

Toryn descended the stairs. He stared at the Archon. The markings on his head had faded and now resembled scars as if inflicted by a keen blade. He kneeled beside Elodi and the crumpled form of their leader. She lifted his pale hands and folded the Archon's arms across his chest. The man opened his eyes.

Elodi gasped. 'Is he blind? He had many colors the last time I saw them. But now… they're cloudy.' She laid her hand on the Archon's brow as he struggled to sit. 'Please, Archon, be still, you are injured.'

The Archon tried to speak, but his voice was barely audible above the breeze. 'She's gone, she's… I can't see. Who speaks?'

'It is Elodi… Lady Harlyn.'

Again, he attempted to sit. 'Where am I?'

'You're at the top of the Caerwal Tower. You were about to open—'

The Archon cried out. 'What have I done? I… I failed. I've destroyed everything... I've…' A tear ran down his cheek, his head sagged forward, his breathing slowed.

Elodi moved to comfort him. 'Uluriel was strong… too powerful. Few, if any, could have withstood her.' The Archon's back arched. He cried out, clutching Elodi's arm. She bowed her head. 'You could not have done more. Had it not been for your efforts at the last battle, all would have been lost centuries ago.' His mouth moved, but his voice could not be heard. A trickle of blood ran from his ear. Elodi leaned forward and whispered. 'Go in peace,

Archon. Find solace in the next world.'

The Archon let out a long sigh and died, setting free his tortured spirit.

Toryn thought he saw his last breath depart his body like a cloud. It rose into the breeze, drifted over the gate, and disappeared into the south. Elodi straightened his robe. 'He should have a monument raised befitting of his stature. The story of Uluriel's betrayal will be made known throughout the land. The Archon should not be held responsible for the actions of a traitor to the realms.' Dust fell from the wall above the steps; the tower shifted. Elodi stood. 'We must leave. The tower is no longer safe.'

Toryn gently lifted Nyomae. 'What of the Archon? We can't leave his body here.'

'We cannot.' Elodi put her full weight on her ankle. 'I will take him. I appear to heal quickly.' Elodi looked to the Archon. 'He deserves a proper sending off as with the Archons of old. The rubble from his tower would not be a fitting memorial.'

They hurried to the shaft, stumbling as the tower trembled. They placed the Archon and Nyomae on the platform. Neither spoke as they descended. Toryn kept his eyes fixed on the circle of light above as they sank into the darkness of the lower levels. The rumbling grew louder. They arrived at the base not a moment too soon and quickly departed the tower.

Outside, a party of Calerdorn's knights took the Archon from Elodi, and Nyomae from Toryn. To his relief, the departure of Uluriel had brought an end to the division among the survivors, and all now worked to free those beneath the rocks. Elodi instructed the knights to take Nyomae and the Archon's body to a nearby healer's wagon.

Elodi sagged against Toryn's shoulder. Her hand went to her mouth as she sunk to her knees. 'So many lost… so many fine people.' Her tearful eyes looked up to Toryn. 'What are we to do? The danger we face is here, on our side of the gate. We cannot resist the darkness that seeks to destroy and enslave us. We have lost the bulk of our forces, we have no leader, and Uluriel has slipped from our grasp. And what of Lord Broon and the elite forces? Surely, if the Golesh are not at the gate, have they gone south and defeated him?'

Toryn kneeled at her side and took her hand. 'We have everything to fight for, ma'am. I don't mind saying it, but there were times when I almost gave up, but others helped me pull through. You are the Lady of Harlyn, a fine realm with a fine history. You have the blood of an Amayan warrior, a potent force if ever there was.' He stood and helped Elodi to her feet, aware of eyes upon them. 'You have to show strength. I would follow you to fight the Evil One beneath the mountains, ma'am. And I'm certain every soldier here would do the same.' He gripped her forearm. 'And we have Nyomae, and my father yet lives, although the enemy hold him. And don't forget the Amayans, imagine what they could do together. Ah! And there are the Nym.' He saw her frown. 'Ancient beings living in Foranfae. I don't know much about them, but I'd rather have them on our side.' He looked into her eyes. 'All is not lost, ma'am. While you live, we still have everything to fight for.'

Elodi straightened and drew a breath. She wiped her face with the back of her hand. She smiled. 'Thank you, Toryn of Midwyche. You're right. I cannot let the enemy's foul deception rob me of my spirit.' Elodi gripped her sword. 'We cannot hand them a victory without a fight. And if we can somehow make allies of the mysterious Nym of which you speak, we may well yet strike back.'

'Ma'am! The tower.' Toryn turned to see an Archonian Guard limp across the rubble as best he could.

For a moment, he thought he saw Hamar as he would have looked twenty years ago.

Elodi cried out. 'Gundrul! You're alive.' She rushed to his side and hugged him, much to the embarrassment of the old captain.

Gundrul patted her shoulder, nodded to Toryn, then to the tower. 'Not for much longer if we don't move. That looks ready to fall, and I don't know about you, but I've had all the rubble I can take for one day landing on my head.' They took Gundrul's advice and hurried away from the tower. When satisfied they were a safe distance, they turned and watched as the pinnacle of the Caerwal Tower toppled. The first stone clattered against the rock wall, sending dull echoes over their heads. The stones bounced back, crashing into the lower walls of the tower, dislodging more stonework until the whole structure collapsed. The ground shook for a second time that day, but this time, thankfully claimed no more victims. When the dust settled, only the lower walls of the base remained of the Archon's last achievement. Toryn regarded the wreckage that appeared to represent what had become of the man — a once-powerful figure of hope, reduced to a hollow shell by the enemy.

46. End of the Age of Shadows

'You did well, young man.' Gundrul held out his hand to Toryn. 'Captain Gundrul of the' — his arm dropped — 'I'm not sure what we should call ourselves following the Archon's act of treason. Perhaps easier to say I serve the good Lady Harlyn here. And thank the Three she led a charge. Many more would have perished had she not woken us from our stupor.'

'Or for this man's skill with a bow.' Elodi gripped Gundrul's forearm. 'And good to see you've survived… mainly unscathed.' She nodded to Toryn. 'And this is Toryn of Midwyche.'

Gundrul's mouth dropped open. 'Toryn? Midwyche? Well, I never. This day has had too many surprises.'

Toryn gaped. 'How do you all know my name?'

Elodi smiled. 'We heard of your deeds at Drunsberg. But what raised our curiosity was why Uleva singled you out from the prisoners and took you with her.' She looked to Gundrul. 'What was that man's name? The one who told us the tale?'

'I believe his name was Roold, and another, a miner by the name of—'

'Jedrul? Did they make it out of the wood?'

Gundrul looked about him. 'They're both here… somewhere. We brought all who could swing a blade. I saw them carried to the wagons. Battered and bruised, but still with us.'

Another guard staggered towards them. Gundrul looked up. 'Ah, Cubric. I see it takes more than half a mountain to crush even your puny body.'

Cubric held out a blackened rock. 'Shreek's Rage, I'd

wager, Gunny.' He turned and shook his head at the scene. 'It must have taken months to bring hundreds of barrels of that cursed powder here. But only the Archon would have had the—'

Elodi held up her hand. 'We have much to discuss, but please let it be known it was not the Archon who was responsible for this slaughter. I'm afraid he was possessed by one named Uluriel who leads our enemy. The Archon did not betray us, sadly he was purely a vessel for the dark forces.'

Gundrul brushed the dust from his hair. 'That is shocking news, ma'am.' He looked to Cubric. 'Does this mean we guards have served our enemy all this time?'

Elodi rested her hand on his arm. 'We cannot know how much control she exerted over him, or what decisions were made by Uluriel or by our Archon. But we do know he suffered great hardship trying to expel her.'

Gundrul nodded to the gate. 'And what of the Golesh, ma'am? I'm surprised, if not thankful, they have not yet launched their attack. I know I wouldn't waste a moment on hearing that blast if I commanded them.'

She shook her head. 'The pass beyond the gate is empty.'

'Empty? But…'

'Toryn climbed to the top of the tower and has looked over. There is no sign of the enemy.'

Toryn glanced back to the gate. 'All I saw was a neglected memorial of sorts. Nothing else, no weapons… or any sign of an army.'

Elodi looked to Gundrul. 'I can only imagine the Archon's report was purely a deception by Uluriel.'

The old captain frowned. 'But to what…? Ah, of course. How else could he justify assembling our full strength here, only to bring down the mountains on our…' Gundrul bowed his head. Toryn turned to see the wagon bearing the fallen Archon and the unconscious Nyomae approach. The wagon stopped. Elodi climbed up and laid her hand on the Archon's shoulder. 'I owe this man an apology. I was critical of his tactics, and came to doubt his intentions, yet all this time he fought an internal battle against the will of a deadly foe.' She explained to Gundrul. 'And this is Nyomae, a powerful ally who fought with the Archon, but not at Gormadon, the last battle took place in the north.'

Gundrul gawped. 'The north? Everything I thought I knew is wrong?'

'I'm afraid that appears to be so… and for all of us.'

The captain looked to Nyomae. 'And you say this woman fought with the Archon? But she looks barely twenty years older than you, ma'am.' He scratched at his chin. 'These are confusing times. Confusing times indeed, ma'am.'

Elodi smiled. 'We have much to learn about what really happened in the final years of the Seven. And when Nyomae recovers, which I dearly hope will not be long, she will aid us greatly, both with improving our knowledge of the past, and with what may yet come.'

Elodi breathed in the late evening air. She stood upon the South Terrace of Archonholm contemplating the events of Midsummer's Day. And she appreciated why it was known as the longest day. So much had happened, it already seemed a week had passed since dawn. And just an hour earlier, she had stood vigil over the Archon's final journey with much sadness and regret. Elodi now understood what had happened when the Archon had attempted to hurl himself from the balcony of his tower. She and Bardon had witnessed a rare moment of clarity when he fought back against Uluriel. He must have been driven to despair, concluding ending his life would be the only way to save the realms. Yet she and Bardon had prevented his gallant act… and thousands perished. And had they questioned him farther on his recovery, could they have assisted the Archon to cast out Uluriel? But as her father had taught her, there was no point dwelling on the past; they had no way of knowing. She had to put that behind and make her next moves uncluttered by regret. But Elodi found the burden of guilt was not easy to shift.

The Archon had looked at peace, dressed in his ceremonial sky-blue robe as he lay in the small boat. The early records of his childhood in Searith revealed he had often sailed out to sea with his father. It was therefore considered fitting the waters of the Menon should carry him back to the Elessyn Sea. As she had watched the boat launched onto the river, she wondered just how many of the events orchestrated by Uluriel were known to the Archon. Unfortunately, Elodi had come to know the mind of the enemy too well, suspecting Uluriel would have gloated at the Archon's agony as she moved to bring down the Five Realms. Without a doubt, it was Uluriel that sent Bardon and the Elites south, knowing they would either come to grief on the strong currents sealing the passage south, or be met by an overwhelming force, forewarned of their coming should they survive the voyage. Her heart broke at the thought that Lord Broon and thousands of elite fighters could already be dead.

Elodi watched the Caerwal Mountains turn pink as the sun began its slow descent, drawing an end to the longest and most tragic day in the history of the Five Realms. When she had first set eyes upon the rock face, she had seen it to be a vital defense, standing defiantly against the evil in the south. But now, the mountain wall concealed a secret. What lay beyond its snowy peaks? Should they shun, or seek out their neighbors?

Elodi turned her attention to the exhausted people on

the terrace. Gundrul, Aldorman and Cubric stood a few paces away, deep in conversation. All three had sustained injuries but none that would prevent them participating in the hastily arranged meeting about to begin. Lord Kernlow had survived the explosion, having been stationed close to the parapet where Toryn had killed the first Nordleng. But Lord Galabrant had died from the blasts on the opposite side of the pass. Lord Kernlow, along with the Castellan, surviving captains of the First Horse, Archonians and Knights of the Archon, gathered at the opposite end of the terrace. But the Vice-Archon was not present. They had returned to Archonholm to discover she had thrown herself from the bridge on hearing of the Archon's apparent betrayal. But while Elodi had been disturbed by the Vice-Archon's hasty and cowardly action, she had not shed a tear for the woman. Elodi had loathed her. She could not forgive her for the apparent delight she had taken on hearing of the fall of Calerdorn. But with the passing of the Vice-Archon, Lord Kernlow, as the longest serving ruler would assume the position of the Steward of Archonholm according to their custom. Elodi watched the old man struggling to stay on his feet and wondered how long he could fulfill the demanding role.

Elodi turned to Toryn. 'Ah. I have a confession to make.'

'You, ma'am? A confession?'

She took his hand. 'Remember, it's Elodi. You, of all people, do not need to stand on ceremony for my sake.' She turned his hand over, noticing his initial resistance. 'I know about your true father… and how you came to be in Midwyche, and therefore appreciate why you had to leave. I sent a rider on hearing of your treatment at the hands of Uleva. And I believe your mother… Miram, when she informed my rider, you were one of the good ones.'

Toryn stifled a laugh. 'Ah yes, a good 'un.' He could

hear Hamar's rasp as he had described the better half of the wyke folk. 'And my mother and father? Are they well?'

'They were happier when informed you had survived the battle at Drunsberg. By some means, news of Hamar's death eventually reached your village. Your mother had assumed you had also perished. But be assured, my rider said nothing of your abduction from Durran Wood. At the time we knew nothing of your whereabouts, or well-being, or even your allegiance. Perhaps now, if I can spare a rider, I could send word to your folks.'

'Thank you, that is very kind. It could be a long time before I could see them.'

Elodi turned to the citadel. 'Alas, it may be some time before any of us can return to our homes. We have much to learn, to discuss, and difficult choices to make. And I am eager to discover what Nyomae can tell us. The healers inform me she's in a deep sleep, but otherwise appears unharmed. I only wish I had the chance to speak with her before the meeting of the Heads of Council.' She looked to Toryn. 'But one thing we can assume, much of the Archon's decrees will have been planned by Uluriel to weaken us.' She shook her head. 'All this time we had our eyes fixed on the threat beyond the gate, while our enemies walked and plotted among us.' She leaned on the balustrade. 'Uluriel has played us for fools. We've been dancing to her tune all this time. The border fences were to keep us penned in, thus hampering our recovery from the desecration caused by the last war. And we fell for her deception.' She turned to the pass. 'Uluriel steered us to sacrifice the bulk of our strength, leaving ourselves much weakened while she has grown stronger.'

Toryn went to her side. 'None could have known. Our enemies appear to be masters at the art of deception.'

Elodi turned. A tear ran down her cheek. 'My father knew. He had his doubts that led him to the Hall of

Scrolls. He found something in the annals that took him to the Caerwal Tower that fateful night. I'm certain he must have gained access to the upper room and looked over the gate. He would have seen the threat lay not to the south. But that sealed his fate.' She spun around and slapped the stone. 'If only he had told someone of his discovery before his visit to the pass. We could have averted this disaster.'

Toryn tried to console her. 'Would any have believed him? And who would he have told? I doubt the Vice-Archon, Castellan or any of the Archon's generals would have listened. He must have been keen to see for himself before he risked speaking out.'

Elodi looked to the bridge. 'How fitting the Vice-Archon chose to fling herself from the same spot my father was murdered.' She turned back and let her eyes wander to the Archon's colors fluttering high above the city. 'Even the banner now tells a lie.'

Toryn read her thoughts. 'Will we see the gold of Kernlow flying in its place?'

Elodi nodded. 'Lord Kernlow is the senior ruler. In normal times, he would become steward, and as such, ruler of the Five Realms until a new Archon can be selected and appointed.'

Toryn glanced to the ample frame of Lord Kernlow. 'But is he really the right person in such times? Even as steward?'

Elodi's jaw clenched. 'You're right.' She leaned closer. 'But these are not normal times.' She looked back to the Archon's banner, speaking to herself. 'Not normal times at all.' Her gaze went back to Lord Kernlow. Elodi straightened. 'I shall dispute his suitability.' Her hand rested on her sword. 'I will put myself forward to lead until a new Archon is found, which I believe should be Nyomae by right.'

Toryn grinned. 'I can't think of any in all of the land

who would make a more suitable steward.'

Her shoulders dropped. 'There is another, but Lord Broon, the true Lord Broon is missing, most likely dead. However, if I seek the necessary support to challenge Lord Kernlow, I believe another may also enter the fray. Bardon's usurper, Nordryn, sits comfortably in his hall in Keld after conveniently being absent at the pass.' Elodi stiffened. 'But should he choose to challenge my claim, then let him ride the long and dusty road and try to take it from me. But I do not wish to sit in the stuffy halls of Archonholm.' Her eyes wandered to the sky. 'I will do as I must to see off the threat, then retake Calerdorn as soon as is possible. But much lies in my way, and with things as they are, it may be difficult to tell friend from foe, who to trust and of whom to be wary.'

Toryn lowered his voice. 'Do you suspect Nordryn could be in league with Uluriel?'

Elodi thought for a moment. 'When Ruan, one of my trusted captains, has his suspicions, I listen. I have no proof, but the fact Uluriel did not demand his forces partake in the attack, does much to settle it in my mind. And now I suspect Nordryn's recall of Ruan's spearmen was to weaken Calerdorn. If he is in league with the Uldalak, he must have known Uleva would send Dorlan against us.'

'Ah yes. Dorlan. Is it truly him?'

'Yet another nasty surprise in these strange times. And sadly, yes, I do believe by some trickery, the enemy have sustained him all these years and brought him back.' She took his hand. 'And I believe you have met him. You knew him as Dohl.'

He laughed. 'Dohl? You cannot mean poor, old, knackered Dohl? But he… wait, there was a moment… yes, I can still hear his words as they sent a shiver down my spine. He said, let me see… *I hope I'm gone before the world changes*, and then, *she knows, she knows what's coming.*' He stared at Elodi. 'But he's truly Dorlan? What would Hamar think if he knew I'd met Dorlan? And… he served my dinner, well what passed for a meal in that place.'

Elodi could not eradicate the picture of the gloating Dorlan from her mind. 'Alas, like the Archon, our legend appears possessed and takes up arms against us. Ah! Of course. I suspect that would be another reason for Nordryn to recall his spears. He knew Broon's men would not be so susceptible to yielding in the face of Harlyn's legend.'

Toryn's heart sank. 'But how do we fight Dorlan? Our knights bear his colors, our soldiers cry his name going to battle?'

Elodi shook her head. 'My hope is we can drive Uleva from his head as we did Uluriel from the Archon, yet I fear that would also mean his demise. But how and when we can achieve that is another matter.' She turned to face the mountains. 'For now, do we need to be concerned by the people beyond the Caerwals? Are they friend of foe?'

Toryn watched the last of the dust drifting over the Lower Gate. 'But what about the attack on the gate? We heard about it at Drunsberg. Who carried out that strike?'

Elodi sighed. 'I imagine it was an act of sabotage. An act to convince the realms to bring their soldiers here to the pass' — her head dropped — 'only to be buried within it.' She looked to the steep slopes in the east. 'Do the Golesh actually exist? We have seen no evidence. Was all of this to keep the strength of the Lost Realms secured beyond the mountains? Do they still thrive, believing we are lost? It would allow the Ul-dalak to recover from their defeat and gain control of the north.' Elodi held Toryn's gaze. 'If the Golesh are indeed a ruse of our enemy, it appears we are on the wrong side of the gate.'

Toryn glanced to the citadel where Nyomae slept.

'Hope... Nyomae spoke of the leader of her Order. She believes he may be imprisoned in the south, but she doesn't know for what reason. She named him Idraman. And although he must be centuries old, older even than Nyomae, she sensed his presence. Perhaps he may also prove to be a useful ally.'

'I know of that name. My father read a revealing scroll penned by Idraman regarding Uluriel, or rather how she came to be corrupted by our enemy.' Elodi turned back to the mountains rapidly turning red as the sun neared the horizon. 'But like the Archon and Dohl, let us hope this Idraman does not pose yet another threat if he is also corrupted by the Ul-dalak. Yet the question remains, if Idraman created the barrier to protect the south, why is there no apparent defense at the southern head of the pass? Where are the guards to watch the barrier should Uluriel attack? Whether it is friend or foe that control the south, why does the pass appear abandoned?' She exhaled. 'Nyomae cannot recover quick enough. We must be wary of making decisions based on the deceptions of our enemy.' Her mood lightened a little. 'Ah. I see this ill-fated day is almost done.'

They turned as the sun touched the edge of their world. The dust from the landslide clinging to the air, acted as a canvas for the sun to daub its colors across the sky. Toryn tipped back his head. He let his gaze descend from deep blue, through to the brush strokes of orange hues, down to pink-tinged, wispy clouds, to arrive at the reds and eventually the dark line drawn across the horizon. He smiled. 'Nyomae promised I would live to see the sunset. But I wish she could be here to share it with me.'

Elodi took his hand. 'Would you be willing to share it with me instead?'

Toryn's fingers tingled at her warm touch. He took a breath. 'Gladly. It would be an honor.' He looked upon her as she marveled at the majestic sky, appearing eager to heal the hurt of the day. Her gentle hold belied her talent for swinging a sword with such deadly precision, but while her warmth soothed the pain in his tired limbs, it set an ache in his heart. Toryn wished the moment could last forever. Yet the sunset no longer held his attention. He lost himself in Elodi's fair face as if the sun had kept its best light for this very moment. But the sky could not compete with her beauty. Her hair gleamed red, brought to life by the gentle breeze; her skin welcomed the caress from the last of the warmth; and her eyes shone. Toryn gazed at the sun's reflection in her eyes, enhanced by the Amayan fire burning bright within. She seemed unaware of his attention, still captivated by the glimmering, red rim as it slipped from their side of the world.

Toryn's chest swelled. 'When I watched the sun rise this morning, I saw you on your balcony.' He squeezed her hand. 'But I never thought I would see it set standing by your side.'

But Elodi's thoughts lay elsewhere. She sighed as the light faded. 'It appears the Age of Shadows has finally come to an end. But I wonder, even dread, by what name the new age will come to be known.'

To be continued…

SEA OF SOULS is due out December 2022

You can sign up to my newsletter at

www.frontrunnerbooks.com/sign-up.html

Made in United States
North Haven, CT
13 April 2023

35402948R00264